The ROAD HOME

MARGARET
WAY

ZEBRA BOOKS
KENSINGTON PUBLISHING CORP.
http://www.kensingtonbooks.com

ZEBRA BOOKS are published by

Kensington Publishing Corp.
119 West 40th Street
New York, NY 10018

All Kensington titles, imprints, and distributed lines are available at special quantity discounts for bulk purchases for sales promotion, premiums, fund-raising, educational, or institutional use.

Special book excerpts or customized printings can also be created to fit specific needs. For details, write or phone the office of the Kensington Sales Manager: Attn.: Sales Department. Kensington Publishing Corp., 119 West 40th Street, New York, NY 10018. Phone: 1-800-221-2647.

First Printing: November 2017
ISBN-13: 978-1-4201-4172-6
ISBN-10: 1-4201-4172-4

eISBN-13: 978-1-4201-4173-3
eISBN-10: 1-4201-4173-2

10 9 8 7 6 5 4 3 2 1

Printed in the United States of America

Chapter One

"Some place, bro!" the cabbie hooted, torn between envy and entrenched resentment of the superrich. "It's a bloody disgrace, all them lights." He spoke like a man committed to having the issue addressed ASAP. "Looks like the *QM2* at sea, don't it?"

Bruno had to agree. The Lubrinski mansion was *ablaze*. Even he, close friend of the Lubrinskis, had to drop his eyes. He reached into his wallet and took out a couple of crisp fifty-dollar bills. "Keep the change." He put the notes into the man's outstretched hand. "You wouldn't expect them to hold a big charity bash in the dark, now, would you?"

"That's what it is then?" The cabbie acknowledged the size of the tip by landing a friendly punch on Bruno's shoulder. "Thank you kindly for that, bro!"

"That's what it is most of the time," Bruno said, stepping out of the cab without further damage to his person. "These people are among the biggest philanthropists in the country."

"Yeah?" The driver wasn't about to let it rest. "All to

do with their taxes, I reckon. Okay, bro, enjoy yourself now. Me, I have to get back to the grind."

He stood for a moment in the golden gleam of the streetlights, watching the cab driver perform a perfect U-turn and then scoot off with a friendly wave. The guy was right. The house did look like a liner at sea.

He was late. Couldn't be helped. He'd gotten caught up with an old university friend he'd made a bundle for, allowing him to pay off his mortgage. There was satisfaction in that. He liked helping people. Just like his dad. As he made his way up the broad flight of stone steps, he could see guests milling around the huge, brilliantly lit entrance hall. They formed a living, moving kaleidoscope of multicoloured gowns, emerald, scarlet, amethyst, silver and gold, set off to perfection against the sea of black dinner suits. It all looked sensational. People had been known to fight for Marta Lubrinski's invitations. Often it came down to hissy fits.

Beautiful music was issuing from the living room, soaring above the hubbub of voices and laughter. It conveyed a broad spectrum of human emotions: joy, love, sorrow, hope. He hadn't started out life as a classical music lover, though he'd been fed a lot of Italian opera in the womb: Puccini, Verdi.

He loved jazz. He had a big collection of the world's greatest jazz musicians. It was Marta, his self-appointed honorary aunt, who had taken charge of his classical music education, starting with *A* for Albeniz, the great Spanish virtuoso pianist and composer. He was still working his way through the *B*s. Bach. Beethoven. Brahms. Marta had unloaded a hundred CDs on him, exhorting him, "Play them, darlink. Listen, listen. Give your soul wings!"

Tonight was one of Marta's famous dos, with wonderful

music and equally wonderful food and wine. It was taken for granted he would attend, especially as he had been, and still was to a certain extent, her husband, Ivor's protégé. Ivor Lubrinski had started his new life in Australia as a seventeen-year-old Lithuanian emigrant with ten pounds in his pocket, an unshakeable belief in his destiny and an incredibly astute business brain. Ivor was also notoriously society shy. He rarely attended his wife's grand soirees. It was Marta who had control of that side of things, as brilliant in her fashion as Ivor was in his.

Bruno was devoted to them both. Their philanthropy was legendary, when he happened to know Ivor was as careful with a dollar as his own Scottish-born dad had been. Neither man ever forgot their roots. Hungarian Marta had to a mind-blowing extent. Marta had the craving for luxury lodged in her very being.

As he stepped into the Rococo-on-steroids entrance hall with its glittering travertine floor, his eyes gravitated automatically to the magnificent Bohemian chandelier at its centre. The hundreds and hundreds of crystals bounced light off every surface. If it ever fell, it would surely kill anyone directly beneath it and injure those in the vicinity. It had been his suggestion to place a large library table beneath it to bear the brunt in such an eventuality. Marta had come up with an extraordinary ebonized and parcel gilt centre table with really weird claws for feet.

The table now held a great pyramid of flowers. It must have been arranged *in situ.* No one could have walked with it. He guessed it was the masses of Asian lilies, pink and white, showing off their beautiful dusky pink faces that gave off the heady perfume that tickled his nose.

Eventually, he was able to move through the throng into the voluminous living room, as big as a football field. A series of open arched and shuttered French doors gave on to a brilliantly lit poolside terrace. It too was paved in travertine, and beyond that a magnificent panoramic view of Sydney Harbour, the most beautiful harbour in the world, and he had seen them all in his travels.

Along his way, he received choruses of hellos, claps on the shoulder, air kisses from the women, some grasping his hand with faintly glazed eyes. He had to know he was one of the most eligible bachelors around. It wasn't a good position to be in. In fact, he hated it. Being a bachelor didn't trouble him at all. He had turned thirty, was coming at thirty-one. Being vigorously pursued by young women and determined cougars did his head in. He was in no hurry to get married. He hadn't met the woman of his dreams. In truth, he was beginning to wonder if he ever would. He *did* have dreams, but they were locked away somewhere, inaccessible even to him. It was too damned hard for him to forget the disastrous breakup of his parents' marriage and the way his staggeringly beautiful Italian mother had taken off and left him and his dad, an incredibly nice guy, to fend for themselves.

He well remembered the waves of grief that had come crashing down on them. They had adored her. Even now, he couldn't think about his mother without feeling a deep, angry hurt. Those early years had been bad, missing his mother. It wasn't until he turned twelve that he had really toughened up.

He'd gotten the hang of cleaning the house, shopping and preparing meals for him and his dad. His mother had been a wonderful cook. He had watched her often enough, so he soon became a dab hand with pasta, al dente of course, matching the right pasta to the right sauce. It'd got to the point when one evening, after a great dinner of spicy calamari followed by Linguini ai Frutti di Mare, his dad had sat him down, asking very seriously, "Do you want to become a chef, son? You know whatever you want to do, I'll back you."

A chef! A great job certainly, if one had a mind to it, but he was on course to secure a place at university. He wanted to finish with a double degree, Master of Laws and Bachelor of Commerce. He could do it in five years, working part time. He was smart. What a good laugh they'd had when he'd explained his ambition. His culinary skills had been inherited from his mother: Italian blood and the love of good food. That was it. Another area where he had shone was organising the household accounts. He saw they were paid on time. He even found better alternatives. He managed the budget far better than his dad. He had made his mark at school, both in the classroom and on the playing field. His father had told everyone who would listen he was meant for big things. Nothing had mattered more than his dad being proud of him. They were survivors. Mates.

Taller than most, his eyes ranged easily over the heads of the usual crowd, the movers and shakers, the society crowd, the hobnobbers and the fringe dwellers. He recognised the piece the quartet Marta had hired were playing. Borodin. The Polovtsian Dances. The reason he knew it was the Polovtsian Dances because it had opened the Winter Games in Sochi. He, Ivor and a couple of Ivor's cronies had been witness to the dazzling opening ceremony, when a beautiful Russian girl had flown across a winter dreamscape to that music. He recalled how the works of Russia's greatest classical composers had filled the stadium, rousing every heart, including his, with a highly emotional Ivor in unashamed floods of tears. The same beautiful Russian music was now being generated in the Lubrinski living room. The musicians were very good, as was expected.

The work came to an end. The applause began. He moved further into the monumental room that certainly had the wow factor, if you didn't shy away from opulence. Sumptuous silk-taffeta gold curtains with tasselled tiebacks swept the floor, a pair of antique Italian chandeliers hung from the elaborately plastered ceiling, a huge portrait of a striking-looking woman stood on a gilded easel. Marta allowed people to think it was a portrait of her great-grandmother. Of course it wasn't.

Loads of Louis XVI furnishings were mixed in with the plush modern stuff. Not Louis style; the real McCoy. Marta had a gimlet eye for such things. It made a praiseworthy balance, because Marta was as devoted to her charities as they were rightly devoted to her.

He was getting his first clear view of the musicians in the group, first and second violins, viola and cello. He started to lift his hands to join in the wave of applause, but they fell back to his sides as shock took over. He couldn't believe his eyes. He probably would have given vent to a gasp, only his breath was lodged in his throat.

The focus of his attention was the cello player, a young woman in her early twenties. He knew the group from other occasions. An attractive, plump young woman showing a lot of bosom played viola. The second violin was a tall, earnest young gent with a mop of unruly black curls, a pronounced Adam's apple and black-rimmed glasses to lend a bit of gravitas.

The cellist was new. A replacement for the evening. She could even be a graduate from the Con. She was that young. In a huge room, surrounded by many attractive, even beautiful women, she stood out as a single red rose would be a standout in a bouquet of carnations. He had no interest in the other members of the quartet. His sole focus was the girl. He was staring, when staring wasn't his style. Not that he was the only male caught out looking his fill. He didn't think he had seen anyone as sexy as this beautiful girl with a gleaming cello propped between her long, slender legs. The length from the knees was tantalizingly on view as the sheer top layer of her long black skirt fell away. Not that she gave off any overtly sexy aura. She looked chaste. Absolutely. Ultrarefined, very romantic. The princess in a fairy tale. A magical creature.

Curling masses of titian hair flowed away from her face and over her shoulders. Her porcelain skin, face, throat, décolletage were shown to priceless advantage against the black lace of the sleeveless V-necked bodice. She would be of above average height when she stood up, and willow slim. She had light eyes. At this distance, he didn't know if they were blue or green. He was prepared to bet they were green, if only because he had seen a blown-up photograph of a large bravura portrait of this girl's double. People did have doubles in life, he reminded himself, only he had the certainty this girl had Hartmann blood.

A Hartmann, for God's sake!

He was so certain, his nerve endings were doing a slow burn.

A seminal moment in your life, McKendrick.

Through his late father, Ross McKendrick, a private investigator and a former ex-chief of detectives, he had developed a fascination with so-called cold cases: mysterious disappearances of certain individuals, male and female, that were never solved. The old Hartmann case was one his dad had laboured over to the point of obsession. It was as much a mystery today as it had been twenty years earlier.

Not anymore.

Tonight had opened up a powerful new lead. The young

woman he had under close observation *had* to have Hartmann blood in her. That was his gut feeling, and he trusted his gut feelings.

At one time of his life, after the untimely death of his father in a hit-and-run accident—the culprit never found—he had wanted to crack the case if only to finish the job for his father and give closure to the Hartmann family. Other ambitions had gotten in the way. He now ran his own wealth management company, The Fortuna Group. His company was getting bigger by the day. He was very good at whatever he did. Consequently, he was doing extremely well. An increasing number of other people were doing well because of him. To be a success had always been expected of him. No way was he going to let his dad down. He honoured his memory.

It was her.

She who had been lost was found.

Well, not the she *his father had never been able to trace, but an offspring?*

The crowd parted like Moses parting the Red Sea as Marta, dressed in one of her eye-popping outfits, a glittering gold kaftan—made of material left over from the curtains?—with a matching jewel-adorned turban, rushed towards him. Marta didn't hesitate to gild the lily. Her arms were spread in rapturous welcome. "Bruno, my darlink, you're here. Mwah! Mwah! Mwah." Multiple kisses were dispensed, landing on both cheeks, one near his mouth.

Marta was followed closely by Penelope Pfeiffer, Sam Pfeiffer's daughter; Sam of the supermarkets. This wasn't the first time Marta had taken on the job of finding him someone *nice.* There had been a very difficult time last year with Gemma Walker. Three dates and Gemma and her twittering girlfriends had started running around like headless chickens, spreading the word the big engagement bash at the Lubrinskis' was barely a month off.

The word had spread like wildfire. He'd had to take steps to call a halt to it. Sweet little Gemma had then shown her true colours, flying into a right tizzy. In the old days, she would have had him up for breach of promise. He had to wonder if many a guy hadn't been caught in this way. He was always on the bloke's side. No surprise there.

Penelope was Marta's current choice for him. At least Gem had held down a job. Penelope didn't. No need, with a doting dad worth just short of a billion. Bruno tried not to be angry. It was hard to be angry with Marta, but he didn't welcome this matchmaker role she had taken on. If he wanted to find a dream girl, he would find her himself, when he was good and ready.

"It's *too* wonderful to see you, Bruno," cooed Penelope, a sight for sore eyes in a figure-hugging scarlet bead-and-sequin number. He kissed her on both cheeks as expected, after which Marta took both their arms with abandon, as if announcing to the crowded room that after a few false starts, Penelope was *the one*. They moved off, a trio, with Marta and Penelope chattering away like geese.

Belatedly, he realized young fire head had been fully aware of his intense scrutiny. She was looking right back at him with surprising directness. Colour flooded her creamy skin, but her gaze was supercool, especially for one so young, and would you believe it, *dismissive* into the bargain. It was obvious she took exception to the boldness of his scrutiny. Had they been in ancient Rome, she probably would have had him thrown to the lions. Such imperiousness unlocked him. He would catch up with the mystery lady later. That was if he could ever fight free of Penelope. A single man on the up-and-up was a positive magnet for women, and men had to understand that.

"So, who's the vision on Faraday's arm?" he asked a hectic hour later, bending his head to Cassie Taylor, his journalist friend who barely came up to his shoulder. Cassie had once done an article on him that had proved very helpful. They had become friends. He was good friends with her husband, Ian, as well. He was godfather to their only child, Josh, who was autistic. Cassie, who had almost died in childbirth, had been advised not to attempt another child.

Cassie knew just about everyone and everything about so-called celebrities. She certainly knew Faraday. She had written many an article on him. None of them kind to the on-the-dodgy-side entrepreneur.

"Phil is showing better taste, huh?" Cassie snorted. "She looks really classy, doesn't she, but way, way too young and innocent. Not Phil's taste. She's standing in for Jonathon Rule. Remember, Jon was offered a place in that German quartet?"

"I seem to remember Marta telling me." He tore his gaze back to Cassie.

"She didn't tell you anything about his replacement?"

"No."

"Well, we'll soon find out. You could do it just bowling up to them. Faraday is a great admirer of yours, though he does his best not to show it. He was really miffed when you left Wallace-Upton."

"I always wanted to do my own thing, Cass. I didn't particularly like working for George Upton. Underneath the day-to-day brush with the man, it was hard to know who the *real* George was."

Cassie fixed her keen hazel eyes on Bruno McKendrick's strikingly handsome face. She felt pleasure and, it had to be admitted even by a happily married woman, a trace of excitement, a *thrill* otherwise missing in her life. Bruno was the stuff of a woman's dreams. He had a great head of hair, wonderful dark eyes, burnished skin, golden even in winter. Any woman would envy the natural *glow.*

"You were a real asset to Wallace-Upton," she said, "but I can see how you felt about Upton. You're no one's yes-man. You would never turn a blind eye. You have a reputation for honesty."

"One I prize."

"So go to it," she urged. "Mosey over to Phil's group. See, he's looking this way. So is his young friend. The really odd thing is that she reminds me of someone." Cassie screwed up her eyes, obviously trying to think who. "I can't for the life of me think who it is, but maybe it'll come to me. She has the kind of face one doesn't forget, don't you think?"

"I do indeed," he said, very dryly.

"Remember Sunday," she called after him as he made off.

"Couldn't keep me away." Sunday was his godson Josh's sixth birthday. He'd bought him a toy he thought would capture Josh's attention, a tall, colourful robot that could walk and flash lights. Josh was receiving the very best attention and ongoing therapy, but it hadn't been easy for Cassie or Ian. Oddly, though Josh usually shunned people, he had taken to Bruno right from the start.

"You've got the knack with kids, Bruno," Cassie often told him, tears of gratitude swimming in her eyes. But then, he had insight into troubled kids. He had been one, hadn't he?

A moment more and he braced himself for a Faraday hug. "Ciao, Bruno, you old son of a gun. Good to see you. You look great."

"So do you, Phil. I'm loving the tie." It appeared to have Philip's winning string of racehorses on it.

"You know I'm a racing man. Hell, you learned to ride on my property."

Philip had a splendid country retreat in the Blue Mountains. "I did too. You're a great host, Phil." It was perfectly true.

"They're missing you over at Wallace-Upton, I hear." Faraday looked up. One thing Phil couldn't buy with all that money: height. He compensated by having his handmade shoes and boots built up. "I know you're doing well, but you could have gone right to the top with the firm had you stayed. Not too late for you to go back."

"Nice try, Phil, but I'm never going back," he said, deliberately shifting his gaze to James Kellerman's companion.

Faraday half-turned, a proprietorial expression on his attractive, fleshy face. "Isabelle, here's an up-and-coming man I'd like you to meet. Bruno McKendrick, Isabelle Martin."

"A pleasure to meet you, Ms. Martin. I thoroughly enjoyed the performance tonight, especially the Borodin."

"Thank you." She did not offer her hand. He'd known she wouldn't. She was clearly on her guard.

Faraday had turned away for a moment to fawn over the governor-general, which was fine by Bruno. "Shall we move on?" He barely touched her elbow.

To his surprise, she made no protest. She went with him through the parting crowd, aware in their wake, that a few of the guests would be prodding one another. For some reason that escaped him, of late people had taken to running bets on how much longer he would remain a bachelor. Especially as Marta Lubrinski had elected to find him a suitable bride.

"Why the interest in me, Mr. McKendrick?" The girl gave him a sideways green glance.

"Oh please, *Bruno*. I have an Italian mother."

"I'd never have guessed. Back to the question. Why the interest?"

"Let me explain. I've no wish to offend you, Isabelle; may I? But you're the living image of someone my late father, a private investigator, had been hired to find. I'm talking just over twenty years ago."

She raised finely arched brows several shades darker than her titian hair. "You'd have been a child."

"Of course."

"Was this woman found?"

He shook his dark head. "Never. Her disappearance devastated her family. She went missing of her own accord."

She considered that for a moment. "Very likely big problems on the home front. That's my guess. Didn't your father investigate that?"

"My father left no stone unturned."

"What has any of this to do with me beyond a superficial resemblance? We all have doubles, so they say."

He shrugged off that theory. "I've seen photographs of the young woman, including one of a portrait painted when she'd turned twenty-one. The resemblance is uncanny, the colouring alone. Redheads make up only about four percent of the population. Your eyes are green. So were hers."

"So that makes me a subject for investigation?" Her green eyes had the sparkle of jewels.

No touch of the usual female flirtatiousness about her. No man-woman challenge, no provocativeness. Rather the reverse. He liked that. Anyway, she was way too young for him. He was a man who applied rules and stuck to them. "Not at all. It's simply I'm finding the resemblance riveting. As would you, if I showed you a photograph, though I agree we do have doubles."

"You carry the photograph on your person?" she asked, so sweetly it had to be sarcasm.

"I meant at some other time. An appropriate time, because you're with Faraday."

Annoyance edged her clear young voice. "I'm not with your friend, Philip Faraday. I was standing briefly with him. I came with the group, Mr. McKendrick."

He held up a palm. "No one calls me Mr. McKendrick."

"Not even your staff?"

"Not even my staff." How did she know he had a staff? Who had passed on the information? Probably Phil. Phil loved to gossip. Nothing bad. Nothing damaging; more titillating. Something appealing about that when other entrepreneurs were so brutally cruel.

"How liberal-minded of you," she said.

"You were about to put me straight?"

"Sorry, I thought I did. Mr. Faraday attached himself to me. Not the other way around. He's old enough to be my father."

He couldn't help it. He laughed. "That would lacerate him. Phil's been married and divorced three times."

"Clearly he doesn't take matrimony seriously. Do you? You're married?"

He fixed his dark eyes on her. "I'm in no hurry."

She looked away, high, slanted cheekbones flushed. "Forgive me. But you set the tone of this conversation."

"I started out wrongly. My excuse is I was stunned by the resemblance. I'm very serious about this. Maybe I could ask you to have lunch with me. Or dinner. Whatever you prefer."

It was her turn to hold up a staying hand: beautiful, long-fingered, delicate but strong.

"Please don't refuse me." He hoped his smile worked, otherwise he was out of luck. "You may think me intrusive, but my father went to his grave without solving the Hartmann case. It took him over."

"I'm sorry to hear that," she said, as though she meant it. "You'd like to solve it for him?"

"I would. For him and for the Hartmann family."

"Isn't it way too late?"

"I would have thought so until I saw you. Were you adopted, by any chance? You're what, English, the accent?"

There was a fleeting beat like uncertainty before she answered. "I'm as Australian as you are, given our forebears hailed from Europe. You're very obviously of Italian descent. My parents are English. They arrived in Australia when I was a baby. I know you'd like to solve a mystery, but your mystery has nothing to do with me. My parents are alive and well. Both are specialist doctors. My father is an oncologist, my mother a highly regarded surgeon. I have no siblings. I've had to produce my birth certificate a number of times over the years. Passports, etc. I've never had the slightest doubt about who I am. Neither has anyone else."

"Grandparents? Your grandparents are still living?" he persisted, driven by God knows what. Instinct. Gut feeling. Mirror images.

"Clearly you're a detective tragic. But I can't help you."

"I'm pretty sure you can. No need to be crotchety."

She looked up at him, blinked in amazement. "I am *not* crotchety. I've never actually heard that word spoken. *Crotchety?*"

"Really? My dad used it a lot." He didn't say it was in connection with his mother. *A bit crotchety today, son!* "Okay, how about vexed? If I've offended you, I'm sorry. Let me make it up to you. Dinner? Lunch is difficult for me most days. We could go to the new place, Leonards. It's highly rated."

"Who said I would enjoy myself?"

"I improve on acquaintance," he assured her. "On the other hand, I'm fascinated by you, Ms. Martin. You're not crotchety, forgive me. Maybe a teeny chip on your shoulder?"

She flipped back her luxuriant hair. A wonderfully feminine gesture. "That does it."

"No, no." His two-handed, up-flung gesture mirrored exactly one of his mother's. "I promise you'll be fascinated. It's quite a story." He glanced at his watch. "Look, it's still early. Why don't we go someplace quiet? At least let me explain. There's some sort of mystery here. Hang on," he suddenly remembered. "I have a small photo in the back of my wallet. It's the same one my dad always carried. I grew up with this photo. And others."

She wanted to resist him. She couldn't. Not many women could, she imagined. It was a feeling she could not and did not want to understand. Not only was he a fantastic-looking man, with all the self-assurance success brings, he looked like a man who usually got what he wanted. For all that, his polished manner, and the humour in his voice, and the darker than dark eyes, he didn't look the sort of man up for casual involvements, or to play women along. He was at heart a *serious* man; her trusty antennae told her that. At twenty-two, she had come to terms with the fact that men looked on her with considerable interest and a whole lot more that she didn't want and actively discouraged. Bruno McKendrick wasn't using his story as a kind of subterfuge for less cerebral pursuits. This was a story he was determined to investigate.

She made her decision, looking away. "I have to say good night to my hostess, to James and the other members of the group."

"Of course. You're finished for the evening?"

"James is staying on. He's a party animal. I feel privileged to have been invited to play with the group. I thought we meshed well."

"You meshed beautifully. You're a fine musician yourself."

"Royal College of Music, London. I have a Master's degree."

"Good for you. You must tell me more."

"You're interested?" She looked up at him quickly.

"Of course I'm interested. I don't say things just for the hell of it. I suppose you were a child prodigy?"

She met his mesmerizing eyes. The irises were almost the brilliant black of the pupils. "Oddly enough, I was regarded as one in my hometown."

"Why oddly?" He quirked a brow.

"It's a long story."

He was intent on hearing it. "No one else in the family was musical?" He knew for a fact the Hartmanns were a musical family. The portrait of the missing young woman had her seated at a grand piano, her face and torso turned towards the painter.

"Isn't Mrs. Lubrinski waving at you?" Isabelle asked,

having just that minute observed she and the dashing Bruno McKendrick were under surveillance.

He looked across to where Marta was standing. She might as well have been bellowing for his attention. Beside her stood Penelope, wearing an exquisitely pained expression. "So she is," he said blandly. "The Lubrinskis are good friends of mine."

"Is the young woman with her a good friend as well?" She was rummaging about in her memory for the name of the often-photographed society figure.

"I've lots of attractive women friends, Isabelle, none of them a fixture. Look, why don't we go over and say good night together?"

"You need protection?" she asked with more than a hint of mischief.

"Every man needs protection from beautiful women." There was no trace of humour in his voice.

"I'll take special note of that." Bruno McKendrick had probably been chased from his teens, but *that* reaction? There had to be a story there involving a beautiful woman.

They walked down the brilliantly lit drive together into the starlit night. He had called a cab to take them to a waterfront restaurant. They would wait for it on the footpath.

"I think your Marta might be a holy terror," Isabelle considered.

"Marta has a lovely nature." It was said tongue in cheek. Marta, though she had remained the gracious hostess, definitely had not approved of Isabelle, who looked like a teenager, even if she were a brilliant young musician.

Isabelle was wearing strappy black heels, yet she had

to tilt up her chin. "I have to ask this. Not idle curiosity. I really want to know. Have you something going on with Penelope?"

He didn't weigh his response. "I thought I was the one who was going to ask the questions." He looked down his perfectly aquiline nose at her.

"So it's a setup. Madame Lubrinski"—it trilled off her tongue—"has made finding you the right partner a calling?"

"There's the cab now."

"I think she's been giving you a hard time," she said with a catch of laughter in her voice. Any of her girlfriends would have felt hurt and intimidated by Marta Lubrinski's disapproval thinly cloaked by brilliant smiles. She didn't. She was well used to intimidating women. On the other hand, if Penelope's looks could have killed, she'd be laid out in the house.

Her skin was luminous under the streetlights. Her hair like rioting flames. If he weren't immune to beautiful women, Bruno thought he'd be having palpitations. Not that Isabelle Martin had arrived at the femme fatale stage. She was still a girl, fresh as springtime. "What is this? You're reading my mind?" he asked with a certain derisiveness.

"You've already given yourself away."

He didn't follow that up. What did she mean anyway? He wasn't used to being put on the back foot.

The restaurant was upmarket. Jolly expensive, as Isabelle was soon to label it. They had a table for two at the window with a view of the starstruck, shimmering water. Isabelle didn't know how he had managed that. The restaurant wasn't crowded; nevertheless, it would have taken some clout to land their table by the window. She hadn't eaten since lunch. Bruno revealed he hadn't been able to manage lunch either, so both of them were hungry. Neither wanted to go past Sydney's marvellous seafood, choosing a menu much like two people who knew exactly each other's taste. At the end, they decided on a series of fancy little entrées featuring oysters, scallops, prawns and lobster.

"A Riesling to go?" Bruno signalled the hovering wine waiter.

"Perfect. Clare Valley." She named the famous wine-growing region without hesitation.

"How do you know so much about Australian wines?"

She shrugged a creamy shoulder. "I've done a little judicious sampling."

"So age bows to beauty."

Her smile was so sweet, so uncomplicated, he saw her clearly as a little girl.

"You're not middle-aged. Yet."

"Before you ask, I'm quite a few years older than you." Looked about ten years, actually. Made him suddenly feel old.

"I wasn't going to ask, as it happens. I could easily check it out if I felt so inclined. It sounded like you were warning me off. I hope you haven't jumped to the rash conclusion I'm after you, Bruno? There's always someone, isn't there?"

"I'm not sure you'd be the one to talk."

She shook her head in demurral. "I can't claim your hectic love life. I have my music. That's more than enough for the time being."

The waiter arrived at their table and highly rated their choice, while giving Isabelle more than a few lascivious glances. Bruno sent him on his way with a crisp *grazie.*

"I'm so sorry for that, Isabella," he said, assailed by an unexpected anger. The guy was only looking. Who could blame him? Still, he hadn't cared for it.

"I'm used to it," Isabelle said gently.

He met her eyes, his serious. "You can be absolutely certain no trouble will come your way if I can help it."

She paused, taking that in. "How, exactly?" She rested her chin on her linked hands. "And it's *Isabelle.*"

"That's the Italian in me." He shrugged. "It's very strong. Could you have a better name than Isabella, *Bella*?"

His smile dazzled. The smile alone had massive sex appeal. "Is that how you get women to fall in love with you?" She spoke as if she were conducting an interview, notebook in hand.

He met the sparkling mischief in her gaze. "I'm not with you, Isabella."

"Of course you are. Even I've spotted women look at you like you're a multimillionaire megastar. I'd be nervous myself, only I've divined you're not into cradle snatching."

"Cradle snatching is a big mistake. I could point out you're over twenty-one and I like redheads." His tone had unconsciously deepened. Hell, what was he doing, flirting?

Ruefully, it dawned on Isabelle she could be the moth drawn to the flame if she didn't watch herself. She let a settling moment go by. "So how are you going to protect me and from what?" she asked.

"We don't know yet." His tone was serious.

"Oh, Bruno, stop that!" she implored. "I'm Isabelle Martin. My whole life is an open book."

An open book? He had serious doubts about that. Soon this young woman would be immersed in asking questions, searching for answers. "Let's just enjoy dinner, shall we?" he suggested. "You said you were hungry."

"I am. Okay then, a cease-fire. I know perfectly well you'll get back to being a private eye over coffee."

"I'm only going to show you a photograph," Bruno assured her.

That should be more than enough.

They were finishing coffee when Bruno pulled the photo out of his wallet and passed it across the candlelit table. "Tell me what you think."

Isabelle took the photograph, studying it hard. She was looking at the unsmiling face of a very beautiful young woman. Not a girl. Most definitely a *woman*, and a very sexy one at that. It was like looking at the picture of an older, far more experienced sister. Isabelle didn't know if she exactly *liked* this young woman. There was something very knowing in the gaze. The face was framed by masses of titian hair. She had large, almond-shaped eyes.

For a time she had absolutely nothing to say. She was, in fact, finding it hard to breathe. Astonishingly, the hand that held the photograph trembled. "This is a complete mystery," she said.

His eyes held understanding and a melting compassion. "I don't think we should do this here, Bella."

"I don't think we should do this at all. The resemblance is extraordinary, I grant you, but this woman has nothing to do with me and my family." Isabelle handed the photo back.

"I've upset you."

"Of course you've upset me," she said with unaccustomed sharpness. "I can't do this."

"We'll do only what you're comfortable with." He signalled for the bill.

Outside the restaurant, he hailed a cruising cab. "I live not far from here. We can talk quietly."

"I don't want to talk."

"What are you afraid of? It's not *me*. I'm here as your protector."

"Look, this is crazy!" Isabelle turned to him, her expression disturbed.

"Then we can sort it out. Trust me."

"I rarely trust strange men."

"Only I'm not strange, am I? It happens sometimes. You're comfortable enough with me."

"God help us, yes."

He placed a light, guiding hand at her back, yet Isabelle felt a sudden surge of sensation. It was as if he had caressed her spine.

When they were inside the cab, he glanced at her. "What's it to be? Your call."

Isabelle felt her agitation growing. "I swear I don't know. I like reading mysteries. I don't relish living one."

"I know you're intrigued."

She shook her head. "Not that. *Intrigued* is too light a word."

The cab driver broke in amiably. He had never seen such a contrast. The guy was the quintessential handsome Italian. The girl was pure Celt. A Celtic muse. "Where's it to be, folks?"

Bruno gave his address.

She knew his luxury apartment block well. She had admired it from afar, never thinking for a moment she would enter it with a man able to afford such a fantastic home.

"The sky's the limit!" she said, throwing up her hands. "Bet this set you back a pretty penny."

"I'm a single man."

"No fool for love, then?"

"Nothing I'm going to discuss with *you,* Bella."

"You must be able to lean out from your balcony and touch the stars," she said. "Fancy waking up to spectacular views in the morning; seeing the city a fairyland at night," Isabelle continued to enthuse. "I might win the lottery and splash it all on a one-bedroom apartment."

"I still can't get used to it," Bruno admitted as they walked into the elegant foyer. He and his father had lived modestly, in the same house all three of them had shared. Sometimes he thought they should have shifted. Too many memories. Especially for his dad.

No one joined them in the spacious lift. They were alone. Isabelle, in her hyped-up state, felt a smidge claustrophobic. Neither spoke a word. They just stood side by side. Isabelle found their being together unreal. She nibbled the inside of her lip while the superfast lift whizzed them to the twenty-eighth floor.

"Where do you live? With your parents?" Bruno asked as they exited into the hushed, thickly carpeted hallway.

She shook her head. "I have a small flat in a respectable neighbourhood, Bruno, because you asked."

"By yourself?"

This time she met his eyes directly. She was very direct. He already knew that. "I think I'm a bit of a loner. *Like you.*"

A strike for her. "How did you work that out?" he asked dryly.

"Woman's intuition."

"Really? Woman's intuition is no joke. Do you see your parents often?"

"Do you see your mother?" she parried.

He released a harsh breath. "No. Obviously, someone has filled you in on me, probably good old Phil. My parents' marriage broke up when I was seven. My father and I adored her."

She patted his jacketed arm, clearly offering comfort. "I'm so sorry. How sad. You were devastated. I understand that. You turned the rage inward."

"What rage?" he asked crisply, opening the door to his apartment.

"Enough to make you fire up. Perhaps *rage* is the wrong word. The hurt, the sadness that simmers deep down. You haven't gotten around to releasing it."

"I thought you were a musician, not a psychoanalyst," he said, turning a switch that controlled all the lighting.

"I know the signs," she broke off as she took in their surroundings. "Oh wow!" She came to a halt, gazing around the huge space with genuine wonder and admiration. "Now this is a showcase apartment for a well-heeled, sophisticated man. A man of taste."

"That's encouraging!"

"I mean it." Her eyes swept over the huge open-plan living area, beautifully furnished Italian style, dramatic like him. A palette of sand, bronze, black and gold. The only vibrant colours came from three dazzling artworks. An ebony grand piano stood in a prominent corner.

"That's a big surprise," she said, glancing towards the piano. "Do you play?"

"I give free rein to polishing the keys."

"You mean you *don't* play. You simply make sure the keys are depressed each day?"

"Right on. Sorry to disappoint you."

"Haven't you got enough going for you?" She flashed him a glance. "I'm really pleased you take time to look after your piano. It's a Steinway, after all. One of your girlfriends isn't a concert pianist, is she?"

"I'm hoping for such a woman to come my way."

"I'll start praying for you," Isabelle said. "And the piano. It needs playing, like all instruments. This place is perfect for you. Did you have a decorator?" She was teasing him deliberately. She guessed he hadn't.

"I did not," he clipped off.

"Good for you," she said approvingly.

"This is where I live. It has to reflect me. No one else."

"Who's arguing?" She put her black satin clutch bag down on a striking black lacquer cabinet, black trimmed with gilded bronze, moving toward one of the paintings, taking a closer look at it. "Next you're going to tell me you painted this."

Under the strong lights, her hair was on fire, glittering, gleaming, dancing with gold and copper highlights. "I wish. Do you like it?"

"Takes a lot of time to figure out, but it's dynamic. You certainly know how to feather your nest. You're a very stylish man."

"Thank you, Isabella," he said.

"And that's the only compliment you're going to get this evening. Do you have parties here? I can see parties."

He nodded. "Often. My people mostly." He took off his jacket, loosened his silk tie and settled them over the back of a chair.

"Your colleagues, the people who work for you?"

"My friends. A sprinkling of others. As long as they're interesting, with something to say."

"You must ask *me*. I'm not your dream concert pianist, but I'll play the piano for you."

"You play the piano?" One black eyebrow shot up.

"You people! Of course I do," she tut-tutted. "The

piano was my second instrument. I started out learning the piano when I was six."

"So, a musical family, then?"

She didn't answer for quite a while.

"You've gone quiet, Isabella. Anything up? The wrong question?"

She sighed. It was quite extraordinary, the way he said her name. It was as though they had known each other for years, the ease off the tongue, so melodic, so *Italian.* "I was a child who needed music. My parents are doctors, as I've said. Not that doctors don't love music. Of course they do. It was just that my parents don't. It's a question of time, I suppose. They don't have a lot of it."

"So how did you manage lessons?" he asked with interest.

She gave a little laugh. "I put on spectacular tantrums, so I'm told. I was determined to learn the piano. Don't ask me why."

"Your soul needed it."

She looked across at him, genuinely surprised. "Gosh, Bruno, that sounded like you really understand. My soul, my spirit, my being, even at that early age, did. I must have been a musician in another life. Once my mother got the message, she arranged a very good teacher for me. Nothing but the best. I started to be a good girl from then on. I had been a difficult child before that, from all accounts. Even I can dimly remember my troubles. My father bought me a grand piano—not like yours, King Steinway; you must have paid a packet for that, but a very good Yamaha. No little upright like other kids. They needed the spur to keep me busy and content. They were—are—committed to their careers. They're dedicated people, just not . . . artistic."

"When did you move out?" They were standing a

short distance apart, facing each other, locked into the conversation.

"When I took up my scholarship in London. It took four years to complete. When I returned, I found myself an apartment in Sydney, close to the Conservatory. My parents live in Adelaide, the city of churches. It's very English in its way. So are they."

"Didn't you want to be close to them?" He started to wonder about that.

"I wanted to be independent. Live my own life. Want me to play something for you?"

"Nothing I'd like more."

Her jewelled eyes lit up. "You're really nice, aren't you, under that top-of-the-pile, exceedingly clever businessman façade?"

He laughed. "Don't believe everything you read in the papers, Isabella. I have to work very hard."

"Me too," she said, sitting down at the piano and adjusting the seat. "Do you like Debussy?"

"All I know is 'Clair de Lune,'" he admitted. He hadn't arrived at the *D*s yet.

"This is one of Debussy's arabesques, the first."

"Great!" He backed up, settled in one of the deep Italian leather armchairs. To his consternation, his heart was jumping in his chest. For the moment, before she started playing, she had struck the very same pose as the Hartmann girl. If only his father had lived to see this. It seemed to him momentous they had met. The truth could even be that their meeting had been ordained.

She began. He gave himself up to the rippling music, the wonderful tone, the lyricism. He had bought the Steinway—very expensive, as Bella said—because he had liked the sound, especially of the bass. Some of his friends were musicians. They played piano, trumpet, sax. Mostly jazz. Great fun at a party. No one had played his piano remotely like this. He found her playing touched him physically. It was tantalizing. Seductive. Darn near erotic.

The piece came to an end. She looked towards him expectantly. He waved his hand. "Please. Keep going. You're a fine musician. This has been quite an evening."

Isabelle had to agree. There was something surreal about it all. "You'll know this one. Everyone knows this one. I play it on the cello as well. A Gershwin prelude." She had never enjoyed such a gratifying reception from her parents. Piano. Cello. Made no difference. Maybe she would have gained a better response playing a mouth organ with abandon. Bruno McKendrick's response, the brilliant flash of appreciation in his dark eyes, came as an absolute if unexpected delight.

"Bravo!"

She finished with a flourish. Rose to her feet. Dipped into her perfected concert bow.

"Come and sit down," Bruno invited. "My musical friends will love you. Can I get you anything?"

"A nice cold glass of water would be lovely. A slice of lime in it. Lemon will do." She began to wander about again. They were at a great height on the twenty-eighth floor. The apartment had two balconies. The city, the Harbour, the Bridge and the Opera House made for a glittering fairyland. It was a sensational view. She couldn't conceive of one better.

He returned with a squat crystal glass filled with cold water, two ice cubes, two paper-thin slices of lime. "Thank you. I know you have some more photos to show me. I don't know if I'm ready to look at them. This could get scary."

"You don't have to do anything you don't want to, Bella," he said. "But I truly believe you should look at what I've got. The Hartmann case obsessed my father, as I told you. A young woman goes missing. Imagine! Dad felt strongly for the family, the grandfather in particular. The young woman was adored."

"As far as you know." Her green eyes moved away from him. "She wasn't around to give her side of things, was she? And why the grandfather? She had parents, siblings?" She all but finished the cold water, handing the glass back to him.

"Dad found the grandfather, the patriarch, most affected." He turned to head off to the kitchen.

"May I follow?"

"Of course."

"Woo-hoo!" She gave a soft, melodious whistle, studying this new space. "How cool is this!" Black cabinetry, immaculate white marble tops, the silver sheen of stainless steel, a stainless-steel wine storage cabinet aligned with the refrigerator. Stainless-steel glass-fronted series of cupboards holding white crockery. Three dazzling gold pendants provided the lighting. She ran an appreciative hand over the white marble bench top. "Who does the cooking?"

"Who do you think?"

He looked down his nose at her. She was getting used to it. "At least one of your lady friends must be able to cook with brio!"

"My mother was a wonderful cook. She—"

He broke off abruptly, obviously about to say more, but thinking better of it.

"What made you tell me that?" One of his bronzed, shapely hands rested on the white marble. Before she knew it, she had rested her hand over his in a spontaneous gesture of empathy.

"I'm damned if I know." He stared down at their hands.

She didn't take her hand away. Neither did he. It was as though each was absorbing the other, through their skin.

"You miss her. You've never stopped missing her."

His answer came in a flash. "And what would you know about loss, Isabella?"

"I know what fills me with sadness," she said. "Maybe we feel the loss of generations. Our forebears." She was looking up into his dark, dark eyes. Deep. For a moment, she forgot to breathe. Even her limbs had turned liquid.

After a second he said very gently, "Bella, let go of my hand."

"Oh I'm sorry, sorry." She hastened to apologize, blushing.

"No need to be sorry." As a total impulse, he bent and lightly kissed her magnolia cheek. He would kiss a young female cousin like that. If only he had one. There was something very endearing about Isabelle Martin. Through her beauty, he also discerned sadness. He could read it in her eyes, hear it in her playing. Maybe that was why they had made an instant connection.

"I should be going, all right?" she announced briskly, as if she had overstayed her welcome. "Could you call a cab?"

"I'll take you," he said.

"You can't." She stared back at him with widened eyes. "You might be over the limit, a man like you."

"All I've had were three glasses of wine," he pointed out. "You've had two. Do you want to drive?"

"A Lamborghini?" She laughed, more a gurgle in her creamy throat.

"Nothing with that amount of impact. A Mercedes."

"Let me take the cab."

"No. I'll see you safely home. Moreover, I'll get to see where you live."

A strange look crossed her face. "You said you had more photos? May I borrow them for a day or two?"

"I'm going to have to say no to that, Bella. You can have one."

A brightening up. "I'll take good care of it. Trust me."

"I do trust you." He had learned the hard way where to put his trust. He trusted this girl.

"Thank you. Shall I ring for the cab?"

"You win. Give me a minute. I want you to see this particular photograph first."

Seconds passed. A full minute. She guessed the photograph would be with bundles of his father's papers. She waited in the living room, taking the piano seat, where she felt more in control.

What was happening here? What had compelled her to listen to him, to come with him, to play for him, to allow him to show her a photograph of—in her view—not an identical twin but an older sister with a sexy stare and a pout to her full mouth. The mouth was the same shape as hers, but she never pouted. At least she thought she didn't. And she didn't invite men's lust-filled glances.

Inside she could feel her emotions shifting like ripples on a pond. She closed her eyes. Opened them. Took a breath. There was nothing but a certain piquancy in this resemblance thing. So why was her mind so agitated? It didn't make sense. Maybe she was too impressionable, and Bruno McKendrick was far too persuasive. Only he hadn't tracked her down. Fate had brought them together. If she hadn't been standing in tonight as cellist for the quartet, they might never have met.

Bruno returned, holding a couple of photographs, one

of which he handed to her. "I haven't even asked you her name," Isabelle said. "This is all *sooo* melodramatic."

"Helena. Helena Hartmann. The Hartmanns are a pastoral family."

"I've never heard of them."

"People on the land have," he said. An understatement.

"German name, Hartmann." She made herself look down. "Oh my gosh!" she exclaimed, seeing herself. "How can this be?" This view of the young woman was completely different from the first photograph. The expression was openly vulnerable, in need of emotional support. This wasn't an adored young woman living in a model family home. She looked like she had been fighting for years to be *herself.* Isabelle had the unnerving feeling she was looking at herself. Hadn't she caught that very same expression in her mirror?

"Do you want to find out what happened to her?" Bruno asked gently. He could see she had instantly identified with the young woman in the photograph. He remembered his father once saying, "That look on Helena's face, Bruno. Makes you want to jump in and help."

Isabelle shook her head. "It doesn't fall to me. An extraordinary resemblance, that's all. I admit it's bizarre. The other photo you showed me is of a different person. An older sister, perhaps?"

"What?" Startled, he looked down at an enlargement of the photo he had shown Isabelle in the restaurant. "Helena Hartmann didn't have a sister. No siblings, in fact."

"Her mother perhaps, when young?"

Bruno was stunned. He continued to stare down at the photograph, compelled to adjust his thinking. Isabelle appeared confident of her judgement. He had already rated her highly intelligent. No suggestion had ever been made that the photographs were of two different young women. They were, after all, identical, save for the differing expressions. It was only after Isabelle had pointed it out that he'd realized she could be right. Anything was possible. The personalities revealed were of one super-confident young woman, the other, girlish and insecure.

"Put the photos side by side on the table," Isabelle suggested. "One is black and white. The other is in colour, I know. We both see the features as being extraordinarily alike. The same mane of curly hair. The same almond eyes, but the *expressions*—the inner selves are totally different. One is a shadow of the other. Surely your dad saw that?"

Bruno frowned. "He didn't have a clue. The photographs were given to him by family. He was told they were of Helena. Why would they lie? What would be the point?"

"The grandfather?"

"Not Konrad. The father actually, Erik. He could scarcely make a mistake. We all do look different depending on whether life is going our way or isn't, surely?"

"What about the mother?"

He paused for a moment, then he met her searching eyes. "The mother, Myra, was killed in a riding accident on the property when Helena was twelve. Rumour had it the mother had been having an affair. Affairs. Could have been exaggeration. The family were all against her, according to Dad."

"Something is wrong somewhere, Bruno," Isabelle said with a shake of her head. "Maybe the husband fixed it that she'd come off her horse. There would have been a lot of venom in him. A beautiful wife. A lover. A jealous, possessive husband. Has all the ingredients. Maybe

Helena ran off to be free of all the family tensions. The dead woman was her mother, after all. It has to be considered: the first photo could be of the mother, Myra."

"You seem so darned *sure*."

"A woman's take. Of course I could be wrong, but I doubt it. The other photo, the vulnerable one, could perhaps reflect grief over the mother's tragedy."

"Over ten years later?"

"Why not? What's time to a grieving soul?"

"Of course there's that, but Helena's father handed over the photographs as those taken of his daughter."

"He could have been playing games," Isabelle said. "He could even hate his own child because she was a constant reminder of the wife who betrayed and humiliated him. The family could well have been trying to confuse your father. Maybe one of them didn't want her found? Maybe one of them helped her get away for whatever reason. It had to be serious. An investigation was mounted by the grandfather, who must have loved Helena. The police would have been notified, then your father. The grandfather might never have suspected another family member was involved, even his own son. So then, which one was the *real* Helena? First subject looks fully capable of running off and establishing a new identity, wouldn't you say? She looks confident, manipulative. Second subject looks just . . . sad and sort of helpless. Anyway, Bruno McKendrick, it's not my problem. I've never met anyone called Hartmann in my life. My parents are Norville and Hilary Martin. My mother's maiden name was Frazer-Holmes." She began to wave the photograph in her hand as if it threatened her. "I don't want this."

"Don't be angry," he said quietly, not taking the photograph from her.

"I'm *not* angry. I'm all shook up. Like Elvis. Heck, Elvis has had dozens and dozens of look-alikes."

"No one, but no one, looked like Elvis," he half-laughed.

"Okay, but lock the photographs away."

"At least you know what I'm talking about. There remains a possibility your parents haven't spoken about, didn't *want* to speak to you about the past."

"By telling me they snatched someone else's baby?" Her voice rose in disbelief.

"Not unheard of. Things do go wrong in maternity hospitals. Wrong tags, no tags, wrong names, mix-ups, babies given to the wrong mothers. Wrong mothers rear wrong babies. Baby gets to adulthood before someone stumbles on the truth. Baby doesn't want to hook up with her biological mother. You read about it all the time, Bella, even if you can scarcely believe it. Surely a mother would *know* her own baby? The smell of it, the look of it. Should we doubt a mother's instincts? I wouldn't have thought so, yet the evidence is there. Babies do go to the wrong families. Moreover, they're accepted."

"Bruno," she said, exasperated. "I am aware of what you say, but it just so happens I *know* they're my parents. I truly do."

"Then you shouldn't be bothered checking things out. Ask a few questions. Show your mother the photograph. See what she says. How she responds."

Isabelle had no difficulty visualizing her mother's reaction. "It wouldn't be the best conversation opener, I can tell you. She'd be affronted."

"How so?" He had to turn that one over in his mind. "If she did react in that way surely you'd have stumbled onto a minefield. I can't see a loving mother being outraged by your extraordinary resemblance to a young woman gone missing decades ago. There could be no possible reason for outrage."

Isabelle sighed. "Want to bet? Everyone has a reason. *Everything* has a reason. My mother is a very formidable woman, and very clever. She intimidates people. I've seen it. She deals in life and death. Not fantasy."

"Who's talking fantasy?" Bruno countered, not liking the sound of her mother. "You have Helena Hartmann's face. You have her colouring. You're a musician. So was she."

She felt dazed. "Maybe you should pay more attention to coincidence? I can't listen, in any case. You're driven to solve an old case for your father. I understand that. You had a father you loved, who loved you. I'm not criticizing my mother. I'm only describing the way she is. Both my parents have been extremely good to me. I've never wanted for anything. They may not have exactly approved of my decision to become a professional musician. They had different hopes for me—I was smart at school—but they supported me on the understanding my ambition was *not* to make a name for myself."

Bruno's shapely mouth compressed. "You can't be serious?"

"I'm very serious."

"Then I'm having a bit of trouble with that. You've spent years studying. You've gained a Master's degree at a world-famous college of music yet all further ambitions are frowned upon. What's their aim? To keep you hidden?" He took a deep and, yes, angry breath.

"More like marry me off." She gave a half laugh. "A good marriage of course. My mother would pick out the most outstanding candidates from within her own circle."

She wouldn't want the dead rising.

"They're not everyday people," Isabelle tried hard to explain. "Just imagine the life they lead."

"They're controllers?"

"Oh, Bruno," she protested. "They want to see me settled. They want grandchildren." Or so they claimed. Maybe they'd be more comfortable with the next generation, a grandchild.

"If you don't want to risk showing her the photograph, it's entirely up to you."

"*Risk* being the punch line?" she challenged wryly.

"Right now, I think it's worth it. If it's sheer coincidence, there's nothing whatever to worry you or your parents. Who knows; we could have *exact* doubles."

"I said it first." She looked back at the later photograph, then up at him. "I wish you hadn't shown me this, Bruno. I see the tears behind her eyes. I *don't* see a much-loved granddaughter or a much-loved daughter. The other woman looks older. Far more worldly."

"I agree." He did, now that he had given the photographs his total attention.

"So what happened in between? It would have been very easy for your father to get so involved. I know instinctively he was a very nice man. A kind man. You obviously loved him a great deal. But what makes you think you can solve a case he couldn't? I'm guessing he was an expert investigator?"

Bruno's explanation was simple. "The best. Only he never got to see *you*."

"And you think *you're* going to nail it?"

"Doesn't her family deserve closure?"

Isabelle lowered her head, shielding her eyes. "All suffering families deserve closure. But this is conjecture. You have no proof of anything. Anyway, the Hartmann grandfather would be dead. Someone in the remaining family could be living with a secret. What do we know? We know Helena Hartmann had problems. She thought disappearing was the only answer. It's a strong possibility she was desperately unhappy. She would have had help to get away. You can't just hop on a bus in the Outback."

"My father was convinced she had hidden away on a freight plane that regularly brought supplies to the station. Probably the pilot knew, but he wasn't talking, not to the police, not even to my dad, who'd made the getting of information an art form."

"The pilot was probably protecting her. You're being very disruptive to my life, Bruno McKendrick."

"I know."

"Do you believe in fate? Karma? That sort of thing?"

"I do *now.*" There was a whole lot of feeling in his deep voice.

Isabelle came to a reluctant decision, but a decision all the same. "I think I'll show this photograph to my father," she said. "He's more approachable than my mother. I'll make it seem like a curiosity."

"You'd have to fly to Adelaide?" He thought he should pay for that.

"No." She shook her head. "There's a medical conference in Sydney starting next Wednesday. I've organised to see him then. He's been very good taking care of me, you know. He loves me. He's not a demonstrative man, that's all. Some men don't find it easy. They don't understand the concept of closeness like physical displays of affection. Perhaps it was the way they were brought up." She omitted to say her mother found displays of affection redundant. Displays of affection were denied her father as well. She had never seen them hug, let alone kiss. They had always had separate bedrooms. Her mother was *different.* She remembered one of her school friends, Cressy, rolling her eyes while confiding *her* mother called Isabelle's "a travelling iceberg." She should have felt bad for her mother, but she didn't. She liked Cressy's mother a lot. She was so warm and friendly. Unfailingly kind. Kindness was very important. Besides, she knew her mother would come across as an icy, unapproachable woman. Certainly not one to stand around chatting with other mothers. But so clever! Everyone thought so.

At that moment, Bruno could find nothing *easy* to say about her parents. "Anyone with red hair and green eyes in the family?" he asked.

"Believe it or not, there is. A cousin on my mother's side. Red hair and freckles. On the horsey side. Long face. Long nose. I don't look a bit like her. But there you are!"

"You've met her?"

"No. I've only seen a photograph of her."

"So what family have you actually known?"

"Tough question. None. It happens like that sometimes. I'd like to go home now, Bruno. There's really no need for you to come with me."

"I feel there is."

"So no argument, then."

Chapter Two

No way could she wear an outfit with evening pants to dinner, not even a very short dress. After a few minutes of indecision, she chose a deceptively simple crepe dress in a beautiful shade of indigo. The skirt hit well below the knee. Her father would like that. Feminine. Ladylike. To further gain his approval, she had subdued her copious hair, pulling it back into an updated roll like the wonderfully stylish Princess Mary of Denmark, Australian born and bred.

Many times over the years she had wondered if her parents had had a choice they would have picked a different child. A child they recognised. A child they identified with. One who shared the same characteristics. Not the changeling they got. A special trial was her riotous red hair. "No restraint about *red*!" her mother, Hilary, a handsome brunette who favoured a short, brush-back style that suited her, had once said. She must have been one troublesome kid, but she had settled down once she got her piano and the household was no longer a "madhouse."

She could well imagine she might have been swapped

at birth. Some new mother, probably with red hair, would have gone home with a dark-haired, dark-eyed changeling who never did fit in. It was possible, as Bruno McKendrick had so kindly pointed out. Thanks to him, she had completely yielded to this crazy idea, but then, the resemblance was incredible. Baby swapping was a conclusion one could reach, though it would have been nigh on impossible to put one over her mother. And there was the horsey, redheaded cousin conveniently living in the wilds of Scotland.

Dr. Norville Martin was a tall, distinguished-looking man in his late fifties. He had a full head of fading fair hair, grey eyes, fine regular features, unlined pale skin that rarely saw the hot Australian sun. He looked like what he was: a man of high moral and ethical standards, a dedicated doctor, recognised in his field of oncology, which was the very serious business of diagnosing with great accuracy the various types of cancers, then advising on treatments best suited to the specific cancer. Dr. Martin was therefore a serious man.

Both her parents dealt in life and death. The making of music wasn't their scene, though she had often thought listening to beautiful music could provide great pleasure and a relief from all the pain and suffering they saw on a daily basis. Her father had the harder time. Her mother coped brilliantly. She had a very different temperament. Or a heart carved out of stone?

He was waiting for her in the lobby of the hotel where he was staying. He rose to greet her. No kisses or hugs, but his fondness for her was apparent in the numerous pats she got on the shoulder. "How are you, my dear? You look well."

"I am well, thank you, Father. It's lovely to see you. How's Hilary?" She had been instructed to call her mother Hilary after her graduation from high school. As though Mother wasn't somehow *right.* As far as that went, she had always thought she should have been allowed to call her father Dad, like all her friends. But the very formal Father worked best.

Her parents inhabited a totally different world from the one her friends' parents did. Few people measured up. She knew *she* didn't. On the plus side, she was no snob, though her mother was among the worst of them.

She almost missed what her father was saying in his quiet, controlled voice. "Your mother is extremely committed, as usual, my dear. Shall we go in? I must admit to being hungry. I missed lunch."

Isabelle found herself ordering much the same thing as her father. Her heart was thrumming and she had butterflies in her stomach. She wasn't hungry. Her father might say he was hungry, but she knew both parents ate sparingly. Unlike the French, they ate to live, not live to eat. She had a mad urge to order octopus but settled for pan-seared snapper with a warm Mediterranean salad. Her father chose chargrilled salmon with a Greek salad. All very healthy and, as it turned out, delicious. Dessert was light and healthy too: lemon curd tarts with fresh raspberries.

"Oh, I do feel so much better," her father said, giving his fugitive smile. It was such a *nice* smile, he should smile more often. "Coffee?"

"Yes, please. I have something to show you. A curiosity."

"Really?" Dr. Martin summoned their waiter. "Two short blacks, if you would. Okay with you, Isabelle?"

"Fine." What she really needed was a short brandy.

"So what is this curiosity?" he asked indulgently when their coffees were set in front of them.

"A photograph. I wanted your take on it." Her stomach was tied in knots.

"Well, then, better show me, m'dear. Is it of you?"

"What do *you* think?" She passed the photograph across the table.

Her father looked down at the photograph. Looked up at her in puzzlement. "Where was this taken, in London? That's not your piano."

"It's not me, Father." She kept her eyes on him.

Norville Martin made a helpless gesture. "It's *not*?"

"It's of a young woman called Helena Hartmann. Ever heard the name?"

He looked back at her in silence. "No, I haven't," he said finally, his grey eyes darkening.

"It's an extraordinary resemblance, wouldn't you say?"

"Certainly. But people do have doubles, my dear." He picked up his coffee, drank it in one gulp.

"I'm her mirror image. She's even a musician, a pianist."

Now his cheeks flushed. "What are you expecting of me, Isabelle?" he asked with unfamiliar testiness. "I've commented on the likeness. There's no more I *can* say."

"And you deny knowing anyone of the Hartmann name?"

He reacted sternly. "What on earth are you talking about, Isabelle? Why are you questioning me in this way? I do deny knowing any Hartmanns. Your mother wouldn't brook such questions. It could be seen as insulting."

"I wouldn't dream of insulting either of you, Father. Perhaps you're overreacting a little. The Hartmanns could well be kin you don't know about."

Dr. Martin sat up very straight. "I know my family tree, thank you, Isabelle. Your mother's family tree is far more illustrious than mine. Hartmann is a German name. No Germans in the family, only English and Scots."

"I know that, Father, but you can see how very intriguing this is?"

"Who gave you this photograph?" he asked, as though denouncing whoever it was.

"Someone I met for the first time a few nights ago."

"And how did this person come to have it, let alone produce it for your viewing? Man, woman? Are you sure you haven't met before?"

"It was a man, Father. A Bruno McKendrick, a respected name in the city. His father was a private investigator. He was hired by the Hartmann patriarch to find his missing granddaughter. This was some twenty years ago. He never did find her. She vanished."

"Australian family?"

"Yes."

He sat back, staring at her. "That settles it. Twenty years ago, my dear, your mother and I were a young married couple living in our homeland, England, where you were later born."

"Go on."

He showed a rare anger. "What do you mean, go on? There's nothing more to say. No story to tell. The likeness to the young woman in the photograph is no more than coincidence. I'm very surprised this man showed it to you. It's a long time ago."

"And you'd be unhappy if I did a little investigating myself?" For a moment, Isabelle thought he was going to stand up and leave the table.

"My dear girl, I see no need whatever. For that matter, why would you want to?"

She put her thoughts into words. "She *speaks* to me, Father. I can see the unhappiness in her eyes. They're *my* eyes." She gave a little off-key laugh. "Maybe it's a case of reincarnation?"

"I think we can rule that out," he said sternly, as though she had lost her mind. "You always were far too imaginative. I hope you don't intend showing that photograph to your mother. You'll get short shrift there."

"Why exactly?" Isabelle asked, not understanding anything at all. "We all know my mother is a formidable woman, but what possible objection could she have to my showing her a photograph of someone who looks like me? Everyone likes a mystery."

"Your mother doesn't. Neither do I. Neither of us have the time to go chasing after mysteries. I can offer you no encouragement, Isabelle. I have no idea who that young woman could be."

"Except she's the image of *me,* Father. You were taken in."

The rare flush in his cheeks deepened. "I'd be obliged if you'd stop, my dear. We've had a pleasant evening. Please don't spoil it. If you've finished your coffee, we should go. Come along now. The concierge will call you a taxi."

Isabelle shook her head. "Not necessary, Father. I'll find one on the street." It came to her with a sense of shock that it seemed as though her father had aged ten years right in front of her eyes.

She kept telling herself not to rush into anything. She had upset her father. God knows what would have happened had Hilary been present at dinner. Would her father tell Hilary all about the incident when he arrived back home? She might be due to get a stern, admonishing phone call. She was on her own now. Whoever Helena Hartmann had been, her parents didn't want to know.

Two days went by. She had taken on a few students at the Conservatorium. Fledglings who would grow. Two with very real promise. Both male. The rest of the time she spent practising with the quartet.

"You play really well, Isabelle," James Kellerman announced, in his smooth, patronising fashion, waving his bow at her. "You've fitted in far better than I hoped." Immediately Emma, the viola player, went into a sulk. She worshipped James. The second violin, Simon, turned shyly admiring eyes on her. He seemed to have developed a crush on her. She smiled, taking little notice of James's condescension. She was quite confident she played better than *really* well. She was a very good cellist. She had studied with the best of the best. Professor Otto Morgenstern would have thrown her out the door if she hadn't met his extremely high standards.

"What say we run through the Schubert today?" said James.

She was happy. She loved Schubert.

When they broke late in the afternoon, James suggested they meet up for drinks and conversation later that night, his blue gaze intent on hers, waiting for her to look delighted and agree.

She had been prepared for something like this. "No can do, James." She smiled at him cheerfully. "I'm seeing my father. He's in town." In fact, her father had flown back to Adelaide that morning.

Always on her mind was the worrying feeling she should get in touch with Bruno McKendrick, who already had profoundly altered her life. He had given her both his unlisted home number and his mobile number.

She waited until 8 p.m. before she rang his home

number. If he were out on the town, as he very likely was, with the very attractive Penelope, who clearly had Madame Lubrinski's approval, she would leave a message. Simple. She would tell him the matter was closed. Her father did not want her to pursue it.

To her surprise, he answered the phone. His voice was so immediate, so deep and sexy, it caused a spontaneous ripple in her blood. She could hear other voices raised in laughter, a woman's voice in particular, in the background.

"It's Isabelle Martin," she announced herself quickly. "You're busy? I can call back another time."

"Where are you?"

"I'm at home." The voices had receded, so he must have moved off. "I need to tell you my father doesn't know any Hartmanns. My parents lived in London at the time Helena disappeared."

No comment on that. "What was his spontaneous reaction to the photograph, Bella?" he asked, cutting to the chase.

"He thought it was me."

"Of course he did. Anyone would. Did he appear rattled in any way?"

"This is my father you're talking about," she protested.

"You sound like you're hurting."

Yet again he surprised her. He had picked up on her distress. "Arrah, not a bit," she lied. "Listen, I won't keep you from your friends. I had to call." She was about to hang up.

He must have sensed it because he called urgently, "Bella? Bella, don't hang up."

She did. He could go back to his guests. He probably had someone over every night. Unbelievably, she was shaking all over.

* * *

Two hours later, she was in bed, rereading a leather-bound book of poems by one of her favourites, Emily Dickinson. Emily, she reckoned, must have been a pretty dark horse. Softly, she recited aloud:

Wild nights—Wild nights!
Were I with thee
Wild nights should be
Our luxury!

Futile—the Winds—
To a Heart in port—
Done with the Compass— Done with the Chart!

Rowing in Eden— Ah, the Sea!
Might I but moor—tonight—
In thee!

Reading the poem had quickened her pulse. Who was Emily's mystery man?

The phone by her bed suddenly rang, startling her out of her little reverie. She knew before she picked up it would be him.

"Hello, Bruno McKendrick," she said.

"Hello yourself, Bella Martin. How did you know it was me?"

"I don't get late-night calls."

"It's only ten-fifteen."

"Late for me."

He laughed. "Come on. It was nearly one a.m. when I dropped you off the other night."

"That was a special occasion. I'm not a party animal."

"You'll have to try a little harder. We have the same initials, by the way."

"No, we don't," she corrected. "I'm I. M. *I* for Isabelle. *M* for Martin."

"You're Bella to me."

"Your guests have gone?" she asked. No sounds from the background.

"My friend Jake and his wife, Sara. I managed to make quite a bit of money for them on the stock market."

"They must *love* you."

"They do. When you meet them, you'll see for yourself."

"I'm going to meet them?"

"There is *no* way, Bella, you're going out of my life."

"Could that be related to the fact that I'm the image of Helena Hartmann?"

"Actually, I'd miss the piano playing," he said smoothly.

"Did you tell them about me? About your father's old case; the resemblance, I mean."

"Absolutely not. That's our little secret."

She was pleased. "Maybe you can make a bundle for me? I'm renting."

"Really? Your parents must be well off, both specialist doctors. Haven't they helped out?"

She tut-tutted. "They've been very good, Bruno. I won a scholarship to the Royal College, but naturally there were many expenses. They bought me a very fine cello before I left. My professor didn't like it much. He traded it in for me and found me one very much better. He knew the lady who owned my current cello, actually a real Lady, and a philanthropist. I've been very lucky."

"There are and always have been patrons of the arts,"

Bruno said. "You are obviously a very deserving case. Marta Lubrinski's husband, Ivor, was a great help to me, opening doors in the business world."

"While Madame Lubrinski wheels out potential wives."

"Don't let's go there," he groaned. "I'm leading the good life as a bachelor."

"Can I be serious now?" she asked, her tone changing.

"That's why I rang you back. I had the idea you were worried sick."

Gosh, he was intuitive. "Why should that be?"

"Maybe it's your destiny—our destiny—to find out what happened to Helena Hartmann. Your father gave you no encouragement, I take it?"

She couldn't help it; she gave a deep sigh. "I have never seen his disapproval so pronounced. He warned me against speaking to Hilary—my mother—about it."

He sounded surprised. "You call your mother Hilary? May I ask why?"

"Obviously because she thought by the time I was seventeen, it was time. I still call my father, Father."

"Can't that be softened to Dad?"

"No. What was your father's first name?"

"Ross. Ross McKendrick."

"I like that. And your mother?"

"I'll be darned if I remember. Chiara," he said, after a moment, with a pure Roman accent.

"I suppose you speak fluent Italian?"

"I do. I'm proud of my heritage."

"Chiara." She had perfect pitch, so his mother's name and the exact inflection he gave to it, rolled easily off her tongue. "A beautiful name for a beautiful woman."

"How do you know she was beautiful?"

She heard the grate in his voice. "You have to look like

someone, Bruno. Someone Italian. You must see your mother every time you look in the mirror."

He did. "It must spook you, not bearing any resemblance to your mother and father," he countered. None of his friends ever mentioned his mother. Isabelle Martin was the first to bring her into the conversation.

"There's the cousin in Scotland."

"I understood she looked like a racehorse. Do you feel you could approach Hilary? I'll come with you."

"To Adelaide?" Her voice soared in surprise.

"There are daily flights in and out," he pointed out dryly.

"You would come with me to meet my mother?"

"Bella, you can't be serious. I meet scary people every day of my life. I've caught all your negative worries about your parents. Your mother in particular. You can bet your life your father has spoken to her about your meeting."

"I am who I am," she said.

"Tell me who you are?"

Some note in his voice turned her heart over. "You'll have to wait until I get my head around it. Say good night, Bruno. I have a full day tomorrow."

He answered not with the good night she expected, but a mellifluous stream of Italian.

That threw her. She knew all the musical terms in Italian. She could toss off the Italian words and phrases everyone knew, but of the words that rolled off his tongue so smoothly, she had no idea. Probably she would never know, but she could listen to his voice all day and all night.

Saturday morning and she planned to do a little shopping: groceries, fresh fruit and veggies. She had just finished dressing in blue culottes with a white camisole, colourful violet, blue and green-printed sneakers on her feet, when she heard her intercom buzzer. She wasn't expecting anyone. She sprinted to the wall fixture adjacent to the kitchen, pressed the button and stared at the video image. For a moment, her mind blanked; then she whispered to herself, "My God!"

It was her mother. In Sydney. This visit meant trouble and no escape. There had never been long, leisurely conversations with Hilary. If it was any consolation, her father didn't have that pleasure either. What else could she do but let her in?

"Open up, Isabelle. I know you're there," Hilary ordered, sharp as a knife.

Had she really expected, "It's me, darling"? She almost asked what proof her mother had. Had she been camped out on the street? She unlocked the security door before snatching up her mobile to leave a message for Bruno McKendrick. She didn't think about it. She just did it.

My mother's at the door. She's on the war path.

Not that he could do anything. Probably he had planned his day sailing the Harbour. She had heard he was an experienced yachtsman.

Heart beating fast, well aware she was going to be given a hard time, she went to her door, opening it to her mother, who regarded her with cold, narrowed eyes.

"Surprised to see me, Isabelle?"

She nearly said, "Naw!" offered instead, "Greetings to you too, Mother. Please come in."

Hilary didn't so much walk as stalk past her, her dark eyes sweeping around the combined living/kitchen space, searching for something that would meet with her disapproval. It was only a small flat, but Isabelle was naturally house proud. She had a flair for design. She always had fresh flowers in the flat, at the moment perfumed yellow roses in a copper bowl on the coffee table, white daisies on the kitchen bench beside a colourful ceramic dish holding lemons and limes. Lemons in the kitchen was a must for her.

"Not a happy face, then?" she dared to quip in the face of icy disapproval. She might have been a badly behaved schoolgirl in need of taming. "You flew in obviously. Can I get you something—tea, coffee?"

Hilary didn't bother to answer. She threw her expensive Bally leather holdall onto a sofa. "To put it bluntly, this is *outrageous,* Isabelle."

Isabelle stood her ground, controlling her strong impulse to run for the hills. "You need to explain, Mother." She fully expected Hilary to remind her she wished to be called by her first name. "*What* is outrageous?"

"Your reckless disregard for the feelings of others. I tell you, my girl, you upset your father terribly."

That was true enough. "Do please sit down," Isabelle invited, thinking Hilary would never change. "You've flown in especially to tell me that? Or are you on your way to someplace else?"

"You can show me that photograph you showed him," Hilary said with severity.

In the old days she would have hopped to. Now an *adult* Isabelle said, "In good time. Shocking Father definitely wasn't my intention."

"Of course it was!" Hilary declared in a controlled rage. "And this person who gave it to you. What's his agenda? What is he playing at? Or rather, why is he playing you? Obviously, he's out to make trouble."

"What possible trouble *could* he make? Where are you going with this?"

No explanation was forthcoming. "Do what you're

told, Isabelle. Go get the photograph. It's quite possible it's been doctored. What's behind it I intend to find out."

"If it weren't you, *Mother,* I'd say you were acting a little crazy."

"Don't attempt to insult me, Isabelle," Hilary said coldly. "Bring me the photo."

"I will, but first, I'm going to make coffee." Isabelle moved behind the kitchen counter. "Who *am* I really?" she shocked herself by asking, staring across the space at the tall, slim, elegantly dressed brunette who was the highly respected Dr. Hilary Martin.

"You stop that!" Hilary looked like she was about to throw something. Maybe the copper bowl of roses. "You know damned well who you are. You're my daughter, even if you are a susceptible little fool."

"Susceptible to what?" Isabelle popped a coffee pod into her machine. "I'd like to hear."

"This is a hoax of some kind," Hilary said, as though she had weighed up the situation and come to that conclusion.

Isabelle felt her heart skip a beat. *Hoax?* "To what purpose?" she asked, suddenly wondering if she could possibly be a victim. Bruno McKendrick was an extremely convincing man. "Please sit down. Surely we can discuss this calmly? The *this* is no more than a photograph of a girl who could be my double."

"You *fool*!" Hilary shot her a look full of scorn. "The name is Hartmann, right?"

"Yes. Helena Hartmann."

Hilary looked like a woman with her feet planted firmly on the high moral ground. "I've been able to make some enquiries about a Hartmann family. Very wealthy people. They own cattle stations in two states. A daughter left home of her own accord twenty years ago."

"Never found." Isabelle poured Hilary's coffee. No

sugar. She placed it on a small tray and then took it over to where Hilary was seated, setting it down on the coffee table. "Where did you get this information from, and so quickly?"

"I have friends in all sorts of places, Isabelle," Hilary pronounced loftily. "Friends with information about many people."

Isabelle nodded. "So you've got contacts everywhere, including God."

"Don't, I mean, *don't* use that tone with me," Hilary cried, her level of ferocity stunning Isabelle. "You owe everything to your father and me."

"Of course I do. But is that so extraordinary? All my friends, my fellow students, had good, loving parents. Many of them had made big sacrifices to get their gifted sons and daughters into college. You and Father are very successful doctors. Am I supposed to go down on my hands and knees and thank you for providing for me, your only child?"

"I'll tell you one thing," Hilary gritted, picking up a spoon and swirling it around her coffee cup. "You've always been thankless, as a child and as a young woman."

Isabelle tried to find answers to all this vehemence. What was behind it all? The photographs of Helena Hartmann had clearly spooked both Hilary and her father. "That's simply not true, *Mother.* No way did I not express my gratitude. I was over the moon when Father bought my piano, then my cellos. I worked very hard for you. I won prizes. Gained lots of attention, got to play the Elgar with a symphony orchestra, yet you never came to see me. Not once in over four years."

Hilary's good-looking face was scrunched. "You know perfectly well we couldn't get away."

"I know that's not true," Isabelle said quietly.

"What?" Hilary's head shot up.

"The Suttons looked me up when they were in London. They told me you and Father had just returned from a trip to Dubai. You loved it. But you don't love me, do you, Mother?" Isabelle said, sad and serious at the same time.

Hilary slipped into top gear. "Don't be absurd! You're my daughter, my only child."

"Yet you don't love me. You've never been cruel or unkind, but you've been as distant as the far side of the moon. I've tried and tried and tried. God knows I've tried to get close to you. You've never kissed me, hugged me, even as a toddler. We've never been pals."

"Pals!" Hilary reared back in astonishment. Any child of hers would need to be a supreme optimist to expect to be *pals* with Hilary. "I have no obligation to be pals with my own daughter. I'm not that idiotic woman, Betty, your school friend Cressy's mother. You were looked after very well, Isabelle. You wanted for nothing. You were handed a future."

"Not a *musical* future. All very well to become an accomplished musician, but my real future was to marry well. Settle down and have children. Definitely *not* with red hair. I bear no resemblance to you or to Father whatever."

"My cousin, Fiona, has red hair," Hilary said, as though that settled everything.

"*Do* you have a very plain cousin called Fiona, or did you rustle up that photograph from somewhere?"

Hilary gave a grim smile. "It's not my fault you're so mixed up and full of resentments. You've been lied to, Isabelle."

Isabelle shook her head. "I don't think so. I do not accept my friend—"

"Your *friend*!" Hilary nearly leapt up from the armchair. "A man you've just met. A man who produces a photograph like a rabbit out of a hat. You've been conned, my dear. Brainwashed, if you like. This is some sort of game. One you should have avoided like the plague, only you have no self-confidence, no self-esteem, no experience of life."

"That really should be the case, but it isn't. The way *you* are, Mother, made me strong. Maybe I was strong all the time. I hung in there, didn't I, until Father bought me my piano. I was that naughty, naughty little girl, remember? Difficult. That off-putting red hair. You've always hated my hair."

"All right, I don't like red hair," Hilary declared, almost savagely for her. "It reminds me of Fiona, ghastly girl, but your father wanted a child. One child was all I could handle. I had the promise of a brilliant career, but I allowed myself to fall pregnant."

"Only neither of you wanted a child like *me.* Can you blame me if I wonder?"

"I do blame you, Isabelle," Hilary said with crushing condemnation. "This man read you right. You're gullible, firing off in all directions. I understand it hasn't been easy for you having both parents in the medical profession. I admit we were both disappointed, even dismayed you chose music as a career instead of following in our footsteps. I know you're gifted, but unless you're a du Pré or the like, it comes down to teaching, getting into one of the symphony orchestras—unlikely where the members never seem to die—join a quartet or keep your music as a hobby, playing for your own enjoyment."

That analysis pierced Isabelle to her soul. A hobby? "Certainly not yours or Father's enjoyment," she said. "Anyone else would call you a couple of Philistines, because that's what you are. Father *is* my father?" She allowed a thread of disbelief into her voice.

"Shame. Shame on you, Isabelle," Hilary retorted, picking up her coffee and draining it. "If you've been persuaded you could be a Hartmann, let me destroy your hopes . . . You're *not.* I'll never tell your father what you just said. It would break his heart."

Isabelle shook her head. "I don't think so. After I showed Father the photograph, he changed. He showed anger when he's such a quiet man. There was no need for anger, surely? Anyone would think I had raked up some awful scandal. He—" She broke off at the sound of the intercom buzzer.

Hilary barked the order. "Leave it. Whoever it is they can go away."

"I'll see who it is first." She already knew. Without speaking, she pressed the button to open the security door. Bruno McKendrick's handsome head came into view.

Hilary looked up expectantly, a frown furrowing her brows. "Well?"

"Just a friend. He'll come up."

Hilary looked pushed beyond endurance. "I *told* you to send whoever it was away."

"I thought you might want to meet him," Isabelle countered. "It's Bruno McKendrick, the man who showed me the photograph. His father was the late Ross McKendrick, a respected private investigator hired by the Hartmann family."

"A private investigator?" Hilary made it sound like Ross McKendrick had been a known associate of criminals.

A tap came on the door. Next, the sound of the lock being tested, then Bruno was inside the door.

"Hi! The door was open, Bella." He knew without being told she had left it that way.

"Come in." She gave him a quick telling smile, standing aside. Bruno's whole aura was one of magnetism and disciplined energy. Here was a man impossible to ignore. A man equal to the likes of her formidable mother.

Bruno fixed his dark gaze on the seated woman who was looking back at him as if she couldn't believe her eyes. "Dr. Martin?" He gave her a semblance of his charming smile.

Hilary didn't respond. She remained staring up at him as if she had never met such an extraordinary person in her entire life.

"What about a coffee, Bruno?" Isabelle asked in an effort to ease the situation.

"Grazie!" For a tall man of impressive physique, he moved with considerable lightness of foot. "May I?" he asked of Hilary, taking the armchair opposite in the absence of her consent.

"You're the young man who has been filling my daughter's head with nonsense." Finally, Hilary spoke, wasting no time launching into accusation.

"Not nonsense at all, Doctor," Bruno replied mildly. "I'm assuming Bella has shown you the photographs?"

"Bella? Bella?" Hilary pulled a stern face. "Her name is Isabelle."

"Most people shorten first names," Bruno pointed out pleasantly.

Isabelle quickly made coffee and brought a cup out to him. "I haven't shown my mother the photographs. Not yet."

"Might be an idea if you go and get them," he said, taking the coffee cup and saucer from her.

"Have you no sense of shame?" Hilary cried, as Isabelle moved off.

"Shame has no part of this, Dr. Martin," Bruno said.

"You're exploiting my daughter."

"Just maybe *you* are," he returned.

A flush spread across Hilary's smooth cheeks. "I beg your pardon!"

"It's not wise to insult *me,* Doctor."

"It's my duty to protect my daughter," Hilary fired back. "She's young and very impressionable."

"She's young, certainly, but I wouldn't call her all that impressionable. Isabelle is highly intelligent, with a fine eye for detail. She's also a high achiever. I've heard her play both the cello and the piano beautifully. You must be very proud of her."

The expression in Hilary's eyes darkened. "We pride ourselves on being excellent parents, thank you. I would love to know what you think you'll get out of this, Mr. McKendrick? What is my daughter to you? She's an attractive young woman."

"Far beyond attractive," Bruno said smoothly. "She's very beautiful. Your daughter honours me with her friendship, Doctor. Does that answer your question? She didn't inherit her looks or her colouring from you."

Was there sarcasm in his smile? "You're a foreigner, aren't you?" Hilary asked, her gaze glued to him as though hypnotized.

"No more foreign than you, madam," he returned suavely. "None of us is original to this country. Our aboriginals, on the other hand, have lived in Australia for some fifty thousand years. I was born in Sydney of an Italian mother and a Scots father. Your question implies you could be something of a racist."

Hilary shuddered all over, as if she had received an electric shock. "I beg your pardon."

"Then I pardon you," Bruno said.

Isabelle hurried back into the living room, holding the two photographs. She was acutely aware of the high tension in the room. Hilary was holding her side as if she'd been wounded.

"I don't want to see those," she cried in a harsh voice as Isabelle approached her.

"Why, Mother? Are you afraid?" Isabelle spoke gently, suddenly feeling very sorry for Hilary. "Please look at them. This isn't just your life. It's *my* life."

"I don't doubt there's some kind of resemblance," Hilary said, making no move to take the photographs in hand.

"Please look, Dr. Martin." Bruno stood up, taking the photographs out of Isabelle's nerveless hand and putting them into Hilary's. He stepped back, took Isabelle by the hand, moving her to the sofa where he joined her.

Hilary's eyes whipped over the photographs. "Are you trying to tell me you see one or other of them as your twin, Isabelle?" She gave another harsh laugh. "They're *different* women," she pointed out scornfully. "One is older than the other."

"I know that," Isabelle said quietly. "I believe they are mother and daughter."

"Possibly. Possibly." Hilary's words dripped contempt. "I have never seen either of these women in my life. It's a superficial resemblance at best."

"There's a great deal more than that, Dr. Martin," Bruno took up from Isabelle, who although she spoke with composure, was shaking. "You're a clever woman. You're a surgeon used to studying bodies, heads and faces. My father—"

"Ah, yes, your father!" Hilary burst out, as if Bruno should feel shame. "He's dead."

"As is the very beautiful Myra Hartmann, Helena Hartmann's mother. I'm convinced Isabelle is directly linked to the Hartmann family. My father, had he lived to meet Bella, would have been convinced too. The resemblance isn't superficial, as you well know. Isabelle is the mirror image of Helena. There's a connection. We thought you would tell us about it."

"Us? Us?" Hilary sounded as if she would like to see both of them hanged.

"There's history there, Doctor. Isn't it time Bella knew?"

"You have some nerve, Mr. McKendrick!"

He regarded her ironically. "I've never lacked it. You must appreciate yours and your husband's reactions have been extreme. There would have to be reasons. There was no intention to upset and offend you. The intention is to discover the truth. Hopefully with your help. If not, easy enough to check these days through DNA analysis."

Hilary's skin burned as though a fire had been lit inside her. "How dare you? You're nothing but an opportunist. You come into our lives and turn our daughter against us with your insinuations and lies. What's in it for you? I ask. Are you going to attempt to pass her off as a Hartmann? I understand they're very wealthy people. This Helena must have a share of their wealth?"

"You *know* who she was, Dr. Martin," Bruno said with remarkable conviction.

"None of which is any of your business," Hilary said, bounding up out of her armchair. "Not one jot of this is true." She transferred her flashing dark eyes to Isabelle. "How very disloyal you are. You've betrayed me and your father."

Isabelle too stood up, confronting the woman she had called her mother all her life. "I'm sorry for all of this, Hilary, but it was meant to happen. Destiny, if you like. My heart tells me you have a secret you don't want to reveal. I have doubts now I'm your biological daughter. I've never *felt* like your daughter. There's no way of knowing without DNA samples."

"You'll get nothing from me," Hilary said, looking incredulous.

"It's on your coffee cup, Dr. Martin, as you of all people would know."

"Now that's a crying shame!" Hilary turned back and swept her coffee cup and saucer into her bag, regardless of what liquid might have been left in the cup. "It's high time to say good-bye." She looked at Bruno with condemnation in her eyes. "I despise your intervention in our affairs. My idiot daughter has clearly fallen under your spell. You've probably had her in your bed."

"Bella is my *friend*, Dr. Martin. Nothing more. I seek to protect her, as she doesn't appear to have you on her side."

Isabelle stood, shocked and mortified.

"Don't come near me, you traitor," Hilary warned in a voice thick with disgust. "After all we've done for you. Your father will be devastated."

"He will be if faced with the truth," Isabelle said with absolute certainty. "I saw his reaction, remember? Nothing remains a secret forever."

Hilary stomped to the front door, head and shoulders thrown back. On line with Isabelle, she suddenly lifted a hand and struck Isabelle across the face. "You've always been the viper in the nest."

"And there we have the key to everything." Isabelle made no attempt to put a hand to her flaming cheek.

"Leave, Dr. Martin, if you don't mind," Bruno said, as though ready and willing to lend assistance. "Isabella may have pity for you. I don't. You're a woman who can successfully lead *double* lives."

Hilary, at the door, whirled back on him. "Meaning?" Spots of red stood out on her cheekbones.

"I see you understand perfectly. Double lives."

Hilary flushed deeper under his mocking gaze. "You're just like your lowlife father, wanting to dig in the dirt. You've made an enemy today, McKendrick."

"I've made worse," Bruno said calmly. "Can I give you a lift to wherever you want to go?"

"Are you mad?" Hilary's handsome face contorted with fury. "You're like a character out of some bad movie, seducing my daughter and filling her head with nonsense." Hilary shifted her gaze to Isabelle. "You'll apologize on your hands and knees before your father and I ever forgive you for your unforgiveable disloyalty, Isabelle."

"I will." Isabelle physically recoiled from the look of enmity in Hilary's eyes. "When and *if* a possible connection to the Hartmann family is ruled out."

"I'm sorry, Bella," said Bruno after Hilary had gone. "You've committed high treason."

"Oh my God!" Isabelle flopped down on the sofa, badly shaken. She covered her face with her hands. "That was as close as it came to a fistfight. Hilary has never laid a finger on me; then she lashes out as if she'd needed to for years. I hope I haven't trusted you too far, Bruno?" The fire in her cheeks was subsiding. She lifted her head. "What were you getting at, accusing Hilary of living double lives?"

"Nothing. I wasn't saying anything at all." Bruno shrugged it off.

"Do you think I'm satisfied with that? There was a decided whiff of threat to it."

"I was overdoing it, I have to admit. Now, I'll have another coffee. That one went cold." He made a move, going behind the counter. "I hope Dr. Hilary didn't make off with part of a set?"

"Did she ever! Wedgwood, Cornucopia. Now I'm down to three."

"You ought to send her the bill." Bruno looked around him. "Why don't you use freshly ground Italian coffee instead of these pods?" he asked.

"Stop complaining." She got up from the sofa, taking the barstool facing him. "The pods are okay. Don't change the subject either. What did you mean, double life?"

He turned his broad back on her. "I just wanted to shake her up."

"You did and no mistake. Your little thrust hit home. Are you going to tell me?"

He turned to look at her, a cup of coffee in hand. "Have you cream?"

"In the fridge. I only take a little."

He opened the fridge door, bent to look at the contents. "You're a neat little hausfrau, aren't you?" He withdrew a carton of cream.

"I'm not a frau anything," she said. "I'm like you, Bruno. I'm happy to live on my own. Not that you're on your own much, I expect."

He knew she was making a gallant effort to appear okay. He reached out a hand, softly pressed a thumb to her reddened cheek. "I didn't like that. That woman hitting you. I did like the way you didn't make a sound or put up your hand to touch the spot."

"Wasn't that just awful!" Without conscious thought,

Isabelle leaned her cheek into his cool palm. "Hilary has never touched me. I was never smacked. My life was normal enough." She pulled a face, realized what she was doing and lifted her head away. "Stop being nice to me, Bruno McKendrick."

"I suppose it's because you're very easy to be nice to. Drink up."

"I must. I have to go shopping. I was on my way when Hilary arrived."

"Where do you shop?"

"Local shopping centre. I like to get my fruit and vegs from the street markets. Lovely and fresh."

He lifted his coffee cup. "Here's looking at you, kid!" He saluted her.

She knew that distinctive voice. It hadn't been all that long since she had seen a remake of *Casablanca*. "Humphrey Bogart? That was *good*."

"I have others. I'll take you shopping."

She opened her green eyes wide. "Now there's a gentleman for you! Don't you have things to do?"

"Nothing more important than shopping for fresh fruit and vegetables," he said.

She held his lustrous dark eyes. "Listen, I'm not a fool."

"Indeed you're not!" He didn't laugh.

"I know perfectly well there was something to what you said to Hilary. Something that worried her. Made her want to run away. It's odd, you know, because I have often wondered about my parents—about Hilary and Norville's—relationship. What you said has brought me face-to-face with a jumbled idea. Were you implying Hilary has been having an affair? Maybe a long-time relationship? My poor father was always far from happy.

Hilary is the boss. No question about it. I don't know if she could actually *love* someone, but she could . . ."

"Want sex?"

She knew she flushed. Twenty-two and she had given sex a wide berth. Casual sex was beyond her. Allowing a man *into* her body had to have real meaning. So far, she hadn't met that man. "I can't see her closing the door on it like she closes the door on . . . poor Norville."

"Sorry, Bella. I can't enlighten you."

"More likely you *won't*." She slipped off the barstool. "Norville would feel so bad if he ever found out. He idolizes her."

"That's where power kicks in," Bruno said. "He would do whatever she said at every stage. He mightn't like it. He mightn't want to go along with it, but her will would prevail."

"Brainwashing. She said no matter what you had led me to believe I was *not* a Hartmann. It was like I was more *not* a Hartmann than I was a Martin. She sounded so utterly *sure*."

"It could be she's a consummate liar and she knows her target," Bruno said. "Are you doing anything tomorrow?"

She looked at him in surprise. "Why? Are you going to take me away from all this?" she mocked.

"It's my godson Josh's sixth birthday. He's mildly autistic. His parents, Cassie and Ian Taylor, are good friends of mine."

"It's a party? There will be other children?"

He shook his dark head. "Josh isn't at his best with people, even other kids, but he is making strides. He gets the very best attention and ongoing therapy."

"I'm sure he does. But why take me, a stranger? I'd only be intruding and Josh could well mind."

Bruno shook his head. "Somehow I don't think he will. Besides, I want you to meet Cass and Ian."

Isabelle gave him a full-on look he couldn't ignore. "Cass?" she questioned, her head on the side. "That wouldn't be Cassandra Taylor the journalist, now would it?"

"The very same."

"She was there at the Lubrinski function?"

"Right again."

"And your Cassandra had me under surveillance."

"Did she? I wasn't aware of that." It was the truth. "She did remark early in the evening that you reminded her of someone."

"Now I understand," Isabelle groaned.

"No, you don't. Please, Bella, keep calm. I want you to come with me, because . . ."

"I'm waiting." She began to drum her fingers on the granite counter.

"Because I *want* you to come with me," he said, disconcerted at how true that was. "You're a truly bright spark. I like that. Besides, the family will love you."

"Sez you!" She began playing with a loose strand of her beautiful hair. "I don't know."

"They own a piano," he said as an inducement. "Cass plays. Nothing like you. Josh loves music. It keeps him calm."

Isabelle let him stew. "Then I'll come for Josh," she said after due consideration. "Not *you.* I'd say you get your own way too often."

He shrugged. "For all the good it does me. Well, chop-chop. Shopping time."

"I'll have to get a present for Josh," she said. "Big box of chocolates for your friends. Who doesn't love chocolate?"

"Actually, I knew a girl some time back who didn't. Zinnia was her name."

"Really? That's brilliant! Names are getting more and more unusual. I think the zinnia is part of the sunflower tribe. You split up?"

"Bella, I assure you it wasn't serious."

She laughed out loud.

Chapter Three

She took one last look at herself. Bruno was picking her up at eleven. She had chosen a cobalt-blue silk top that hung loose from shoestring straps over a short, crossover orange skirt cut like a piece of origami. The combination of colours was arresting, but it worked. The orange was almost the colour of the glints in her hair. Gold sandals on her feet. She had left her hair loose, at the last moment fixing heart-shaped gold earrings to her pierced ears.

She hadn't slept much. Why would she, with a mind in turmoil? A thousand thoughts moved around and around through her head. She couldn't clear them.

The confrontation with Hilary had deeply disturbed her. She could have ruined everything. What if her instincts were wrong? What if Hilary *were* her mother, however different they were as people? She couldn't claim she resembled the man she had called Father all her life either. Not in looks, characteristics, interests. God forbid what she and Bruno had started turned out to be a betrayal, as Hilary had claimed.

On the other hand, if she really were connected to

Helena Hartmann, the two people she had been raised to believe were her parents had lied to her all her life. She had seen and had to produce her birth certificate a number of times over the years. All had appeared to be in order. She wasn't adopted. According to her birth certificate, she had been born to Hilary and Norville Martin at a private maternity clinic in London. If she were connected to Helena, if Helena was her mother, how could she possibly have handed over her baby to another woman?

How could she?

Helena couldn't have been penniless. She'd had sufficient money to get her to London and find herself someplace to live. She would have had help. Even the pilot of the freight plane had been under suspicion for helping her to get way. He would have been grilled, but he'd continued to claim innocence, and the police and Ross McKendrick had not been able to prove otherwise. Helena would have had assistance to change her identity. No Helena Hartmann had appeared on the manifests of ships and planes travelling out of Australia for an extended period after her disappearance. Isabelle supposed if one had the money, the chances of changing one's identity would significantly increase.

The Taylors lived in the affluent, leafy suburb of Double Bay, with a blue water view, a hop, step and a jump from the marina. Isabelle found whatever expectations her host and hostess had for her, she was greeted with open pleasure. No sign of the little boy, Josh. He did appear as they walked inside the house, running at Bruno but not calling his name. Bruno bent and lifted the blond-

haired, blue-eyed child into his arms. "How's it goin',
Josh! Six years old today."

For answer, the little boy bent his head into Bruno's neck. Isabelle was within his range of vision, but he didn't look directly at her. So much depended on how the little boy felt with a stranger in his midst. Isabelle turned to her hostess. She was carrying a gift bag, from which she produced the big box of Lindt chocolates. "For later." She smiled. "I have a little present for Josh. I hope he likes it. And me."

"I'm sure he will." Cassie looked both pleased and surprised. "You didn't have to do that, Isabelle." Their guest was much younger than Bruno's usual women friends, but she looked perfectly at home with him, as comfortable as Bruno was with her, for that matter.

"Of course I did. I'll wait a while before I show Josh. Let him get used to me."

"He'll probably think you're the princess out of one of his storybooks," said Cassie in a gentle, kind voice.

Lunch was set in the lovely, secluded sanctuary of the garden, under the broad, feathery dome of a jacaranda. The beautiful shade tree was due to burst into exquisite mauve-blue bloom by November. That was the month when the city with one of the best climates in the world to grow the Brazilian jacaranda was hazed with purple, much to Sydneysiders' delight.

As Isabelle helped Cassie bring the various salads, the prepared sauces, the herb butters and the little crunchy bread rolls out of the kitchen, Josh hovered. Once or twice he walked out into the garden with them. Silent. Expression withdrawn. Mostly he stuck close to his father and Bruno, who were tending the barbeque. The sizzle alone was making Isabelle hungry.

"What a lovely setting!" she exclaimed with pleasure.

"I love the way you've done all this, Cassie." She looked down at the attractively set picnic table. Cassie had placed little glass vases at intervals, each containing two perfect yellow tulips folded within their green leaves. The colour was echoed in the yellow, pink and turquoise stripes of the tablecloth and napkins.

"Well, thank you." Cassie's anxious gaze slipped past Isabelle to her little son. Isabelle had already noticed Cassie was always looking to see how Josh was getting on. "I haven't told you how much I admired your playing at the Lubrinskis', Isabelle," she said as her hazel gaze came back to her guest. She looked ethereal in the glittering, green, subtropical sunlight raying through the branches of the jacaranda. "Bruno tells me you have a Master's degree from the Royal College of Music in London."

"I do." Isabelle inclined her head. "Did he tell you I also play the piano? I bet he did. I can see you're good friends."

"Actually, he did," Cassie admitted, looking over at Bruno as he put some beautiful big prawns she had marinated in lime juice and zest onto the barbeque plate. He and her husband, Ian, a quiet, studious man, headmaster of a leading boys' school, had always gotten along just fine. She and Ian had been late starters as parents. Just when they had thought they would never have a child, along came Josh as she turned forty. Her beloved boy. Josh loved Bruno, his godfather. Sometimes she thought Josh responded to Bruno more than he did to her and Ian. "He told me he was utterly enchanted. Those were his exact words."

"That was nice of him. Better not tell Madame Lubrinski."

Cassie gave an amused grimace. "Marta likes to take full credit for picking Bruno's female friends."

"Be certain I'm not trespassing on Madame Lubrinski's turf. Bruno sees me as the young cousin he never had. As for me, I have no designs whatever on his splendid body."

Cassie burst out laughing. "Isabelle, honey, he's got enough women doing that already."

"It's all that handsomeness and sexual energy, don't you think? Better still, he has a great sense of humour and he's *kind.* I rate kindness highly. Now this Penelope—I keep forgetting her name."

"Penelope Pfeiffer. She's actually quite nice. Nothing like the last one, Gemma. She's the daughter of Super Sam."

"I know. My dearest wish is to remain Bruno's musical friend. Has he discussed my background with you?" she asked openly.

Cassie leaned over to pat Isabelle's arm. "Bruno wouldn't do that without your permission. *I* admit to being aware of your striking resemblance to a young woman who disappeared when I was a girl. Helena Hartmann."

"Ah, yes, the mysterious Helena," Isabelle sighed. "Please let's not talk about it now, Cassie. I want to enjoy myself."

"And so you shall, my dear," Cassie said.

It was Isabelle's turn to laugh. "That's exactly what Cinderella's fairy godmother said when dressing her for the ball."

"I've no difficulty visualizing you in Cinderella's beautiful ball gown," said Cassie.

Platters of delicious barbequed seafood were placed on the table: prawns marinated in different sauces, lemon scallops, calamari, succulent lobster. Bruno had even taken the grilled spanner crabs out of their shells so Cassie and Isabelle wouldn't have that messy job, although there were little bowls of ice water to dip one's fingers into.

Josh evidently didn't like seafood because Cassie had placed a sausage with a liberal dollop of tomato sauce inside a slice of bread and handed it to him. She had also prepared a bowl of chips. Isabelle had already been told Josh objected to most foods. It had been impossible to get him to eat vegetables until Bruno suggested she turn vegetables into a puree and use it as a sauce over different pasta shapes, like farfalle, fusilloni and radiatori. Josh wouldn't eat her gnocchi, but he would eat Bruno's.

"I tell you, he's a real catch!" said Isabelle, sounding utterly convinced.

Cassie started laughing again. Young Isabelle was very good company.

Bruno sat beside her, handsome face and tall, athletic body a powerful living sculpture. He was wearing a stylish navy shirt and navy stretch chinos, a mustard-coloured belt slung around his waist. She liked a man to dress well. She fancied she was a bit of a fashion plate herself. "A glass of wine?" He held up a bottle of Riesling for her inspection.

"Lovely. Just one glass, I think, in the heat. Everything looks wonderful. I hope your lady friends know you're a serious cook."

"They haven't seen my skills put to the test, Bella."

"Really? You haven't asked anyone over for a quiet, romantic dinner for two? Dinner of course prepared by you."

His dark eyes beneath his black brows pinned her in place. "I don't know what you're imagining, Bella, but I usually wine and dine a woman friend at a good restaurant."

"Safer that way?"

"Drat your impudence!" he said, mock darkly.

"If you want to put your skills to the test you could ask me over one night. I'd love to come. No strings attached, which is as safe as it gets."

He laughed. "You like a bit of mischief, don't you?"

"It works for us," she answered breezily. "Josh loves you."

"Calm and understanding," Bruno replied. "That's the secret."

"And a gentle manner. He's a lovely-looking little boy. He doesn't seem to mind me?"

"I'd say you remind him of the princess in one of his pop-out storybooks."

"That's funny. Cassie said the same thing."

"I'll find the storybook later," Bruno promised. "What are you going to have?" He picked up her plate.

"A bit of everything," she said happily. "Thank you for asking me today, Bruno."

"Another one of my brilliant ideas." Bruno began to select small portions of all the seafood he and Ian had barbequed, arranging it neatly on her plate.

"This looks marvellous!"

"I'm going to ask you a favour later," Bruno told her.

All four had their barbequed food and a side salad in front of them. They charged glasses, not saying "Happy Birthday" in case Josh felt overwhelmed but making do with a "Cheers!"

They began to eat. The conversation flowed with ease, covering all manner of relaxing topics. Josh didn't sit down. He wandered around the table, as content as his parents had seen him.

Once he stopped beside Isabelle, watching the flash of the sun off her copper-red hair with his eyes. Cassie passionately hoped Josh wouldn't object to the attention Isabelle was getting from Bruno and make a big fuss, but somehow, he remained stable and connected to the party. He even sat down at the table beside Bruno while he ate two little cupcakes she had decorated with funny faces especially for him.

Afterwards, Cassie and Ian insisted they go into the living room while she and Ian made short shrift of cleaning up.

"Time to give Josh his presents, now he's settled." Bruno bent over Isabelle to murmur in her ear. She was wearing a lovely light perfume with floral top notes. It was perfect for her. Perfect for him, for that matter. An intoxicant. He was susceptible to a woman's perfume. Anything that cloyed wasn't his idea of enchanting.

"I hope he likes mine," Isabelle said, suddenly feeling nervous. Josh had made no effort to communicate with her. Neither had he looked directly at her. He could speak; she had heard him speaking to his mother. He had sounded perfectly normal. His voice had the same soft, gentle quality as his mother's. No way was Josh an emotionally deprived child as she had been; his parents clearly loved him. Cassie doted on her boy.

"It's okay," Bruno reassured her, sensing her fears. "He likes you."

She threw him a little shimmering glance. "How do you know?"

"He'd have soon let us know if he didn't," Bruno told her, walking across to a mahogany and brass cabinet where they had left their birthday presents for the little boy.

Josh, who had been watching while not appearing to do so, moved quickly to catch hold of Bruno's trousered leg.

"Let's see what this guy can do," Bruno said, handing

the loosely wrapped robot to the child. Josh stood for a moment, obviously processing Bruno's words before he fell to his knees, tearing the paper away. He had no difficulty with the sturdy toy. He simply picked it up, got it started. The colourful robot began to walk and flash its lights.

"Ah, a success!" Bruno murmured to Isabelle in a quiet, triumphant aside.

"Let's hope I *top* you," she punned. Her main gift was, in fact, a colourful spinning top.

To her great relief, the brightly painted and decorated present was almost as well received as the robot. Bruno had introduced her as Belle. Isabelle used that nickname as she'd handed her present to the child. "Hello, Josh. I'm Belle."

"Belle," Josh repeated, meeting her glance briefly before he looked away.

The star turn of the day came later. Bruno and Isabelle were sitting on the floor with Josh when his parents rejoined them. Both had made constant little peeps into the living room, thrilled their son had accepted their young guest. Josh, in fact, was leaning against Bruno, then Isabelle in turn, as if they were a pair of comfortable bookends.

"Play something." Bruno caught Isabelle's eye.

"Is that the favour?"

"Something bright to take Josh's attention."

"You take advantage of your seniority, Bruno McKendrick."

"Thank goodness we've got *that* sorted," he said, looking down his perfectly aquiline nose at her.

Isabelle glanced over at Cassie, pointing to the baby

grand in the corner, silently seeking her hostess's approval for her to play it.

Cassie understood perfectly. She nodded. Music was a powerful therapeutic tool. She knew it worked for Josh. She was in the habit of playing to her little son as often as she could because he was so receptive. She watched Isabelle go to the piano, lift the lid—which she seldom did, though a highly trained pianist would—then sit down on the long upholstered bench. Cassie wondered what Isabelle would choose and whether Josh would like it. She clutched her husband's hand, experiencing a rush of adrenaline.

Isabelle launched into Mozart's *Rondo alla Turka*.

Perfect.

Just perfect!

Immediately, as Bella's fingers came down on the sparkling opening, Josh's blond head shot up. Bruno moved quickly to help the child to his feet, watching with great satisfaction as Josh moved across to the piano, standing close to Bella's moving left elbow. The piece required considerable manual dexterity. Anyone would know that, but Bella didn't show any signs of being cramped. No change of expression on Josh's face, but to those present who loved him, it was apparent his interest had been captured. Moreover, it was being held.

When Isabelle finished the piece, she didn't stand up as Bruno expected. She started to play a snatch of some melody Bruno knew. Grieg's "Morning." She played the opening bars over and over, miraculously enticing Josh onto the piano bench. Bruno stood back, not crowding the piano, watching what was to unfold.

Bella spread the long, beautiful fingers of her right hand over the keys and then brought them down. She played two bars of the lovely, atmospheric melody and then she moved off the bench, standing up beside the piano. Josh, to the watching adults' astonishment, took her place on the piano bench, as if this was a regular piano lesson. Isabelle the teacher, he the dutiful pupil.

Cassie clasped her hands tightly against her chest. *What was Josh going to do?* she thought in a sudden panic. Would he begin thumping the keys wildly? Would he work himself into a rage of frustration? Would the wonderful atmosphere of Sunday peace disintegrate? Cassie half-expected he would, but she had seen enough of their young guest not to have to worry about Isabelle's reaction. Isabelle would handle the situation. She was a highly trained musician. She was also a born communicator, in Cassie's view.

Her fears did not eventuate. There was no explosive reaction. Josh began to *play.* Play like a very young, aspiring pianist. Marvel of marvels, he reproduced the musical fragment with absolute accuracy.

Dear God!

He might be a savant! Cassie, overcome, ran back into the kitchen, swallowing down a gush of highly emotional tears. Josh's father, equally stunned, followed her. Bruno continued to stand nearby, transfixed, while Bella sat down again, demonstrating several more bars of the music. She was playing the melody an octave higher, as Josh was centred middle C, but he had no difficulty repeating the motif from where he sat.

The exercise went on for another ten minutes. For Josh, it was manifestly clear this was serious business. His verbal communication skills would take time, but his musical skills appeared unique, especially in such a young child. Towards the end of what had become an important lesson, Isabelle demonstrated for her highly attentive pupil a three-note chord to play with his left hand, thus engaging both hands. Josh had no difficulty there either.

The implications of this were enormous, Bruno thought. Here was a child apparently very capable of musical achievement. He was thrilled for Cass and Ian.

Josh continued to play, unaware and uncaring of who else was in the room. He was locked into his own performance. He was even adding tonal colour.

Isabelle moved over to where Bruno stood, full of a born musician's satisfaction and hope for the child. Her heart lost a full beat as, with a strong, muscular arm, Bruno pulled her into his side, giving her a spontaneous hug. "Bella, you're a miracle worker!" He went further. Inclining his raven head, he landed a kiss on her temple.

Immediately, her temple throbbed. Isabelle couldn't for the life of her suppress a huge rush of excitement. The scent of him was on her skin and her clothes. She'd had countless hugs from male friends. Nothing remotely like this. She couldn't look at him when he was only a breath away. To look at him was to feel what she shouldn't. She knew what a magnet Bruno was to women. She was conscious of the pulse beating away at the base of her throat. To save herself, she closed her eyes. As soon as he let her go, she prayed her heartbeat would slow.

A moment later, she was able to speak normally. "Josh is gifted," she said.

"My God, so are you!" Bruno's passionate dark eyes moved down over her. "That was fantastic!"

"Such responsiveness is," she agreed. "You can write me a cheque for a million dollars."

"It's yours," he said.

He sounded so utterly serious she produced a sweet, shaky laugh. "Don't be silly, Bruno. I'm joking."

"What has been accomplished is worth all of it." Bruno found himself staring into her beautiful green eyes. He was feeling a little dazed. Come to that, the entire afternoon had had the sense of a dream.

"You honour me," Isabelle said. "But dinner at your place will do. I really *love* Italian cooking. It's so . . ."

"*Squisito!* Italian food is the best ethnic food in the world. I would have you know, Bella, my cooking would pass muster in Rome or Milan."

"Skite!"

"Bella, you have a lot to learn about me."

"We have a lot to learn about *me.* Have either of us asked if it could be dangerous?"

Bruno shook his head, trying to find an adequate answer. "You won't be on your own. I'll be right there beside you. You realize we have to take a trip to the Hartmann stronghold?"

"Have we got to?" she asked with a curious little shiver.

"Yes" was Bruno's quiet reply.

"They might refuse to see us."

"The older members of the family and the extended family will remember my father. Remember his name. I'll get in touch with them. A photograph of *you* should secure a meeting."

"They may not want to revisit the past," Isabelle warned. "It could be too painful."

"Or too problematic. Nevertheless, I'll get in touch."

"God knows what the response will be," said Isabelle.

Cassie, still tearful, came back into the living room, Ian's arm around her. "What can we say, Isabelle?" she asked, a poignant expression on her face. "My baby!"

"Josh is gifted, Cassie," Isabelle said with gentle certainty. "We were all witness to that. I took a chance. I tried an experiment. It might not have come off, but it did. Autistic children have little or no impairment when it comes to music, I believe. Josh had no difficulty processing the notes I was playing, along with my fingering, the *correct* fingering. I suggest you have him taught. He engaged with me. He will engage with someone else, providing they have a calm presence. The right teacher can be found. I can help there. I don't know if you've tried singing to Josh, but I had a friend—a fellow student—who stuttered painfully but sang fluently when we were at choir. I suggested he take singing lessons. They really helped. In time, his singing lessons rid him of the stutter."

Ian Taylor said in his quiet, cultured voice, "We can't thank you enough, Isabelle." He turned his head in their great friend's direction. "We can't thank you, Bruno, enough for bringing Isabelle to us."

Bruno sketched one of his elegant, expressive gestures. "I can say for all of us, we're thrilled with what has happened this afternoon. I'm certain none of us will forget it. There are little miracles and there are wondrous miracles. I would say it's the latter in Josh's case. Now, what about opening those chocolates, Cass?" he said with a brisk change of tone. "I'll make the coffee."

"He'll want me to help," Isabelle explained as she quickly moved off after Bruno.

Cassie and Ian, starstruck by their son's gift, sat down and listened to bar after bar of Grieg's "Morning."

There are indeed miracles, Cassie thought. Their son had to be given every opportunity to live the fullest life possible. There had to be a reason Isabelle had come into their lives. It had a feeling of *rightness*, of fate about it. Yet all wasn't right with Isabelle's world. Who *was* she?

She had a highly memorable face. An experienced journalist, Cassie had no difficulty putting two and two together. She would look further into what was virtually a cold case. What had happened to Helena Hartmann? Past and present family had to be checked out. Helena Hartmann would have had friends.

She also would have had enemies, Cassie thought. Perhaps close to home?

Helena Hartmann's story demanded an answer.

The last thought Isabelle had in her head Monday morning was that the man she called Father would make a return visit. She had a rehearsal with the quartet in thirty minutes, yet here he was on her doorstep. Was she going to be subjected to more abuse? No, not from him. Norville wasn't an abusive man.

She opened her door, inviting him into the flat. Her heart smote her. He didn't look like a man ready to demand apologies. He looked deeply distressed, a *broken* man, if one looked closely.

Isabelle led him by the arm to an armchair. "Father, you don't look well." She had decided she was going to call him Father until it was proven otherwise. "You must tell me what's the matter. I know Hilary was furious. She would still have been furious when she reported to you. My intuition tells me I haven't had the whole story. Perhaps the *true* story."

Norville Martin slumped over, one hand massaging the back of his knotted neck. "Can I get you something?" Isabelle studied him with pity in her heart.

"No, nothing, thank you, my dear." He straightened. "Hilary doesn't know I'm here. I fly back this afternoon. I have no intention of telling her I've seen you. Not until I have time to *think.* The very last thing I want is to create a scandal. Please sit down, there's a good girl. We must talk."

"I have to make a phone call first, Father," Isabelle said, half-turning away. "I'm supposed to be at a rehearsal in thirty minutes. I'll cancel."

"I'm sorry about that, my dear, but this is important." Norville went back to massaging his neck.

She couldn't get James on his mobile, so she left a message. He would be far from pleased. She could even lose her spot. A number of fine cellists would be delighted to take her place.

Norville didn't even ask if her apology was accepted. He was too preoccupied with his own troubling thoughts. Isabelle sat opposite him, waiting.

"You know how much I love your mother." He gave her an imploring look. "There has never been another woman for me. Not from the moment I met her. I considered myself the most fortunate man in the world when she chose me. She could have had anyone. She was so clever. So many people envied her. She left her male admirers in the dust. I have to say she was a little cruel in that regard."

I bet she was! "So you won her hand and married her," Isabelle said, wondering how and why that happened. Hilary was self-obsessed. Norville was a man obsessed. She had never seen her parents as two people who loved each other. The big distinction: only one did the loving. The full weight of that had fallen on Norville. "Please get to the point, Father," she urged. "The time has passed for deception."

Norville Martin threw back his head, the muscles of his face working as if in physical pain. "I'm *not* your father, Isabelle," he said starkly. "I have no idea who your father is."

Isabelle now found she wasn't immune to rage. "You're not my father and you've kept silent all these years?" she cried. "How could you!"

"I beg you to forgive me," Norville said. "The whole business is monstrous, a nightmare. I know all about your mother's affairs. She's a woman of strong passions. I could never satisfy them, but I loved her so much I was prepared to turn a blind eye. She has never asked for a divorce. She made it plain we were going to stay together. I suited her, you see."

The explanation left Isabelle utterly cold. "She knew she could rely on you not to intrude into her extramarital affairs. There's a world of sorrow and shame in that."

"There is. There is." Norville was back to hanging his silver-grey head. "When you showed me those photographs, it was too much for me to handle. I've known if only in my heart you weren't my child. You were some other man's. Seeing those photographs sent Hilary off her head. I'm convinced she recognised that young woman, but in what context I don't know."

"Of course she recognised her." Isabelle gazed at Norville as if she had never seen him before in her life.

Norville covered his face with his hands, desperate to be left in peace. "I managed to get the full story out of her. She was very fierce at the start, but she broke down. She admitted I wasn't your biological father. Her interest in whoever it was—I'm guessing a colleague, and may be connected to the young woman—had only been sexual."

"Hilary, the nymphomaniac! So what was the young woman's name?" Isabelle's voice was quiet and grave. "Hartmann?"

Norville fell back against the armchair like a man on the verge of a nervous breakdown. "God knows!"

"You couldn't get it out of her?" Isabelle's whole body felt tremulous.

"Isabelle, there was no point in my trying. Hilary doesn't give up her secrets. I've always been terrified of losing her if I pushed her too far. She seemed terrified. In all our years together, I have never seen her like that."

"You know better than anyone she's a consummate actress."

"In certain lights, you look a bit like her." Norville tried a weak smile.

"Rubbish!" Isabelle relished the denial falling off her tongue. "I look *nothing* like her."

"No," Norville admitted, the blood draining from his cheeks.

"So I'm to believe Hilary is my mother but you are not my father. Is that it?"

"Dear girl, I swear I didn't know for *certain* until last week. Showing me those photographs changed my entire world."

"*Your* world!" Isabelle could hardly believe her ears. "What about me? I *still* don't count, do I? I'm the changeling."

Norville sighed deeply. "Please don't use that word. You do count. That's why I'm here. I'm very fond of you. You must know that. You're a beautiful, very gifted young woman. You're a *good* woman."

"Whereas Hilary is *not,*" Isabelle said bleakly.

"Some of the finer feelings are absent," Norville was forced to admit. "I haven't been able to sleep since I found out."

Isabelle laughed. There was no humour in it. "In your *own* room. You and Hilary conspicuously sleep apart."

"Sometimes she allows me into her bed," Norville said, a man long enslaved.

"And that's sufficient, is it?"

"She loves me in her own way."

"So easy to lie to yourself," Isabelle said sadly. "I pity you, Norville. You've been kind and generous to me."

"I held to the belief you were my daughter."

Isabelle cut him off brusquely. "That kept your soul in line, did it? If I were you, I'd divorce Hilary. Get your self-respect back. She'll always have a lover on the side. Those appetites of hers! You still have time to find a good woman to love, who will, in turn, love you."

Norville gave her a defeated, self-mocking look. "I know what I am, Isabelle. I'm a weak man held hostage by a strong woman. Hilary will have to leave me. I will never leave her."

For once in her life Isabelle was tempted to be cruel. "That's what leeches do," she said. "They cling."

Her life up to this point had been shadow play. After her father, in name only, had gone, Isabelle, even in the worst kind of pain, still managed to retain a measure of calm. She was sick to her stomach. She had been dealt with so badly.

If she had wanted one of them, Hilary or Norville, to be her biological parent, her choice would have been Norville. The thought that Hilary was now established as her birth mother made her laugh so hard her chest ached, scalding hot tears rushing into her eyes. She knew Norville meant it when he said he was fond of her. She had to accept he would have little in the way of love left over from his obsessive love for her mother.

She had thought, in secret, even from childhood, that she didn't fit. Only in retrospect could she slot all the pieces together. Well, not all. It remained to find her biological father. She wasn't Isabelle Martin. She was, in all probability, Isabelle Hartmann. It could be a life-changing existence. She knew families could be complicated, but hers was more complicated than most.

Midafternoon, she had a visit from James Kellerman. She wasn't happy to see him arrive at her door. She was well aware of his roving eye. She also knew it had landed on her. She wasn't in the least attracted to him, however much he was a hit with the other ladies. It was all so unwelcome. She would have to move cautiously. She so enjoyed being with the group, all fine musicians, but if the price of entry was an affair with the leader, she would have to move on.

"How did you know where I lived?" she asked when he arrived at her front door.

"You're in the phone book, Isabelle," he said, swaggering past her into the apartment, blond, blue-eyed, handsome and well aware of it. She remembered now his wife had left him. Rumour had it he had taken up with a very attractive blonde violinist in the Symphony Orchestra.

"Of course. Please sit down. I must apologize again for not being able to get to the rehearsal. A family matter came up. I had to attend to it."

He swung back to her with a piece of advice. "I hope you're not going to have to attend to family matters often, Isabelle," he said, returning to roaming about. "Our rehearsals are extremely important."

"I do realize that, James. It won't happen again."

"Good." He was very much playing the leader. He who had to be obeyed. "Your parents live in Adelaide, don't they?"

"Yes." She nodded. She couldn't bring herself to mention Norville's visit. Her psyche had been rubbed raw.

"Both doctors?"

"I've told you that, James. Can I offer you coffee?" Tea or coffee, the universal specific.

"Coffee would be lovely," he said expansively, as though he were ready to settle in for the afternoon. "Where do you practise? You couldn't practise here."

"At the Conservatorium," she said. "I've made arrangements. Soundproof room. I practise the piano there too, although I have my own in storage."

"They have lots of good things to say about you at the Con," he said, as though she were dying for a compliment. "No harm in giving the Young Performers a shot. I won it some years back."

Ten years, she knew. "I do intend to enter," she said. "My biggest award was in Belgium." Her former professor's opinion of her was all that she had or would ever need in the way of confidence building.

"I'm not surprised," James drawled. "You're very good. A black coffee and a sandwich would be great, if you could manage it. We didn't stop for lunch."

"No problem," Isabelle said, wondering how much longer he intended to stay. She hadn't been able to contact Bruno. She had left a one-word message for him: "News." She could have made it two: "Bad news." She knew he would ring back when he could.

James made short work of the chicken and avocado sandwiches. "That was lovely!" he enthused, his blue eyes sliding all over her as she sat in her leather armchair. "Filled the spot for the time being. If you're free, we could do dinner?"

It was the second time he had asked her. She was supposed to say yes. She knew a lot of women would accept, including Emma, their viola player. She was madly in love with James, but Isabelle knew James would never invite Emma out to dinner. "Don't you have a partner, James?" she now asked.

His gaze hardened. "I do. No matter." He threw up a hand. "It's not a soul-shaping love affair. Both of us feel free to have dinner with . . . friends."

"That sort of arrangement wouldn't suit me," she said. "It would break my heart if the man I loved felt free to go out with other women."

"Isabelle!" He laughed, steadily trying to magnetize her with his eyes. "You're not a born-again Christian, are you?"

"I am a Christian, James. I have ethical standards. I should tell you, I do have someone."

His blue gaze went oily. "You just made that up, Isabelle. No need to be nervous. I don't bite. You're a very interesting girl. I was merely hoping to get to know you better. The better I know you, the better we'll perform together. As a quartet, of course. I can see you're nervous with me."

She shook her head. "You're quite wrong, James. I'm a great admirer of yours as a solo violinist and the leader of the quartet. That's as far as it goes."

"You're not *trying*, Isabelle." He reached across the coffee table to grasp her hand.

She glanced away quickly as the intercom buzzer echoed through the flat. "Excuse me, James," she said, retrieving her hand and making towards the intercom wall unit.

The cavalry had arrived. It was Bruno. She felt like bawling in relief. "Come up, Bruno," she said, aware her voice sounded quavery.

He was there in seconds flat. She all but walked into him, white cotton shirt, blue jeans, tooled boots. Warmth and fresh male fragrance. He had his arm hard around her, his eyes making a sweep of the living room, taking in James Kellerman's presence.

"James is here," Isabelle said unnecessarily. "I had to miss rehearsal."

"Hi there, James," Bruno called, and then proceeded to take Isabelle by storm. He tilted her chin, bent his head and kissed her mouth. It was a profound experience and completely unexpected. Wave after wave of sensation began swooshing through her bloodstream. She was reacting as if she had been totally deprived of such a kiss. By the time he let her go her heart was pumping wildly and her head was reeling.

Watching this from the sofa, cold lights flared in James Kellerman's blue eyes. He stood up, a man full of disappointment and discord. "Time to be off," he said in a clipped voice much at variance with his practised drawl. "Many thanks for coffee, Isabelle. I'll be in touch."

"Nice to see you, James," Bruno said suavely, opening the door for him, then shutting it afterwards with an air of satisfaction. "Can you beat that?" He gave a short laugh. "James Kellerman might be a fine musician, but he's a serial womaniser."

"Aren't most men?" Isabelle was having some difficulty speaking. Her mouth was still throbbing. "He's going to sack me, you know." To her surprise, she wasn't all that worried.

"His loss! I'm just appalled at his trying to make a move on you."

"I had to tell him I had someone." Now she was deeply inhaling. She could feel the blush of colour in her cheeks.

"You *do* have someone," Bruno said. "You have me."

"I mean a *someone* someone, though I guess that was a pretty convincing kiss. A lot of chivalry in it."

"I'm an expert when it comes to reading situations," said Bruno.

"You're an expert at kissing as well. Fair warning. You might have to kiss me a thousand times more before we're finished." She was attempting to turn a heart-stopping moment into a joke. No need for him to see her vulnerability. It was clear kissing her had been no earthshaking event for him.

"No problem!" he confirmed. "Actually, you're lovely to kiss, Bella *mia.* I can see a long line of future admirers coming to swords and blows. So what's the news?" he asked, steering her into an armchair. "Have you been crying?" His dark eyes had turned very intent.

"It's a sad story."

"Bella, Bella," he groaned. "I'm guessing the ceiling has fallen in on you?"

"Something like that," she said. "Norville isn't my dad." Her heart contracted as she said it.

"I knew that." Bruno spoke gently, taking the armchair opposite.

"'Course you did. I'm getting used to your impressing me. My entire life has been a circus."

"And I am so sorry for your pain. We're going to get your fake parents out of your life, Isabella."

"Hilary is *not* my fake mother," she told him in a melancholy voice. "She's the real thing. God, what a mess! You and your dad got me into this, Bruno."

"Don't you want the truth?" he asked.

She gave a pained laugh. "The desire for the truth only comes in fits and starts. I'm afraid of what we might turn up, Bruno. Didn't you tell me your father was killed by a hit-and-run driver? Any decent human being couldn't run from such a scene. Could the accident have been deliberate? Maybe your father was stirring up trouble? Maybe he had found out something the Hartmann family wanted kept quiet?"

Bruno looked down at his clenched hands. The knuckles were white. The pain of his father's violent death and the fact that it was never solved would never go away. Bella was only asking what he had asked himself innumerable times over the years. The driver of that car remained a shadowy figure. Police investigations had turned up nothing. No witnesses, not even a witness who was determined not to get involved. The murderer had slammed his car into his father and gotten clean away.

"So." He looked at her, internalising her anguish. Isabelle in no time at all had managed to get under his skin. "Time to pass on your news in its entirety."

Isabelle did.

"Why should we believe him?" Bruno asked, after Isabelle had told him word for word the meeting with Norville Martin.

"He's absolutely sure of it, Bruno."

"He isn't," Bruno flatly contradicted. "There's no bitterness in you?" If there was, she was showing no sign of it.

Isabelle shook her red-gold head, almost abstractedly. "What good would that do? Bitterness is corrosive. Besides, I felt sorry for him. The man I called Father was good to me. Hilary ruined him."

"Very revealing, don't you think? He's not a real man, Bella. He's a puppet on a string."

"He *loves* her," Isabelle said. "Don't they say love is a madness? Maybe you've never loved a woman, Bruno. Maybe you don't *want* to love a woman? You know all about loss. Perhaps that's why you're on the run from Penelope and the rest of the pack?"

"As long as you aren't one of them, Bella." He spoke crisply, a cool glitter in his jet-black eyes.

"Never me," Isabelle protested. "I told you. We're *partners*. We've buddied up, as they say. You don't believe Hilary is my mother?"

"I'm having it checked out."

"Really?" she gasped. "You're a fast mover."

"I'm like that. Whatever the outcome, our next stop is the Hartmann Outback stronghold. Eaglehawk Downs. A small spread," he said, an attractive quirk to his mouth, "some five thousand square miles."

"Goodness me, that's *huge*!"

"There are a couple bigger. Australian Outback stations are the biggest in the world. They have to be, given stock have to forage over a vast arid area. Eaglehawk is in the Channel Country, which you probably know is the semidesert region in the corner of the South West, crisscrossed by innumerable rivulets. When in flood, those rivulets can run fifty miles across."

"It's now I ought to tell you, I do watch the weather on the TV, Bruno. Most of the Channel Country is in Queensland, isn't it? It runs into South Australia, New South Wales and the Northern Territory. I remember seeing the fantastic coverage of Lake Eyre that was turned into an Inland Sea years back."

"Cyclone Olga. That was 2010. My good friend and mentor, Ivor Lubrinski, hired a helicopter to fly a small party of us over a magnificent inland sea. It was the most awesome sight I've ever seen. And the birds! They arrived from all over. The Channel Country is a major breeding ground for nomadic water birds. The Lake, every billabong, waterway and lignum swamp were literally alive with birds, pelicans, ibis, spoonbills, herons. We were flying at about two hundred metres. An area of the lake was covered in green algae. It looked for all the world like grass with thousands of pelicans at rest on top. It was a fantastic sight. We couldn't look away, including the pilot. It was then he told us how two light planes had crashed into one another over the Lake because the pilot had forgotten to check the altimeter."

"So what happened?"

"They took a dive straight into the Lake. They managed to exit, shocked but unhurt, but the planes are still in the Lake. Too expensive to salvage. When the flood subsides and all the waterholes shrink, the enormous bird migration takes off again."

"I expect they're nomads because they have to be," she said sensibly.

"Right. Though Eaglehawk and the other Channel Country stations, even in drought, have access to water via numerous bores that tap into the Great Artesian Basin. The Diamantina River crosses Eaglehawk Station."

"So tell me what you have to tell me," she invited. "What's the Hartmann history? I'm anxious to know."

"Listen closely, because it's fairly involved. The lease was first taken up by pioneer pastoralist Adler Hartmann in the 1860s," Bruno said. "Adler is German for—"

"Eagle, I know. Hence, the Eaglehawk. I studied German for four years. German and French."

"What a pity, not Italian?"

"Italian wasn't on offer. Japanese."

"Italian is the most beautiful language in the world."

"Mozart thought so. I agree."

"You would do; you're a musician. I'll teach you Italian, if you like. You have a trained ear."

"Perfect pitch. One is born with it."

"I'm in awe of your talents," he said with sardonic humour.

"I suppose I am quite remarkable," she answered, tongue in cheek.

"I think you might be. Too early to say. To continue with our discussion, from all accounts, our intrepid Adler was a high-flying adventurer keen to make his fortune in the New World. He brought his German-born wife, Viktoria, from a minor aristocratic Prussian family, with him. They had four children, three girls and a son. Two of the girls died in childhood."

"How sad!"

"It is indeed. Going down the family tree, we come to Helena's grandfather, Konrad, who instigated the search and hired my father to investigate when police enquiries came to a dead end. I suppose they'd come to the conclusion she'd taken off like a lot of other young people sick of the isolation. Money was no object, though my father wouldn't have taken advantage of anyone, let alone a grieving family. Konrad was a fine man, according to my dad. 'A true gentleman.' His first wife died giving birth to their son, Erik, Helena's father. Konrad remarried about eighteen months later. A young Englishwoman, Lillian, he met on a trip abroad. They had a son, Christian."

"So two half brothers?"

"Yes. Very different personalities, according to Dad. Erik, the heir, was supremely arrogant. Christian took after Konrad."

Isabelle tried to crystallize her thoughts. "And the offspring?"

"Erik only fathered one child, Helena. Twelve years later, his allegedly promiscuous wife, Myra, took a fatal fall from her horse. Christian had two children by one Abigail Hartmann, a boy and a girl, cousins to Helena.

There's a grandson, Kurt. The granddaughter lives with her mother in Adelaide. Divorce in the family. Christian came to a sticky end. He was the victim of a shooting accident on the station. They had guests that weekend. The men went out on a duck shooting party. An inexperienced shooter picked off Christian by mistake. The death was investigated. The official verdict was a tragic accident. The family appear jinxed."

"Jinxed or targeted?" Isabelle asked. "What did this shooter take Christian for, a marauding lion?" She spoke as though she doubted the verdict was proper.

"Accidents happen on properties, Bella. Accidents happen with guns."

"Too *many* accidents," Isabelle said. "What if they take it into their heads to feed us to the crocodiles?"

Bruno's serious, even grave expression turned humorous. "You won't find a crocodile where we're going."

"I know that. Okay, giant goannas, perenties, aren't they?"

"For all we know, they could be very nice people," Bruno said, thinking just the opposite.

"Your dad didn't think so," Isabelle remarked darkly.

"Would you be ready to make a start next week?" Bruno asked.

"Next week! What do you think I am, rich?" She opened her emerald eyes wide. "Bruno, I should be chasing a job. James is bound to give me the push. He can easily find someone else."

"Not as good as you. He'd be a fool if he let you get away."

"I could be a fool to stay. James is not the man to tolerate slights."

"Then he can go to the devil. Anyway, I'm paying for this. You're doing *me* a huge favour."

"Letting you pay for everything is just about as low as it gets," she protested.

"Nonsense, Bella. I don't give a damn about spending money. You're in need of help and I'm here to give it."

It would be very easy for a woman to work up a grand passion for Bruno McKendrick, Isabelle thought. She had enough turmoil going on inside her already. "So my knight in shining armour, then?" she asked.

"It's in my blood." He slanted a smile, thinking there couldn't be a more romantic looking creature than Isabelle. It was easy to picture her in some gorgeous medieval gown with a garland of spring flowers on her titian head. "My dad was that kind of man."

"Hallelujah!" Isabelle exclaimed. "I'm very sorry I never had the pleasure of making his acquaintance."

Bruno gave her a long, approving look from his fathomless eyes.

Chapter Four

She couldn't wait to exit the Hartmann bumblebee, a Bell helicopter painted yellow and black with a white stripe. In one way, the flight was thrilling. This was the land of legend to city dwellers like her. The land of endless mirage and far horizons; of parallel lines of blood-red sand dunes that made up the Simpson Desert, fourth largest in the world, and the fearful desolation of the great Sturt Stony Desert, covered in gibbers that blinded the eyes with their silvery glitter.

The *vastness* of it all affected Isabelle deeply. The antiquity! The white man had inhabited this ancient land for a mere two hundred years, the aboriginal people for some fifty thousand, living in harmony with the land they identified with so strongly. It was said when the aboriginal tribe living on Botany Bay's headlands saw the first fleet arriving in the January of 1788, they turned their backs in fright, not having any understanding of what they were looking at. They had been looking at the end of their way of life. Witnessing the beginning of the white man's Australia.

She wasn't airsick, but from time to time her heart and

her stomach threatened to come right into her throat. Then she had clutched at Bruno, who had settled her jitters by holding firmly onto her hand. Now she stared in fascination as a table-topped escarpment, glowing fiery red, loomed up before them. She had a feeling the station pilot was showing off for her benefit. She knew the signs. For a few heart-rocking moments they hovered over the eroded monolith so low she could clearly see the dark golden cloak of vegetation. Then they were flying on, making their descent into the Hartmann ancestral home, Eaglehawk Downs.

Thank God!

After hours in the air she needed to stand on her land legs.

From the air, Eaglehawk Station looked like a small town one might encounter on planet Mars, such was the fiery red landscape. Thousands upon thousands of square miles of empty open plains stretched to the horizons, the land heavily dotted with dark golden mounds of spinifex.

The isolation, the loneliness of it all, had Isabelle thinking of all the incredibly brave Outback women who had gone with their husbands to pioneer this savage, strangely beautiful land thousands of miles from medical help. The landscape was so flat, the ancient escarpment aside, it was possible to see how a phenomenal area could be flooded by the big three rivers, the Diamantina, the mighty Cooper Creek and the Thomson.

The town was, in fact, the Hartmanns' sprawling homestead, surrounded by its many satellite buildings, including the giant silver hangar with the name of the station and its logo painted on top.

They had taken a domestic flight to Longreach, an Outback town that sat on the Tropic of Capricorn and one of the far western towns associated with the national carrier, Qantas—Queensland and Northern Territory Aerial Services—and the Royal Flying Doctor Service, founded in 1928 to give vital medical help to everyone living in or passing through the remote Outback. The Hartmann helicopter, a Bell used for mustering, had been waiting for them at the aptly named Longreach, as Bruno had been advised.

"You're safe now, Bella." Bruno tightened a hand on hers as they stood on the all-weather tarmac.

The shimmering heat bounded up at Isabelle, hitting her in the face. Bruno, with his golden skin and Mediterranean heritage, looked quite at home, but she thought she might melt. The Big Sky Country was a cloudless intense blue, in startling contrast to the bright rust red of the desert fringe soil. Isabelle could feel the dry heat off the tarmac lancing into her body. She could never stand in this Outback sun for long without a wide-brimmed hat. She had brought two straw hats with her and a ton of sunscreen.

"It was no Black Hawk, was it!" she pointed out wryly.

Inside the hangar, she could see a handsome twin-engined light aircraft, white with three narrow different-coloured stripes along the fuselage.

"Beech Baron," Bruno told her, following her gaze. "Let's move," he said. "It's too hot for you here."

"It's a very long way from Sydney."

"We won't stay a moment longer than we have to," Bruno promised.

Shielding her eyes from the blazing sun, Isabelle looked up at him. "Why do I feel guilty about something when I'm perfectly innocent?"

"If there is a guilty party, Bella, it's not you," Bruno said. "Brace yourself. Here comes the welcoming party."

"Surely he doesn't intend crashing into us?" Isabelle

asked in faint alarm. A jeep was coming down a long winding track at high speed. On a city highway, he would have been pulled over, breathalysed and then arrested.

There was a sardonic glitter in Bruno's dark eyes. "Face it, Bella. Men tend to show off when you're around."

"I know, and it's a real pain."

The jeep came to a screeching halt at the corner of the hangar. A young man, dressed in immaculate riding clothes, made quite a production out of swinging nonchalantly from the vehicle, striding towards them with, of all things, a riding crop in hand.

"Think of *King Solomon's Mines*," Bruno suggested below his breath.

"Maybe he's just anxious to meet us."

"*Anxious* might be the right word."

The young man's clean-cut appearance, his dress and his confident stride, alerted them this was one of the Hartmann family. Not a redhead. His hair was golden blond, straight, sleeked back. He was good-looking, tanned, fit, an inch or so below six feet.

"Good trip?" he called as he strode towards them. "I'm Kurt, by the way," he said, much as Prince Charles, dedicated to egalitarianism, might say, "I'm Charles."

Bruno held out his hand. "Bruno McKendrick and this is—"

"Don't tell me. The girl who claims to be one of us." He was staring at Isabelle with extraordinary intensity, all the while flicking the whip against his leg.

"Isabelle." Isabelle had to polish up a smile. She wasn't taking to this handsome young man. Woman's intuition again. Only she had to remember that honey caught more flies than vinegar. She extended her hand. "Please set your mind at rest. I'm not here to claim anything at all. Just a visit."

"Good. Good." It sounded like *gut, gut*. "English?"

"I studied in London for four years." She no longer felt she could claim English parents.

"Studied what?"

"The cello," Isabelle said.

"Which adds up to what?" he asked, with what could have been a derisive snort.

"A musical career," Bruno intervened, his tall figure looming. "Isabelle is very gifted. She has a Master's degree from the Royal College in London."

"Classical music doesn't move me," Kurt said, still on the disdainful side.

"When the Hartmann family boasted some fine musicians?" Bruno's face tightened.

Kurt swallowed back a rejoinder. "I've got it!" he said, tearing his ice-blue gaze off Isabelle and turning it towards Bruno. "You're that investigator's son."

"Indeed I am," Bruno said with just a touch of steel in his voice. "Ross McKendrick was my father. Your great-grandfather, Konrad, hired him to find your aunt Helena, who I believe was an excellent pianist. There's a portrait of her seated at a grand piano at the house."

"Oh, that one!" Kurt said vaguely. "It's long been shifted from the drawing room in the main house. My father had it hung in the East Wing. I can't imagine why anyone was surprised when she ran off. No one talks about Helena anymore."

"Maybe it was convenient to forget her," Bruno said.

Even in the heat, the temperature dropped. "Come with me," Kurt said after a fraught pause. "I'll drive you up to the house. My great-uncle is waiting."

"It's very good of him to allow us this visit," Bruno said. He felt strong irritation at the way Hartmann couldn't tear his ice-blue gaze off Isabelle. In fairness, he couldn't blame him. Isabelle was born to get attention. Only more significantly, Kurt Hartmann would have been living with Isabelle's image all his life, despite what he said. He trusted his instincts. His instincts told him *not* to trust Kurt Hartmann. What manner of friendliness Kurt had shown, Bruno thought it feigned. He looked more like a young man who thought his secure world might be in jeopardy.

"My father is out on a muster," Kurt informed them, once they were on their way. "A lot of it is still done on horseback, though we have two helicopters involved in the big musters."

Bruno sat up front beside the driver. Isabelle had the back to herself, charmed by the way Bruno's glossy crow-black hair was curling up at the temples and the nape in the heat.

"Rounding up clean skins. Know what they are?" Kurt asked as though they couldn't possibly guess.

"Obviously unbranded cattle," said Bruno, just beating Isabelle to it.

Kurt shrugged. "He won't be back until late tomorrow. If then. My mother and my sister, Kimberley, live in Adelaide. I dare say you know my parents are divorced. People just love to know all about us Hartmanns. I guess you could say we're Outback royalty. My mother *hated* the isolation of station life. She hated the heat. When we aren't in drought, we're in flood. My mother was a social butterfly when my father met and married her six months later."

Not a marriage made in heaven then, Isabelle thought.

"There's just Uncle Konrad and me and the household staff and of course we travel a lot. I get on very well with my great-uncle. I don't get on nearly so well with my father. He's a workaholic. Expects me to be. Dare I say

I'm a big disappointment to my father? He'd be perfectly happy sleeping in his swag beneath the stars for the rest of his life. I'm not cut out to live a stockman's life. It's dirty, dangerous, back breaking work for the stockmen, for the horses. My father thinks his horse is his best mate. They all do. Uncle Erik doesn't mind I'm not a bushman. I'm a big help to him, though. I'm his heir."

"Sounds like your father manages the station alone?" Bruno said, turning his head to study the young man at the wheel.

"He does no such thing!" Kurt bridled at this. "Uncle Erik runs everything from his desk. Uncle Erik is the cattle baron. He doesn't have to go out with the men. He delegates."

"Lucky for him," said Bruno.

Eaglehawk homestead boasted a very impressive exterior; a central double-story structure with single-story wings to either side. All three buildings were washed a golden ochre. On the down side, it didn't appear welcoming. To Isabelle's eye, it badly needed a woman's touch. She suspected the departure of the Hartmann women had precipitated the decline. She could see there had once been numerous garden beds. Now date palms with their enormous cascading heads dominated the huge area the homestead sat in. Date palms and grevilleas, waterfalls of brilliant bougainvillea pink and tangerine, all suited to the dry conditions. A magnificent three-tier stone fountain stood in the centre of the circular drive. Rearing horses held up the largest basin. It looked as if it hadn't played in a long time.

"'Honour the date palm for it is your mother,'" she said, aloud.

Bruno gave her a smile. "Mahomet?"

Isabelle nodded, pleased he had picked up on the quote.

"Mahomet, the great prophet. In all the desert fringes of the world the date palm is life. I really like dates."

"I'll get you some when we get back," Bruno promised.

"Might I suggest you learn how to make a scrumptious date cake?"

"What are you two on about?" Kurt all but snapped.

"Just a private joke." Bruno shrugged the question off.

Kurt was trying hard to shrug off their guests' easy camaraderie. It seemed to him inappropriate. Wasn't the big guy supposed to be Isabelle's legal advisor? He had the look of success and all that came with it. A don't-mess-with-me aura that could be extremely useful. And intimidating. Kurt didn't like him.

The girl, Isabelle, was something else again. She was the living image of Aunt Helena. She was very beautiful, younger than he by a couple of years. The big guy, the macho Italian, was years older, maybe seven or eight. He didn't see that they were sexually involved, for all the guy's powerful charisma. The two presented as would-be claimant and highly protective hotshot advisor. Going on the extraordinary resemblance, there was no way the girl didn't have some family connection. She had the flaming, riotously curling mane and the green eyes Great-Uncle Erik's wife, Myra, the bitch who had betrayed him and met with her comeuppance, had brought into the family. Why had Uncle Erik allowed them to come here? It could only mean trouble. Worst case scenario, she could be Helena's daughter. Helena was Uncle Erik's only child. If she were alive, she would be his legal heir. If she were dead—and he had already started praying she was—the girl had a legitimate claim.

* * *

"Do you ride?" Bruno bent to whisper into Isabelle's ear.

"Like the wind," she whispered back. "No, really, I haven't been in the saddle for ages. A friend used to ask me to stay for weekends at her parents' lovely country home. We used to ride there."

"You'll go nowhere unless I'm with you," Bruno said, thinking he would check their saddles first.

She leaned into him conspiratorially. "There's a killer out there?"

"No joke," said Bruno.

They were stepping into the splendid entrance hall, parqueted floor, partially covered by a glowing Persian rug. The walls were painted a pleasing apple green, hung with huge paintings in ornate gilded frames. All landscapes. No tempestuous Turneresque seascape. She was a great lover of the arts. She had haunted all the major London galleries during her student days. The homestead was an imposing colonial residence, more European than English. One could see fine examples of colonial architecture in any of the major capital cities, but the Hartmann mansion looked totally bizarre set down in the remote Outback.

Archways led to the main reception rooms to left and right. A grand central staircase with barley sugar twist balusters swept up to a landing with a ceiling-high stained-glass window set into the exterior wall high above it. The light streamed through the stained glass, sending down multicoloured rays: blue, violet, red, green and gold. It should have been a marvellous feature, yet it seemed more like a heavy curtain.

The staircase divided at the landing into two to access the upper level, the gallery. It didn't look unlike the entrance hall of her English girlfriend's country home, except there were no lovely flowers on the fine console table, and the welcoming atmosphere was sadly lacking. It felt like a house where untoward things could take place, Isabelle thought with a suppressed shiver.

This was her last-ditch attempt to find out whether she was a Hartmann. She felt in her bones this trip wasn't going to be any harmless adventure. A deeply unsettling force had entered her life. She would have to ask the questions the two people she had believed to be her parents had spent a lifetime avoiding. She would never have come here without Bruno, who was looking around him with great interest. His father would have described to him Eaglehawk Station's homestead, and now he could see it for himself. He moved closer to murmur, "This isn't the house for you."

She couldn't hold back the comment. "Nor Helena."

A woman suddenly made her entrance. She began moving from the gallery down the left side of the staircase, coming to a halt on the landing with the multi-coloured lights from the stained-glass window splashing all over her. A tall, slim woman, dressed in what could be a dark-coloured uniform? It was hard to tell her age. Isabelle was a great reader, so Mrs. Danvers, the housekeeper in Daphne du Maurier's famous novel *Rebecca*, immediately sprang to mind. The image grew the longer the woman stood there. What was she waiting for, a summons?

"Ah, there you are, Mrs. Saunders," Kurt called, his voice so loud it bounced off the walls.

Not Mrs. Danvers, then. A look-alike.

"Our guests have arrived. Perhaps you can show them to their rooms."

"Certainly, sir." At last the woman was free to get mobile.

No friendly Christian names, then. Clearly this wasn't an everyday establishment, Isabelle thought.

"Mrs. Saunders has been with us since before I was born," Kurt chose to inform them. "She runs the domestic side of things. She's our housekeeper."

First impression: *scary*.

The woman came down the flight of stairs, not looking down as an older woman might in case she tripped, but head held high. All the while she was subjecting Isabelle to a piercing scrutiny.

Those eyes had seen Isabella's like, was Bruno's thought as he stood, a keen observer.

"This is Isabelle Martin," Kurt made the introductions. "And her advisor, Bruno McKendrick."

"I remember your father well." The woman turned her head towards Bruno. "Although it's many long years since he was here. If you'll come this way?"

"Uncle Erik is expecting you both to join us for predinner drinks. Say seven o'clock?" Kurt was already moving away, most probably to report to his great-uncle.

"Fine," Bruno answered for both of them. Isabelle felt too dumbfounded to reply. She half-expected a form of dress to be nominated, but no such request was made. She had brought with her two dresses suitable for evening. She hoped they measured up.

"I've put you in the Chinese Room, Ms. Martin," Mrs. Saunders, midfifties, said. For a woman who lived her life in the blazing Outback sun, she had a remarkably unlined olive skin, suggesting it was not often exposed to the elements. Possibly she didn't get much time off, but she did carry a decided air of clout. "Mr. McKendrick, you'll be on the other side of the gallery," she announced, staring off to the right of the gallery. "The rooms are kept aired. They're big and comfortable. If you want for anything, you have only to let me or one of the house girls know."

Bruno's answer was perfectly calm and courteous. "If I understand you correctly, Mrs. Saunders, our rooms are a good distance apart. This is a very large house."

"Indeed it is," she said, as though the homestead was on a par with one of the great houses of England. "There are twelve bedrooms."

"Then may I request one on Isabella's side of the gallery?" he asked. "I do hope that's no bother?" He smiled down on this deeply reserved woman with wings of silver in her copious raven hair. "My job is to keep watch on Isabella." Which was something of a fib. "I wouldn't want her to be nervous in such a huge, strange house." Now there was the softest taunt to his words.

Mrs. Saunders appeared to pick up on it. "Really, Mr. McKendrick, the rooms have been made up. The wall sconces are left on should anyone get up for something in the night."

"I would be grateful if you would indulge me, Mrs. Saunders," Bruno pressed the point. "With twelve bedrooms, it shouldn't be a problem for me to choose another?"

The muscles in the housekeeper's throat locked rigid. She was a handsome woman, striking in appearance. Probably, in her youth, she had been a beauty. Isabelle was happy to leave the negotiating to Bruno. The truly bizarre thing was, Mrs. Saunders put Isabelle in mind of Hilary. The same rigid discipline. The same air of being enclosed in barbed wire. Bruno might have been smiling, but he looked, quite simply, a formidable man.

"Please come this way," Mrs. Saunders said, keeping her hard composure. "I dare say something can be arranged."

"I'd be so grateful."

Isabelle risked a look at Bruno. Pulled a little face. There was a devil inside Bruno. But a good devil, if there was such a thing.

Mrs. Saunders paused outside a heavy mahogany door halfway down a wide, thickly carpeted corridor lined with more paintings and antique chairs set at intervals. She opened the door and then stood back, like a soldier at attention, waiting for them to enter.

Bruno was the first to speak. "To put it into words, this is a room fit for an Asian princess."

"Is it ever!" Fascinated, Isabelle moved farther into the large room, studying the chinoiserie furnishings. A white marble mantelpiece, the pilasters of winged female figures, above it an enormous painting of two white herons standing in jade-coloured water beneath some tall green plant with exquisite white flowers. On the walls was an antique wallpaper featuring peonies, with colourful little birds in green branches. A lovely red-lacquered desk and chair at the end wall. But what dominated the space was an extraordinary Chinese four-poster bed. It stood on carved legs, with fretwork on three sides, the canopy intricately carved. It was fully made up, with a beautiful embroidered green silk coverlet.

"Beautiful as it is, I could sleep badly in that," Isabelle murmured, thinking she would dream of the young woman who had lived here, slept in that extraordinary bed and then felt forced to leave.

"I assure you it is most comfortable," said Mrs. Saunders in a stiff voice.

"Perhaps this was Helena's room?" Bruno looked down at the woman to ask.

The charge in the atmosphere turned up. For a moment, it looked as though the housekeeper didn't intend to answer, then she said, unsmilingly, "It was."

Isabelle glanced over at Bruno. *One question at a time.*

"It's the most beautiful bedroom in the house," Mrs. Saunders said, her voice implying they would have little knowledge of such splendid things. "It has an en suite—Mr. Konrad had it put in for her, although it took quite a slice out of the adjoining bedroom. Whatever Miss Helena wanted, she got."

That sounded so *sour,* it prompted Isabelle to find a question of her own. "If she were so indulged, why did she leave?"

The housekeeper swept her a cold look. "It is not for me to say, miss."

"Didn't you want to know?"

Mrs. Saunders pursed her lips. "I'm not family. I'm the housekeeper. I know my place. If you want to come with me, Mr. McKendrick, you can choose another bedroom, although you will have to use the bathroom at the end of the corridor."

"No problem," said Bruno obligingly. "Care to come along, Bella?" He held out his hand.

Such was his natural magnetism, Isabelle went to him, making a grab for his warm, strong hand. In all her years, she couldn't recall ever once making such a grab for the hand of the man she had called Father. "Certainly," she answered now. "I like to be helpful."

"May I ask where the family sleep?" Bruno asked, when they were once more in the corridor.

The housekeeper appeared disconcerted by the question. "Mr. Hartmann has the West Wing," she replied stiffly. "Mr. Stefan and Mr. Kurt occupy the East Wing. My rooms are on the ground floor. Staircases connect the wings to the main house. You'll be joining Mr. Hartmann in the drawing room downstairs. You won't have any difficulty finding it. The drawing room is to the right as you go down the staircase. The dining room is to the left."

Bruno made his choice of a large room on the opposite side of the corridor. The Turkish Room. Isabelle wondered why this room hadn't been made available for Bruno in the first place. It suited his exotic air. Mrs. Saunders had been in the process of directing them farther away from Helena's bedroom. It was Bruno who had made his own choice, asking to see the bedrooms closer to Isabelle's.

The Turkish Room won hands down.

"I'll need to send one of the girls up to air this room and make the bed." Mrs. Saunders's expression, if not her actual words, conveyed this was an imposition. "Believe me, this room can get very dusty with all those hangings, the Kurdish rugs and all those cushions lying about. I have been told not to shift anything. Merely dust and vacuum. This is exactly as it was left."

By whom? What family member?

Evidently Mrs. Saunders didn't like the exotic furnishings or the rich clutter. There were books everywhere. On the floor, on the desk, piled up on a collection of inlaid brass bound travelling boxes. Cushions covered in beautiful Turkish fabrics were scattered all over the place. The room had been painted a shade of dark red, the colour picked up in the rugs with their beautiful central medallions and glowing dark sapphire or ruby fields. The mahogany bed was huge, made for a big man.

Who? was the burning question.

Mrs. Saunders supplied the answer. "The old gentleman, Mr. Konrad's second son, Christian, brought it all back from a trip to Istanbul. This was his room." She could barely keep a quiver of distaste from her voice. "Towels will be put in the bathroom at the end of the hall for your use, Mr. McKendrick."

"Perhaps your house girl can do what she has to do when we're at dinner," Bruno suggested.

Mrs. Saunders's mouth puckered, as if she'd sucked on a lemon. "As you wish. Your luggage is being sent up. It will be here shortly."

"Many thanks, Mrs. Saunders," Isabelle said, cool and calm. "Perhaps you are able to tell me, do you think I resemble Helena? You've been studying me closely."

For the first time the woman showed a degree of torment. "The answer, miss," she said, a fine tremor rippling beneath her smooth, unlined skin, "is in your mirror. You will see her image there."

"Did you love her?" Isabelle asked very gently.

The tremor under the woman's excellent skin intensified. "*Love* is hardly an appropriate word, miss," she retorted. "Miss Helena Hartmann hardly knew I existed."

"I see," Isabelle said gently. What else was there to say?

"I'll be off, then. I have much to attend to."

"We wouldn't dream of keeping you from your duties, Mrs. Saunders," said Bruno with the merest suggestion of an ironic bow.

"You're a devil, aren't you?" Isabelle accused him when Mrs. Saunders had left. Bruno had gone to the door, checking on her progress down the staircase.

"I'm one of the good guys, Bella." He came back into the room. "In order to be a step ahead, one has to know the enemy."

"Mrs. Saunders is the enemy? Tell me quickly."

Bruno's strikingly handsome face grew serious. "You

do realize she's going to protect 'the Master' with her life?"

"What?" Isabelle nearly laughed but reined it in. In truth, the Hartmann mansion itself was freaking her out without throwing in the inmates.

"I'm asking you to pay attention now."

"I *am* paying attention, thank you," she said tartly. "What I'm asking *you,* Bruno McKendrick, is how in the world did you figure that out? I'm assuming 'the Master' is Erik."

All at once Bruno laughed.

She couldn't help it. She laughed too, rattled or not.

"Mr. Hartmann of course. If you took that woman out of her dreary gear, slapped a bit of makeup on her, she'd be a striking-looking woman."

"She is now," Isabelle said.

"But a shadow of what she could be."

"Agreed. I can't comment on her sexuality, but I see you've cast her as the sex interest, if not the love interest?"

"Erik Hartmann doesn't strike me as the loving type," Bruno said. "Controlled as Mrs. Saunders appears, she's passionate about something. Clearly she hated Helena."

Isabelle felt her once-settled world had been blasted away. "Hated?"

"You bet! She wouldn't have mourned Helena's departure."

"What do you intend to do, write a book?" Isabelle asked facetiously.

"There's a story here, Bella. *Stories*. These people live so close to one another, they must hear the others breathe. This is real *isolation.* There are no weekly, monthly dinner parties for friends, no weekend outings, no trips to department stores and the supermarket. No cinema.

No theatre. No opera. No ballet. Only interaction with one another."

"Hang on," Isabelle protested, "I need to get a handle on this. Are you implying incest is rampant in the Outback?"

"Incest is fairly rampant everywhere, but I'm not saying that at all. I'm saying lives can become *too* entwined. I don't imagine the Master and his heir make pals of the station staff and invite them up for dinner. Kurt thinks he's an aristocrat, so much nonsense has been fed him. Okay, the family is rich, but they're living like they're in another age."

"Even another country. This is the twenty-first century. Maybe that's why the women took off: male domination."

"We'll know more after we've had the honour of meeting the Master. The house girls would be aboriginal or part-aboriginal girls, women; wives or daughters of station employees. Aboriginal men have been the mainstay of the cattle industry in the Outback. They're wonderful bushmen, horsemen, trackers. In a way, this is a closed community. Living in such isolation makes for dependence on one another. The extreme isolation of our continent made for legendary mateship. The reliance on one another to survive began from the first day of settlement."

"I understand that. Kurt does give off an arrogant air. You don't. Not when you're with me anyway." She couldn't resist the little jibe.

"Arrogant? Why would I be?"

"Well, a man who looks like you and is as successful as you could easily be."

"So what do I look like?" He suddenly caught her arm, turning her towards him and pinning her eyes.

For seconds, she went into free-fall. Seconds more before she recovered enough to manage lightly, "I'll leave that to your girlfriends to tell you. I guess the Hartmanns and the likes of Mrs. Saunders are given over to keeping up appearances. Mrs. Saunders was born a century too late."

"What's the betting she worships the ground Mr. Hartmann walks upon?" Bruno asked, releasing her.

"I don't have money to bet."

"All right, a titian curl from your head?" He reached out and tweaked one, wrapping it around his finger.

She knew it wasn't possible, but she felt her heart flip over. "You can't be serious?"

"I really am. A symbol of trust. It's not as though you can't spare one."

"You really should confess you enjoy teasing me."

"To be fair, I haven't missed *your* little jabs, either." There was a mocking expression on his face, but his tone was almost tender.

"Okay, we're even," she said shakily.

"And the lock of hair?"

"I have no idea why you want it, but it's a done deal."

"Great! I'll have to buy one of those Victorian lockets."

Such was his blazing masculinity, he could even get away with it. "You're not planning on wearing it around your neck?"

"I'll keep mine in my breast pocket."

So he wasn't exempt from trying to seduce her, even if it were only with his voice and eyes. "Don't practise your charms on me, Bruno McKendrick," she warned.

He placed one hand over his heart. "Bella, I had no idea you find me charming."

"Well, you do have enough going for you, which doesn't mean, however, I fancy you. We're colleagues. Colleagues hunting down a possible crime."

"As if I could forget."

"We can't afford to." She looked around at all the exotic appointments. "Gosh, this is some place. Some people would even call it a madhouse. This beautiful Kurdish prayer rug I'm obliged to stand on would look wonderful hanging on a wall." She stared across at Bruno, who was examining a piece of militaria, a scary-looking war ax. "There's a ghost in this room," she said. "Don't you feel it?"

Bruno put the war ax down. He too was experiencing the odd sensation. "There are ghosts all over this house."

"There you go again. We're in the homestead family mansion, Bruno, not the family cemetery."

"Which must be somewhere on the station." Bruno picked up a weighty leather-bound tome. He flicked through it, then put it down again on the travelling box. "I'll make a good search of this room. I could very well find something interesting. Something that will tell us what we need to know, or at least point us in the right direction."

Isabelle gave him a long, measured look. "I could help you, even if we choke on the dust. People who've lost their lives violently leave something behind, don't you think? There was Erik's wife, Myra, the adulteress, if that's to be believed, and Christian, who managed to get himself shot."

"Out of stupidity, inexperience or perhaps because he broke the rules?" Bruno pondered. "How do we know if Christian wasn't having an affair with his ravishing sister-in-law?"

"Once removed?" Isabelle reminded him. "Erik and Christian were half brothers. I'm sure the much-maligned Myra had good in her. Perhaps whoever took that photograph of her was her lover? It had that look about it, seductiveness shimmering out of her. She looked very sexy. Women can get into a lot of trouble being sexy."

"You're telling me!" Bruno exclaimed, giving an expressive shrug of one shoulder. "They get us guys into a lot of trouble as well."

"Wasn't some girl running around town telling everyone you and she were on the brink of announcing your engagement?"

"And I didn't give her an inch of encouragement." Bruno suddenly held a finger to his lips. "Someone coming."

"Gosh, you've got good ears." She had heard nothing. Why would she? She'd been too busy following Bruno's every word.

"A lot of practise," he explained.

"Practise! Oh come on, you don't—" She broke off when she realized he was having her on.

A moment more and they saw a tall, whipcord-thin figure in khaki working gear put Bruno's luggage down and then pop Isabelle's two pieces inside her room. "Time for us to step out."

Bruno had his suitcase in hand when the houseman reappeared.

If he had been a woman, Isabelle was certain he would have screamed. As it was, he said on a hoarse gasp, "Gawd, you startled me!"

Not only did he look astonished, he looked fearful, as if he were seeing a ghost.

"Sorry," Bruno apologized. "We were taking a look at my consigned bedroom."

"No one goes in there," the man said, looking furtively past Bruno's tall figure.

"It's the room I've picked," Bruno said. "Is it supposed to be haunted?"

"Wouldn't be a bit surprised." The man swallowed hard.

Bruno held out his hand. "I'm Bruno McKendrick and this is Isabelle Martin. Thank you for bringing up our luggage."

"No trouble, mate." The man took a deep, shaky breath and then shook Bruno's hand. "Liam O'Connor. I'm the handyman." He shifted his disturbed glance from Bruno to Isabelle. "S'truth, young lady, I just can't believe my eyes. It's like Miss Helena has come back."

Nailed it in one, Bruno thought.

"You knew her?" Isabelle asked the man, before he could get away.

"Well, not exactly *knew* her. She always said hello to all of us, but of course she wasn't one of us. She was family. I was a young apprentice stockman in them days, but I remember her. She was beautiful like you, miss. All them red curls, the white skin and green eyes. She was tallish and very slim like you too. No one ever recovered after she ran off."

"Hard to credit she would," Bruno said.

"Mind you—" Liam inclined his head, obviously about to say more, when he appeared to come to his senses.

"Mind you?" Isabelle prompted.

"Pays to keep one's mouth shut around here, miss," Liam said. "Anyways, pleased to meet yah both," he mumbled. He then turned on his high-heeled boots and moved off as though a hand would reach out to prevent him.

"We get affirmation all the time," Bruno said. "Miss Helena has come back. I have to speak to that guy." He rubbed a hand over his chiselled chin.

"Could be a bad move."

"I can and I will," said Bruno. "Mind you, what? That's the question. Someone in the family was a monster?"

Isabelle's green eyes went wide. "Wouldn't your dad have sussed that out?"

"My dad was never able to speak to anyone on the station outside the family. Very convenient, these musters. They go on for weeks at a time."

"You heard what he said. Am I a Hartmann? Am I?"

Bruno met her eyes. "There's a possibility, I suppose, you could be Helena's child."

"Which has to mean Hilary is well and truly in the frame for snatching me. Or Helena handed me over. Helena's child, but by whom?"

"At this point, we don't know," said Bruno. "Look, why don't we take a look around your room?"

Isabelle turned away. "Good idea!"

The time for truth was at hand. Both of them were determined to find out as much as they could about the family and the family secrets. Both were convinced Isabelle was part of the family. Had she been born out of wedlock? Had Helena's mother, Myra, been pregnant with her lover's child, not her husband's? There was much to discover. Much to understand.

Chapter Five

Five minutes before they were due to join Erik Hartmann and his great-nephew and heir, Bruno knocked on Isabelle's door. She opened it almost immediately, the two of them face-to-face, each intent on the other, both covering up reactions that were finding their way to the surface.

"You look beautiful," he said lightly, giving her an approving nod. "What else could you look?" Bella had a genius for looking chic. She was wearing a dress with a fitted top and a flowing, calf-length skirt, the colour of an amethyst gemstone. Her crowning glory was pulled back from her face and arranged in some sort of elegant roll at the back. Large amethyst pendant earrings swung from her ears, throwing lights onto her cheeks. God knows how Erik Hartmann would react when confronted with this vision.

A blush warmed Isabelle's flawless skin. "Thank you, Bruno. You look good too." Instinct told her not to enthuse. His outfit comprised a blue linen jacket over a black tee that hugged his taut, muscled torso, with narrow-legged black pants. "The truth is, I'm extremely nervous, if you aren't. These people are strangers to me as I am to them."

"Not too strange," Bruno said. "Kurt will have filled in his great-uncle. You're the living image of his aunt Helena."

"Maybe, but we don't know who I am."

"We're going to find out. Come along, now. Got everything?"

"Yes." Bruno took her hand in his like her very best friend. That alone gave her the confidence and courage she needed to meet this family that could end up hers.

From the base of the staircase they heard men's voices in the drawing room beyond, one deep and educated, the other higher-pitched, less cultured, raised in anger. "What the hell do you mean, keeping this secret, Erik, damn you!" The angry voice sounded as though the news he had just received had totally blindsided him. "And why didn't you tell me, Kurt? Or are you so bloody gutless? I'm your father. Not him. And you ought to thank God for it!"

Isabelle darted a highly perturbed look at Bruno. He increased the pressure on her hand, his thumb soothing her palm. "I'd say Kurt's dad has come home unexpectedly."

"Oh God, Bruno!" she breathed. "What do we do now?"

"What we came here to do," he said purposefully. "Confront them."

"Can't we wait until the argument dies down?"

"A minute more might be helpful," he conceded, but with a certain finality.

Erik Hartmann's voice came again. "This is *real,* Stefan,"

he said. "The girl is here. You should meet her, or aren't you game?"

"Game?" The angry voice turned up a few notches to near ferocity. "I don't want any part of this, Erik. Leave me out of it," he shouted. "Everything you do stinks to high heaven. Our poor Helena is dead. How could she not be, never getting in touch with us. We loved her, Father and I, though you did bloody well keeping any love from her. This girl is a fraud made up to look like Helena."

"Why don't you wait and see?" the darker voice taunted. "I invited them down for drinks right about now. I will admit to a few misgivings myself, but it should be easy enough to tell. Women can do a great deal to alter their appearance."

"Time to go in," said Bruno, looking down at this beautiful young woman whose life he had turned upside down. "You have nothing to fear."

"If I have I don't care." Isabelle tilted her chin. "Who are they to talk about frauds?" she scoffed, stepping off the big Persian rug onto the parqueted floor, allowing her high heels to tap out their arrival.

"Okay, we're on!" Bruno announced, as if they were going onstage. He dropped her hand so as not to give the appearance they were in any way hooked up beyond client and advisor.

The voices had stopped. The house fell silent, as if it had been waiting for this moment for years.

Inside the drawing room, Isabelle knew immediately which man was Erik. She would have known even if the two men had been dressed exactly the same. The family resemblance was strong. Both men were tall, dark haired, dark eyed, with very black straight eyebrows, handsome, the man Stefan noticeably fitter than the much older, heavier Erik, who wore a Paisley evening jacket with a cravat.

Did anyone wear a cravat these days? Bruno wondered. This guy really was a throwback. Probably he had his newspapers ironed.

"Ah, there you are!" their host called with a pleasure they knew perfectly well was feigned. "Come in. Do." He swept a hand toward the younger man dressed in clean, neat khakis. "This is my nephew, Stefan, Kurt's father," he said with practised bonhomie.

For all the playacting, a flash of something akin to fear surged through Isabelle. She had an instinctive distrust of the man who was Helena's father and, God forbid, her grandfather. The other man, Stefan, was standing stock still, clearly in shock. In the background the silent Kurt was nervously twisting his hands around and around.

Erik Hartmann began to make civilised introductions, his voice purring as though they were honoured guests and this was the start of a very enjoyable evening. Bruno shook hands with both men. Isabelle felt she couldn't without triggering some kind of adverse reaction in herself.

Stefan Hartmann appeared struck dumb, but there were many signs of emotion. The muscles of his face were working. His dark eyes appeared glazed. It seemed to her, though she could be quite wrong, that he was a sincere and honest man, where his uncle was not.

At the corner of her vision she saw Mrs. Saunders, dressed more formally, appear through a doorway that must connect with the kitchen, then go to a long serving table placed at the back of a sofa. It had been set with a large silver salver with a beaded rim. It held four long-stemmed crystal flutes. She was carrying a silver wine cooler with garlands on it and rams' heads. Valuable. She placed it alongside the salver. It held a chilled bottle of French champagne. Isabelle recognised the label. Louis Roederer. Their host was splashing out, or maybe he dined on the best of the best French champagnes every night of the week.

"Thank you, Mrs. Saunders," Erik said expansively. "We're all going to enjoy a glass, aren't we?"

"Nothing for me." Stefan Hartmann broke out of his stupor. "Excuse me, please. I've only been home an hour. I wasn't told of your visit until I came into the house." He targeted Bruno, then Isabelle, as he spoke.

"Couldn't you join us?" Isabelle asked with gentle courtesy. "I would like that."

"Why not, Stefan?" Erik joined in sardonically. "Isabelle and Mr. McKendrick have come all this way."

Stefan's dark head shot in Bruno's direction. "McKendrick?" He gave his uncle a fiercely quizzical look before turning back to Bruno. "You have some connection to Ross McKendrick, the private investigator who came here many years ago?"

"My father," Bruno replied. "I regret you weren't at home to be told of our visit."

Stefan frowned heavily. "When was the visit arranged?"

"A day after you left," Erik Hartmann cut in smoothly. "You really didn't give me the opportunity to explain, Stefan."

Bruno bestowed a wry look on Isabelle. No point in flatly contradicting their host.

"I'm sorry, but please don't include me." Stefan Hartmann fixed Isabelle with such a strange look. There were actually a glitter of tears in his eyes. They seemed to speak to her of a deep wound, as if the shock and the grief of Helena's disappearance would never go away. "I'll say good night," he said, moving awkwardly when he wouldn't normally have been awkward, such was his haste to be gone.

"Perhaps we could speak tomorrow?" Isabelle asked. "That's if you have the time. I know no more than you do, Mr. Hartmann. All I know is my resemblance to Helena is such it startles everyone, including you. All this is very new to me. I knew nothing of this family until very recently and only through a photograph of Helena and, we assume, one of her mother. Ross McKendrick had the photographs in his possession. I'm as much a mystery to myself as I am to you."

"Helena's mother? You surely can't be talking about Myra?" Stefan spoke in a rush, even further amazed.

"No, no, the photographs were of Helena," Erik Hartmann said calmly but emphatically. "I gave them to your father myself."

"Wherever did you get the idea you had a photograph of Myra?" The words were wrested from some place deep inside Stefan Hartmann.

"I believe the two photographs I was shown were of two different women who shared a remarkable resemblance," Isabelle explained. "Bruno's father did not see it. I did." No point in adding Hilary had spotted the difference too. She knew most people wouldn't, but they would be merely observing whereas she and Hilary, women, had considerable powers of observation.

"My dear girl!" Erik Hartmann appeared to be marvelling she could have jumped to such a conclusion. "I *do* know the difference between my wife and my daughter. You're entirely mistaken."

"Is she really?" Stefan swung aggressively on his uncle. "I'd know which was which. Do you have the photographs with you?"

"I do," Bruno said.

"So you came here." Stefan's whole demeanour had changed.

Erik suddenly waved a hand to hush the housekeeper away. "That will do, Mrs. Saunders. Dinner in thirty minutes."

"Yes, sir." There was no humility in her voice; nevertheless, the ever-faithful housekeeper moved off as if she couldn't wait to be gone.

"If it's only coincidence, and not some connection by blood, that can be easily proved," Bruno said, crossing to Isabelle's side.

Stefan Hartmann turned away abruptly, took a few steps out of the room, then faced Isabelle again. "How long are you staying?"

"A very short time."

"All we need is the answer to a few questions," said Bruno with swift decisiveness. What were these people hiding?

"I know. DNA testing?" Stefan said, anger resurfacing in his eyes.

"Don't you all want to know if Isabelle is in some way connected to you?" Bruno asked, the voice of reason.

"You mean like we have a choice?" Kurt suddenly entered the fray. "You're after money, aren't you?"

"We most definitely are not!" Bruno answered the younger man almost amiably. "We can all wonder about the extraordinary resemblance Isabella bears to your relative, or we can rule out any blood connection."

"Or rule it in," Stefan said. "Which firm do you represent, McKendrick?"

"I run my own wealth management company in Sydney, Mr. Hartmann. The Fortuna Group."

"Impressive too," Erik Hartmann interjected. He had checked McKendrick out.

"I've involved myself in this because of my father," Bruno continued. "He was obsessed with finding Helena. He wanted to bring closure to the family. He thought very highly of Mr. Konrad Hartmann, who hired him. I'm doing this for Isabella, my father and, of course, Helena." He stopped short of telling them whom they now knew had fled to the U.K. Or maybe they did know. Maybe Erik Hartmann knew, if his nephew, Stefan, didn't.

"Why don't I get the photos?" Isabelle said. "It will only take a moment."

"Leave it, my dear," Erik said, shaking a grave head. "We can see them later."

"I want to see them *now*." Stefan Hartmann didn't appear to trust his uncle one inch.

Bruno brought the disagreement to an end. "I'll get them," he said.

"Good man!" Stefan nodded.

Bruno moved as soundlessly as a big cat down the corridor. He had a fair idea who he would find when he reached the Turkish Room. He was a past master at intercepting communications between employees, competitors, people in general. Erik Hartmann had given a silent signal to Mrs. Saunders, possibly his long-term mistress. The woman could look vastly different if she took the trouble. Whether his nephew and great-nephew were aware of a possible arrangement between the two, he had no idea. Both Hartmann and the housekeeper were consummate actors.

The door of the Turkish Room was open. He had shut it. The woman had her back to him.

"Whatever are you doing, Mrs. Saunders?" he asked.

She turned, drawing herself up. She did not lower her eyes. She looked fixedly back at him, as brazen as you like. "I was just checking you would be comfortable for the night, Mr. McKendrick. I have trained my staff well, but I always check things myself. Why do you look at me like that?" she asked abruptly. She wasn't the first person to be unnerved by Bruno's regard.

Bruno only smiled. "Thank you for going to the trouble, Mrs. Saunders. I expect you want to get on with dinner?"

"I have everything in hand."

"So do I, madam," Bruno said. "You appear to have touched my suitcase. It's not where I left it."

A look of confusion crossed the housekeeper's face. "I swear—"

"No need," Bruno said pleasantly, holding up a hand. "You probably lifted it off the bed?"

"Exactly," the woman said. "Now, if you'll excuse me?" She was studying Bruno's smiling face with little idea of what lay behind the charm.

"Of course." He didn't know whether she'd had the time to find the photographs and form an opinion that would be passed to the Master one way or another. One young woman? Two young women? One Helena? One Myra? Mrs. Saunders would do anything Hartmann asked.

He wasn't such a fool as to leave the photographs on display. He located a specific book on the Ottoman Empire, spread the yellowed pages and found the photographs.

He had learned a great deal from Isabella. His father had never questioned the photographs were of Helena.

The same hair, the same features, the same colouring. He had taken them on good faith from Helena's father as both being of his daughter. Why would a father lie unless he had something to explain? What if Erik were not Helena's father? How could such a thing be? With the exception of Kurt, who probably had inherited his mother's colouring, the Hartmann men were dark eyed, dark haired. Myra—the family pronounced it *Meera*—Hartmann had been a dazzling beauty. She would have attracted most of the men who came into her orbit.

Myra and perhaps her daughter were nothing but bones, as was Erik Hartmann's half brother Christian. He knew DNA testing was accurate. He had consulted a medical scientist friend. He had asked and learned if half brothers underwent a paternity test, the biological father would be easily identified. Only identical twins would have the same DNA, not half brothers, as Erik and Christian had been.

"If only walls could speak!" Bruno exclaimed aloud. "Did you love Myra, Christian?" he asked the dusky air. "Did she love you? Was Helena your love child?" Stranger things had happened. Or was there some other man involved? A family friend, a frequent visitor? One from overseas? How did one get the Hartmann men to consent to DNA testing? Both would be affronted by any such suggestion. And he wouldn't blame them.

What wouldn't I give to hear your story, Christian? he thought. Christian long buried, as was the beautiful Myra. That to Bruno seemed most peculiar. Two members of the family who had suffered accidental death. The family was so influential, even more so in those days, when stations were run like private kingdoms, their accounting of the two tragic events would have been accepted. Such accidents in their part of the world weren't rare.

Bruno arrived downstairs to a group reduced to silence. His gaze went immediately to Isabelle, bypassing Eric and Kurt. She gave him a faint, encouraging smile. She was all right, then. He crossed the room to where Stefan Hartmann was sitting, handing him the two photographs. But would he be an expert on Myra, his aunt?

It appeared Stefan thought he was because after a brief perusal, he burst out, "This is Aunt Myra, your wife, Erik." He jabbed at the larger photograph with a finger, before waving it aloft.

"You don't know what you're saying," Erik countered with weary contempt. "You wouldn't have been that old when my wife was killed. You've forgotten her."

"I've forgotten nothing," Stefan said, not even bothering to defend himself. "This photograph is of Helena," he said, having put the larger photograph down before picking up the other. An expression of great sadness crossed his face. "It's the photo of a heartsick girl. Your wife overshadowed your daughter in all departments. Aunt Myra was a great femme fatale. I remember her well. She had so many attributes. She played the piano beautifully. She was a wonderful hostess, a great rider, a fine markswoman. I remember how she used to draw all the male guests like bees to honey. You hated that. You wanted all her attention, but you never got it. Aunt Myra had a *presence,* a vibrancy Helena lacked, for all she was just as beautiful as her mother. Note the expressions are quite different. One woman has all the self-confidence the other lacks. Helena looks so unsure of herself, unhappy. *Why?* What was making her so unhappy? She'd lost her mother, and then she lost my father, her uncle Christian. She loved him, might I remind you, Erik. She loved him and he loved her."

"If we can trust your recollections," Erik Hartmann said mildly, unimpressed by what his nephew had to say. "You were a long time at boarding school. The smaller photo of Helena was taken when she had become somewhat rebellious. Occasionally she did foolish things. She had to be cautioned for her own good. The trouble was, my father overindulged her, especially after she lost her mother."

"She didn't *lose* her mother," Stefan suddenly shouted. "Her mother was killed here on the station. Myra was a superb horsewoman. No one ever worried about her when she went out. She could handle any horse. She could even break in brumbies. She could jump fences with her eyes closed. Everyone admired her. I'm not making all this up. I know. I saw."

"So what are you trying to say, Dad?" Kurt asked, appearing honestly shocked by his father's outburst.

"I don't know what I'm trying to say," Stefan admitted, shaking his head sadly. "What I *can* say is one is a photo of Helena, the other is of her mother. It's a mystery how you, *Uncle* Erik, couldn't pick which one was of your wife and which one was of your daughter. God help me if I'm wrong."

"You are wrong, Dad. You have to be," Kurt cried, the blood draining from his tanned face.

"We've got a captive audience here," Erik Hartmann pointed out almost languidly, as if immune to family outbursts.

Stefan looked across at Isabelle. "I'm sorry if I've upset you, young lady. I had to speak my mind."

"I'm glad you did," Isabelle replied.

"Not that it makes a great deal of difference if both the photos are of Helena or they aren't," Bruno said in a sombre voice.

"So what are you sweating on?" Kurt asked him angrily.

"Be quiet, Kurt," Stefan snapped, turning his head to reprimand his son. "This young lady only seeks to find out if there's a family connection. Isn't that right, Isabelle?"

Quietly, Isabelle replied, "I have spoken at length with my parents—the people I have always believed to be my parents—but could I have been adopted?"

"That being so, there would be adoption papers," Erik Hartmann said, as if that settled the matter, as it would. "Obviously there aren't."

"I don't look anything like either of my parents," Isabelle couldn't refrain from commenting.

"I'm certain that's not a unique state of affairs." Erik studied Isabelle at length. "Are there no redheads on either side of the family?"

"My mother has a cousin in Scotland with red hair," Isabelle admitted.

Erik Hartmann spread his hands. "There you are, then. Look at young Kurt. He takes after his mother's side of the family, blond, blue eyes."

"There's nothing for it but we settle this thing." Stefan Hartmann, brow furrowed, took a stand. "I don't know a lot about DNA testing, but it's accepted by the courts. I'd be happy to give you a sample of whatever is needed."

A bitter look flared in Erik Hartmann's eyes. "I absolutely forbid you to do such a thing," he said in a low, angry voice.

"Could you tell us why, sir?" Bruno asked, his tone courteous. "We're sorry if you've been made to feel offence, but you did allow us to come here."

"A big bloody mistake, I'd say!" Kurt leapt in again.

It was obvious he couldn't control his own anger. He was 100 percent behind his great-uncle.

His father curled his lip in disdain. "What's it got to do with you, Kurt? I'm beginning to think all you really care about is keeping in with Uncle Erik."

Kurt stopped, unsure. "These people are after something, Dad."

"Your inheritance?" Stefan scoffed.

Erik Hartmann interrupted. "How do you know I haven't learned to my sorrow that my daughter is dead?"

Kurt blinked in astonishment, but his father jumped to his feet with all the energy in his tall, strongly muscled body. "You store up information like a miser, Erik. You've learned—you've *learned*—the hell you have! You're a liar!" He rejected his uncle's claim out of hand.

"Have you, sir?" Bruno was very conscious of what all this was doing to Bella.

Erik Hartmann didn't answer directly. "Helena destroyed this family," he said, pulling at his silk cravat. "She was given everything she could possibly want and she ran off."

"I'd like to know where." Isabelle's green eyes sparkled with challenge. Helena didn't destroy the family. The family destroyed her. She didn't have a shred of proof, but that was what she believed.

"My dear, you don't have a role in this," Erik said, sounding very kind. "You may have dreams you're a Hartmann, but I know you're not. I grant you a remarkable resemblance, but we've all seen doubles."

"Why won't you allow testing?" Stefan demanded of his uncle. Clearly, they weren't close, rather at loggerheads.

"Because, my dear nephew, it's an affront to our family,

of which I am head. Your grandfather would totally agree with me."

Isabelle gave their host a long look, trying to judge the sincerity of his words. "Surely Konrad Hartmann, were he with us now, would change his mind?" she asked.

Stefan was frowning, leaning his hand on the back of a sofa. "Of course he would. Anything to establish what could have happened to Helena."

"My father is not with us now. I make the decisions now. Isabelle here is very beautiful, but she could have dyed her hair. You notice her eyebrows are naturally dark. She could be wearing contact lenses. She could even have had plastic surgery."

"None of which is true," said Bruno flatly. "If you, Stefan Hartmann, are willing to undergo DNA testing, it should be all we need to prove a familial connection."

"For the love of God!" Erik burst out, showing the first sign of agitation. "I won't have this. I am head of this family. Not you, Stefan. You have a stake in Eaglehawk. That's all."

Isabelle stood up. "I am truly sorry if our coming here has upset you all. We *were* invited. What I don't understand is why?" She directed her gaze at Erik Hartmann, lounging back in his chair.

"Because of the McKendrick connection, my dear girl," he said, settling back into his confident, rich voice. "My father, Konrad, thought Mr. McKendrick a fine man who did his very best. The invitation was intended as a courtesy."

"My father *was* a fine man." Bruno entered into the discussion. "We have reason to believe Helena may have fled to the U.K." He expected that to badly shake them, even the Master of Eaglehawk.

"She did," Erik Hartmann said with enormous calm.

Kurt sat staring at his great-uncle as if he didn't know what to say, but his father placed himself squarely in front of Erik, drawing a furious whistling breath through his teeth. "I would never have imagined even *you* would keep that piece of information from us," he cried in undisguised shock. "What right did you have not to tell us?" He threw a heated glance at his son. "Wouldn't you want to know, Kurt?"

"Yes, Dad, yes," Kurt answered immediately, touching his forehead with his fingers, as though he had a terrible headache. "When did you find out, Uncle Erik?" he pleaded, looking immensely bothered.

"Would you believe only recently?" Erik Hartmann replied calmly. "At the same time, I learned Helena had died."

Stefan brought his fist down so hard on the serving table everything jumped. "That isn't good enough!"

In the middle of it all, Mrs. Saunders appeared, no doubt waiting in the wings as instructed. "Excuse me, sir," she addressed the Master, "dinner is ready."

"Dinner?" Stefan bellowed. He was swaying back and forth on his booted feet. "Who wants bloody dinner at a time like this?"

"I do, Stefan," Erik said mildly, "and I'm sure our guests do as well. They've come a long way. The least we can do is feed them."

"What did that bloody woman tell you before?" Stefan asked, watching his uncle closely.

"*That bloody woman* has devoted her entire adult life to serving this family," Erik shot back with ice in his voice and possibly his veins. "I'm shocked you should attack her, and in front of our guests. Now, why don't we put further discussion aside and go in to dinner?"

Stefan shook his head. "Not for me, thanks. Tell our splendid housekeeper to send my dinner over."

"I think I'll go with Dad," said Kurt, of a sudden finding his bond with his father the stronger.

"Whatever, my boy!" Erik Hartmann smiled benignly, presenting his arm to Isabelle. "Shall we go in? I must confess I'm hungry."

Isabelle's appetite had fled. She had no option but to accept her host's arm when she had already formed an instinctive dislike and distrust of the man. She was deeply disturbed by what she had heard and the tensions within the family. If they had existed in Helena's youth, small wonder she had run away to find some peace and harmony.

Stefan levelled his dark eyes on Bruno. "I'll see you both in the morning. McKendrick, we have things to discuss. Forgive all the anger. It happens when painful memories resurface."

"In the morning, then, sir." Bruno extended his hand.

Stefan took it. "I like the look of you, McKendrick," he said. "I trust you. I trust you to look out for that beautiful girl. She's the living spit of Helena, even if she's far more spirited. It can't be coincidence."

"No," said Bruno.

Isabelle was *blood.*

Dinner was pure theatre. Erik Hartmann presided, the most gracious, most practised of hosts. Mrs. Saunders moved back and forth, her helper a pretty young part-aboriginal girl, who smiled shyly. The table had been laid to perfection with plates and dishes from a beautiful porcelain dinner service, "been in the family ever since I can remember, Royal Crown Derby's Old Imari." There were two silver candelabra, silver flatware, crystal glasses. No flowers, but an ornate German silver centre-piece. A large cut-glass and ormolu chandelier hung over their heads. The three courses were up to restaurant standard, beautifully presented.

Isabelle couldn't wait to get away. Bruno, clever, highly educated, well travelled, had no difficulty matching Erik Hartmann's cultured conversation, but Isabelle sensed Bruno too was keen to escape. Bruno didn't bring Isabelle's musical abilities into the conversation, waiting, Isabelle sensed, for their host to pursue the subject, but he never said a word. She might have been a doll sitting at the table. Both she and Bruno were certain Kurt, who had defected to his father, would have relayed every word they had exchanged on arrival.

No background music had floated in the air all evening, but the grand piano, a Bechstein, the one Helena was seated at in the portrait, was prominent in the drawing room. Erik Hartmann was like some character out of a Gothic novel, playing the role of betrayed husband, betrayed father. The crimes were against him. The crimes could well have been the other way around. Isabelle felt sure of it now.

"Thank God that's over!" Isabelle whispered as they made their way up the divided staircase to the gallery. "Relief, that's what I feel."

"Whatever is the man playing at?" Bruno's voice was as soft and potentially dangerous as the purring of a big cat.

Isabelle drifted closer to his side. This was one heck of a scary place. "I have no idea. Did Helena know something about her father that caused her to run? Did *your* father come to find out something about Erik Hartmann that got him run over?"

"That would take him right down to Hell." The purr had turned into a growl. "Everything turns around the same thing. *Why* did Helena run? She was only twelve when her mother was killed. What would a child know?"

"Maybe she knew nothing then, but she could have found out something years later."

"Then why didn't she go to the grandfather?" Bruno asked as they moved down the corridor.

"Maybe her grandfather wouldn't have listened to a word against his son and heir. Old school thing."

"I can buy that," Bruno said. "It's like we've stumbled into a foreign country. Konrad would have trusted his son against the suspicions of a nerve-ridden girl, even if she were his granddaughter."

"That's men for you." Isabelle exhaled a puff of disgust. "I think Konrad Hartmann would have been the classic definition of a well-born European patriarch. They brought their homeland with them. I bet they all speak German. They certainly did a lot of travelling around Europe with their buying trips, even as far as Turkey. With the family occupying both wings, we have the central core to ourselves," she pointed out, a little tremor in her voice. "This is one spooky house. The height of Goth, don't you think? I'm glad you're with me, Bruno. Sometimes it's handy to have a big, strong man around. Though the trusty Mrs. Saunders has rooms downstairs."

"When she is where she's supposed to be," Bruno said very dryly. "I take it I'm the big, strong man?"

"You are. I depend on you, Bruno. You got me into this after all. At least Kurt went off with his dad."

"That's a good thing," Bruno agreed.

They were outside her door. "Come in for a while," Isabelle entreated, a strung-up expression on her face. "I feel way too unsettled to go to sleep. I could have nightmares."

"I suppose I could sleep right outside your door like that guy slept outside Queen Victoria's door," Bruno suggested with a smile.

"John Brown, her Highland ghillie," Isabelle said. "'The best, the truest heart that ever lived,' Victoria said when he died. Apparently, she had a huge appetite for sex, a bit at odds with all the 'life of purity' she tried to force on her sons. Prince Albert, described in his day as 'effeminate,' was finally driven to putting a foolproof lock on his door to escape her advances."

Bruno had to laugh. "Is this true?"

"Absolutely. She was the one on the rampage, not Albert. That great love affair was very much a fiction. She used to knock on his door, screaming at him in German to open up. According to records and her own letters reviling her sons, she was a manic personality who was unbelievably cruel and controlling with her children. They must have done a little jig when she died. She even put John Brown's bully of a brother in charge of one of the princes. He gave the child hell. The courtiers on the side of the prince reported it, but the queen ignored them. Isn't that just awful? Not mom of the year. I've always been interested in history, even historical trivia. Absolutely sickening, the facts as opposed to what's dished up for public consumption."

"That occurs at all levels of power," said Bruno. "I may not sleep outside your door, but you can be sure I'll keep an eye on it."

"Gee, thanks. You're not only the sort of guy women

ogle, Bruno, you're the sort of guy who comes to a damsel's rescue."

"I'd like to think so at least." He opened her door and then stood back for her to enter the extravaganza that was the Chinese Room. "Stefan has agreed to see us in the morning."

"That's good news. Do you suppose Helena was happy in this bedroom?" she asked as she moved to the centre of the room, looking tantalizingly young and beautiful in her amethyst dress. "Do you suppose she had an idyllic childhood?"

"Hardly. Losing one's mother must come a close second to the terrible trauma of losing a child."

"You lost your mother," she said gently. She didn't think Bruno had even now come to terms with it.

"You mean she took off without saying good-bye." Bruno swallowed down a harsh response. "She's doing well. The guy comes from some old, illustrious family. God knows where she got to meet him."

"Waiting at the lights, crossing the road?" Isabelle suggested. She'd had her fair share of desirous glances at such places. "Men dream of meeting a beautiful woman with the power to attract all their senses, don't they? Your mother would have given off a powerful magnetism." She didn't say, *like you*. "You've no desire to look her up?"

"No, Isabella," he said with great firmness.

"So both our mothers took off," she said sadly.

"If we're correct, they did."

"I refuse to believe Helena was happy here," she said. "This room is far too overpowering to be restful. It's like a niche in the Oriental section of a museum."

"It is," Bruno agreed.

"Why ever did Konrad Hartmann have his granddaughter's bedroom decorated like this?" Isabelle asked in wonderment.

"If it was he who did the decorating," Bruno pointed out. "It could have been done in his father's time, although we know from the dour Mrs. Saunders that Konrad had the en suite put in."

"Taking space off the adjoining bedroom, don't forget. Clearly Mrs. S. was jealous of Helena. She could even have conspired against her."

"The Turkish Room is downright dowdy by comparison." Bruno's dark eyes were making a clean sweep of the large room, searching out details. "Everything the same as you left it?" he asked.

"Well, no one has shifted the bed," she said.

"I'm not joking."

"Aren't you?" She gathered herself, staring across at him.

"The estimable Mrs. Saunders was in my room when I went up to get the photographs."

"And just when were you going to tell me?"

"Ah, well, yes. I'm telling you now. You must be aware we're being watched like hawks."

"Well it is Eaglehawk Station." Isabelle let out a nervous laugh. "I know, don't tell me. She was checking on our photographs?"

"Bella, if I went into business, I'd want you as my off-sider."

She shook her glowing head. "I think you mean *partner*. Do you think she found them?"

"I'm certain she didn't," Bruno said with satisfaction. "I'd picked a book at random and hid them in it. She didn't have a lot of time."

"So the Master managed to tip her off?" Isabelle sat herself down on the ornate bed, waving Bruno into a deep armchair. "Those two are cohorts," she said, her emerald eyes fixed on him.

"I thought that was a military unit in ancient Rome?" Bruno said, fascinated by the sight she made as she sat on the extraordinary Chinese bed with its green embroidered silk coverlet. His eyes were flooded by colour: Bella's radiant hair, her jewelled eyes, the pearlescent skin. Her amethyst dress was a perfect colour foil for the silk quilt. Such was the link that had grown up between them, he felt as though he had known Isabella since she was a little girl. Her beauty and her engaging personality never paled but gained strength, yet their first encounter had taken place such a very short time before. Time didn't seem to have meaning. One either caught the fast train or took the slow one. He had never believed himself capable of being so enchanted. But he knew what impulses were in him; the elemental fire had to be banked and contained. He was determined on maintaining the correct moral boundaries.

"I actually meant cahoots, not cohorts," Isabelle was saying.

"Co-conspirators."

"Do you suppose Stefan is as belligerent all the time? I'd hate to be around him if he had a gun in his hand. Must be hard to live with, uncle and nephew at each other's throats. That could be one of the reasons Kurt reaches out to his great-uncle. His father must show his disappointment Kurt isn't made in his mould."

"Why doesn't he leave?" Bruno asked. "He's obviously not tied to the land. He acts more like a grown-up kid. I fully expected him to stamp his foot or chuck something at me. Surely he needs some life. He must have a dream. Where are the girlfriends?"

"Maybe he's got one and we haven't seen her? He's handsome enough."

"You've been keeping your eye on him?" Bruno regarded her with a mocking expression.

"For heaven's sake. I feel sorry for him, if you want to know."

"Compassion is a strength," Bruno remarked, liking that quality in her.

"Kurt has all the makings to be handsome, but there's something missing," Isabelle considered. "He's a couple of years older than I am, yet he seems immature. All in all, we've got off to a very dismal start."

"What else? Isn't it what we expected? Erik doesn't appear to want the mystery of Helena's disappearance and supposed death solved. How unbelievable is that?"

"I'd say they've all had a lot of practise forgetting Helena."

"Kurt, of course, is hanging in there for the money. I can check how much the family is worth."

"Who cares?" Isabelle exclaimed. "Go on. You want to say something."

"You already know what I want to say. If you turned out to be Helena's daughter, you would have the stronger claim."

"When Erik Hartmann clearly doesn't want me in the picture. That's a complete aberration for a possible grandfather. What is he up to, claiming he had word of Helena's death in the U.K.? Who told him? And very recently . . ." She stopped, uncertain.

"You're thinking Hilary?"

"I can't rule out the possibility. I was born in a London maternity hospital. Was Helena in the same ward?"

"God knows! From what I saw of Hilary, she's the sort of woman who could come up with solutions to hers and other women's problems. What if Helena were in no position to keep her baby? Alone, frightened, traumatized, without money. What if Hilary lost her baby? Was there a swap?"

"No, no, no!" Isabelle shook her head. "I can't believe that. I won't believe it. What I *can* believe is Hilary might have contacted Erik with some information she had."

"Then why didn't he do what everyone else would do? Inform his family."

"Hilary told me she'd made enquiries about the Hartmanns from some influential friend. But to say Hilary and Erik Hartmann had made contact would be to take a massive quantum leap."

"Here's another leap: Erik could have staged his wife's accident. He could have spent time working it all out."

"A theory without proof. We will *never* know."

"Then Christian gets accidentally shot."

"One suspicious death is hard enough to cover up. But two? Two is a pattern. The police would be all over it, Bruno."

"They would need hard evidence. Suspicion is not enough. This house is talking to me, Bella. This room. Christian's room. This is no ordinary family. No ordinary house. Secrets are imbedded in the walls. Couldn't Christian have fallen in love with his sister-in-law? Yearned for her?"

"What about his wife?"

"She could have been very stout."

"Be serious," Isabelle said, knowing he was trying to lighten the atmosphere. "Why don't we hear a thing about her? It's as though she never existed. It's all Myra, Myra, Myra. What about the wife, Abigail? She bore Christian a son, Stefan."

Bruno was struck by a moment's sadness. He would

always miss his father. He would always feel anger over the way his dad had died. "Dad would have checked her out," he said. "He described her as a pretty woman, reserved in manner but perfectly pleasant when they met. I have to double-check this, but Dad thought there had to be a lot of repressed emotions there."

"Nothing strange about that!" Isabelle blew out a breath. "If Christian had fallen in love with his sister-in-law, Abigail would have known about it. He wouldn't have been able to conceal it. His every glance would have given him away."

Bruno couldn't ignore that piece of insight. "Christian may well have loved his wife. He married her. Had two children by her. There are all degrees of loving. Myra may have seduced him and he surrendered gladly. A sort of love, if you like. They would have had plenty of secluded places they could go to be alone."

"What! Behind the spinifex bushes?" Isabelle asked facetiously. "So Erik finds out and decides they must die. Abigail might even have alerted him to what was going on right before his eyes. She could have been horrendously jealous, not accepting at all. Who knows if Helena were Christian's daughter? Maybe that's why Erik doesn't want any DNA testing. They can tell these days, can't they, who the father is even within families?"

Bruno nodded. "Stefan is willing to give us a sample."

"What, a mouth swab? How do we go about it? How do we store it?"

"One thing at a time."

"Okay, Doc! You realize Stefan could be ignorant of so many things that went on. We should ask him about his mother. She could easily be alive and living elsewhere. All the women took off. Erik would be a fearsome man if he found out he'd been cuckolded. Why did he invite us here? Does he propose to kill me too? We have been poking our toes into pretty murky waters."

"He might be a devil, Bella, but he's not a fool. It will all come out now. Either you're one of the Hartmanns or you're Hilary's baby, as Norville claims. The facts will come out."

"I hope so. We have nothing really to go on but my extraordinary resemblance to Helena Hartmann and her mother."

"Isn't that enough? Your appearance has lit the fuse. It's put them all in a panic."

"We're so *close*," she agonized.

"Yes, we are. Think you can sleep now?"

"Sure, with one eye open."

Bruno laughed. "I'll wait until you're ready for bed. Hang on, I'll go get a book. Lovers never seem to throw away their love letters. Who knows? I might find a stack hidden away in Christian's retreat from the world."

"Surely he shared a room with his wife?" said Isabelle as she slid off the bed. "There would have been an adjoining room for their child."

"This was his *retreat*, Bella. Here it was far easier to be left alone. Christian and his wife may have had the East Wing. We can ask Stefan. Did his mother, Abigail, leave her husband for most of the time, like his own wife spends most of her time in the city with their daughter?"

"I wish we'd stayed out of it, Bruno."

"We need to find out who you are. We need to find out the truth."

"Sounds so noble, doesn't it, finding out the truth? But bad things can happen to people trying to find out the truth."

"Nothing bad is going to happen to you, Bella."

Her green eyes locked on his. “You say that with such surety . . .”

“It would have to be over my dead body. And *that’s* not going to happen.”

She sighed deeply. “Go get your book, Sir Lancelot. Or is that Sir Galahad? I seem to remember Galahad was Lancelot’s illegitimate son.”

“God, I have a lot to learn to catch up with you,” Bruno said, making for the door.

“The more I think about it, it’s Sir Lancelot. Anyway, you’re elected.”

Chapter Six

It might look desperately uncomfortable, but Isabelle found as she bounced up and down in her white cotton and lace nightie, the Chinese bed was well upholstered with an excellent mattress. Thank God for that!

She knew wall sconces along the high-ceilinged corridor were burning, but no light reached under the heavy mahogany door. She looked around the large room for ghosts. There were none. Bruno was right across the corridor, yet she wanted him to be closer. She would have no hesitation banging on his door should some creaks in the night frighten her. Though all old houses creaked, didn't they? Bruno's rock-solid presence made her feel safe. Yet she was reluctant to close her eyes, much less fall asleep.

Again and again, old memories of her childhood threatened to overcome her. Norville believed Hilary to be her mother. She now didn't. But what did Norville actually know? Hilary led him around by the nose. Had Hilary lost her child and somehow persuaded Helena to hand her baby over? Her heart ached for all the young women who had been forced to do so all down the centuries. Nothing much seemed to change.

"Oh God!" she muttered, winding her arms around herself. "Don't worry about things you can't alter. Go to sleep. Go to sleep." It had been a very long, upsetting day, with the promise of a worse one on the morrow.

She had pulled back the floor-length silk curtains, letting the bright moonlight and the night-sky stars shine in. She hadn't felt brave enough to open up the French doors. The wind was tapping at the panes of glass and creeping under the gaps between doors and floor. A lovely, subtle fragrance rose from the freshly laundered sheets and pillow slips. She could identify the fragrance. Boronia. By the light of the moon, she could see the elaborately carved white marble fireplace with a luxuriant green fern filling the interior space. She knew the high temperatures of the day could drop dramatically at night as the desert sands gave up their heat.

She closed her eyes, clutching the top sheet tight. She wasn't afraid of the dark. Well, not until now anyway.

She couldn't open her eyes or find her breath. Where was she? She threw out an arm and hit hard, glossy timber. "Damn!" Her fingers were poking through holes. Of course: the fretwork on the Chinese bed.

She opened her eyes as memory flooded back. The white moonlight that had rayed across the room before she had fallen into an uneasy sleep had dimmed. She had been dreaming. Hilary and Helena were in her dream. Both of them sunk in sadness. Mother and daughter. She wanted to get out of that dream. It was too distressing.

Fully awake, she became aware of a sound. Surely that sound had been in her dream? It was a soft moaning, extremely unsettling. She sat up in the Chinese bed, struggling to get her bearings. Surely the previous owner of this room could mean her no harm? Her plait had come loose. Her hair was spilling all over the place. The moaning continued apace. It was like a *grieving* in the partially relieved blackness.

Have to get out of here.

She kicked off the covers, thrashing her long legs. She needed to find her feet as quickly as she could. She was shivering, feeling a little faint.

Get a grip on yourself.

Why the hell didn't she have her flashlight? She had brought one with her. Reaching for her white robe, thankful it glimmered in the semidark, she shouldered into it. The moaning held a faint vibrato. It continued, shifting pitch. Close to a demisemi tone. She knew the sound of the wind. The wind had dropped.

Oh, oh, oh, I have to get out of here.

She made a rush for the door, not stopping to turn on the lights, throwing the door open, before running on bare feet across to the Turkish Room, where no doubt Bruno had fallen fast asleep the minute his head hit one of those cushions. She had to wake him; it couldn't be helped. She wanted Bruno as witness to the moaning sound. She hadn't conjured it up. The sound had played around the room, joltingly ghostly. Was it such a terrible thing to feel frightened in a vast, strange house full of strange people? Even Hilary might have a fit of nerves.

Bruno's door was open, which made it easy for her to run inside. She was feeling her way, yet something touched her cheek. She nearly screeched aloud in panic.

Damn, it was only a wall hanging. The bloody things were everywhere.

She could see Bruno's lean body at rest. Here she was with goose bumps breaking out on her arms and he was fast asleep. Thank God he didn't snore. She ran at him as if he were the only person in the world capable of saving her from falling off it.

He was lying with his bare back to her, his skin so smooth and golden. She wanted to jump in beside him. Instead, she grabbed at his shoulder with cold fingers, intending to shake him and tell him to wake up, when she was suddenly seized by strong arms, thrown over the top of him, bent back against the bed, all squished up against his side. For a second it was so wildly exciting she didn't want to move. From cold she went to hot and dreamy in an instant. She wanted Bruno's weight, the wonderful muscular density pressing down on her. She wanted to do what she had never done before. Raise her legs, lock them around him. Raise her hips. She had to face it. She wanted Bruno to make love to her.

Bruno, however, had other ideas. He shot up, leaning over her, poised on one elbow. "God Almighty, Bella, what are you doing here?" For a moment, he didn't know if she was real or a figment of his imagination. Only he had clamped her willowy body with his hands. His fingertips had brushed her white breasts, grazed the flowering coral-pink buds of her nipples.

"What am *I* doing?" she cried, spitting like a kitten. "I don't believe this. What are *you* doing? I was only trying to wake you. It was you who hauled me into the bed." She tried to sit up. He lifted her in an iron grip.

"Bella, my bed is private," he said.

"You're not making a joke of this surely?" She knew she sounded overexcited.

He took a very deep breath. "Of course I'm not." In the semidarkness, he stood up and moved away from the bed. He couldn't stay a second more beside her. The obvious was obvious. Just holding her, he was fully aroused. He reached for his robe, thankful he had pulled it out of his suitcase.

Isabelle began to inch across the uncomfortable bed. "All right, you're so tough. Let's put it to the test. There's a weird sound sailing around my room. It sounds like a grief-stricken moan."

"Bella!"

"Don't Bella me." She pressed her two hands over her heart as though holding it in. "Come and have a listen."

"I hope you're not trying to seduce me?" He half-laughed, only it wasn't a laugh at all.

She picked up a heavy cushion and threw it at him, which of course he fielded. Then, all of a sudden, out of nowhere she wanted to cry. Longings and desires. She had them. Why else would she want to cry? Only what possible good could come of that?

"You're not crying, are you, Bella?" Control was slipping out of his fingers. He knew there would be danger in comforting her.

"Are you going crazy? Of course I'm not crying." She denied the charge, astonished that she was. Tears were trickling down her cheeks.

"Damn it, you are. Don't cry, Bella. Please, please don't cry."

The anguish in his voice made her heart leap right into her throat. He actually sounded as if she was breaking *his* heart. She touched a forefinger to one cheek, then the other, flicking away the beads. "You really should come and listen to this," she said huskily. "It's not night terrors, I swear." She went to move past him but accidentally stumbled over one of the many objects lying on the rug.

To prevent her falling, Bruno had to make a grab for her. There was nothing else he could do.

It was ecstasy.

Agony too. He was nearly breaking up. He knew if he started kissing her, which he desperately wanted to do, he would be very harshly judged. By himself and whoever was up there. That was his religious upbringing, started by his mother, who had conveniently left her religious scruples behind. Isabelle was in his care and protection. He was determined to be the good guy to the end. All this wasn't helping one little bit. Especially in the adrenaline rush of the dark. Temptation that had been there right from that very first night but kept seriously in check was getting stronger with every passing hour. When had he ever wanted to kiss a woman and hadn't? This was a first. Bella was a first. He was treating her like a princess.

Her glorious hair was falling all around her face and down her back. Her body come warmly against him seemed barely covered when she was wearing a long white nightdress and a robe, half-slipping off her shoulders. It would be so easy to slide it the rest of the way. She had a natural, very special scent. That scent was on him. The scent was everywhere, like a powerful aphrodisiac. All he had to do was pull her in by her supple waist. Let what was going to happen, happen. He had to remind himself a beautiful woman could break a man into a million little pieces.

"Bruno," Isabelle whispered. "Are you going to let me go?" It was the last thing she wanted, but she had to gather all her strength. How strange yet how familiar they were to each other, she thought. This wasn't any casual fling. What was it? They were actually treating one another with kid gloves. Bruno, without knowing it, had become her centre. It was a secret she couldn't confide. Marta Lubrinski might shoot her.

Bruno's heart was tolling heavy beats. He could feel

the heaviness in his groin. "You should have put on a light," he said, deciding the best course was to admonish her. It was safer.

"If I could find one. Gosh, there are a lot of things in here." She clasped his hand, urging him to follow her. "Come and listen."

"I'm coming." He had noted the time: 3 a.m. The witching hour, deep in the night. An hour for lovemaking with all the senses raging. God knows he was in the mood, but he didn't fancy being sent straight to hell. He just had to put up with the ache in his heart, in his head, in his groin.

"Don't turn on the light," she warned as he put out a hand. "Come right in. Keep quiet."

"Bella, I'm getting a little too old for this," he protested.

"I said *keep quiet*."

The bright moonlight had dimmed, but he could see all the fine details of this extraordinary and undeniably spooky room. It was difficult to pay attention to anything but Isabella. He thought he might even be deaf to the most beautiful music or it would surge through his whole being, washing away all his good intentions. As it was, he could hear nothing but the hammering of his heart. Anyone would be susceptible to the atmosphere in this house. He was himself. Isabella, with her exquisite sensibilities, even more so.

Nothing. His teeth were actually locked together in concentration. He couldn't hear a peep, let alone a moan. "I think our ghost has cleared out," he joked. He wanted to reach for her. Say it was only the sound of the wind whistling around the huge house. He wanted to offer comfort. He could *love* Bella, his heart told him. It was a very worrying thought.

"Wait."

It was clearly an order. Her short fingernails bit into

his skin. "Tomorrow is a working day, Bella. For both of us," he reminded her.

"Hush!"

"Most ghosts are invisible, aren't they? Or spotted maybe once or twice?"

He had hardly finished his little taunt when, as if whooshed out of a tunnel, a soft, poignant moaning that even Bruno found disturbing issued from within the fireplace and floated into the bedroom.

"What did I tell you?" Isabelle hissed between her teeth. "It sounds utterly desperate."

Bruno hadn't reached that conclusion. He moved nearer the fireplace. "Precisely!" He gave a brief laugh. "It's doing what it's supposed to do, frighten you." He uttered a mild curse beneath his breath. "It's a trick, Bella. A ploy. The bloody nerve!"

He was giving the strong impression of a man who might very well raise the household at 3 a.m. demanding answers. That alone cleared Isabelle's head. She rushed to switch on the lights. Why hadn't she thought of that? A trick! She *hated* the fact Bruno had. Hated anyone who would play such a callous prank on her. The sound had sounded so perfectly *authentic.*

Immediately, the large room was flooded in a golden glow. She bit her inner lip, waiting for Bruno to come up with something resembling a plausible answer. She watched him move to the marble fireplace with those winged women, get a hand on the luxuriant fern, jerking it out roughly. In the process, the plant hit one of the gilt-metal andirons. It fell over, clattering loudly in the silence. Bruno then stuck his head under the chimney breast. Stared all around him.

"What are you looking for?" Isabelle went to him, tapping him on the shoulder.

"Have you noticed the moaning has stopped?" He

swung his head to look down at her. How much smaller she seemed without heels.

"All right. Don't get angry."

"I'm somewhat off angry. I'm furious. This room they put you in? It was all planned. It might be an Oriental extravaganza, but it's no place to sleep."

"Agreed, but it was Helena's room. I'm sure of that."

"And I'm sure someone was trying to drive Helena mad. She was a sitting duck."

"Sleeping duck, don't you mean?"

"She'd have been lucky if she got much sleep. The sound was coming from the fireplace, right?"

"Well, I haven't known you all that long, but as it turns out you are mostly right."

"The sound could be ducted into any number of rooms. These old houses had their own system of servants' bells to ring. Things to yank. A servant could easily turn some device against a nerve-ridden girl. I've a good mind to go downstairs and wake up Mrs. Saunders. She's as sinister as it gets."

Isabelle blinked. "Well, yes, but I wouldn't call her a fiend!"

"I'm more used to fiends than you are, Bella," he said darkly. "Can't you see poor Helena sitting up in bed, full of woe, crying?"

"It's good to know you have a feminine side."

"Let's not get into that. A young girl raised without a mother she may have believed had been killed by her father or someone prepared to do his bidding. We can't forget Christian. Probably he was shot as a matter of urgency."

"Possible, but it's also possible your theories are skewed."

Bruno looked down his straight nose at her. "I hate to

mention this, but you were so frightened you ran across the hallway and jumped into my bed."

Isabelle was all the more indignant because it had been so nearly true. "I've been warned against jumping into strange men's beds, thank you. A bit of a change for you, but there was no flying leap to hop in beside you. You pulled me right across you, and none too gently either."

"I'm wary of beautiful women," said Bruno self-righteously. It was perfectly true.

"No need to fret. I bear that constantly in mind. Surely Helena didn't suffer in silence? We intend to have the moaning sound investigated in the morning, don't we? It wasn't the wind."

"More like someone blowing through a tube," Bruno said with a frown.

"Playing it like an instrument."

"Probably had plenty of practise," he said grimly.

"You're deadly serious, aren't you?"

"You bet. I doubt you'll hear the moaning again. Just to be sure of it, I'm going to spend the rest of the night on that settee, sofa, whatever the heck it is." He jerked his head over his shoulder to the furnishings.

"It's a chaise longue." Isabelle set him straight.

"I regret I'm ignorant of such matters."

"Gosh, you sound like Mr. Darcy. Anyway, you're too big for it. It would probably collapse. I'll take it."

"Great, that's settled." He bent to pick up the fallen andiron.

She hadn't expected him to agree so quickly. "I can't believe you mean that."

"I don't. It might seem unfair, but women always get the best of everything."

Now she found herself smiling. "What about the

armchair? We'll find you something to rest your long legs on. A footstool. There's an ottoman in your room."

"Perfect! I'll turn my armchair with my eyes trained on the door. We've got the message loud and clear. Erik Hartmann wants us out of his territory. That's when Mrs. Saunders moves in, with or without his knowledge. She's perfectly capable of any amount of mischief."

"Why doesn't it horrify me?" Isabelle asked.

"That's easy," said Bruno. "You've got me."

They were the first in for breakfast, or the family had already had theirs. No surprise there. It was eight o'clock, the time stipulated. Stefan Hartmann would most probably be on the job from first light as he appeared to run the vast station alone, with only the aid of his stockmen.

Isabelle moved over to the sideboard. This was the breakfast room adjoining the kitchen. A collection of lovely old plates, probably from some nineteenth-century dinner service, had been attached to the Wedgwood blue walls and set within frames. Someone with impeccable taste and money to burn had organised the design of the downstairs rooms.

They could hear the murmuring of voices from inside the kitchen, which no doubt would be state of the art. The long mahogany sideboard with three drawers was set with all manner of plates, dishes, flatware, a jug of orange juice, a big bowl of fruit compote, another of muesli, a basketful of muffins. There were a number of silver entrée dishes with covers, sauce boats containing condiments. She lifted the lid of one of the entrée dishes. Steam rose.

"Scrambled eggs. I love scrambled eggs." She lifted

the next lid. "Bacon and sausages for you, Bruno. At least we won't go hungry. I would like some toast, though."

The words were no sooner out of her mouth than the same aboriginal girl, sweet faced, black curls, lustrous dark eyes, who had helped serve dinner, came out of the kitchen door carrying a very fancy silver toast rack that held at least ten slices of toasted bread. She smiled shyly. Isabelle and Bruno returned her smile with a friendly, "Good morning. It's . . . ?"

"Nele," the girl supplied. "Anything else you would like?" she asked, looking from one to the other with a great deal of interest.

"No, thank you, Nele. This looks lovely. I'll have coffee afterwards, if I may? What about you, Bruno?"

"Black for me," he said.

"Any chance you would be able to make me a cappuccino?" Isabelle asked. She liked a cappuccino in the morning.

"Certainly, miss," the house girl told her cheerfully. "Mrs. Saunders has all the machines she needs." With another beaming smile, she turned about.

"Clearly Mrs. Saunders doesn't want to see us," Bruno said, when they were alone.

"Why would she? We'll just have to invite her to explain where the sound might be coming from. Though I'm sure she will deny ever having heard it."

"We have a bit of time to fill in until Stefan Hartmann meets up with us at ten," Bruno said, pouring orange juice for them both.

"Do you suppose we could see something of this incredible landscape before we leave?"

"We can ask." Although he'd made several trips to the

wild heart of the continent, he was keen to see as much as he could of Eaglehawk.

After a good breakfast that restored a measure of well-being, they made their way back into the grand drawing room. Mrs. Saunders had not appeared with a cheery, "Good morning. Was everything satisfactory?" She stayed well out of sight and sound. There was no one around. The house was all but empty. Probably Kurt was with his uncle in the West Wing. Too much to expect he had joined his father in the great outdoors.

"This has to be the piano in Helena's portrait, wouldn't you say?" Bruno signalled Isabelle to come over. "Play something."

"Not here. Not now. It wouldn't be polite."

"Polite?" Bruno laughed harshly, his dark eyes burning. "Who cares about polite? Don't worry. You're here with me. Everything will be just fine. If nothing else, it might draw the family out."

"I'd feel safer if you had that battle-ax with you."

"Mrs. Saunders?" He raised his black brows in surprise.

"That's one battle-ax. I'm talking about the piece of militaria in the Turkish Room." As she was speaking, Bruno was opening up the lid of the grand piano.

"What's it to be?" She went to touch the keys, stopped short.

"Something as loud and bravura as possible."

"Something to shatter the silence."

The moment Isabelle's curled-up fingers actually came down on the keys, feeling their weight, which was important, she felt a pang of fright. The keys were about to start talking to her.

"What's wrong?" Bruno stared down at her in surprise. Isabelle the accomplished pianist was acting like a beginner, unsure of where to start. "Are you okay, Bella? What are you waiting for?"

She shook her head a little, flapped an authoritative hand at him. He stood back at her command.

The first rebellious chord of Chopin's "Revolutionary Etude" in C minor rang out like a battle cry. That was what it had been intended to be. Chopin had poured his emotions into the famous etude, inspired by the Russian attack on Poland's capital, Warsaw, in 1831. The chord echoed right through the house, rapidly filling the drawing room with tumultuous sound.

Isabelle was underway, her left hand a dazzling, relentless accompaniment to the right. Bruno couldn't imagine anyone not coming to a halt, hearing a piano being played with such power and technique. Where was the power coming from? he wondered. Isabelle couldn't have weighed more than 105 kilos. It wasn't until the final chords had died away before they heard heavy, fast footsteps on the staircase.

A moment later, Erik Hartmann strode into the room, his face working like a man overcome by some terrible dread. "How dare you!" he shouted, as though Isabelle should have to beg for forgiveness. "How dare you! The impertinence!"

Such a reaction was completely over the top. One might have been forgiven for thinking Isabelle had taken to the grand piano with a sledgehammer. Bruno came swiftly to her side, intending to intervene, only she stood up from the piano, walking slowly towards Erik Hartmann with astounding self-possession, given she was a guest in his home, which was about as remote as one could get. "I dare," she said, in a voice not quite her own.

It wasn't at all what either Erik Hartmann or Bruno expected. Hartmann stared back at her as though he didn't have the faintest idea what to say next because his opening salvo hadn't worked.

"Sometimes it's possible to pick up vibrations from musical instruments," Isabelle continued in the same tone. "Great artists, particularly string players, have made that point. I'm no great artist but I know a little about such things. Hands that touched those keys were holding tight to their sanity."

Instantly, Erik Hartmann's expression changed to one of scorn. "What, piano tuners?" he cried. "Those are the only hands that have touched that piano for nigh on twenty years, young lady. Tuning it. You should be careful with your tricks."

"No trick," Bruno broke in, unsettled by something in Bella's manner, but ranging himself beside her. "Speaking of tricks—and it was pretty good as tricks go—what causes the moaning sound in the Chinese Room?" he asked.

Erik Hartmann gave him such a queer look. "Moaning sound? I have no idea what you're talking about. What you heard would have been the wind."

"The sound was coming from the fireplace." Bruno ignored the protest. "We thought—"

"We?" Erik Hartmann drew himself up as though some scandalous romp had occurred under his roof.

"I assure you. it's not what you're thinking, Mr. Hartmann," Bruno said calmly. "Isabelle found the sound very disturbing. She came across to my room to wake me."

"You're making it all up!" Erik Hartmann was reduced to a kind of panting, as though his heart hurt him.

"You don't believe us?"

"I do not."

"Sir, I don't lie. Neither does Isabelle. The sound would terrify a child. Even an adult. Initially, it frightened Isabella. It even disturbed me until I figured out what might be causing it. Perhaps we might take a look at all the bells and whistles that were used in the old days to alert the servants. The family would have had servants?"

"Of course," Hartmann said pompously, as though no one need to ask.

"Could you indulge us?" Bruno's suggestion was prompt.

Erik Hartmann's dark eyes were markedly fixed on Isabelle. "You're a very fine pianist," he said with a strange, unexpected emotion. "My wife, Myra, was just such a pianist. Helena was good, but she could never match her mother. In anything, sadly."

"Her mother taught her?" Isabelle asked, thinking what they knew of the dazzling Myra, she wouldn't have made a good teacher, if a fine performer. The two didn't often go together.

"No, no." He shook his head. "Well, only for the first few years," he amended. "Myra didn't have the patience, but fortunately, Helena showed a lot of early promise. We finally hired an excellent teacher. A fine young man. He lived with us for some years. Helena liked him. I liked him myself. Myra was capable of being very unkind to him from time to time. She was like that. She wanted you to feel *uncertain* of where you were with her."

"A tutor? Why wasn't my father told about him?" Bruno asked, shooting a quick glance at Isabelle.

"For the simple reason he had gone back to England almost a year before. He was well out of the picture."

"When did he actually arrive?" Bruno asked. All sorts of theories were exploding in his mind.

"Myra had hired a woman teacher before then, ex-Sydney Conservatorium. She was effective, certainly, but she didn't really fit in. Piers was hired when Helena was around twelve. He left when she was seventeen and had gained all her diplomas. That was five years after her mother was killed. May she rest in peace."

"If you could please tell us his full name?" Isabelle asked.

For a moment, Erik Hartmann appeared incapable of formulating a name. "Piers . . . Osbourne," he said finally, hitting a hand on his forehead. "English. Such an air about him! One would have thought he was the aristocracy, yet he was only a piano teacher. But absolutely first class. Helena blossomed under his tutelage."

"Did he keep in touch?"

"I believe he kept in touch with Helena for a time. Then the contact fizzled out. He returned to his family in England. We never heard from him again."

"Helena didn't go to boarding school, then?" Isabelle asked the question. She had assumed Helena, like many Outback children, especially the offspring of the well to do, attended private boarding schools.

Hartmann shook his head. "She could learn all she needed to learn here. Piers was a great help there too. He was obviously highly educated, of good family. Her aunt Abigail supervised her studies too. Abigail is a very clever woman, although she hides it beneath the proverbial bushel."

"How old was Piers Osbourne when he arrived?" Bruno asked.

Erik Hartmann took his time answering. "Early twenties, I believe." His tone had gone from fairly amiable to aggressive. "I believe he wanted some excitement in his life and picked out Australia. No great culture clash, with the huge migration from the British Isles."

"May one ask where Mrs. Abigail Hartmann lives?" Bruno looked to his host.

"All these questions!" Erik Hartmann was clearly displeased. "Don't think I don't know what your reasons are."

Bruno answered for them both. "Isabella is making no claim to anything, sir. It's as I told you. I was the one who brought her extraordinary resemblance to Helena and her mother to her attention. She wanted no part of it, but subsequent conversations with the two people who raised her have given rise to serious doubt and a whole lot of speculation. This is a crisis time in Isabelle's life. All she wants to know is whether there is a Hartmann connection."

"So this DNA testing is the answer?"

"The definitive answer. There's nothing easy about any of this, sir. We do understand that. You said you were contacted with news of Helena's death. Have you been sent papers? Have you sighted them?"

"God no!" Hartmann burst out angrily, and then caught himself up. "You'd do well to go away. Someone helped Helena to run away. It killed my father."

"Someone killed *my* father," Bruno said on a harsh note. "Hit-and-run accident."

Hartmann gaped at him. "How monstrous. I didn't know." He appeared genuinely shocked. Either that or he was a fine actor. "I had heard he had died. I assumed of natural causes."

"*Unnatural* causes," Bruno said. "The driver of the vehicle that hit him was never found. The police investigated of course."

"The police, the police!" Erik Hartmann threw up his

hands in disgust. "The police are bloody useless. Couldn't find Helena. Thought she'd simply done a bunk. Thought we were a bunch of wankers. Murderers, maybe. Your father didn't think that. He saved us all from going mad. He had *heart.* You thought I might have been the one to make Helena run? Not me. I could never, ever go so far, although I had come to question whether I was her father. Oh, don't look like that!" he all but shouted at Isabelle.

"That must have opened up a great deal of rage?" Bruno asked, his contained tone in marked contrast to Hartmann's belligerence.

For a moment, there was naked grief in Erik Hartmann's dark eyes. "Anger, humiliation certainly, but that doesn't mean I was not completely broken by Myra's death. Such a mystery! She was a splendid horsewoman. So is Abigail. They used to go riding together. Alas, not on that fatal day."

"So Mrs. Abigail Hartmann loved to be outdoors too?" Isabelle asked, stunned by how many new trails were opening up.

"Why wouldn't she?" Erik Hartmann asked, making a chopping gesture with his hand. "Abigail is a Stirling. Surely you've heard of the Stirlings of Moorooka Downs? The family pioneered the South West, just as we did. It was considered a great coup when my stepbrother, Christian, managed to win her hand. Abigail had many suitors. I would have considered her myself but for Myra. No woman could hold a candle to Myra."

"The two women were good friends?" Bruno spoke casually, so as not to appear too prying as indeed he was.

"Good enough." Hartmann shrugged. "Wise woman that she was, Abigail quickly got into the habit of accepting she could never measure up to Myra. Actually, in her own way she used to minister to Myra. She certainly deferred to her."

"Not a good place to be in?"

"Whatever do you mean?" Hartmann stared across at Isabelle, who had made the observation.

"She wouldn't have been human if she weren't a little jealous of your wife's position as number one," Bruno suggested.

"It was a great comfort to us Abigail understood what her place was," Hartmann said stiffly. "Abigail may not have been a vivid personality, but we all liked her. She was—is—very pleasant. My father always said Christian was lucky to get her. I thought so too. No one could ever accuse Abigail of letting the family down."

"My father had the idea Mrs. Abigail Hartmann hid her understandable resentment."

Their host threw up his arms. "That's monstrous!" he cried. "There was no bitterness or envy in Abigail. She was a great comfort to us all, especially after Myra was killed. We owe a lot to Abigail. There was no rancour whatever in the woman."

"Where was she on the day?" Bruno asked, keeping his tone respectful.

Erik Hartmann could hardly speak for anger. "What are you suggesting?"

"As the police say, just a routine question, sir."

"Question time is over," Erik Hartmann said curtly, making no attempt to hide his agitation. "But I can put you straight on this. Abigail was in her room the entire afternoon. From time to time she suffered severe migraines. A servant looked in on her *twice*."

Isabelle longed to ask the name of the servant, but it was clear Erik Hartmann wouldn't hear another word on the subject of Abigail Hartmann, his half brother's widow.

Despite that, Bruno gave it one more try. Like Isabelle, he was disturbed by all the things they didn't know and, to the best of his knowledge, his father had never recorded. "I'm surprised Mrs. Abigail Hartmann didn't choose to remain with you. There must have been a very close family bond, and she *is* Kurt's grandmother."

"Abigail went back to her own people," Erik said in a dull, defeated voice. "There was no persuading her to stay."

"Would she not have been a supportive figure in Helena's young life?" Isabelle dared to ask.

"Oddly enough, that wasn't the case," said their host. "The answer lies in Helena's difficult nature."

"She crossed swords with you?"

"No, no." Hartmann dismissed that sharply. "Helena didn't have aggression in her. She had *problems*, obviously to do with her mother's death. We all thought it would pass as she grew older, except it didn't. Helena had a timid side to her character. She became fearful of every last little thing."

"Such as?" Bruno knew he was pushing it.

"The house. The house she had lived in all her life. Our beautiful ancestral home. There was even a time when she thought someone was trying to harm her. Absolute nonsense! No one would have dreamed of harming a hair on her head. It all had to do with her mother's accidental death. Myra was so *alive* it was impossible to accept she could die."

"Thank you, Mr. Hartmann," Isabelle said gracefully. "Thank you too for letting us in to this illustrious family's history." She hoped she wasn't piling it on too thick.

Hartmann appeared charmed, and then he rallied. "You're not one of us, my dear, although you give every appearance of it."

"That's precisely why your nephew is taking steps to prove or disprove our case," Bruno said.

Erik Hartmann let out a long shuddering breath. "If my nephew is loyal to me, as his son is, he will refuse any DNA test. It's an insult to our family name. Your father found nothing here, McKendrick. Neither will you or Isabelle."

"Perhaps, sir, you don't know your nephew as well as you think?" Bruno suggested. "We have a meeting with him right about . . . now." Bruno glanced down at his watch.

Erik Hartmann's smile was a pained grimace. "I think you'll find he won't return to the house. My nephew, in the absence of his wife and daughter, a frivolous little thing like her mother, is married to the land, Eaglehawk, our family inheritance. It means more to him than anything in the world, including his own son."

"So I don't count? Mum and Kim don't count, *frivolous little things*!" Kurt made the second tempestuous entry of the morning. He gave his great-uncle a look of tremendous disappointment. "That's what we mean to you, is it, Uncle? We're family."

"My boy, my boy, I can't believe you thought I meant *you*. I love you. You're my heir."

"You've given up on Mum and Kim? They're inferior, are they? Mum said you always made her feel like that. Kimmy was really frightened of you when we were kids."

"Why don't you go to your mother and sister?" Bruno asked, keeping the conversation on the boil. "Strike out. Live your life. You're not a cattleman like your father. What talents you have, you could be wasting."

"What I should do is kick *you* out right now," Erik Hartmann shouted. "Who are you to come here, telling my family what to do?"

"Maybe I'm trying to be helpful, Mr. Hartmann," Bruno said.

They all turned as a man dressed in working gear, with an Akubra on his head and heavy black boots on his feet, thundered into the drawing room. "What the blazes is going on here?" Stefan eyed his son first, then his uncle, whose cheeks had swelled with anger.

"Uncle Erik has been mouthing Mum and Kim off big time." Kurt wore unaccustomed rage. "He called them 'frivolous little things.' What do you call them, Dad?"

Stefan Hartmann didn't hesitate. "I married your mother because I loved her. I still love her. Nothing has changed for me there. Kimmy is my darling daughter. You are my son. I can't bear the way you've turned away from me, Kurt. I don't care you're not cut out to live a life on the land. I want you to be happy. But as long as you're under your great-uncle's thumb—I can just imagine the sort of stuff he feeds you—you'll never get yourself sorted. I love this place. I love this land. It's in my blood. Don't blame me for that."

"I don't!" Kurt cried. "But I do blame you for not going after Mum. How sorted are *you*?"

Stefan threw off his wide-brimmed hat. "Why don't we take a trip into Adelaide sometime soon? Just the two of us."

"And what? Ask them to come back here? You having me on or what?"

His father shook his head. "They'd have been okay only for the great-uncle you so admire. When did you ever take their side? When did you ever do the *manly* thing, Kurt? Stand by your mother and sister against *him*. No, Erik promised you a great prize. Or so you thought. His heir. Don't you realize if I pulled out, Eaglehawk would fail as a working station? I work twenty-four/seven to keep it afloat. It's not your great-uncle who runs Hartmann Holdings. It's *me,* for God's sake. Everyone but you knows that. I could, with a little bit of help, buy Erik out. It could be three against one. You, me, and Kimmy."

Bruno broke in. His tone held a hint of challenge. "I could, perhaps, help you there, Mr. Hartmann."

"*You're* leaving," Eric Hartmann rasped, his body tensed like an animal about to spring.

Kurt, however, sounded almost friendly. He turned to Bruno. "Could you do that?"

"I run a very successful wealth management company, Kurt. If your father needed help, I'm certain I could provide it."

"You bastard!" Eric Hartmann spat out. "You think I'm so easy to intimidate?"

"You've rolled over everyone and everybody who has got in your way," Stefan cried in condemnation. "But that's all behind you. I must take a stand. This young lady here"—he indicated Isabelle—"is the living image of Myra and Helena. A finer version of both. I promised McKendrick a DNA sample. I'm going to stick to that promise. My *heart* holds to the fact Isabelle is one of us. My head needs the final proof. Of course if she *is* one of us, she is entitled to shares in Eaglehawk."

Kurt, of all things, burst out laughing. "You're serious, Dad?"

"Try me."

"What do you say you solve a little problem for us, Kurt?" Bruno asked, turning to the younger man.

"Like what?" Warily, Kurt started to juggle some keys in his pocket.

"Last night Isabelle was awoken by a sound of moaning that appeared to come from the fireplace in the Chinese Room. She came across the hall to me because she was frightened."

"It was the wind, more than likely," Stefan said, crinkling his already deeply lined brow. "Why do I have this sense of Helena speaking about moaning in the night?"

"Helena had psychological problems." Erik Hartmann gave a laugh that stopped short of being contemptuous. "The truth of it is, she was unhinged. She never got over her mother's death. Myra haunted the girl."

Bruno ignored him. "Bella and I had the idea it might have been someone blowing through a pipe of some kind. Perhaps a pipe connecting upstairs and downstairs that was in use way back."

"Someone?" All of a sudden, Kurt appeared much younger and freaked out.

"We believe so, yes. Someone wanted to frighten her. For what reason we're not sure. Maybe for the hell of it."

"We'll want Mrs. Saunders in here," Stefan said.

"I forbid it!" Erik roared.

"Go get her, son," Stefan said to Kurt.

Immediately, Kurt sprang into action. "Right, Dad."

"Is that it? Is that your answer?" Erik Hartmann cried. "It's Mrs. Saunders playing a joke?"

"Some joke!" Bruno said.

Kurt was back with the housekeeper in double-quick time. As ever, she looked to Erik Hartmann. "You wanted me, sir?"

Isabelle glanced over at Bruno, who looked simply wonderful brooding. A Mr. Rochester. "We wondered, Mrs. Saunders, if you could show us the bell system that is probably ducted into various rooms of the house?" he asked in a polite enough tone.

Mrs. Saunders, looking astonished, sought the Master's approval. "Sir?"

"Do what you're told, woman," Stefan broke in, like a man going mad.

The woman went to protest, but Stefan Hartmann took hold of her arm. "Lead the way, Mrs. Saunders, if you want to keep your job."

"I beg your pardon!" Mrs. Saunders refused to heed him. She wrenched herself away.

"Do it," Erik suddenly roared.

Face rigid with mortification, the housekeeper led them through the house to the corridor outside the huge kitchen area. As expected, up on the wall was a long panel with coded letters beneath, identifying different rooms of the main house.

None for the adjoining wings, Isabelle noted.

"What are we looking for here?" Kurt asked.

The overpowering personalities of his great-uncle and father explained a lot of his immaturity, Bruno thought. He gave Isabella a quick look. Both had hoped, indeed expected, to find something that could have been used to create sounds. Some piping device. There wasn't one. At least not one hanging on or beneath the panel.

"Perhaps you can tell *me*," Mrs. Saunders spoke through tight lips.

"Something with the capacity to make a moaning sound," Bruno said, aware Isabelle had moved off. She was walking down the corridor to a tall Victorian mahogany hall stand. Several hats were hanging on the various pegs, uniforms, an apron, outdoor shoes and tall Wellingtons in the space beneath.

"There is absolutely *nothing* there," Mrs. Saunders said with great emphasis.

Bruno turned on her. "Let's see, shall we?"

Isabelle, meanwhile, was shuffling around the boots

and shoes. They all saw her pull out a long, tapering hollow piece of yellowish wood, painted with aboriginal symbols.

"That's a didgeridoo!" Kurt stared at all of them in turn, his mind awhirl.

"We all know what it is, you fool!" his great-uncle snarled.

Mrs. Saunders was taking deep breath after deep breath. She appeared to have an excellent lung capacity, Bruno thought.

Isabelle walked back to them, handing the aboriginal musical instrument from ancient times to the housekeeper. "You can play this, can't you?" she asked, showing no sign of doubt.

"Of course she can!" Kurt's voice had gathered strength. "She has aboriginal blood in her, hasn't she, Dad?"

"Which doesn't mean she can play it," Isabelle said. "It's a very difficult instrument unless one has mastered certain techniques, like circular breathing. I could probably get a moan or two out of it. It's been kept in good condition, water run down it frequently, maybe some kind of wax inside."

Stefan Hartmann's voice shook. His entire powerful body shook. "What-have-you-done?" he demanded of the housekeeper, barely able to keep himself in check.

"Play it, Mrs. Saunders," Bruno urged. "You can. We all know it."

There was a fierce anger on the woman's face. Anger and something more powerful. Pride. She took the instrument from Isabelle, wiped off the mouthpiece with her pocket handkerchief, and then set the tapering end to her encircling mouth.

Immediately, her lip tension and the controlled air flow

caused the primitive instrument to vibrate. It was clear Mrs. Saunders had command of the woodwind instrument. It started to *moan.*

Both Stefan and his son looked stricken. Erik Hartmann slammed back into the wall, wringing his hands so hard his fingernails had turned white.

"I should have guessed," Isabelle murmured to Bruno beside her. "That was really stupid of me. I knew it had to be a horn of some kind. I was thinking Afghan, Turkish, something Christian had brought home, but we're right here in the home of the didgeridoo."

The moaning, the grieving sound, continued. Mrs. Saunders didn't check herself. She considered herself an artist as indeed she was.

"Give that bloody thing to me," Stefan continued to roar, his expression hostile and bitter. "Give it to me, witch!"

The resonant if eerie sounds stopped. The housekeeper passed the native instrument to him. There was a strange, triumphant expression on her handsome face. "I'm as much one of you as she is," she suddenly announced, in a hate-consumed voice. "Don't you remember how beautiful I was when I first came to this house? Beautiful. Beautiful as that bloody woman Myra, who was horrible to me. She treated me like dirt, yet I was one of you."

"You should be in the madhouse." Erik Hartmann let himself drop slowly into a hall chair as though his legs could no longer support him.

"What the hell is she talking about?" Stefan Hartmann's ruddy, tanned face had lost colour.

"Go on. We're listening, Mrs. Saunders," Bruno urged, reaching for Isabelle's hand and clasping it tight.

"Bin sleepin' with yah own kin," Mrs. Saunders rounded

on Erik Hartmann with undisguised contempt. A further shock. She had dropped her educated accent for a bush-woman's slurred speech.

The Hartmann men were transfixed with shock, their expressions blank.

"I chased that girl away," Mrs. Saunders jeered. "I felt sorry for her, but I did it."

"The same burning resentment that brought about Myra's accident," Bruno's tone seared. This raised even more questions, he thought.

"A ghost did that. Not *me*," she said with a flash of emotion.

"What in hell is she talking about, Erik?" Stefan rounded on his uncle, his big body tensed.

"Don't you dare touch me." Erik slunk back further against the wall, as though his nephew, a tough cattleman, was about to physically attack him. "I have no idea, Stefan. Truly. The woman is delusional."

"Thought the old man was a saint?" Mrs. Saunders sneered. "He couldn't help himself. *No* man is a saint. He took my mother. Not by force. No way. He was a gentle-man. She worshipped him like he was a god."

Everyone was in their own way in a state of confusion. "You expect us to believe this fantasy for one instant?" Stefan exploded. "My grandfather slept with your mother?"

Kurt gave a little moan, then before anyone realized it, he crashed to the floor in a dead faint.

"Half caste," Mrs. Saunders corrected him, totally ignoring Kurt's dramatic collapse. "Beautiful. Like me. You people are pathetic. You know nothing. You know nothing of our magic."

"We know enough about the Kadaitcha Man," Bruno threw over his shoulder. "The magic man, the tribal executioner." He and Isabelle alone had sprung to Kurt's aid. Bruno began tapping the young man sharply on his cheeks, calling his name.

"You know it's you two who have opened up a whole new world to me," Mrs. Saunders went on as though nothing was happening. "DNA testing. Never crossed my mind! But now! I could be entitled to a share in the station. It's sitting on sacred land. Our sacred land. You have no right to it, the lot of you. But I don't think I want to make trouble. You can pay me out. I'll go away like Miss Helena."

Stefan swung on her, looking capable of real violence. "You frightened her away." He stared at the woman as though she had crossed some uncrossable divide.

"Not me who chased her away from here," the woman said. "Ghosts. Phantoms. Maybe the Kadaitcha Man, like Mr. McKendrick says. The Kadaitcha Man could have put a spell on her. Or it could have been a powerful female member of a tribe charged to cause death. Maybe it was the outside world calling. She asked for help to get away and got it. Many possibilities, don't you reckon?"

Neither Erik nor Stefan spoke, though they appeared absolutely united in thought. They had lived all their lives close to the wild heart of the continent. They had lived with aboriginal culture. They knew all about the Kadaitcha Man and magic rituals. They knew all about curses put on certain individuals, the methods of execution used. In Erik's childhood, the station's head stockman had died without being either poisoned or injured but through bone pointing. A method of magic that never failed to kill. The practise still continued, but very much in secret. The Kadaitcha Man wasn't any mythical figure. The Kadaitcha Man was real.

Kurt had come around, shuffling his booted feet on the floor.

"You're okay. You're fine. Stay still for a moment," Isabelle reassured him, brushing a lock of his blond hair from his clammy forehead.

"My whole world has changed," he muttered hoarsely. "I'm not the person I thought I was anymore."

"Neither am I." Isabelle looked with kindness into his colourless face. "I'll get you a glass of water."

"I'll get it," Bruno said. "Stay with him."

Bruno was only gone a moment. He handed the glass of water to Isabelle, who held it to Kurt's lips.

"Thank you. Thank you." He handed the half-empty glass back to her, wiping his mouth with the back of his hand.

"Let's get you up." Bruno extended a strong arm, drawing the younger man to his feet.

"All right, son?" Stefan finally emerged from his stupor.

"What do we do now, Dad?" Kurt asked timidly, ill with shock.

"God Almighty, I want nothing else but the *truth*," Stefan cried. "Helena was forced out of this house."

"Sir, I don't believe Mrs. Saunders is the answer," Bruno intervened, speaking calmly and with a good deal of persuasion. "Admittedly, she had formed the habit of playing cruel pranks on Helena. Revenge, I would suggest. Revenge against the entire Hartmann family, who lorded it over her, if not mistreated her. Mrs. Saunders—I believe the *Mrs.* is a courtesy title—hated everyone at the house. Understandable, if she actually is, as she claims, Konrad Hartmann's illegitimate daughter."

Erik Hartmann's still handsome face had become deeply grooved. He tried to clear his throat. "She's lying," he said, as if with his last breath. "That woman could never be my half sister. Christian's half sister. It's not possible. You talk about the Kadaitcha Man; our God should condemn her to hell."

"He's not going to do that." Mrs. Saunders was unperturbed. "The old man didn't know. My mother never told him. She feared we would be banished to some other station or even killed. Easy enough out here. Especially then. My mother made a respectable marriage. Her husband, my *dad*, died only a few years back, as you all know. She died when I was fourteen and I started work in this house as a maid set to do all the hard cleaning and the polishing, helping out in the kitchen. That's all any of you thought of me, a servant. Only I had a taste for power, even if it was only in small things. Years later, I became *Mrs.* Saunders, the housekeeper. No husband. No children to cling to me. I wanted a better life."

"You wanted my wife out of the way?" Erik accused her with burning eyes.

"I hated her sure, but I didn't lay a finger on her. Didn't have to. Didn't the tongues wag about her? She craved sex, that woman. She was having it off with that boy."

Isabelle interjected, "What boy? Piers Osbourne?"

"Him and your dad." Mrs. Saunders wagged a cruel finger at Stefan. "The fool couldn't get enough of her."

Stefan Hartmann's dark eyes were glazed over. "You're lying. Tell us you're lying."

"I'm not. Mrs. Abigail Hartmann could back me up. She knew all about the secret love affair. I didn't need to tell her—she's a smart woman—though I tried to protect her. She was kind to me. Not like that cruel bitch, Myra."

A loud, disturbing groan emanated from Erik's throat.

"Do you mind if we leave this for a while?" he begged, holding up his hand in a desperate gesture. "I can't take anymore."

Stefan Hartmann's head was bent, as if in defeat. "Neither can I. None of us is going anywhere. We can speak of these matters much later in the day. My wife always said this is a house of secrets. She was right. But not even she could guess at how much has been hidden, and so deep."

"I love you, Dad," Kurt abruptly burst out, his voice trembling.

"I love you too, son," Stefan said quietly, before he turned to address Bruno and Isabelle. "Look, I can see this is a big shock to you both as well. Even your father couldn't have known what we've heard this morning, McKendrick. Will you both be all right on your own? Why not take a look around the station? You can take one of the jeeps, but remember, don't go far."

"What if we take a couple of horses?" Isabelle asked. "Bruno and I both ride."

Stefan nodded. "I'll get someone to look after you. Hard hats, mind."

"Of course," Bruno answered.

"Look at the two of you, shattered, humiliated, brought face-to-face with reality!" Mrs. Saunders crowed, giving Erik and Stefan a smile that offered no quarter. "I don't lie. The tests won't lie. Much as you wish it otherwise, I'm one of you. And so's *she*!" She threw out a hand to include Isabelle. "You can't bear to hear it, I know, but I'd say she's Christian's granddaughter. Not yours, Erik, my longtime secret lover. Don't dare to deny it."

Erik Hartmann's features looked carved out of stone.

"You've learned very little if you think you can cross me, Orani."

"You don't know how good it is, seeing you lose control," Mrs. Saunders countered. Her still-arresting face was filled with such immense hatred, the sensitive Isabelle could feel it rolling over her in waves.

Chapter Seven

The stables complex was a short distance from the house. It was huge, with a traditional timber barn that took pride of place. The massive doors at one end of the structure were fixed back in place. Flanking the doors were brassbound wooden planters filled with verdant lemon trees, the golden citrus fruit out of season. The courtyard for mounting and walking the horses was equally impressive.

It was only midmorning, yet the sun was blazing from a cloudless blue sky. Isabelle was wearing plenty of sunblock, a silk scarf to protect her nape and a long-sleeved white shirt to protect her arms, though she had rolled the sleeves back some way. Bruno, with his Mediterranean skin, was wearing a short-sleeved blue shirt with his jeans, but he had tied a protective red bandana around his neck. He looked enormously dashing but totally unconcerned with his appearance.

"Can't see anyone about," Isabelle said, her voice uneasy. She felt thoroughly unnerved by the events of the morning. Life was becoming way too complicated. Hilary, for all her intimidating aura, wasn't in the same league as Mrs. Saunders when that lady got underway. Mrs. Saunders, aka Orani, was a genuinely frightening woman, shaming Erik Hartmann, who had stood mute and staring until a fierce denial had been forced out of him.

"Bound to be someone," Bruno said, striding ahead. "I'll take a look."

He reappeared a moment later accompanied by an aboriginal boy, around sixteen. "Mani here will help us," Bruno said. He had an arm clapped around the boy's shoulders while the boy was looking up at him with a kind of wonder on his face. *Fascination*, Isabelle thought. Bruno had the capacity to fascinate men and women alike. It was a quality beyond physical beauty. It had life, movement, vibrancy.

"Mornin', miss." Mani gave Isabelle a jaunty smile. He waved them both inside the barn. "Come in, please. Take yah pick."

"Thank you."

Most of the stalls were empty. Mani led them along the wide passageway. At their approach to the right, a gleaming dark bay threw up its handsome head, nostrils flaring. "Now there's a beauty!" Isabelle said, not sure she could handle such an obviously spirited horse.

"Not for you, miss," Mani said with a note of warning, "Rega is a one-woman horse. He belong to Orani. Mrs. Saunders," he corrected himself quickly.

"She's an accomplished rider, then?" Bruno caught Isabelle's eye. Another piece of unexpected news.

"Bin ridin' since she was a kid. Like me. Can ride anything. I reckon a brumby. Best woman rider I ever seen. Rega would be dangerous in the wrong hands. Not for you, miss. You need be safe. What about Honeysuckle?

Honey for short. She's as sweet-natured as they come and a lovely ride."

Isabelle approached the chestnut mare, putting out an upturned hand as her English friend, Emma, had taught her to do. She hoped Honeysuckle would lick her palm. The mare did.

"Honey will be fine," Isabelle said, her spirits picking up. It was a long time since she had been in the saddle. She would probably be a bit sore afterwards, but she loved riding. With the right horse, she was sure she could acquit herself well enough.

Bruno pronounced himself happy with a big gelding called Rommel, which begged a question. Field Marshall Rommel, the Desert Fox, had been a greatly respected German general during WWII forced to commit suicide for being implicated in a plot to assassinate Hitler that had sadly misfired.

It was a simple matter to saddle up. Mani handed them both a hard hat from a collection hanging on one wall. It was apparent to them both that he took his duties seriously, holding himself responsible for the safety of guests.

"We're off! Let's make the best of it." Bruno reined in beside Isabelle. He looked wonderful mounted, tall figure upright, back straight, easily controlling Rommel. The gelding looked keen for a gallop. Isabelle already knew the mare would be no match for the powerful gelding, but the mare was giving off signals she too was ready to fly across the desert sands.

Budgerigar exploded in their thousands, emerald and gold as they were in the wild, turquoise beaks, fine black stripes on their backs. Crimson chats and little zebra finches fed on the ground, taking no notice at all of the predatory hawks until one made a leisurely swoop, picking up a bright little victim.

"Oh!" said Isabelle, feeling a pang of pity for the little zebra finch.

"Wedge-tailed eagle!" Bruno pointed out the country's largest bird of prey with a wing span of seven feet. It sat resting on a thermal cushion high above them, ready in an instant to dive with lightning speed. "That's one effective killing machine. Believe it or not, they can take a fair-size kangaroo."

"As long as they can't take a fair-size woman." Isabelle shivered. "It's kill or be killed, isn't it?"

"Rule of the wild. Man is the only animal that kills for pleasure. The animal world kills to survive."

"We're what? Twenty minutes out from the home compound, and we're in the wilds. This is as far remote from our lush eastern seaboard as the far side of Mars. I didn't know soil could be baked furnace *red* until I'd come face-to-face with it."

"This *is* the oldest continent on earth, Bella."

"And it looks it. Still, to our amazement, it *blooms*."

"That's the wonder of it all."

Ahead of them, the legendary mirage was abroad. It created silvery waterholes where none had existed since prehistoric times. "Easy to see how the early explorers were tricked into thinking they had found deliverance and lifesaving water," Bruno remarked. "From the air it's a flat landscape, but it doesn't appear that way on the ground."

Isabelle agreed. All around them were stands of acacias and scrubby-looking mulga trees that supported many squawking families of pink and pearl grey galahs. From a distance, the birds looked like huge, fantastic flowers. To their west lay a long unbroken chain of low-lying hills, ancient ranges eroded down to what the family called the Hill County.

Seams of opal matrix had been found there, so they had been told. The sand plains, the sand hills and the ranges were thickly sown with the most extensive vegetation type in the continent, the spinifex. The "abomination," as one explorer had called it.

"Watch the needles," Bruno called to her. "Get too close and they'll scrape the mare's legs."

"Difficult not to," she called back. "The bushes are everywhere. It's almost like a wheat field." The burnt gold of the spinifex plains stretched away to the far horizons.

"You'll handle it," Bruno told her, confident she could do so. He had known that from the moment she had without assistance swung up into the saddle, gathering the reins. "The mare will help you. There's a Big Red over there wanting to say hello."

"Where?" Her eyes swept around. "Oh, yes, I've spotted him," she lilted, genuinely entranced. She had never seen a kangaroo in the wild. "Isn't he just beautiful! Our boxing kangaroo." Semicamouflaged by a great spray of olive-coloured leaves, a Big Red was standing upright on its powerful long legs, tail acting as a balance, calmly surveying the intruders into his world.

"Herds of them ahead," Bruno said. "The kangaroos and emus on our coat of arms are indigenous animals; camels were brought in from Pakistan and India by the British with Afghan handlers. They used camels in the early days as beasts of burden in the Outback and for exploration. Burke and Wills used them. They've thrived here to the extent they've become a real menace. Basically, they destroy everything in their path. We're bound to see a few, considering there are well over a million in the wild heart. The largest population in the world. They love it here. We even export them back to the Middle East, where they're superior to the homegrown beasts."

"Any tips on snakes, goannas?" Isabelle asked. "I need to be prepared. I've never in my life been on wild terrain, on foot or on horseback."

"There's a slight possibility a five-foot log will suddenly morph into a sand goanna," Bruno only half-joked. "When confronted by riders, they usually take off at high speed."

"Thanks for telling me that."

"A need to know." He laughed.

The land was in far better condition than they had expected. Mani had told them vast areas of the Outback had received much-needed rain some months before, as well as floodwaters coming down into the Three Great Rivers system of the Inland from the tropical North that had been lashed by not one but two cyclones. Vegetation was, as a consequence, abundant.

One area they rode through was still covered in thousands of white paper daisies with yellow centres. They illuminated the red soil. In another area, the pink parakeelya reigned, a succulent the cattle could feed on. Further off in the distance, a huge area of desert hibiscus, a beautiful flower that favoured the spinifex country.

"This lovely display will soon disappear under the heat of the sun," Bruno told her with regret. "The millions of dormant seeds will regenerate with the next good rains."

"'All the flowers of all the tomorrows are in the seeds of today,'" Isabelle said. "An old Indian proverb."

"I really like the way you come up with these things," Bruno said. "The Inland goes in cycles. Drought. Drought. Drought. Then, a floral wonderland. What we're looking at now is the end of the display. The flowers are fading, as you can see. At their peak the flowering annuals create the most amazing desert gardens. They go on and on, right away to the horizon. Saltbush, cottonbush, hopbush, carpet of snow, fan flowers, poppies, spider lilies, green or lilac pussy tails waving in the wind. I came out this way once with a couple of friends, one a well-known botanist, the other equally celebrated as a wildlife photographer. The desert and the desert fringe is their hunting ground."

"I can see why." Isabelle looked around, enchanted. "It seems like a miracle such exquisite blooms can not only adapt but thrive in this harsh environment. One would expect the millions of wildflowers around us would wither away in the fierce heat of the sun, yet they continue to hang on to delight the eye. I'm so glad we came, a lovely memory to store up."

"We'll come back." Bruno spoke with perfect certainty. "I'll bring you when the flowering is at its height."

"Really? That sounds wonderful."

"I mean it."

"So I'm going to stay in your life?" she asked, not looking at him but straight ahead.

"Yes," he said.

"What if you're married? What if Madame Lubrinski finds you the perfect bride?"

He laughed. "Marta has no real idea of the sort of woman I want."

"Better tell *her* that," said Isabelle. Madame Lubrinski had not looked on her favourably.

A little while later, through a screen of trees, they could see an outfit of stockmen driving a sizeable lowing herd of cattle across a gully with diamond needle points of light flashing off the brackish waters. "Probably to a holding yard," Bruno made the comment. "What do you say we take a break at the next billabong?" There was a constant glitter of water now. Swamps, waterholes, deep and shallow pools, curving billabongs with verdant banks, shaded by the ubiquitous coolabah trees.

"That's a great idea!" Isabelle was feeling a little sore, with sets of muscles brought into play for the first time after quite a while. "We have water, I hope."

He clicked his tongue, his brilliant dark gaze brushing over her. "Bella, one can't go anywhere in the Outback without water. I have a full canteen."

"My hero!" she said.

The horses were easily led, grateful, like their riders, for the blissful shade. They tethered them loosely to some low-lying coolabah limbs and then walking a short distance down the slope sown with constellations of tiny lilac into purple wildflowers.

"The air is so *sweet*!" Isabelle slowly drew in a breath. She had the feeling of never having been so happy in her life.

"It's a bit like lavender," Bruno said, inhaling the fragrance. "Would you just look at those waterlilies?"

"Glorious, aren't they? A handful would cost a fortune at a city florist. I know I've bought them, but here there are masses and masses of them, white through to creamy yellow." A thick canopy of waterlilies adorned the still-deep waters at the far end of the lagoon. Tiny long-legged birds were skipping from one green pad to another.

"Like kids playing hopscotch," Bruno remarked with a laugh.

Flights of birds were circling the tops of the trees, flying in and out, up and down, playing their own games. Their calls, ringing, trilling, echoed all over the wilderness.

"There are always birds and birdsong even when you can't see them," Isabelle said. "This is just beautiful, isn't it? Everything turns on nature, its beauty, its majesty, its awesome power."

"I agree." Bruno quickly rid himself of his hard hat, running a quick hand over his tousled dark hair. "No aches and pains?" he asked, watching her every movement with a deep running pleasure. Their journey out had been wonderfully companionable, lifting all the dark shadows of the morning. He bent to pluck a purple flower.

"I'm fine," Isabelle said. "I'll be a bit stiff tomorrow, but it's worth it." Hands at her waist, she began swaying her willowy body in a limber up.

"You're a good rider, a natural." Bruno walked over to her. Every nerve in his body was jumping with a kind of fierce exhilaration. He pushed the short stalk of the wildflower into her red-gold hair, positioning it. Their faces were mere inches apart.

She flushed, making a business of finding a hair pin to fasten the little flower. "Thank you for the flower and the compliment. My friend, Emma, used to tell me I was a natural too. She was a good teacher. Who taught you, or did you simply jump on a horse and ride?"

"I tried and landed on my backside." He gave a remembering grin. "If you must know, I learned at Phil Faraday's Blue Mountains estate. Phil has a very serious love of horses. He has a string of winning racehorses and lives to win the Melbourne Cup. He's a fine rider himself, only he's allowing himself to put on too much weight. He's a great host. Actually, it was an old guy over seventy, Terry Bailey, who taught me the ropes. Irish. A fine jockey in his heyday. He used to ride for Phil's late father.

Phil kept him on. Phil has good qualities as well as a couple of dodgy ones."

"Terry taught you well." Isabelle sat herself down on the carpet of springy little wildflowers so prolific hundreds of tiny blooms were crushed beneath the leaves. Bruno stayed on his feet, pouring her water from the canteen.

"Don't spill it. Each drop is precious."

"I'm well aware of that, thank you."

Isabelle took the beaker from him, tilting her head to take a long draught. "That was good!" she pronounced. "There's nothing better than cold, clean water." Running down her throat, it had been wonderfully refreshing. She handed the container back, watching him pour himself water before putting his lips to where hers had been.

Isabelle had to shake herself to break the little spell. "I don't think I can go back and face those people," she said, pulling the remaining pins out of her hair and dropping them safely inside her hard hat. That done, she shook her glistening copper and gold hair free, enjoying the light breeze on her nape. "Miss Marple would have her work cut out, finding the culprit with that lot. They just kept on coming. Abigail Hartmann, born and bred in the Outback, probably sat her first pony at three. Living out here, she would have known how to handle a gun. Probably a crack shot. The mysterious Piers Osbourne we've never heard of, alleged lover of Myra, Helena's piano teacher and part-time tutor. He would have been no more than nine or ten years older. Very handsome. A cultured young man. Then there's Mrs. Saunders, who has to be one of the scariest women on the planet; Erik's longtime mistress, who *might*—I emphasize *might*—be his half sister. Can you believe these people? And to think we've gone eyeball-to-eyeball with Orani. She could easily be a close relative of a Kadaitcha Man."

"You believe in that stuff?" Bruno asked. "There are more things in heaven and earth, etc.?" He sat down beside her, stretching his long legs.

"Outback cops believe in that stuff," Isabelle said. "I swear, I've never seen a face so full of hate as on Eaglehawk's housekeeper."

"And lust," Bruno added.

"Lust, yes," Isabelle agreed. "Sex is very dangerous," she said solemnly. "People get murdered all the time over sex gone woefully wrong."

"Is that going to stop you?" Bruno glanced sidelong at her. He had an idea Isabella was still a virgin. He knew she was a very fastidious and serious-minded young woman.

"It hasn't stopped *you*," she retorted. "I was very surprised young Mani called Mrs. Saunders by her aboriginal name."

"Orani."

"Shouldn't he have been more respectful? After all, she is Eaglehawk's longtime housekeeper."

"How do we know they're not related?"

Isabelle shrugged. "Wouldn't surprise me. Am I the one ordained to set a match to the Hartmann bonfire?" she asked. "If we hadn't turned up, Mrs. Saunders might have taken her secret to the grave. You could see how thrilled the family would be to take her into the fold. Even in this day and age it would create a scandal."

"They're scandal prone, Bella," Bruno said. "The old guy, Konrad, charmed my dad completely. Dad thought him a fine man, a gentleman."

"Having sex with a consenting adult isn't a crime. It

doesn't make you a villain. It might have been in-between wives."

"I suppose nothing passes all understanding. It's not as though would-be mistresses are thick on the ground out here."

"I've never actually believed in people like the Hartmanns, which is pretty naïve. Well, not here in the down-to-earth Outback. More like Transylvania. Twenty years ago, someone had plenty to worry about. They've got plenty to worry about now. One of them is an A-list villain."

Bruno nodded. "I won't argue with that. Our first task is to collect samples for DNA testing. You included."

"Of course. Do you think the family is going to enter into the spirit of it?" Isabelle asked with real worry.

"We could turn our findings over to the Australian Federal Police."

"Meaning?"

"The National Missing Persons Coordination Centre. A lot has happened in the past twenty years. DNA samples now confirm relationships where all else fail. We're sure of Stefan and probably Mrs. Saunders. It doesn't really matter about the rest. You wouldn't have any cotton tips with you?"

"Not with me, but there's an unopened packet of them in the bathroom cabinet. I suppose you could use unopened small plastic bags as containers. I don't mind telling you, I want to take my leave of this family. They're the classic definition of weird." She waved an expansive arm. "Yet Eaglehawk is such an extraordinary place."

"As beautiful as it's savage."

"I only wish the Hartmann family members were ordinary, hard-working station owners, but there's nothing vaguely ordinary about them. I admit at the beginning I felt a surge of elation that we might be on track to find Helena. Now I want to beat it out of here just like her. She might have formed the terrifying idea someone was trying to kill her."

"More likely that someone had killed her mother. Christian's premature death might have been an accident. Maybe Dad had found out something and decided to check it out."

"Only he too was put out of the picture."

Bruno stared at her, highly responsive to what she was saying. "Dad's briefcase full of papers was never found."

"So no one knew what was in it."

"No."

"You carry a heavy burden."

"It hasn't been easy, I admit. I had quite a few nightmares after it happened."

"I bet. It must be the worst kind of pain for the families of victims, not being able to find out the truth. No little grace notes like closure."

"DNA is solving a lot of cold cases thirty and more years on."

"And that's where we're heading."

"Yes." Bruno stared across at her. Her face and hair was caught in a filtered shaft of golden sunlight. He had never seen such bright, beautiful hair. He had never even dated a redhead. It was becoming increasingly difficult being alone with her. Cracks were appearing in his armour. He could almost hear them.

"Questions, questions, questions and no answers," Isabelle was saying. "Let's go back." She began twirling her long hair into a roll and securing it with pins. "Under different circumstances, our trip could have been an adventure, but now? My every thought is of mayhem. How do we know *we* won't get targeted?"

"One would have to be a lunatic to try," said Bruno, diamond glints in his eyes. He sprang to his feet in one lithe movement, extending a helping hand. "This was a dead-end case for my dad. It's open again. I'm here with you, Bella. I'll keep you safe."

"That's a promise?" She looked up at him, wanting to suspend the moment in her memory.

"With my life." He struck a fist to his breast.

She smiled at his gesture, putting out a hand to rub the exact spot. "I welcome that and your presence. What sort of riding accident was it that killed Myra?" she asked. "I haven't seen anything obvious, like crumbling walls here and there. Lots of fallen branches blocking trails. On the other hand, someone could have jumped out from behind a tree, startling Myra and spooking her horse to the extent it reared and then threw her heavily."

Bruno's answer was grim. "Breaking her neck."

"God, what a thud! What were the circumstances leading up to it? I wonder. The Kadaitcha Man was available to do the dirty work."

Bruno's handsome mouth compressed. "The police checked all avenues. There was no one near her when she died."

"Sez who? Myra had enemies. A few people would have been happy to see her gone. Helena grew up knowing all this. No wonder she cleared out," Isabelle said.

"To head for England? Hilary knows so much, only it will have to be dragged out of her. Still, the lies are all over. It's coming up Judgement Day."

Isabelle slowly exhaled. "It's taken years and years."

"Sadly many, many cases do that," Bruno reminded her.

* * *

On the opposite bank came such a rush of spectacular wings, the air echoed with the sound. “Brolgas!” Bruno cried, his eyes fixed there. “Is this a good omen or what?”

“The day has turned magical!” Isabelle moved down farther towards the emerald waters.

A pair of silver-grey cranes with bright red heads alighted at a skipping run on the golden sand of the opposite bank.

“Do you think they’ll dance for us?” She turned to Bruno excitedly.

“We’ll be privileged if they do. They can just as easily take off again.”

“Let’s wait and see. We could easily have missed this, Bruno.”

“Maybe it was meant for us,” he said.

The elegant waterbirds, the most treasured in all the land, were famous for their legendary dancing.

“Not even the aboriginal people know the secret of their dance,” Bruno said, joining her. “Long ago, in the Dreamtime, there was a beautiful young girl called Brolga. Brolga’s dancing was so graceful, so elegant the swooshing of her arms, tribes from near and far would come to see her dance. She always chose the banks of billabongs where her favourite tree, the coolabah, grew.”

“Like here.” Isabelle reached out to take his hand, locking her fingers through his. “Sit by me, Bruno. They’re going to dance. I’m sure of it.” Fascination was in her voice.

Neither spoke again. They were the audience. The brolgas bowed low to each other, the introduction to their famous pas de deux. Upright, their two-metre wingspan outstretched, the brolgas went slowly into their polished performance. Their movements were extraordinarily balletic. Their long, dark-grey legs lifted into the air in splendid jetés. Bruno and Isabelle watched almost without breathing. The cranes continued their dance, back and forth, back and forth, up and down, up and down without lull, until finally they bowed once again to each other, signalling the end of the dance. The performance ended as it began, with a deep bow, thought to be a symbol of their love and lifetime commitment.

Almost three silent minutes passed.

Isabelle found her voice. "I'll never forget that. I don't think I've ever felt so close to nature."

"My first time as well." Bruno too felt they were honoured.

"A precious memory."

They were adding up with Bella. "Brolgas mate for life," he said as they watched the cranes use the long, dry, sandy bank as an airstrip. A short run-up and then they gained lift-off, rising into the air, clearing the treetops, with legions of birds applauding their flight. "Maybe their dancing together confirms their lifelong bond. Who knows?"

"My thoughts exactly. Don't we all want a lifelong bond?" she asked. "A truly meaningful lasting relationship. That's what I want."

"I hope that's what you get, Isabella," he said in a deep, sincere voice. "To be loved. Utterly loved. To *feel* love."

"Is that what you want?" she asked.

He answered quietly. "What one wants and what one gets are most often two different things. I know what happens when love turns cruel."

"Your mother's leaving you and your father left a very deep wound."

"Okay, you've solved it, but you haven't solved me. Dad took the brunt of it. He adored her. There was a divorce of course. He never thought to remarry."

"So you cling to your bachelorhood?"

"So I do. Above and beyond that, I've never met the woman I can't live without. I've fallen a little in love from time to time, but at some point, for whatever reason, communication breaks down."

"Making you afraid of taking the plunge?"

He turned his night-dark eyes on her. "I suppose I'm like you."

She blushed. "What, pray, does that mean?"

"*You* give it time. Unless I'm very wrong and you've had a hectic love life?"

"That would have interfered with my studies, Bruno. I'm twenty-two. I'm in no kind of hurry."

"Look before you leap?" he asked.

"You could say I've taken a leaf out of your book." She hesitated a moment. "Want to know what I *really* think?"

"Nothing I'd like more," he said, his eyes on her lovely profile.

"I'd say we're a couple of incurable romantics, Bruno."

He laughed. "Then I'd have to ask what proof have you got?" He met her green eyes with the challenge.

"I know we'd be heart-broken if our love was betrayed."

She was coming too close to the truth. "I'd like to know how at twenty-two you've acquired so much understanding."

"It's just a question of observation, Bruno, and reading about the lives of others. Take the often tragic lives of the great composers. The sublime emotions they were still able to pour into their works despite everything that had gone terribly wrong in their lives. Beethoven's *Ninth* says it all."

"It just so happens I know it," he said with a thankful smile. He had to keep up with Bella.

"Not many people realize Beethoven wasn't just the brooding genius of his most famous painting."

"The one with the bold red scarf?" Bruno asked. He was familiar with that one. He supposed every music lover was.

"That's the one. Painted around 1820 by Joseph Karl Stieler. A Jewish family, the Hinrichsens eventually came to own and treasure it. It was just one of the many paintings the Nazis stole. Henri Hinrichsen died in Auschwitz, but the family managed to get it back after the war, which was the rightful outcome. Anyway, from letters we know Beethoven was a witty man with a great sense of humour. He was said to have had a beautiful smile and exceptionally good teeth."

"That would have been a plus in that day and age. Beethoven expressed the whole range of human emotions in his music, so he may just have had a sense of humour as well as his profoundly serious side. Marta undertook my classical music education. She gave me whole collections of classical CDs. I've worked through A to C. I haven't had a chance to get to D. Remember Debussy?"

"I do." She would never forget that night. "That was nice of her. I believe we get to know who we are through music."

"The universal language?"

"Can I say something else?" Isabelle asked, almost haltingly.

"Sure. You can tell me anything, everything you like, Bella. I'm your friend. I will never betray you."

"Do you know I believe you, Bruno." She gave him a lovely smile. "I've never had a sexual partner, Bruno. I'm pretty sure you've guessed. I had plenty of male friends as a student. My life could have been very different of course. I could have taken sex as lightly as some others, but I don't think that's possible. Not for me anyway. I had to console a few of my girlfriends, in floods of tears, who thought they could embrace that lifestyle with no ill effects. Someone has to suffer and it's usually the girl. I don't believe a woman should give her body lightly."

"So why don't women practise that?" he shot back.

"Maybe your lot got brainwashed?" Isabelle suggested.

"I beg your pardon!"

"Oh, come off it, Bruno. Arguably you're the most-chased bachelor in town."

"What, women galore trying to entice me into their bed?"

"Something like that."

He grimaced. "Bella, I don't kiss and tell."

"You're a dying breed. A lot put their exploits on Twitter."

"I hesitate to ask this, but are you a man hater?"

She laughed. "It's proving difficult not to be. I don't hate *you*, Bruno."

"I needed to hear that." He gave a mocking sigh. "As it happens, I do believe a woman should be approached with a certain reverence." His dark eyes had turned serious, thoughtful, focused on her and what she was saying.

"That would win you a lot of approval, Bruno. It's my belief there should be a *preparation*."

"A courtship?"

"Yes." She nodded. "I know it's considered old-fashioned."

"The woman sets the parameters," Bruno said from experience. "The man conducts himself accordingly."

"Hard when women throw themselves at you."

He was trying very hard to preserve his calm objectivity, though it was rapidly escaping him. "That's what I love about you, Bella. You don't. You're absolutely right to take your time. You're at the beginning of everything."

"We're good pals?" she asked, her radiant head to one side.

His feelings were way too fierce for palship. "We are, Isabella."

"That's lovely. I trust you, Bruno. It's not every man who gives a woman a feeling of safety. You do. The gods have been kind to us. We've witnessed a spectacular bush sight together. One, as a city dweller, I never thought to see. That's further bonding, surely?" On a little wave of euphoria she leaned sideways, lightly kissed his cheek. "My whole being is filled with healing blessings. What about you?"

"You give your heart and soul to things, don't you?" He felt unnerved by her trust in him. A trust he could never break.

"I suppose I do," Isabelle admitted.

"That makes you an optimist." He knew her kissing his cheek was a perfectly innocent, spontaneous gesture, yet it was all he could do not to pull her into his arms, knot his fingers through her hair and tilt back her head so he could see the lovely line of her throat. He felt like crushing her to him, his hands tracing the length of her, the imprint of her small, tender nipples against his chest. If he weakened and kissed her, the whole world would be lost. It was as simple as that. He knew all he had to do to arouse her desire. Isabella was a creature of passion, of strong feelings, revealed in her playing. He could not test her vulnerability. He didn't through pure force of will. He craved her. Only his duty was clear.

It was his job to follow protocol.

At the same time, her idea of *preparation* for a love

affair struck him as a beautiful concept. But how to keep someone like Isabella at arm's length?

Back in the saddle. All around them thousands and thousands of square miles of raw bushland. No sign of the grazing cattle. No sign of human life. Only the phenomenal birdlife and marauding hawks and falcons. Sand and spinifex. Silence. Infinity. It would be all too easy to get lost, especially near the lignum swamps, where the pelicans made their nests.

"The budgies are leading us out of here," she said, her eyes following their path. Her heart was beating way too fast. Despite all her talk, which she did truly believe in, she felt herself open to powerful sensations she had never before experienced. As for Bruno's experience in sexual matters? He had plenty. How many women had he kissed? How many women had he taken into his bed? She had registered the tension in him. The silence that lay between them was like a forerunner to something . . . unstoppable? If that happened, Bruno *knew* she would surrender, for all her talk of holding off. His decision had been not to allow that to happen. That took matters out of her hands.

The sunlight after the golden-green oasis was blinding. Isabelle shaded her eyes to look up at the great flock of budgerigar flying in their natural V formation. A trickle of sweat was running down between her breasts. Heat was getting to her. Inside and out.

She had to confront the fact she wasn't just falling in love with Bruno. She had been insane enough to fall in love with him on sight. Nothing he had done or said had diminished that. She was the virgin who wanted to be taken. To be his. Her heart was in his hands. Like many a woman before her, she could be in for a hard fall. If that happened, it wouldn't be easy to get up again. The wisest thing would be to listen to one's head not one's heart, yet wisdom was so often abandoned for what was sometimes termed madness.

Bruno, the object of her desire, rode up alongside her. "We won't get lost, Bella," he said, noting her unusually tense expression. "I've got a good sense of direction. Better yet, I have a compass."

"God bless you." The best thing she could do was settle back into their normal easy banter. "Those tall seed stems on the spinifex look a bit like aboriginal spears, don't you think?"

He didn't answer.

Isabelle glanced at him sharply. There wasn't even a flicker of a smile on his face. "Bruno?"

"Sit your horse. Keep still," he ordered beneath his breath.

She stared at him in astonishment. "I hate to ask, but what for?"

Again he kept silent, causing her to visualize an aboriginal man staring out at them from behind the screen of mulga. He would be wearing the Kadaitcha shoes woven of feathers and human hair, stuck together with blood. Orani had sent him. Nothing seemed impossible in this ancient wilderness. She couldn't rule out attack.

"Not a witch doctor, if that's what you're thinking," he said, reading her mind. "It's a bit hard to make out, but there's a lone camel, a dromedary, keeping a close eye on us. His dirty, dusty ginger coat acts as a good camouflage. He's standing well back in the clump of acacias at two o'clock."

She turned her head very slowly to the two o'clock position, keeping a tight hold on the reins. "Dear Lord!

We're being staked out. I don't believe it! It's huge! Six feet or more. Just look at the hump!"

"It may well mean us no harm," said Bruno.

Her answer held dismay and incredulity rolled into one. "Are we going to ask it? Hey, camel, please explain. What are your intentions?"

"I said keep quiet." Bruno's attitude was totally serious.

"I'm *whispering*, in case you haven't noticed. All wild animals are dangerous, aren't they? Don't camels bite?"

"I've heard they resort to it from time to time. It could see us as a threat, but we don't want it to think we're intimidated. We sit tight. Apply universal bush rules. Don't panic. We are *not* moving on, Bella. We sit quietly, not annoying it in any way."

"As if I'm likely to do that." Her voice quaked. "I'm certain I've read somewhere camels can do grievous bodily harm. How fast can they run?"

"I haven't actually clocked one, but I believe around forty miles per hour."

"So Honey and I couldn't outrun it." She was so outraged, she almost shouted. "The gelding probably could."

"The gelding isn't a racehorse, Bella. I'm not going to leave you. We sit tight and wait for it—"

"To charge?"

"In that case, we split to the left. Worst-case scenario: you kick your feet out of the stirrups and gather yourself. I'll pull you over onto the gelding. The mare can find its own way home."

"And I'm supposed to believe you can do that?" Her voice rose in panic.

"I'm damn sure I can," he said tersely. "Have a little faith. But it's not going to end that way, Bella." He was speaking with remarkable calm. "There, what did I tell you?" He creased his dark eyes against the blazing light. "It's turning away."

"So it is!" Isabelle crossed herself. "Boy, do I have a heap of dinner-party stories to tell." She took a deep breath watching the camel move off laconically on its huge feet. "I expect you've been on big-game hunting trips in Africa with your friend Lubrinski?" There was a note of accusation in her voice.

"I'd be too scared. No, Bella, I'm very much against big-game hunting, though I have been to South Africa and visited a lion park. I can't understand why intelligent people are lulled into believing wild animals won't attack. You have to be there to understand how tourists let down their guard. It's not unlike the way tourists elect to take a dip in our crocodile-infested waters. Even our own people get taken."

"That won't be my story."

"Nor mine. Destroying beautiful endangered animals is not my scene either. It's a sin."

"All the same, I wouldn't come out here without a shotgun," Isabelle said, staring around her. Six-foot goannas had been known to attack horses and riders.

"Someone was messing around with a gun when Christian was killed," Bruno pointed out. "We can move on now." He turned his handsome, dynamic face towards her. "Come along now. We have a full program before we leave. I'd like to see that portrait of Helena. It's in the East Wing, where Stefan had it hung."

"I don't know that I want to go there," she said, showing signs of rebellion.

"You can wait outside."

"Shut up, Bruno." It was enormously important to sound normal.

He only laughed. "See that ghost gum right ahead?" He lifted a hand to point out a beautiful eucalypt that stood in splendid isolation. The most beautiful tree in the desert, its pristine white bole and branches were in sharp contrast to the intense blue of the sky and a rust-red pile of boulders. "Race you there," he said.

She didn't ask for a start. She gave Honey's sides an encouraging little kick with her heels. "You're on!"

Stefan Hartmann was waiting for them at the house, still wearing his dust-spattered clothing, his face drawn. "I'll have one of the girls fix us coffee and sandwiches," he said. "I don't want that woman anywhere in my sight. I know evil when I see it. I've never liked her. I've never wanted her in the house. Now I loathe her. I'm horrified to think she could have Hartmann blood."

Bruno took pity on him. "We don't yet know, sir, if she does. She could be making it all up. Why don't we wait on the truth?"

"She could be mad," Stefan said, clinging grimly to hope. "She wouldn't be the first to make false claims. Maybe she even believes them. Maybe she's delusional? She's Tom Saunders's daughter. Hell, she even looks like him at certain times. Her mad mother poisoned her mind. She turned her own crazy dreams into an actual reality. Orani Saunders has been poisoning the air for years, though I have to say she's run the household well. My uncle has retired to his rooms. He's in a shocking mess. I've never in my life seen him like that. Whether her story is true or not, there'll be hell to pay." He broke off, clenching and unclenching his fingers. "How was the ride?" he asked, making a piteous attempt to be normal.

"Very memorable," Isabelle told him gently. "We had the privilege of seeing a pair of brolgas dance, which was amazing. Then a lone camel had us under close observation."

"I hope you stayed in place, returned its stare?"

"We did."

"Good. They're an absolute bloody menace. Occasionally, we get a real rogue that only a bullet will stop. They're belligerent beggars. They will charge if you appear in any way to threaten them. Now, you'll want to wash up. Don't let me keep you. We'll eat in the breakfast room, say in an hour? Kurt is devastated. He just can't get his head around anything. I've allowed Erik far too much influence over my boy. The thing is, running the station requires massive effort and long hours. In many ways, I've been an absentee father. I plan to send him off to his mother."

"Does he want to go?" Isabelle asked.

Stefan nodded. "Yes, thank God. His mother can care for him until we get these other matters straightened out."

Upstairs, Isabelle showered, shampooed her hair and changed her clothes, choosing a cool cotton dress in a shade of leaf green. Fantastic as the Chinese Room was, she wanted to move out as soon as possible. She saw the room as distinctly museumish, not somewhere to sleep.

Even now, she was astounded by the cruelty of Mrs. Saunders's actions. It was unbelievable really. Orani could well be cast as a witch, for the housekeeper enjoyed frightening people. Possibly she was clinging to the belief she shared Hartmann blood without any proof except the stories she had been told by her mother.

Wasn't *she* a case in point? She had believed all her life she was Isabelle Martin and Hilary and Norville Martin were her parents. Things had progressed at a frantic pace. If progress was what it was. All that remained was DNA testing. If it was proved she had Hartmann blood, the next step was to establish how Hilary had come to get custody of her and rear her as her own. She couldn't bear to think Helena might have arranged to hand her over. She wasn't finished with Hilary. She had never had occasion to go to the police, but she needed Hilary to believe she would do so if Hilary didn't reveal the true story. Hilary would never wave away her and her questions again.

Kurt joined them for lunch looking so vulnerable he was almost childlike. Clearly, his opinion of his greatly admired great-uncle had taken a nose dive. His father's devotion to the station had come at a price. Stefan had nearly alienated his son. Kurt had taken a certain position, proven a mistake. His father, not Erik, ran Eaglehawk Station. His father was an honest, honourable man. His great-uncle was an egoist lounging around the house all day, reading, writing the family memoirs, telling Kurt, his captive audience, lies or at the very least falsehoods. As for a sexual relationship with the housekeeper . . . That was too horrible to bear contemplation.

The same sweet-faced aboriginal girl, Nele, served them a light lunch, the choice of open sandwiches of marinated lamb and English spinach and/or smoked salmon with shaved fennel, cucumber and zucchini. There was cold tomato juice in a tall glass container and tiny round cheesecakes to go with the coffee.

Somehow they all kept to the decision to put painful matters temporarily aside. Afterwards, Stefan consented to show them the portrait of Helena that had once hung in the drawing room but had caused so much upset after her disappearance, Erik had ordered it be taken down. At that point, Stefan had stepped in with no intention of banishing the portrait of his beautiful cousin to the attic.

Kurt didn't move off as Isabelle expected he might. He came with them, as though he needed the comfort of his father's presence. The East Wing was huge. They entered it through an ornate stained-glass door. Inside, in the open hallway that served as a place to read or write, they found an entire wall covered in leather-bound books. Sunlight fell through the series of tall windows with matching pointed arches into a vaguely melancholy atmosphere. The furnishings were Victorian, comfortable in style, with none of the grandeur of the central core of the homestead. All was quiet, tidy, ordered. It was rather like a gentleman's club.

In the adjoining room, which was undoubtedly the most decorated in the wing, there was a gleaming polished timber floor, huge Persian rug, lighter-in-style furnishings, pictures, ornaments, rather grand curtains and walls a delicate yellow. A large portrait of Helena dominated the end wall. The light glanced off the carved and gilded frame. In silence, they all walked towards it, stopping in front of it, a saddened group.

"It's a wonderful painting!" Bruno said after a while, taking a step forward to note the signature of a famous artist.

"Helena was a beautiful little girl, a beautiful young woman," Stefan said, real grief in his voice. "She was extraordinarily sensitive. She suffered from not having a mother. She suffered from having a mother who dazzled. Helena, had she ever found an antidote to all her troubles, would have been even lovelier. The most remarkable part is that this could be a portrait of *you.*" Stefan turned his head to study the silent Isabelle.

Isabelle slanted him a poignant smile. She didn't altogether agree despite the remarkable similarities.

"In many ways, yes," Bruno was murmuring absently. "But there's a recognisable difference. One can see it in the expression. Isabella is a confident young woman, sure of her abilities. She knows she has a great deal to offer. Helena looks much frailer in character. She looks like she was at a stage in her life when she felt she was floundering. Her expression is one of *appeal.*"

"There were reasons," Stefan said bleakly. "If it's to be believed, that witch of a woman terrorized her. Claims she kept it up for years. I don't accept that. Helena could have told me. I would have checked it out without hesitation."

"Probably you wouldn't have found anything," Bruno said. "If it were the didgeridoo, one could count on Mrs. Saunders hiding it away."

"She wouldn't have found it hard to come by one," Kurt interjected, a look of strong condemnation in his voice. "They're all frightened of her, the aboriginal stockmen, aren't they, Dad? They reckon she's a sorceress."

"She damned well isn't," Stefan only said coldly. "I don't want her on the station. She has to go into exile. Move on."

"Uncle Erik won't allow it, Dad." Kurt was visibly torn.

"Your great-uncle has lost control," his father returned firmly. "Things are going to change around here, Kurt." He turned to Bruno. "Now, there's the matter of DNA samples.

My uncle wants no part of it. I want this matter cleared up. I suppose you will have to approach Saunders?"

"One way to shut her up, Dad," Kurt cried in a fury of intention.

Stefan looked down on Isabelle. "Your mother—the woman who has always claimed to be your biological mother—obviously had contact with Helena. Was there something between them? Of what did Helena die? If she *did* die. If Helena bore a child, perhaps the father didn't want the child or even abandoned Helena. But she had friends. She had to have had. Someone helped her flee the country. That fellow Osbourne perhaps? It's a wonder your father didn't follow up that lead?" He turned back to Bruno.

"For whatever reason, a lot of information was kept from my father," Bruno said. "What I do know was that my father never gave up on the case. He had a good number of files on it. Instead of being given the full picture, it now appears important details were withheld by your family. The family wasn't united. That's very clear to us all these years later. Abigail Hartmann, your mother, was judged to have known nothing about Helena's disappearance. She was never suspected of being involved, yet might she have taken pity on Helena and helped her get away?"

"You can't go bothering my mother," Stefan said with a vigorous shake of his head. "My mother is a woman of honour. She would have lost no time telling us she had helped Helena and why. The woman you should really be talking to is the one who claims to be *your* mother, Isabelle. I'm much struck by the fact that if the two of you hadn't met, and there hadn't been the McKendrick connection, we would have gone on mourning Helena behind closed doors."

"Only Fate has stepped in. Once we have the DNA samples, we need to get a flight out of here." Bruno fixed his eyes on Stefan. "I can arrange a private flight, but I'd like your permission to land here."

"God help us, you don't have to do that!" Stefan protested. "I can organise a private flight into Brisbane, where you can hook up with a flight to Sydney. Would that suit? I'd take you myself only there's too much work to do."

"I can help you, Dad," Kurt jumped in.

His father put a warm hand on his shoulder. "Fine, son. Tomorrow morning, say eight o'clock?" he asked Bruno. "The sooner we deal with this, the better."

Chapter Eight

They didn't have to go in search of Mrs. Saunders. She found them. They were in the Turkish Room, systematically searching through the piles and piles of books.

"Who knows if we won't find a revealing letter inside?" Isabelle said hopefully. "It wouldn't be the first time something like that has happened. I leave lots of stuff inside books. I once put a couple of hundred dollars inside a textbook for safety's sake. It took months before I remembered which one." She turned her head. "Hello, who's that?"

"I shudder to think." When Bruno opened the door in response to the firm knock, he found the housekeeper—or the soon-to-be ex-housekeeper—standing outside.

She didn't beat about the bush. "You'll be wanting my DNA." She wore a bitter smile on her striking face. Today, she had thrown open her wardrobe. She wasn't wearing her house uniform. She was dressed in riding clothes that showed off her trim figure. Her raven, silver-winged hair was drawn back into a heavy knot. She wore makeup, lightly but perfectly applied. The *real* woman, not the shadow, would turn heads.

"Come in, Mrs. Saunders," Bruno invited smoothly. "I'm going to be straight with you," he said, as he closed the door. "We have serious doubts you're related by blood to the family."

"What would you know?" She shrugged, as though his opinion was of little value.

"It's not what I *know*; it's more intuition. You claim Konrad Hartmann was your father. He and your mother had a sexual relationship?"

"Ah, come off it!" She laughed crudely. "Is that so unusual?"

"Perhaps not. But my father was a good judge of character. He thought Konrad a fine man, a gentleman. He didn't see him as a man who would seduce a young girl in his employ. A part-aboriginal girl, which would have made her so much more vulnerable."

The woman's brilliant dark eyes flashed. "Ah, spare me the fine-gentleman stuff. I know what my ma told me."

"But you don't actually *know*. You never saw anything with your own eyes; otherwise, I'm sure you would have told us all. Mr. Hartmann never acknowledged you. Never let down his guard for one moment, or tried to make things up to you in some way. Have you sent away to be educated."

She froze. "He wanted me around. Just like he wanted my ma around." It was clear Orani and not her alter ego, Mrs. Saunders, didn't want to deal with those questions.

"The other members of the family had no sense of kinship," Bruno continued.

"They *hated* me."

"Mightn't it have been the other way around?" Isabelle gave the woman a long, searching look.

"Mrs. Abigail used to ask me questions about all the terrible things that happened."

"What terrible things?" Bruno asked briskly.

The woman drew in a sharp breath, held it, then released it on a sigh. "Never you mind. Mrs. Abigail believed me."

"You sound incredibly proud of that fact," Bruno commented.

"Mrs. Abigail Hartmann told you she believed you?" Isabelle asked, feeling a sense of pity.

"She acted kindly to me. Not like that bitch, the Missus. The two ladies did not compare. As for that Helena, my God, was she a wimp! All she could do was play the bloody piano. I ask you!"

"So you selected her as the one you would punish?" Isabelle said bleakly. "How cruel was that?"

Mrs. Saunders responded with a harsh laugh. "Cruel? Oh, that's good! No one cared about *me.* I wasn't as beautiful as them."

"You're a beautiful woman, Mrs. Saunders, though you've done your best to hide it," Bruno said. "Your aboriginal blood has made you even more striking, though you could equally as well be Greek. Your features are finely cut."

"Why wouldn't they be? I have Hartmann blood."

"There's no genetic resemblance. You don't look remotely like Erik Hartmann, for instance. Or Stefan Hartmann. Kurt obviously resembles his mother's side of the family."

"Look, are you ready for me or not?" the woman flared, a feverish look in her eyes. "This family *owes* me. Once we know I share their blood, they'll pay."

"Okay," Bruno said, as though giving in. "This whole business can be easily resolved. If you want us to help you, you might tell us who helped Helena get away. If you don't actually know, an educated guess will do."

The woman gave Bruno an amused look. "Some man. Some man who worked here. Some man who visited. Even the piano teacher. He was a handsome young guy. He was kind to her. She could have contacted him. Who knows? The thing is, *I* don't know who it was. I would have shaken their hand if I did. It could even have been Mrs. Abigail. Those sharp eyes of hers missed nothing. She was the only one who didn't fall under that Myra's spell. Her and me."

Isabelle broke in. "I thought the two women were close friends? They went riding together."

Mrs. Saunders appeared genuinely shocked. "How d'you become close friends with a woman who stole your husband? Go on, tell me that!" Her tone was so strong, so challenging, it rang round the room.

"All this is hearsay, Mrs. Saunders," Bruno said. "Lots of suspicions, lots of conjecture, but no actual proof."

She shrugged her straight shoulders. Her cream shirt, Isabelle had noticed, was silk, not everyday denim or cotton. What else did she have hidden away in her wardrobe? "Believe what you will," the ex-housekeeper said in disgust. "Now, are you going to take this sample?" She reached in her riding pants' pocket. "I cut a lock of my hair as well. I already know the answer. It's you two who have to make sure."

"Laboratory testing will do that, Mrs. Saunders," Bruno said. He picked up a clean cotton tip. "If you wouldn't mind opening your mouth. This will only take a moment."

The woman complied without a word. Clearly, she thought she would soon be in a position to give the family hell.

"Either way, you intend leaving the station?" Bruno asked, sealing off a plastic bag similar to the one that contained the lock of hair. The woman's position had become untenable. She would have to go. But where? When all was said and done, Eaglehawk Station and the Hartmann family had been her life.

"Of course," Mrs. Saunders confirmed. "I've contacted Mrs. Abigail. She's coming for me this very afternoon. She's the best of them all. She's promised me she will help me find a position in the city. Hers is a respected family. Establishment. She has influence."

"That's very kind of her, I must say," Bruno commented. "We would be very pleased to meet her, however briefly."

"I can't promise you anything," the woman said.

"I understand." Bruno spoke gently. "It's a very emotional time for you."

Mrs. Saunders jerked up her raven head to look at him, searching his eyes. "It is," she said, as though reading compassion there. "I'll speak to Mrs. Abigail," she offered. "If the occasion presents itself, she will. She's a very kind woman."

"And she will be wanting to speak to her son and grandson," Isabelle added.

For the first time, Mrs. Saunders looked unsure of herself. "I'll leave it all up to Mrs. Hartmann. She will decide." She turned to go. "You will continue taking your meals in the breakfast room. Nele will look after you. I've trained her well."

They had the Turkish Room to themselves once more. "Abigail Hartmann is coming to whisk Mrs. Saunders away. How about that?" Isabelle exclaimed in a tone of wonder.

"Dad spoke to Abigail." There was a vertical frown between Bruno's black brows. He was starting to think he didn't believe in anything anymore.

"*Spoke* to, yes," Isabelle said, noting his unsettled, upset expression. "She really needed to have been interrogated."

"Police do that, Bella. Not private investigators. They can only ask questions. Elicit comments. Dig deeper."

"*We* have to speak to her," Isabelle said.

"I don't think she's going to fall into that trap. What's the betting?"

"No bets. Maybe her curiosity will be aroused? Maybe she'll want to see me? It would be good to get her reaction. What I don't understand is why, if she's such a lovely woman, a woman of honour, she's not closer to her son and her grandson. If she's coming, surely she will want to see them? No nice grannie would simply fly in and fly out. Or maybe she's having someone drive her overland?"

"I seriously doubt it," Bruno said. "They all use helicopters for mustering these days. She'll come by chopper."

"We ought to speak to Kurt," Isabelle said.

"If he's around. He seemed very anxious to support his father all of a sudden."

"Especially when his father can, if he so chooses, use the whip hand," Isabelle said, picking up another leather-bound book.

"Surely Abigail would get through a message? She *is* very much family."

"So why is she giving them such a wide berth?" Isabelle put the book down to ask.

"We don't know that exactly. Both Stefan and Kurt may well intend to come back to the house to greet her. If that's the case, we have to make sure we join them."

"I can't wait." Isabelle picked up the book again. "Sir Walter Scott," she identified the author.

"'Oh, what a tangled web we weave . . . when first we

practise to deceive,'" Bruno came up with the familiar quote.

"Wasn't he right about that!" Isabelle met his darker-than-dark eyes. Always the little butterflies in the stomach. The feeling of instability she desperately wanted made stable. "Sir Walter was enormously popular," she said. "The first blockbuster author. A close friend of Byron, who admired his work. Christian must have loved his books too. There are a lot of them here. This is *Ivanhoe,* the knight returning from the Crusades only to find he's been disinherited and thwarted in his love affair with the Lady Rowena."

"Classic ingredients for a romantic tale." Bruno gave one of his elegant shrugs.

"I ought to read it." Isabelle opened up the dusty book, giving a start as something fell out. "What's that?" she cried.

Bruno made a grab for it before it landed on the Kurdish rug.

"Pray it's a love letter." She was trying to stay calm.

Bruno scanned the single yellowing page. "Here's the tricky part. It's in German."

"Give it here," she said quickly, holding out her hand. "I may be able to read some of it." Suddenly, her heart was pounding.

"It could be anything, Bella," he said, warning her against false hopes. "No envelope. Something Christian jotted down. It's a man's writing. Pen and ink."

"It's a poem," she said.

"Can you read it?"

"Not only read it, I *know* it. It's one of Rainer Maria Rilke's short poems."

Bruno grimaced. "I give up. Who might Rainer Maria Rilke be? I never found him in my law books."

"Arguably one of Germany's greatest poets," Isabelle replied, nibbling her lip. "Have a look to see whether there's a book of his poems shoved in with the rest."

"I will when you tell me what the poem says."

Isabelle lifted her eyes from the sheet of paper. "It seems to me this is lightly perfumed. What do you think? Men are supposed to have the better sense of smell." She waved the page under his nose.

"It is," he confirmed. "Musky but discernible."

"Myra's perfume? Abigail's?"

"It was a long time ago, Bella," he said.

"We're never free of the past," she countered. "It's only one verse. I studied this poem among others at college in London. It was in connection with the life of a brilliant Australian violinist, Alma Moodie, born in Brisbane. She was regarded as one of the finest female violinists of her time. She made Germany her home, obviously to further her career. She died in Frankfurt where she was a teacher at the Conservatorium in 1943 during a bombing raid. Her friends thought she committed suicide. It's on record Rilke had greatly admired her playing."

"Is it going to help us?" Bruno asked. He wasn't feeling a lot of hope. A scrap of unsigned paper? A love poem? Not original. A famous German poet.

It is life in slow motion,
It's the heart in reverse,
It's a hope-and-a-half:
Too much and too little at once.

"That's deep," Bruno said, feeling the weight of emotion that was inside him. Bella's speaking voice had a quality that pierced his heart. It excited and consoled him at one and the same time.

"It's called 'The Wait,'" she said, meeting his eyes.

He drew a breath. "I get that. Their love affair—if we're right about that—never did move forward."

"Both of them were killed."

"Or got themselves killed. Crime and punishment." Bruno rose slowly to his full height, beginning once more to riffle through the crowded, dusty bookcases.

It was Isabelle who located the volumes of German poetry. "Goethe, Schiller, Heine," she said, pulling out the volumes and placing them precariously on top of a high stack. "Schiller wrote the 'Ode to Joy'; Beethoven set to music in his *Ninth*. Goethe you must have heard of. I won the Goethe Prize for German my last year at school. Heine wrote the lyrics for a lot of German *lieder.* Schubert, Schumann songs."

"The stuff you know!"

"Lots of it. I'm a great reader. And there you are, only making a fortune!"

"Well, at least that's something positive."

"The family brought their German heritage with them, just as the British and the great influx from Europe in the twentieth century brought theirs," Isabelle remarked, a student of history. "They came from everywhere all over the British Isles and Europe to live in peace."

"No wonder. They must have had a brutally cruel time in Europe from the Great War right through World War II and long after that. My Italian grandparents and my mother were assisted migrants."

Isabelle looked up. "You've never spoken of your grandparents."

"Much like you. I didn't know them."

"Don't you want to find them? They could still be alive."

"I suggested it once to my mother. That caused major

trauma. Apparently, one of the reasons she married my father was to get away from her strict parents. Or so she said. Could even have been true. My mother didn't have a lot of heart."

"You do," Isabelle pronounced with considerable approval, peering closely at something she had just found. "Read this." A shiver passed through her as she passed Bruno a slim volume.

"To the centre of all my labours and my loves.
Forever yours, Myra."

"No one wrote that to someone they didn't love," he said.

"Christian?" she asked the question.

Another rap came on the door, so heavy Isabelle jumped. "Who is it *this* time? I wonder."

"If that door weren't solid mahogany, they'd have put a fist through it," Bruno said. He opened the door to find Kurt waiting outside. "Hi, Kurt! Can I help you?"

"My grandmother is here," Kurt announced, as if on an important mission. "She'd like to meet you."

"We'd be delighted to meet her," Bruno responded, his natural charm to the fore.

"She's having coffee with my father and me," Kurt continued in the same ambassadorial tone of voice. "If you'd like to join us in, say, a half hour?"

"It will be our pleasure," Bruno returned suavely.

"*Gut*." Kurt turned away.

"Why the hell does he pronounce good as *gut*?" Bruno asked, irritated by the younger man's manner.

"I don't think it's an affectation. I expect Kurt speaks German. One doesn't like to lose a language."

"No, of course not." He had to agree. "I didn't lose my Italian. I never anticipated the grand invitation, did you?"

"That Abigail might ask to meet us?" Isabelle asked.

"Most likely to take a good look at you."

"I expect so. But we don't need her to prove if I have Hartmann blood. DNA will do that for us."

"Certainly, but the woman has all the information my father needed and didn't get. It's pretty clear now Myra and Christian were lovers."

"In which case, we can assume Abigail would have been the first to know."

Bruno sat poised on the edge of the massive desk. "If my dad knew what Abigail kept hidden, he might have been able to solve the mystery of Helena's disappearance. Only much of the truth was kept from him for a very good reason."

"Too much to cover up. Myra could have ridden right into a trap, you know. Christian as the man who betrayed her obviously had to go."

"Abigail won't want to talk about it," Bruno said. "Hence, we'll never know."

"I'm not so sure," Isabelle said. "The truth has already started to emerge. On the afternoon Myra met her fate, Abigail was confined to bed with a bad migraine."

"With Mrs. Saunders in and out of the room, checking on her."

Isabelle picked up. "Mrs. Saunders who looked at Abigail as a friend and supporter. Terrible to contemplate a family member could commit murder."

"We've all been shocked at how the most unexpected people do that. Desperate situations call for desperate measures. How did Helena manage to become invisible? There has to be a record of her baby's birth somewhere."

"That's if she had a baby," Isabelle said. "Our resemblance could be nothing more than freakish."

"At least we'll have an answer to that. We can't explain Dr. Hilary Martin's reaction though, can we? If your history is straightforward and she is your birth mother, why did she react as she did? Why did Norville react as he did? The two of them, at least, left a trail. Both young doctors at the time. Their background has to be looked into. The hospital records at the time have to be double-checked. My dad had no idea whatsoever about you, let alone the Martins. He was investigating the case of a young woman who simply vanished. It wasn't thought all that baffling. It was known she was deeply unhappy at home. Young people do go missing. They move away. They change their names. They live a new life."

"It's a puzzlement and it's giving me a headache," Isabelle said.

"That's the dust. The place needs a good cleaning out." Bruno hesitated for a moment. "I do think there was a reason for Dad's accident. Maybe years later, he came across some lead? Some lead that had been concealed. Why did so many of his papers disappear; files in his office? There was no break-in. The police checked on that. Many of them knew him, attended his funeral. He'd been one of them. He was well liked and respected. I know a lot of questions were asked on and off the record. The missing brief case, for a start."

"I've come to think of all this—your father's valiant efforts—as *Finding Helena*," Isabelle said. "I feel her loss strongly. She could have been my mother." Of a sudden, her voice broke.

What affected her affected him. Bruno reached for her. Pulled her in tight, his chin resting on the top of her red-gold head. He felt her whole body relax against him. His strong arms held her up. "We'll find her, Bella," he said.

They had reached the landing before Bruno said quietly, "I'll go in first. You follow after a minute."

"You want to get the best view of the reaction?"

"Indeed I do. Who knows, she might find it an occult experience. I'm most interested in meeting Abigail."

"I've got my hand up as well. We're hoping to nail her?"

"On something," Bruno said. "She knows more about the disappearance of Helena than she has ever said."

"That's why you told me to leave my hair out?" She already knew the answer.

"Of course, Bella. I want to leave her gasping. Why would she have worked at a friendship with Orani? She was family. Her loyalty was to family."

"Not if her husband was having an affair with another family member. There's little doubt she used Mrs. Saunders. I think Orani suits her best."

"It's her name. I'm going in," said Bruno, looking the picture of energy and purpose.

"Go right ahead." Isabelle waved him off. She remained on the landing, feeling the oddest mixture of excitement and fear.

She heard uplifted voices. Stefan's query as to where she was. Bruno's ready answer. "She'll be here in a moment, sir."

That was her cue. She wanted to take the stairs at a nervous rush; instead, she walked down slowly, controlling herself as if this weren't a momentous meeting. If it turned out Myra was her grandmother, wouldn't Abigail automatically hate a young woman made in Myra's image?

"I'm sorry if I kept you waiting," she said, looking smilingly from one to the other as though this was another everyday friendly introduction.

"Not at all!" Stefan Hartmann answered immediately. "Mother, this is the young lady I've told you about."

"Ah, yes, Isabelle." Abigail Hartmann, to their surprise, was a little woman, but of apparent robust constitution. She was no more than five two or three, but with considerable presence. She was smartly dressed in a two-piece outfit, upmarket denim jacket and skirt with a white silk blouse beneath. Ankle boots on her narrow feet. She had beautifully cut and styled white hair and far-seeing hazel eyes. She returned Isabelle's smile with a gracious one of her own, even if a strange spasm momentarily distorted her expression. "You believe you are a relation, my dear?" she asked in a most kindly way. "Do please sit down," she invited. "Beside me." She indicated a chair.

Isabelle obeyed. Something told her that in the days before DNA testing, there was no way Mrs. Abigail Hartmann would have owned her, for all the graciousness she was displaying. The facial spasm was tiny, but it had an effect. Abigail Hartmann could well create the illusion of any emotion she so chose.

Abigail glanced over at her son. "Why don't you leave Isabelle and me to have a nice chat, Stefan dear?"

"Whatever you say, Mother." Stefan held out a shepherding arm to his son, whose expression said plainly he didn't want to go.

"I'd like it if I may stay, Mrs. Hartmann." Bruno looked directly at the very-much-in-command-of-herself lady. "I promise I'll keep quiet." Quick to assure her, he had no definite intention of doing so. He too had noted the facial twitch. Whatever emotion she had felt the moment Abigail laid eyes on Isabelle, it was very real.

Now she smiled at him benignly. "Isabelle might find it difficult to speak to me with a third-party present," she suggested. "Just the two of us will bring more ease."

"That's very thoughtful of you, Mrs. Hartmann," Isabelle spoke up. She had the strong feeling Mrs. Hartmann was her enemy when she really didn't know anything much about the woman. All she had to go on was intuition. "Bruno and I are here together. He knows my story. Not the full story of course, which we intend to find out, but the very possible Hartmann connection."

"Easily provable of course." A strained patience crept into the confident voice. "I've heard about the DNA samples, but I simply can't take it in, my dear. You must forgive me. You could well bring to light things none of us as a family want to know."

Was that revulsion in her heart? Bruno thought. He kept out of it, allowing Isabelle to take the lead.

"But you do see the strong resemblance?" Isabelle inquired quietly.

"I see red hair and green eyes." Abigail's reply was calm. "A not unusual combination."

"I think it's more than that, Mrs. Hartmann. For a fleeting moment when you first saw me, you were deeply disturbed."

A tight smile touched Abigail's mouth. "You know that, do you?"

"It was an involuntary twitch."

"You certainly read a lot into that. The fact is, you're making no sense, my dear. I had been warned. I was fully expecting a young woman who looked uncannily like Helena." Abigail directed a cool, sharp-as-a-knife glance at Bruno, seated apart. "You're McKendrick's son?"

"I am."

"You don't look the least like him."

"I take after my mother's side of the family," Bruno said.

"Ah yes!" Abigail spoke as though she was well aware of the McKendricks' entire history. "I believe he was killed in a tragic hit and run?" she said in a sympathetic tone. "It must have been a bitter blow when the police could find nothing."

"It was. My father did mention in his files that you were very pleasant and helpful when he was making his enquiries here on the station."

"A nice man. A gentleman. I told him what I could, which wasn't a great deal. Helena was a very secretive girl. She was always like that, from childhood. Some girls are."

Bruno thought swiftly. "When did you hear of my father's death?" he asked.

Abigail answered automatically, as he hoped she would. "From Erik, of course. How would I have known otherwise?"

"From Mr. Erik Hartmann?" Bruno repeated with an enquiring inflexion.

"I did say that, Mr. McKendrick." She gave him a buttoned-up frown.

"I have to say, I find that odd. Mr. Hartmann was quite shocked when I told him only a day ago."

Abigail's response was patient this time around, even wearily so. "I can't think for the life of me why. Poor Erik hasn't been himself for years now. Myra, then my husband and another great blow with his daughter running off."

"What kind of a young woman was Helena?" Isabelle asked. Apart from being secretive, she thought.

"She was beautiful certainly and talented. At one time, we had high hopes for her," she said unsmilingly.

"This was when?"

"When would you imagine?" Abigail countered, sounding displeased for all her poise. "Before her mother was killed. Afterwards, well. She seemed to shrink inside. It was clear to all of us she wasn't going to make a woman of substance."

"Weren't you judging her a little harshly?" Isabelle asked. "She was scarcely out of her teens."

"We know for a fact Mrs. Saunders, the woman you had taken under your wing, was tormenting Helena using the didgeridoo to make moaning sounds during the night," Bruno said, his tone openly accusatory. "Mrs. Saunders has admitted it. She seemed quite proud of it. I'm sure your son has told you she claims to have Hartmann blood."

Abigail gave an unladylike snort full of subterranean anger. "What I judge most likely is that her insane mother filled her head with foolish tales."

"Yet you encouraged her to believe those foolish tales?" Isabelle charged.

"I did nothing of the kind. I would remind you, my dear, you're a guest in this house. Mrs. Saunders never heard any such nonsense from me. It was a fantasy she and her truly unstable mother wanted to believe."

"She has given us a DNA sample," Bruno said.

Anger must have flooded Abigail's being because her small face flushed. Her voice, however, gave no sign of it. "She'll be devastated I know, when the results come back in the negative. Poor Orani is Tom Saunders's daughter. You only had to see them standing side by side. As for her claiming she's Konrad's daughter, the idea is preposterous. Konrad Hartmann and a servant? You can put that idea out of your heads at once. You might as well say I had an affair with one of the stockmen. Konrad had two wives. He did *not* have a mistress."

"It's a pity you didn't make this perfectly plain to Mrs. Saunders. You would have saved her a lot of grief," Bruno said.

"Please don't blame me," Abigail said with a fussy little shake of her body. "No one was going to convince Orani her mother hadn't fallen pregnant to Konrad. Total make-believe. Psychotic, I suppose you could call it."

"Can you tell us anything more about Myra Hartmann's fatal accident?" Isabelle swiftly changed the subject.

"My dear, the police as well as Mr. McKendrick's father investigated that. It was thought something spooked Myra's horse, causing it to rear and throw her. She was a splendid horsewoman. There could have been no other explanation."

"You didn't join her that day?"

Abigail flashed him a sad smile. "Alas, a bad migraine. I lose the sight in my right eye for an hour or two. No pain, but very limited sight. It's a great source of grief to me that I wasn't with her on that fatal day. I might have been able to prevent whatever happened. We shall never know."

"Of course you and Myra Hartmann were very close. I imagine you would have been," Bruno said in a deep, soothing tone.

"We were the greatest of friends." Abigail examined her rather chunky hands folded in her lap.

"Forgive me, but there was a suggestion—" Bruno began, allowing a hesitation to gain her reaction.

He did that. "What are you talking about?" Mollified by his previous sympathetic tone, she rounded on him swiftly, imperiously.

"Well, we know Mrs. Saunders—Orani—played nasty games with Helena. Wasn't it possible Orani could have had something to do with Mrs. Hartmann's accident? She told us she hated her."

"As well she might!" For once, Abigail couldn't control an abrupt outcry.

"You're saying Myra Hartmann was as cruel to Orani as you are kind?"

"Myra was my dear friend." Incredibly, Abigail's sharp hazel eyes misted. "We were sisters-in-law after all. But I can't deny she had a malicious side. *I* never saw it, but others did. I saw Myra as she was with *me*. As for what Orani was doing that day . . ." She winced.

"Wasn't she supposed to be looking in on you?" Isabelle asked.

"She was, but how could I say for sure? The room had been darkened. I fell asleep. All I know is that she was in a terrible state when Myra was brought in. We all went to pieces, I'm afraid. Myra was so vivid, so vital, it didn't seem possible she was dead. I wish you hadn't brought all this up. It's very upsetting. This young woman might well have Hartmann blood. We'll soon find out. The connection could only be Helena who abandoned her loving, generous family and ran away."

"My father knew nothing of the existence of a Piers Osbourne, the piano tutor." Bruno changed tack.

Abigail gave another derisive snort. "Why would he? Piers was long out of the picture. He had returned home."

"Surely Helena would have kept up the connection? Possibly a strong friendship. They weren't that far apart in years," Isabelle said.

"Piers fell head over heels in love with Myra," Abigail said, condemnation all over her. "He was a very susceptible young man, and let's face it, Myra enjoyed having men fall in love with her. She was a great beauty, you know."

"We intend to find Piers Osbourne," Bruno said, meeting Abigail Hartmann's eyes.

"Any special reason for needing to do that?" Abigail challenged, looking even more condemnatory.

"Helena had to look to someone. She needed to get away. She had her reasons; we don't yet know what they were. She could well have asked Piers Osbourne's support. We know she did get away to England. Obviously under a false name. It wouldn't be the first time a flight passenger gave a false name."

"Well, I wish you every success," Abigail barked, clearly wiping her hands of the whole business. "All I know is Helena betrayed her family. She put a curse on us. It has never gone away. After Myra was killed, I was especially kind to her. I helped her with her studies, but I'm afraid she didn't look on me as her friend. Helena wasn't easy to deal with. She spread a lot of trouble."

"How?" Isabelle was quick to ask.

A flush of anger spread over Abigail's good skin. "Helena was a liar and a troublemaker. There, I've said it. She couldn't be allowed to continue. It was like having a serpent in the house."

Bruno's raven head jerked up. "That's very extreme, isn't it?" he asked, taken aback by the image of the serpent and the vehemence with which the remark had been delivered.

"You did ask," Abigail said sardonically, a flicker in her eyes. "I loathe being put in this position, young man. So far as I'm concerned, Helena no longer exists."

"But *I* do," Isabelle said quietly.

Abigail gave an odd laugh. Obviously, she found Isabelle's statement very funny. "Are you hoping for some kind of payout, my dear?"

There was an edge to Bruno's voice. "We're sorry you

think that, Mrs. Hartmann. If there's any possibility Helena is Isabelle's mother, that's all we want to know. That and what happened to my father and a good many of his files on the Hartmann family."

"Then I wish you every success." Abigail spread her strong, chunky hands. "Could you please find my son? I've done my duty. I've met you. I've sighted you, young lady. The resemblance is more to Myra than Helena on a number of counts. I grant you, it's uncanny, but I can't possibly help you."

"I think you have a few dark secrets, Mrs. Hartmann," Bruno said quietly.

Abigail's expression was set and closed. "Do you know anyone who doesn't?"

"You're taking Orani with you. Finding her a job?" Isabelle asked.

"Orani trusts me."

God knows why, Bruno thought. Orani by this time was so sure she was a Hartmann, the truth that she was not could send her over the edge.

"Yet you've used her," Isabelle said. "She thinks of you as a friend. As a supporter of her story."

Another derisive snort. "More fool she."

"And when she finds out?"

"Finds out what?"

"That you've been allowing her to believe a lie? That she is not the late Konrad Hartmann's daughter?"

Abigail spread her hands. "What else could I do? Get her locked up for life? Her mother should have been. I'm doing my bit for the family, my dear. I'm taking Orani Saunders off poor, gutless Erik's hands. Orani got her claws into him long ago. All part of her plan. He's been screwing her for years, if I might use that crude term. I'm letting him off the hook. I'm taking Orani away. I'll give her enough money to keep her going until she finds a job. I'll even provide her with a reference. At least she's a competent housekeeper, if mentally unstable."

"Is that your way of easing your conscience a little?" Isabelle asked. "I have to say, despite all she's done, she did get a lot of malicious encouragement from you. I feel pity for the woman. Her mother wasn't the only one playing with her mind, and from such an early age."

"It isn't easy counteracting fantasies placed in a young mind. No doubt I should have tried, but in my case, it was protecting my own interests and the interests of my family. They will back whatever I have to say if I ask them. Now, I must go. Young man"—she turned to Bruno—"you can come with me. We have to round up Stefan and Mrs. Saunders. Maybe she's having a last little chat with Erik. Who knows? I have always placed the blame where it belongs."

"Which is where?" Isabelle asked.

"I will not answer that question," Abigail said. "Come along, young man. I haven't got the entire day to waste. I want to get on home."

"You were piloted here in your station helicopter?" Bruno asked, fully expecting for that to be the case.

"Good God, why would I need a pilot?" Abigail simply asked. "I'm a woman of the Outback, Mr. McKendrick. If I have a need to do something, then I learn. I've had a licence for many years. Plenty of experience. I love flying. It's a way of life out here." She turned back to Isabelle. "I suppose Helena just could be your mother, my dear. I think you'll find she's dead. Traitors usually come to a sticky end."

"So do people who have committed crimes in the past," said Isabelle.

* * *

After Abigail and Bruno had gone off in search of Stefan, who would most probably be driving his mother to the airstrip, Isabelle stood still in the middle of the huge empty room. She was full of banked-up emotions. Abigail Hartmann was a complex character whose conscience appeared to fall into a moral grey zone. She hoped she would never see her again.

She was about to put two chairs back in order when a light flashed at the corner of her eye. She spun around in time to see Orani move from behind a chinoiserie leather screen at the far end of the room. The flash was sunlight on her crystal earrings. Tears were streaming down her face.

"She betrayed me," Orani cried, locking eyes with Isabelle.

"How long have you been there?" Isabelle gasped, her brain working overtime.

"From when Mr. Stefan left. I came in through the French doors. None of you noticed, so I slipped behind the screen. I wanted to hear what Mrs. Abigail would say."

"I'm so sorry," Isabelle said. She was. She was human. She recognised how this woman would feel.

"She lied to me," Orani continued, her devastation plain to see. "All these years and she deliberately let me believe Mr. Konrad was my father."

"In all likelihood, fantasy. Something your mother dreamed up and fed you from childhood. Believe me, I know what that's like. The two people who reared me lied to me all my life. They aren't my biological parents. A *new* reality is very hard to come to terms with. For your peace of mind, your DNA will be tested. You can contact

Bruno through his wealth management group, Fortuna, in Sydney."

"She lied to me," Orani repeated, barely acknowledging what Isabelle was saying. "She got me to lie for her. I did it willingly. She knew what was happening between those two."

"Myra and Christian?"

"Who else?"

"Can you be sure now Mrs. Abigail didn't want them dead?"

"I'm not sure of anything," Orani said, "but she weren't in the house that afternoon. She weren't in her bed. There was no migraine. I didn't look in on her." She spoke with great bitterness. "I don't know where she was. Maybe she went out thinking to speak to Mrs. Myra. Maybe something went wrong. Maybe they had a furious argument. Who knows? Mrs. Abigail was badly wounded, badly wronged. I was questioned. I said what I was supposed to say."

"Which was that Abigail had been laid up with a bad migraine?"

Orani shrugged. "Everyone knew she got them from time to time, but she was as strong as an ox. Still is. Don't let the littleness fool you. She was one of the shooting party the day Mr. Christian was killed. Could have been her that put the bullet through his back. Nobody said anything about the fact she is a crack shot."

Isabelle's heart skipped a beat. "You have suspicions about that day as well?"

"Not then. But *now*!" Orani spoke with so much venom, Isabelle felt pinpricks on her skin. "There was enough evidence—just barely, mind you—to indicate an accident. No one would ever think to point a finger at Mrs. Abigail. She was recognised by everyone as a member of the landed gentry. Why would she want to kill her husband? She adored him. She did too until she found out about them."

Isabelle felt vaguely nauseous. "How? Surely they would have been very discreet?"

"We're all too close," said Orani, "if you know what I mean."

Isabelle was amazed she did. By comparison, she had lived a very quiet, even monastic life. "So you spied on them for her?" She kept her voice nonjudgemental.

"I did from time to time," Orani admitted. "Mainly she did the job herself. They couldn't have known what was going on in her mind. She half-scared me. All those smiles and acting like she cared, and behind it maybe murderous thoughts."

"'One can smile and smile and still be a villain,'" Isabelle said, making use of the quote from *Hamlet*.

"Kept them guessin' anyway. If she did confront Mrs. Myra that last day, she wouldn't have been prepared for it. That was the problem for us all. We didn't know the *real* woman. She was kept hidden. She was so *nice* to everyone. So nice to me. Always doing me little favours. Keeping me on her side."

"You should have spoken out, Orani," Isabelle risked saying. "If Abigail wasn't in the house the day Myra had her fatal accident, she didn't have an alibi."

Orani looked away, perhaps guiltily. "Not as though I cared about Mrs. Myra. I could live with her being dead. But I wasn't going to make Mrs. Abigail look bad. She was kind to me. She told me my day would come."

"Like Anne Boleyn."

"Don't know the name." Orani dashed the last tears from her eyes. "Never really knew Mrs. Abigail, did I?"

"No," said Isabelle. "You weren't the only one."

"Did you hear the way she spoke about my mother?" Orani cried, splaying her long fingers across her tear-stained face. "Insane, isn't that what she said? And I'm mentally unstable. She's had those thoughts for a long time." Her expression conveyed a painful surfeit of memories. "She turned me against Helena. She hated her almost as much as she hated Mrs. Myra. She was fragile, that girl, not physically but emotionally. She was living the life I was convinced should have been mine."

"You believed what you were told as a child," Isabelle said. It was her own experience after all.

"And that woman backed it." Orani stared at Isabelle, as though studying her from a new angle. "You're a good person," she said.

"I try to be." Isabelle felt irreparably tangled in Hartmann affairs.

"He did come back after all, you know."

"Who?" Isabelle drew in a sharp breath.

Orani's huge black eyes filled with tears again. She turned away abruptly, her expression sombre in the extreme. "No one. A ghost. I must go. What Mrs. Abigail said was bad for her. Bad for us both. I intend to hold her to account."

Not only the words but the way she said them filled Isabelle with dread. "Mightn't it be best for you to simply forgive, forget and move on? Take nothing from her. Make no attempt to bribe her. It could be a huge mistake. You could possibly be risking your life."

"It's always the quiet ones, isn't it?" Orani said, such an agonized smile on her face. "In my heart, I believe Helena could still be alive. If she is, I hope you find her."

"I have every hope we will," Isabelle declared. "You had a relationship with Erik Hartmann, didn't you? Have you said your good-byes to him?"

Orani shook her head violently. "I could never satisfy him," she said. "Not ever. Not once. I even tried a few love potions. Didn't work. There was only one love in his life and that was his beautiful, adulteress wife. Can't blame her in a way. Christian was the better man. Most likely the better lover. She got her hooks into him. I swear, Erik knew Helena wasn't his daughter. But Erik wouldn't kill anyone. He doesn't have the guts."

"I can't think *guts* is the right word," Isabelle said in horror. "More like a level of brutality and a lack of godliness to be able to take another human being's life. Murder gets people locked up forever."

Orani smiled grimly. "Then Mrs. Abigail has been on death row for a long time."

"There's a good chance she didn't do anything." Isabelle dragged in a breath. "We don't *know.* You didn't help. You could have talked, Orani. You didn't. You chose to keep quiet. Helena suffered the loss of her mother. Probably, as she grew older, doubts sprang into her mind. She was fearful of someone. Not you and your cruel little games. Someone else. Now it's too late for retribution."

"Maybe it is. Maybe it isn't," Orani said. She closed her eyes as though inviting some plan of action to come to her.

"Well, good-bye, Orani," Isabelle managed with quiet compassion. There didn't seem to be anything else to say or do.

"Be a better person than the others," Orani responded, surprising Isabelle by taking her hand. "Don't stop here. Go away. Your Bruno will take you. He can help you sort out your life."

It was a stunning shock to Isabelle, this turn of events; still, she found herself saying, "Go with God, Orani."

The woman's face, a mask of suffering, suddenly

softened. "What did I say? You're a good person. But I go with my gods, not yours."

With that, she walked off, back straight, head up, like a proud, strong woman bound for the gallows.

Bruno returned minutes later, on his own, which was a great relief.

"What is it?" he asked urgently. Isabelle looked as distressed as he had ever seen her.

"I have a bad feeling about all this, Bruno."

"Understandable." He went to her, turned her towards an armchair. "This is one weird family, damn near Gothic. We'll go home tomorrow, okay?"

"Did you pass Orani?" she asked.

"I did. She was weeping, believe it or not."

"She heard everything Abigail had to say," Isabelle told him.

"Oh God!" Bruno dropped into the armchair opposite. "Where was she?"

"Behind the screen, down there at the end of the room." Isabelle gestured. "She came in through the French doors, probably looking for Abigail. None of us noticed her, so she decided to hide behind the screen and listen to what we had to say."

"So she got an earful!" Bruno said grimly.

"She feels bitterly betrayed. Full of anger and hate."

"Well she's no angel, is she? She even tried to frighten you with her stupid pranks."

"She's been brainwashed from childhood, Bruno. She lived her life in a closed environment. Her mother must have been a woman with her head full of dreams."

"Very likely she would have been diagnosed with some

kind of emotional illness," he said. "Orani too. It's a genetic condition, isn't it?"

"Most disorders are. She more or less thought her friendship with Abigail was sacred. Then she heard Abigail speaking of her mother and her with open contempt. That would have been an immense shock. An immense loss of faith. You saw her tears. Orani wouldn't be a woman given to tears."

"Fool that I am, I interpreted her tears as some kind of sadness. I mean, this has been her life. Now she's more or less been kicked out. She went with Mrs. Hartmann. You know what they say, beggars can't be choosers. I'm pretty sure Abigail meant it when she said she would give Orani a good reference and enough money to get her settled. It would be in her own best interests to do so."

"I'm very concerned," Isabelle said. "Orani believes in love potions and spells. They could even work, for all I know. What I do know for sure is that Abigail is in Orani's sights."

"Let's hope she wasn't packing a pistol," Bruno only half-joked. "She's not perfectly sane, that's the problem. Abigail brought it all on herself. Let her sort it out."

Isabelle lifted her eyes to meet Bruno's. "Abigail wasn't in the house the afternoon Myra was killed."

He nodded sharply. "Orani told you of course."

"She said what that great lady told her to say. Abigail didn't have a migraine. She was somewhere on the property. She might have intended to have it out with Myra."

"Easy for things to get out of hand." Bruno made the mental leap. "Abigail mad with jealousy. Myra perhaps mocking her?"

"Abigail was one of the shooting party the day her husband was accidentally shot," Isabelle added.

Bruno answered with a great sigh. "God, I'm speechless."

"Orani said she's a crack shot."

"Now that I do believe. She can even fly a helicopter. She should be taking off by now."

"You don't have a million dollars, do you?" Isabelle asked in a grave voice.

"What's the bet?"

They looked into each other's eyes. "No bets. Something very serious and bad is going to happen," Isabelle found herself predicting. "Orani will put out a hand for far more than a huge cheque. She'll very likely—" She broke off, suddenly jumping out of her chair. "Bruno, I'm afraid."

He too was on his feet. The French doors of the façade were lit up by a red glow. Even from inside the house they heard the explosion, followed by screams and great wailing yells.

"Dear God, it's the chopper. It's down." Bruno felt like his heart was losing vital beats. He held out his hand to Isabelle, taking it in his own.

"I don't want to see this," Isabelle said, her whole body trembling.

"For one solitary moment," Bruno said. "You were one of the last people to talk to Orani. There will be an investigation."

"Does history never stop repeating itself?"

"I'm afraid not."

From the attic windows, they could see the site of destruction. The Moorooka Station helicopter had slammed into the escarpment, bursting into flames. No one could have survived such a horrendous crash.

Isabelle held a hand to her throat. It was aching painfully

with suppressed tears. "It was no accident," she said. "None of them were."

Bruno looked down at her. "You're alive. You're safe," he said. It didn't seem odd to him now that his father had been cut down. His father had gone too far with his investigation and paid the price.

It was a truly horrible day played out in brilliant sunshine. Eaglehawk Station wasn't that remote that emergency services didn't quickly swing into action. Pilot and passenger had been killed on impact, as everyone had feared and expected. An emergency services helicopter had taken the bodies away. It was considered on the face of it a great tragedy. Mrs. Abigail Hartmann was a very experienced pilot, fixed wing and helicopter. She had been flying for years. She was in her late sixties. It was possible she could have suffered a stroke or a heart attack. The two women on board were known to be on excellent terms, despite the difference in their station. An autopsy would be held. Four police officers flew in, no doubt thinking the Hartmann family was cursed. It sometimes happened that way. Look at the Kennedys! Each member of the family was interviewed. After that came Bruno and Isabelle's turn.

So far as Isabelle was concerned, it was all too late for words. She gave an edited version of her last conversation with Mrs. Saunders. Orani. The surviving members of the family had suffered enough. There was no need for the general public to know of the sexual relationship between the housekeeper and Erik Hartmann. No need for them to know Abigail could well have brought about the deaths of her husband and her sister-in-law, his mistress. Bruno too kept silent, even about his suspicions regarding the death of his father. It was thought by both of them that the perpetrator of these crimes had been brought to justice.

"Sadness, such sadness!" Erik Hartmann said that evening when they all came together in the drawing room.

Isabelle could think of nothing to add.

It was Bruno who was thinking of the results of the DNA tests and what they would reveal. He started to speak, but Erik cut him off. "Yes, yes, McKendrick," he said. "If you're very kindly trying to warn me Helena wasn't my daughter, I have to tell you I already know," he cried, looking utterly grey and shattered.

"God Almighty!" Stefan sat, stunned. "So who then was her father?" he asked after a full minute.

"Wake up, Dad!" Kurt suddenly shouted, nearly out of his mind with shock. "My grandfather, Christian. Who else?"

"Stop!" his father roared. "Stop it this minute. Is this true, Erik?" he asked his uncle scarcely less quietly.

Erik didn't look up. He sat hunched.

"It's true, sir," Bruno answered for the broken man, Erik. "The DNA will confirm it."

"So Helena is my half sister?" Stefan shook his head, not in frantic denial but acceptance.

"And *my* auntie," Kurt cried, furious at constantly being treated like a child.

"What did you tell the police?" Stefan asked, ignoring the boy.

"Neither of us spoke about private family matters," Bruno said. "They aren't relevant to today's fatal crash. Isabelle had a final conversation with Mrs. Saunders. Mrs. Saunders confirmed she knew Helena was Christian Hartmann's daughter."

Stefan pondered all this. "She could only have got it from my mother," he said, ageing in front of their eyes.

"Don't go there, Dad," Kurt pleaded, jumping up from his chair and going to stand behind his father. He placed his hands on Stefan's broad shoulders.

"What kind of a man would betray his wife?" Stefan asked, patting his son's hand with one of his own.

"Perhaps Abigail couldn't give him what he wanted," said Erik. "She wasn't much of a mother to you, though we all pretended we thought her perfect." Erik looked across at Bruno with saddened dark eyes. "Your father thought Abigail knew a lot more than she was willing to confide. He had the idea she would have many hidden wounds. They kept in touch," he confided. "She told me that once. I was amazed. Abigail, God rest her soul, was a woman of many secrets. Secrets we hope she took to her end."

"Is Mrs. Saunders involved in this?" Kurt asked, making his fears clear.

Bruno shook his head. "We will never know." So his father had been in touch with Abigail Hartmann? How close to his premature death?

"We will just take this as it comes," Stefan said heavily.

"That will be the way of it, sir," Bruno said respectfully. It was painfully obvious the three Hartmann men were absolutely shattered.

"It means a great deal to us that neither of you told the police of family matters they didn't need to know," Stefan said, taking over from his uncle as head of the family. "Not now, at any rate."

"We still have to find Helena," Isabelle said. "That's *my* quest."

"And ours," Stefan said. "None of us had the slightest

suspicions about my . . . mother," he hesitated painfully. "Helena had to be frightened of someone. She had to have found out something."

"We have a new lead," said Bruno. "Piers Osbourne."

"Heavens no!" Erik jumped on that suggestion promptly. "He went back to England."

"As far as you know," Isabelle said. "Orani said something to me. She said, 'He came back, you know.'"

"Who did?" Kurt asked blankly.

"She said, 'no one, a ghost,' when I questioned her. I believe now she could have been talking about Piers Osbourne."

"Didn't the young fool fancy himself in love with Myra?" Stefan asked. "As I recall, he was a very uppity young man. Acted quite superior. Myra often remarked on it."

"We don't believe he *was* in love with Myra," Bruno said. "We believe he would have grown fond of Helena and she of him. We could suppose both knew of the relationship between Myra and Christian." He didn't mention the loving inscription they had found in the book of German poetry.

"And you think Helena wrote to Osbourne, asking for his help?" Stefan asked.

"He could have been in the country, for all we know."

"Then we find him." It was Kurt, surprisingly, who spoke up.

"We intend to," Bruno said. "I have a good friend, a top journalist, who claims with some truth she can find anyone. As soon as we get back to Sydney, I'll enlist her aid. She's very discreet. Better still, her newspaper has far-reaching resources."

* * *

The family retired early, greatly shocked. The search team would be back early the next morning. The police would have more questions. The news of the fatal crash had already gone out via bush airways. The Stirling family had been contacted. They had pronounced themselves devastated when they had spoken to Abigail about giving up flying at her age. Stefan had contacted his wife in Adelaide. Stunned by the news, she told him she would be flying in as soon as she could get a private flight organised. Life moved on, no matter what.

"I don't want to sleep in the Chinese Room," Isabelle said, feeling as if all her mental and physical strength had drained away and she was running on empty.

"I don't expect you to," Bruno replied. "Will we both be finding some love letters, do you suppose?" In truth, his interest in them had vanished. It had been a terrible day and it had taken its toll on everyone. The family. Him. But all his concerns were focused on Isabelle. She was twenty-two years old. A baby in terms of a full life. Moreover, she had led a sheltered life. She was handling herself extremely well, but no sooner had they learnt one terrible thing than another had popped up.

He had no difficulty with the scenario of Orani accusing Abigail of treachery from the very moment they were airborne. Abigail being Abigail would have revealed her true nature, telling Orani in no uncertain terms to shut her mouth. There would be nothing left to hold Orani back. She had wanted vengeance, just as Abigail had cried out for vengeance against her husband and sister-in-law. His own father had to be quietened. What had he found out? Whatever it was, Abigail had come to know of it. Maybe his father's "accident" had been meant as a warning only? Maybe it was meant to silence him forever. Bruno would never know. It hurt him unbearably. He had so loved and admired his father.

Isabelle was opening the door of the Turkish Room. “We’ll give it an hour,” she said, gritting her teeth. “I don’t want to go to bed. I’m bound to have nightmares after all this.”

“Bound to have a few myself,” Bruno admitted.

“The whole place wants clearing out,” Isabelle said. “Too much history. Too many bad memories. I’m sure a museum would take a lot of this stuff. Or it could be put up for auction. The rugs alone are superb.” She stumbled a little dazedly over the mounds of cushions that lay everywhere. Probably once had provided a love nest?

“Are you sure you want to do this?” Bruno asked, steadying her on her feet. He thought she had lost much-needed weight. Of light, willowy build, she was looking a bit on the fragile side. Courageous as she had shown herself to be, she couldn’t continue to sustain these shocks. He felt guilty now that he had brought her to Eaglehawk. The ghosts of the family members who had died violently were here. Now there was another one.

“What did we get ourselves into, Bruno?” Bella was asking, turning to meet his eyes. No accusation there. A near-despairing question.

“Your family,” he said wryly. “You can thank your lucky stars you weren’t brought up with them.”

“What lucky stars?” She sighed. “Not a whole lot of joy with Hilary and Norville. We have to speak to Hilary again.”

“Would it be all that impossible to switch babies?” Bruno pondered.

A shudder passed through Isabelle. “I wouldn’t put anything past Hilary. Norville wanted a child. Not her.

But she agreed to have one and get it over with. There was never going to be a second. Hilary needed a well-respected husband to add weight to her own position. One who would allow her to lead her double life. For over twenty years she dominated Norville's life. Talk about a monster!"

"So Hilary's baby dies not long after birth and she talks Helena into handing over her baby?" Bruno asked.

"Worse." Isabelle came up with her scenario, seeing they were without a single vital clue. "How's this? Hilary being a doctor realizes something is wrong with her new-born baby. She thinks long and hard, then decides her course. She switches her baby for Helena's. Wrist tags, toe tags, identification, whatever is necessary. Helena's sickly little baby dies. Hilary goes home with me."

"But that's criminal!" Bruno burst out, shocked. "One would have to be a monster to do that."

"Monsters look like everyone else, Bruno. You know that. How many killers out there go unrecognised, unpunished? We see photos. Nothing about the faces suggest what crimes they're capable of. You're going to speak to Cassie when we get back?"

"If she's not on the information highway already," Bruno said. "Cassie will do anything to help you."

"How lovely! It means a lot to me I was able to help Josh and find the right teacher for him. Music unlocks many doors. You saw with your own eyes an autistic child behaving normally when listening to me, then when playing those black and white notes for himself. It's extraordinary really! More should be done. Music has a very powerful effect on us all, even pop music, which isn't my scene. Jazz I do like."

"Thank God for that!" Bruno gave a theatrical sigh. "I have a jazz collection to die for."

"The great Daniel Barenboim, concert pianist and conductor, husband of the late, great Jaqueline du Pré, is said to be a marvellous jazz pianist," Isabelle told him.

"So jazz is *real* music," Bruno said.

"Absolutely."

They were just about ready to give up when Bruno picked up an old Bible he had previously put aside. Both he and Isabelle had been searching out German poems of all kinds. The Bible was in English. This time he opened it up fully. "Hello, just look at this." He turned his head to her. "A nifty little hidey-hole."

Isabelle moved quickly to join him. "A hollowed-out book!" she exclaimed. "They were all the go at one time. You wanted to hide a key, a piece of jewellery, a gold watch, anything fairly small and of value, a hollowed-out book would do. Pretty hard for a burglar to search a library to uncover something the owner wanted kept secret."

"Like a bunch of letters," Bruno said, taking out the letters tied with a narrow red ribbon.

"Another minute and I'm going to start singing 'Amazing Grace,'" Isabelle said. "Please?" She put out her hand to take the little pile of old letters Bruno was holding.

"They're probably from your granddad," Bruno said, passing them over. "To the love of his life, Myra."

Isabelle sank down on an ottoman covered in a striking Turkish fabric. Radiant head down, she read through one page, then the next. The letter was of a very intimate and erotic expression of love and longing. She passed the pages to Bruno, making no attempt to read further.

"I don't think we're meant to see these, Bella," Bruno said after he had read what he considered enough.

"No, we're not." Tears filled Isabelle's eyes. "They really did love each other, didn't they?"

Bruno gave a soft groan. "It was a love that came at a heavy price. Please don't cry, Bella."

"Let me cry," she almost wailed. "It's my turn to cry."

"For the love of God, Bella," he protested. "I can't sit and watch." Dark clouds were moving across his handsome face.

"Okay, I'll stop." Isabelle threw up her arms in defeat. "Seeing you're so desperate to get out of here."

Bruno put out an arm to haul her to her feet. "Let's check on the other bedrooms," he said briskly. "I don't want to sleep here anymore than you want to sleep in the Chinese Room."

"I'm not surprised. We're all alone with the ghosts."

"It's not the ghosts I'm worried about," said Bruno.

One of the bedrooms near the bathroom housed good-sized twin beds with blue quilted-satin coverlets. A small inlaid mahogany desk separated them with a Tiffany style—it could well have been Tiffany, Isabelle thought—table lamp with an alabaster nude, slender arms upraised, standing beneath it.

The matching chair stood against the wall beneath a gilded mirror. Four large botanical prints hung behind the beds. Two on each side. The walls were painted the same duck-egg blue as the beds' coverlets.

"What do you think?" Bruno asked, his voice decidedly on the tense side.

"This should do." Isabelle nodded, sitting on one of the beds and bouncing up and down. "Tell me you won't let me sleep here alone, Bruno? We have the desk between us for propriety. I can think of you as my big brother."

"As if that is ever going to happen," he returned, super-sharp.

Isabelle's green eyes filled with tears again. "Don't jump down my throat. I'm feeling a bit emotional, okay? I need a little time to deal with it. I just don't want to be on my own. I'm not afraid exactly. It's just that my mind and body aren't at peace. Once I would have thought it a bit of fun sleeping in a house that was supposed to be haunted. This one actually is."

He gave a short laugh. "Let's see if they're made up." He pulled the quilted satin coverlet from the other bed.

"There must be a linen closet somewhere," Isabelle said.

"Probably downstairs. I'll go." Bruno half-turned away.

"I'm coming with you."

She looked so young, a vulnerable softness in her expression, a slight quiver to her lovely mouth, that Bruno held out his hand. "Keep your eyes peeled," he said, deliberately injecting humour.

To his relief, Bella laughed.

An hour later, showered, they were ready for bed.

"I take it I'm nearest the door," Bruno said, wondering how the hell he was going to get through the night. There was Bella, so beautiful, so desirable in the other bed, and he couldn't touch her. If there was a humorous side to the situation, he couldn't see it.

"Of course you are, Bruno, my knight in shining armour." She plumped up a pillow.

The lovely, fresh aroma of the native boronias filled the room. Isabelle had elected not to wear her usual night-clothes. She had pulled a cotton kaftan over her head instead. Bruno had decided on a T-shirt and a pair of khaki shorts. Neither had wanted to draw attention to the fact they were sharing a bedroom, however platonically.

Appearing in total control, inside Bruno's whole system was racing. He thought he needed a drink, so he had tossed off a shot of brandy when they were down-stairs. "I'll have what you're having," Bella had said.

"You wouldn't be used to brandy," he said repressively.

"It will help me sleep."

"Ah, I suppose." Though he muttered against it, he gave her less than a shot.

"That tasted awful," she complained, putting down her squat crystal glass.

"I never said it would taste good."

They were safely tucked up in their respective beds with the light from the hallway sconces filtering through the half-closed door. A half hour passed. Bruno, thoroughly awake, thought Bella had fallen asleep until he heard what sounded like the faintest sob.

"You're awake, Bella?" He lifted himself on one elbow, compelled to whisper.

"Of course I'm awake," Isabelle replied crossly. "You're doing a bit of tossing and turning yourself."

"Hard to relax." Having her a few feet away from him was driving him mad.

"Reach out your hand," she said, suddenly sitting up in her bed.

"You want to shake it?" he asked with heavy sarcasm.

"Do it. I want to feel your hand just for a moment," she said softly.

"Ah, Bella," he groaned, extending a long arm across the divide.

She clutched at his warm fingers. "Would you kiss me good night?"

His heart rocked, even as he felt a great surge of excitement. "If I do it once, I mightn't stop." His tone was far from warm. It was harsh.

"You will," she said, full of trust. "Just for once, Bruno, reach out."

"Bella, I don't dare. Don't you know you're in protective custody?"

"It's not an invitation into my bed," she said. "All I'm asking for is a good-night kiss. Is that so hard?"

"You really expect an answer to that?" He could see her small face in the dim amber light, her luminous skin, her delicate, delicious mouth, the masses and masses of soft, curling hair.

"All I'm hoping for is a good-night kiss. I'm not proposing anything else. I deserve it. I've been having an awful time. I want to forget for one blessed moment. I want release. We know each other well enough by now for a good-night kiss."

A woman can tear a man to pieces.

His dad had said that.

The bottled-up forces inside him exploded. Bruno threw off the coverlet so wildly it fell to the floor. He stood up, a tall, powerful male figure, and then came around to the far side of her bed. "There's only so much I can take, Bella," he said sternly, without allowing himself to look down at her.

"You're more than happy to kiss everyone else," she was quick to remind him.

“You might be sorry you said that.” He reached for her, pulled her willowy body right up into his arms, enfolding her. She didn’t resist. Instead, she wrapped her arms around his neck. He could feel her heart beating, the catch in her breathing. The protectiveness he had always felt for her was turning into a driving passion. The drive to take her. She opened her mouth to him and he fell into kissing her, breaking up the unbearable tension. He would have done nothing against her will, but she wanted this as much as he did. He didn’t kiss her once. He kissed her over and over until soft cries came from her.

All at once he couldn’t endure the impossibility of the situation. This was neither the time nor the place to take off the single garment Bella wore, lay her back on the bed and make love to her. Their time would come. He no longer had a single doubt. But not now. For all he knew, he could make her pregnant.

“You were mad to ask me.” He lifted her like a child, putting her back on the coverlet.

She gave a palpitating laugh. One that held thrills in it. “That was as close to heaven as I’ve come,” she exclaimed. “I think you love me a little, Bruno McKendrick.”

“You can tell, can you?” He all but threw himself down on his bed, not even bothering with the quilt.

“Truly, I think I do.”

“Well, you are a beautiful creature,” he said. “You got what you wanted; now go to sleep.”

“Oh, I will!” She drew a deep, appreciative breath, as though what she had prayed for had been granted.

Chapter Nine

They were back in Sydney over a week before the results of the DNA testing came from the laboratory. It was confirmed Isabelle was related by blood to Stefan Hartmann. This was no great surprise. Neither were the findings on Orani Saunders. Her mother's claim that Orani was Konrad Hartmann's love child was no more than a sad and ultimately tragic delusion.

It took longer to test Isabelle's relationship to Hilary Martin from dry saliva, but it was proven Hilary was not Isabelle's biological mother. For almost her entire twenty-two years, Isabelle had been living with a lie. It was decided between them that she and Bruno would confront Hilary and Norville with the laboratory findings. Not that Hilary didn't know the truth. She had just lied. Sometimes pathological liars were hard to spot.

Cassie Taylor had gone full speed ahead tracking down Piers Osbourne, making full use of her far-flung sources and a fair bit of Internet searching. Some of what she found was readily available, if only one had known where to look and who to look under. Cassie had agreed to come over to Bruno's place for an hour, and then she had to get back to work. She had a deadline for her column and she always delivered on time.

"Piers was born Piers Egerton," she told them with unconcealed excitement as they sat around the coffee table. "Osbourne was his mother's maiden name. Lady Mary Osbourne. His father was a member of the British peerage, the fourth Baron Wyndham, having inherited from his childless uncle, the third Baron Wyndham. That was some fourteen years back. His bride was a Miss Helen Stephens. They had two children, fraternal twins, Christopher and Anne."

Cassie had laid the photographs she'd had printed off on the glass-topped table. Several were of Lord Wyndham, a substantial landowner. Several of the twins with their father. None of Lady Wyndham, who was said, however, to be a beauty. It could be concluded Lady Wyndham had red hair because her husband didn't. The twins did.

"Lord and Lady Wyndham spend most of their time at the family estate in Scotland," Cassie said, jabbing a blue nail at a photograph of a stately manor house. *Wyndham Hall.*

"Good grief!" Bruno sat back, momentarily at a loss for words.

"So we know where to find them?" Isabelle said, strongly resisting the urge to burst into tears.

"We do," Cassie said, still amazed by what she had been able to unearth. "The Hartmanns' Piers Osbourne was really Piers Egerton. It's fairly certain he was the one who whisked Helena out of the country."

"He was probably still in the country," Isabelle said.

"He must have fallen in love with Helena but felt she was too young to do anything about it. His solution to his seeming dilemma was to take himself off."

"But obviously they kept in touch," Bruno said, taking Isabelle's hand in his. "You have a real story there, Cass."

"One I don't intend to tell." Cassie stood up with reluctance. She had wanted to stay on. "I have to get back. I'm doing a piece on Muriel Ballinger. Wonderful woman!" Muriel Ballinger had been a prominent Parliamentarian for the last fifteen years of her life and a great advocate for women's rights. "If you're both free Sunday, Ian and I would love to see you, not to mention Josh. You'll be thrilled at his progress on the piano, Isabelle," she said. "You too, Bruno, of course."

"Thank you for everything, Cassie," Bruno said. "You're a national treasure!"

Isabelle reached out for Cassie's hand, kissed her cheek. "Thank you from me, Cassie."

"I think that makes you the Hon. Isabelle Egerton, doesn't it?" Cassie said.

"You're saying Piers is my father?"

"Aren't you?"

"Really, Cassie, we have no proof."

"Go to Scotland," Cassie urged. "I know and pray you'll find the truth there."

They decided to confront Hilary not at home but at the hospital where she did nearly all her surgery. As it was, they had an anxious wait of several hours before their luck was in. A young intern told them where to find her. She was having coffee in the hospital canteen.

They stood for a moment watching a small queue line up for a meal before they decided to join Hilary. She was facing them, her striking face alive with interest in what her companion was saying. Opposite her sat a male colleague. Even from the back one guessed he was in his midforties, most probably good-looking and charming if Hilary's smile was anything to go on.

"Could be her boyfriend," Bruno said beneath his breath.

"Why are you whispering?" Isabelle asked.

"Bella, that's a woman with big ears. She could easily jump up and run away."

"She's not running this time," said Isabelle, surprised by the amount of adrenaline surging through her.

They were almost at Hilary's table before she dragged her eyes away from her companion. Colour flooded into her face. Her eyes sparked. She looked livid.

Isabelle moved forward, unperturbed. "Sorry to interrupt, Hilary. An intern told us where to find you."

Instantly, her male companion stood up, turning to them. "Isabelle, isn't it?" he asked. "Of course it is. Who else is so beautiful?"

Isabelle gave the smiling man her hand. "How are you, Dr. Sommerville? It's a long time."

"Years," he said. "You look wonderfully well."

"I am. May I present my friend, Bruno McKendrick?"

Sommerville couldn't keep the pleasure out of his voice. "That would be the McKendrick of the Fortuna Group?" The two men shook hands.

"It would." Bruno smiled. He had come to the conclusion, based on nothing more than his gut instinct, which was almost always right, that this man had nothing to do with anything. He was merely having coffee with the predatory Hilary.

"If you could give us a moment, Richard," Hilary said, having a struggle injecting normality into her voice. "I haven't seen Isabelle in quite a while."

"Of course." Richard Sommerville was already pulling

back his chair, preparatory to moving off. "Good to meet you, McKendrick. Still studying your cello, Isabelle?"

"I have my Master's degree from the Royal College of Music in London," she said.

"Wonderful, wonderful!"

By the time they sat down, Hilary had almost regained her equilibrium. "How dare you come here?" she asked in a furious undertone. "Confront me like this?"

"We thought you might like to read this," Bruno said, withdrawing the laboratory letter from the inside pocket of his suit jacket.

"And what is that supposed to be?" Hilary asked haughtily, giving the letter a brief glance.

Isabelle found it difficult to remain quiet. "Proof positive you are not my biological mother," she said. "You are, however, a pathological liar!"

Hilary didn't even bother to pick up the letter. "So what?" She shrugged. "Feeling deeply sorry for yourself, are you? Poor little Isabelle who lost her mummy."

"You deliberately falsified the records," Bruno said, looking at Hilary with distaste. "We will make sure this all comes to light. You could be left with your reputation in tatters."

"I doubt that." Hilary was back to looking supremely self-confident.

"The truth will destroy you, Hilary," Isabelle said. "DNA testing proves I'm a Hartmann. Stefan Hartmann supplied a DNA sample, as did I. It's highly likely Helena Hartmann is my mother. We believe, Bruno and I, that you were in the same ward in the London maternity hospital where Helena gave birth to a child. A little girl. Just like you did."

Hilary narrowed her dark eyes. "If you want to blame anyone, blame some idiot nurse at the hospital. My blood pressure was high. I was being sedated. I scarcely knew what was going on. It took time for me to realize you weren't my baby. Helena's baby had, sadly, died."

"So you're saying it was all a terrible accident? You were given the wrong babies by mistake?" Isabelle's hand started to shake. She was no match for Hilary. Hilary was a woman without scruples.

"Try to prove otherwise," Hilary said. "One stupid girl who shouldn't have been a nurse at all screwed up? Mistakes happen. We all know that."

"We don't believe you," Bruno said. "You were a doctor. The staff would have known that. You would have had access to areas where other new mothers might have been denied or supervised. We believe you realized your baby wasn't going to make it, so you stole Helena's baby."

"Just like that!" Hilary threw one hand up.

"Just like that," Isabelle said. "You weren't going to go through another pregnancy. One was bad enough. You didn't carry well. Helena was young. She could have more babies. She would be upset for a time, but she would get over it. That would be your thinking."

Hilary sucked in her breath. "You're mad."

"No, I'm not mad. I'm *right.* I know you, Hilary. I've had a lifetime to study you. You don't care about anyone but yourself. You don't recognise another's pain."

Hilary didn't bat an eyelid. "There's no point in going over this. It is as I told you. A tragic mistake. I'm prepared to swear that before God."

"You don't believe in Him either," Isabelle said. "He may forgive you. I don't. We're going to find Helena. We know where to look."

"She's dead," Hilary said flatly.

"You've been taken in for a change, Hilary," Bruno said. "Helena is very much alive."

Hilary's face whitened. "It was an accident. The hospital would have covered it up."

"Norville still thinks you're my biological mother," Isabelle said. "Set him straight or I will. You've destroyed a good man."

"Whatever you say, Norville will stand by me," Hilary declared as a given fact.

"You sound a bit uncertain," Bruno said.

"Norville is witness to the fact I brought you home as my child. I did everything possible for you. You were well looked after all your life. You wanted for nothing. Now you've turned traitor. Go to any lengths you like; you will never prove I switched babies."

"But you did, didn't you?" Isabelle stared into the older woman's eyes. "You didn't care about the massive trauma Helena was about to have. You *needed* a live baby."

Hilary sat bolt upright. "Go away before I call security," she hissed. "I'll have you arrested."

"Nonsense!" Bruno said briskly. "We could hand over this letter you don't want to read. You've known the contents for over twenty years, Dr. Martin. I don't think your long-suffering husband will be too pleased if and when he hears the true story. You can't forget he too knows you. Knows what you're capable of."

A security guard actually arrived at their table, apparently alerted by Hilary's loud voice. "Everything okay here, Dr. Martin?" he asked with considerable deference.

Isabelle gave the guard a sad smile. "Some upsetting family news," she explained.

Hilary was forced into nodding.

"Sorry to hear that, Doctor," the guard said and quickly moved off.

Hilary leaned forward, making sure she spoke clearly. "If I were you, I'd think long and hard before opening up Pandora's box. The hospital made a regrettable mistake. It took me a very long time before I realized what had happened."

"And me with my *red hair*?" Isabelle shot back. "You *knew* I was Helena's."

"Sorting out these cases can prove a very harrowing business," Hilary warned. "Some secrets are best kept just that. Secret."

"It's a bit more complicated than that, Doctor," Bruno said. "It will be for Helena to decide."

"Her baby is no less dead," said the callous, unrepentant woman who was Hilary.

Days went by after the upsetting discussion with Hilary. Isabelle had to put it all behind her as an important audition was coming up—a chance for a place with the Symphony Orchestra.

On the suggestion of a violinist friend, she had made a tape and sent it off some weeks back. Apparently, whoever had heard it was impressed enough to grant her an audition. She thought she might cancel, only she knew that was a very bad idea. Her not turning up would be remembered. It was her long-established habit to practise for a couple of hours daily. She was out of practise, but within an hour or two the tension fell away. She thought her playing acceptable enough to be judged. She had chosen the Elgar because she knew it so well. She had won the award in Belgium playing the Elgar.

She had received a letter from James Kellerman,

advising her she had lost her place with the quartet. It upset her for a moment. Then it was a relief. She actually thought he needed her more than she needed him. She had an idea to form a trio of her own.

The audition went well.

"An extraordinarily beautiful sound," she overheard one of the judges, an eminent musician, say, and her face lit with pleasure. "A serious, concentrated musician."

She had to tell Bruno. She almost set off there and then but remembered Bruno had come back to a lot of work and some necessary decision-making. She could wait until evening. She had bought a lovely new dress especially for him. Yellow. The colour of sunshine.

Around seven she set off. She could think of nothing but seeing him. He knew about her audition. She had fully expected him to ring her. She would beat him to it. A couple were coming out of his building. They smiled at her. She smiled back, slipping in past them, amazed it was so easy. Either they had caught sight of her with Bruno or they thought her no one to worry about.

She stood outside his door, knocking lightly on it. Bruno! She had given her heart into his hands. She felt they were in total harmony. It was the most wonderful feeling in the world. They surely were meant for each other. Why else had Fate brought them together?

A moment passed. The door opened.

She felt great, coursing humiliation flooding through her entire being.

It was Penelope, Super Sam's daughter. She was wearing a sparkling short dress and a brilliant smile that didn't falter. "Why, it's Isabelle, isn't it, the cellist?" she asked in pleased surprise. "Are you coming in? Bruno and I are off to a function in about five minutes. But no matter! Do you want me to get him for you? He's taking an important overseas call."

"No, actually I won't bother him," Isabelle said. "It will keep."

"You sure?" Penelope asked kindly, looking doubtful about letting her go.

"Quite sure." Isabelle turned away, doing a very good job of hiding her stunning shock. "Enjoy yourselves," she called over her shoulder. She wouldn't let the mask slip until she got home. From elation, eager to talk about her afternoon, she felt only wretchedness. It was her own fault. She had let herself believe what she wanted to believe. The same old story. She had even dressed for him. How stupid!

She was almost at the elevator before Bruno came charging out the door and down the hallway. "Bella," he called with enough urgency to stop her.

"Sorry," she said. Her every instinct was to run away.

Like a miracle the lift arrived, but before she could step in, Bruno grabbed her none too gently, sweeping her off her feet and pushing her back against the wall. "Where do you think you're going?" His brilliant eyes blazed with sparks of light.

"Home," she said, equally fiercely. "I came to tell you about my audition. I can't think why."

"I was trying to ring you."

"I forgot my mobile."

"What made you run off?" He eased his powerful hold on her.

"You're going to a function with Penelope What's-her-name, aren't you? She said you were off in five minutes. You don't look dressed for a function to me." He was wearing a stylish business shirt and suit trousers, but his tie had been removed.

"What bloody function?" he asked angrily.

"You marry Penelope and you'll get your just deserts," she warned. She was near spent. "Let me go, Bruno."

"Marry her? Forget it. I'd never let you go." He lifted her in a tight grip. "I love you." He kissed her with a passion that left her breathless. "You don't mind, do you? I love you, Bella. I've loved you from the moment I laid eyes on you."

"You do?" She was flushed, confused, enraptured.

"I do."

"Then what are you doing with Penelope Pfeiffer?"

He cupped her face, said, "Forget Penelope, Bella." His deepening tone couldn't have been more loverlike.

"I will if she never darkens your door again." She broke off hastily as Penelope walked elegantly towards them.

"Good night, you two," Penelope said playfully, as though they were the best of friends.

"Good night to you too, Pen," Bruno said too smoothly.

"It was a nice try, but it didn't work," Penelope said.

"No hard feelings." There was a sardonic curve to Bruno's handsome mouth.

"So you've found the love of your life?" Penelope just managed not to sound crushed.

"The answer is yes. It's bound to get out."

"How will Marta feel?" she asked, as though Marta's favour was important.

"Marta will assure me I've made the right choice," Bruno said gently. And he laughed. He hugged Isabelle close. "And I'm the luckiest guy in the world."

"Well, I'm happy for you both, then." Penelope moved past them and stepped into the waiting lift.

Bruno put his arm around Isabelle's waist leading her

back to his apartment. "Ivan and Marta have been good to me."

"They have. They're your friends. They'll be my friends too. In the end, all they want is to see you happily married, Bruno."

He bent to kiss her, wrapping his arms around her. "I think we can manage that, don't you?"

Isabelle looked up at him, her face reflecting her joy. "I'm sure of it," she said.

"So that's settled." Bruno took her hand, raising it to his lips. "By the way," his highly appreciative dark eyes ran over her, "I love your dress, Bella *mia.* I want to take you out."

"Lovely!" said Isabelle. "I bought it especially for you."

Epilogue

Four months later . . .

They spent several idyllic weeks of their honeymoon in Europe. Paris first, then Rome, on to Florence to take in as much of the Uffizi as they could, ending their whirlwind tour in Venice, Queen of the Adriatic. It was time to return to their base in London and from there make the trip to the Scottish Borders in the hope of finally meeting up with Helena.

Although they had agreed they wanted a smallish wedding with only close friends, it hadn't turned out that way. There just had been too many people who would have been devastated not to be included in the celebrations. Stefan Hartmann had given Isabelle away. His very stylish wife, Robyn, had taken him in hand. Primped and polished, beautifully dressed in the updated formalwear the bridegroom had chosen for the wedding party: long black dress coat, double-breasted waistcoats in a colour of their choice, dark grey trousers, dress shirt and tie. Stefan had cut a fine figure.

Stefan and Robyn's daughter Kimberley, Isabelle's new found cousin, had been thrilled to be asked to be one of the two bridesmaids, the other Isabelle's best friend at the Royal College. Bruno had taken care of all Marianne's expenses, flying her in. Cassie had acted as matron of honour. Bruno's great friend from university days had been his best man. Kurt had acted as a groomsman. Several of Bruno's team happily took over the role of ushers. Bruno's wedding was a great excitement for all of them. They all thoroughly approved of his beautiful bride.

Marta Lubrinski couldn't be kept entirely out of it. No way! She had set her heart on arranging the reception at the Lubrinski mansion, so both Isabelle and Bruno gave way on the condition that she run all her splendid ideas past Isabelle. In no time at all, Marta had found she was able to love Bruno's most beautiful and talented bride. Isabelle had even asked her opinion of the wedding dress, to be made by a top designer house. The most exquisite, delicate white lace over taffeta. A strapless gown with a sweetheart neckline and a wide taffeta cummerbund to show off Isabelle's tiny waist. Marta had pronounced it perfect for a young bride.

The evening before the wedding, Bruno had presented his bride with his wedding gift. It was a time of high emotion for them both. His gift took Isabelle's breath away. An emerald and diamond pendant necklace and earrings to match her lovely engagement ring. Even Isabelle, who had never focused on her looks, thought she looked radiant on her wedding day. It was a day that would forever be remembered by all who had had the good fortune to attend. Weddings were known to work magic. Bruno and Isabelle McKendrick's wedding was judged more magical than most. It was such an uplifting feeling to see two people so much in love.

It was a cloudy day with intermittent grey drifts of rain, more like drizzle to anyone born and bred in Australia. They had hired a 4WD in Edinburgh, and now they were in Sir Walter Scott Country. They had taken in his favourite view overlooking the River Tweed valley. Lord and Lady Wyndham's country seat, which stood by the Tweed, would be their final destination.

"Does it ever stop raining?" Bruno asked, his eyes narrowing against the rain spatter on the windscreen.

"The short answer to that, dearest husband, is *no.* That's why it's so lovely and *green.* I think I can spot a patch of blue," she said hopefully. "With any luck, the sun will come out. I always feel better when the sun is shining like at home."

They had left the upland hills behind now they were driving through a spectacular all-shades-of-green valley.

"Nervous?" Bruno asked. His own nerves were churning. If things didn't appear welcoming, they would leave. He wasn't going to have Bella upset.

"Of course," she breathed. "Though they mightn't even be there."

"Most probably are," Bruno said. "Like a lot of the grand country homes, they've had to open up parts of the house and gardens to cover the huge maintenance costs. They probably run various events as well."

"What am I going to say?" Isabelle asked rather desperately.

Bruno reached out to place his hand over hers. "I don't think you'll have to say anything. Your face will do the talking."

"We believe I'm Lady Helena's daughter stolen in infancy?"

"We do. If we're blessed with a meeting, we let Helena take the lead."

"Of course."

"What will she do when she hears my story?" Isabelle asked with a quiver in her voice.

"Up to her, my darling. She's either going to believe the accidental swap was made by the hospital or take it further."

"That would shake a lot of people up," Isabelle said. "Most of all Hilary, though she will stick to her story to the death."

"Or go to jail. We still don't know why neither Helena nor Piers ever contacted her family."

"I expect if we're lucky we'll find out. They must have had a good reason. Maybe Abigail?"

"Most probably. Whatever happens, you and I are going to have a wonderful life together, Bella *mia.* I'm going to do everything in my power to make that possible."

She turned her head to smile. "I love you, Bruno McKendrick."

"I love you too, Isabella McKendrick," Bruno said. It was a declaration that came from the bottom of his heart.

They passed through the huge gates of the estate, with their enormous pillars, a lodgelike building to the right, coming on the house through a long tunnel of trees with wonderful open woodlands, oaks, ash, sycamores, with slopes of spring flowers to either side. One huge area was carpeted in blue bells. Another, yellow daffodils.

"May in the British Isles! It's an enchanting sight."

The beauty around her was calming Isabelle's nerves. She couldn't help comparing Eaglehawk's home compound with the entry to Wyndham Manor. The one set down in the remote desert heart of the continent, the other a magnificent green woodland sown with flowers. They could see as they approached the eighteenth-century house walls of glorious blood-red rhododendrons in full flower half-tucking out of sight the various outbuildings with signs posted outside.

"We're here now," Bruno said in a perfectly calm and composed voice. He didn't park near the outbuildings, as Isabelle had expected. He ran the 4WD right into the great courtyard that fronted the four-story house with a city of chimneys atop, its portico held up by six huge columns.

"Ready, my love?" Bruno asked, unclipping his seat belt.

"I'm ready for anything with you by my side." Isabelle met his dark eyes, her pride and trust in him apparent.

A young girl was watching them from the top of the stairs. She was wearing riding gear. The sun had come out, lighting up the clouds of Isabelle's titian hair. Almost hesitantly, the girl, in her early teens, came down the stone steps. Her hair shone a glossy red, woven into a thick pigtail that hung down her back.

The girl shaded her eyes. "Do you have an invitation?" she asked politely, clearly surprised to see them.

Bruno answered in his usual charming manner. "I'm Bruno McKendrick. This is my wife, Isabella. We were hoping to see Lady Wyndham."

"We've come a long way," said Isabelle. "From Australia. But I was born in England."

"Australia?" The girl's lips trembled.

"Who is it, darling?" A tall, slender woman, also in

riding dress, moved from the entrance hall out into the portico.

The girl's eyes darted back to her mother, who came down the steps, a look of intense concentration fixed on Isabelle. It was obvious the closer she came, the more deeply she was affected.

In a dreamlike state, Isabelle moved off towards the beautiful woman who now appeared on the verge of collapse. She caught the woman in her arms, saying over and over, "Helena. Helena, Helena. It's *you*! I think I got stolen from you in the hospital where you gave birth to me. Another baby was switched into my place."

The young girl turned her eyes on Bruno. "Who *is* Isabelle?" she cried. "Why does she look so much like my mother?"

Bruno didn't hesitate. "We are hoping she's your long-lost sister," he said.

"Really?" The girl's voice rose in astonishment. She was greatly struck by the fact that her mother and the young woman from Australia were hugging each other as though they would never let go. She gave Bruno's words due consideration. She knew her mother was from Australia. She also knew her mom had had a baby before she was born and her mother's heart had been broken when the baby died. Maybe she didn't die . . . "I can live with that," she said finally, giving Bruno the sweetest smile.

Her mother turned, the beautiful young woman who looked so much like her mother and she too for that matter, turned towards her as well. They waved, clearly inviting her into the circle of their arms.

Bruno watched the young girl run to join them.

No explanations appeared necessary. This was his idea of the power of blood. Of recognition. A *knowing* that needed no words. It had taken over twenty years, but they had found Helena. He knew his beloved father, Ross, could rest in peace. He would eventually go back and investigate his father's death. He believed Abigail had been behind it.

Lady Wyndham called to him, her beautiful face aglow. She was clearly in a state of euphoria, as was his adored wife. "Bruno, Bruno, please join us. We're going into the house. You must stay with us." The words came out with absolute joy.

And afterwards, Bruno thought, they would talk, and uncover the mystery that had surrounded Helena's departure from Australia. But he pretty much knew the answers—fear for her life, and she had left with the love of her life.

She who had been lost was now found.

Mallory knew the route to Forrester Base Hospital as well as she knew the lines on the palms of her hands. She had never had the dubious pleasure of having her palm read, but she had often wondered whether palmistry was no more than superstition, or if there was something to it. Her life line showed a catastrophic break, and one had actually occurred. If she read beyond the break, she was set to receive a card from the Queen when she turned one hundred. As it was, she was twenty-eight. There was plenty of time to get her life in order and find some happiness. Currently her life was largely devoted to work. She allowed herself precious little free time. It was a deliberate strategy. Keep on the move. Don't sit pondering over what was lodged in the soul.

The driver of the little Mazda ahead was starting to annoy her. He was showing excessive respect for the speed limit, flashing his brake lights at every bend in the road. She figured it was time to pass, and was surprised when the driver gave her a loud honk for no discernible reason. She held up her hand, waved. A nice little gesture of camaraderie and goodwill.

She was almost there, thank the Lord. The farther she had travelled from the state capital, Brisbane, the more the drag on her emotions. That pesky old drag would never go away. It was a side effect of the baggage she carted around and couldn't unload. It wasn't that she didn't visualize a brave new world. It was just that so far it hadn't happened. Life was neither kind nor reasonable. She knew that better than most. She also knew one had to fight the good fight even when the chances of getting knocked down on a regular basis were high.

It had been six years and more since she had been back to her hometown. She wouldn't be returning now, she acknowledged with a stab of guilt, except for the unexpected heart attack of her uncle Robert. Her uncle, a cultured, courtly man, had reared her from age seven. No one else had been offering. Certainly not her absentee father, or her maternal grandparents, who spent their days cruising the world on the *Queen Mary 2*. True, they did call in to see her whenever they set foot on dry land, bearing loads of expensive gifts. But sadly, they were unable to introduce a child into their busy lives. She was the main beneficiary of their will. They had assured her of that; a little something by way of compensation. She was, after all, their only grandchild. It was just at seven, she hadn't fit into their lifestyle. Decades later she still didn't.

Was it any wonder she loved her uncle Robert? He was her superhero. Handsome, charming, well off. A bachelor by choice. Her dead mother, Claudia, had captured his heart long ago when they were young and deeply in love. Her mother had gone to her grave with her uncle's heart still pocketed away. It was an extraordinary thing and in many ways a calamity, because Uncle Robert had never considered snatching his life back. He was a lost cause in the marriage stakes. As was she, for that matter.

To fund what appeared on the surface to be a glamorous lifestyle, Robert James had quit law to become a very popular author of novels of crime and intrigue. The drawing card for his legions of fans was his comedic detective, Peter Zero, never as famous as the legendary Hercule Poirot, but much loved by the readership.

Pulp fiction, her father, Nigel James, Professor of English and Cultural Studies at Melbourne University, called it. Her father had always stomped on his older brother's talent. "Fodder for the ignorant masses to be read on the train." Her father never minced words, the crueller the better. To put a name to it, her father was an all-out bastard.

It was Uncle Robert who had spelled love and a safe haven to her. He had taken her to live with him at Moonglade, his tropical hideaway in far North Queensland. In the infamous "blackbirding" days, when South Sea islanders had been kidnapped to work the Queensland cane fields, Moonglade had been a thriving sugar plantation. The house had been built by one Captain George Rankin, who had at least fed his workers bananas, mangoes, and the like and paid them a token sum to work in a sizzling hot sun like the slaves they were.

Uncle Robert had not bought the property as a working plantation. Moonglade was his secure retreat from the world. He could not have chosen a more idyllic spot, with two listed World Heritage areas on his doorstep: the magnificent Daintree Rainforest, the oldest living rainforest on the planet, and the glorious Great Barrier Reef, the world's largest reef system.

His heart attack had come right out of the blue. Her uncle had always kept himself fit. He went for long walks along the white sandy beach, the sound of seagulls in his ears. He swam daily in a brilliantly blue sea, smooth as glass. To no avail. The truth was, no one knew what might happen next. The only certainty in life was death. Life was a circus; fate the ringmaster. Her uncle's illness demanded her presence. It was her turn to demonstrate her love.

Up ahead was another challenge. A procession of undertakers? A line of vehicles was crawling along as though they had all day to get to their destination. Where the heck *was* that? There were no shops or supermarkets nearby, only the unending rich red ochre fields lying fallow in vivid contrast with the striking green of the eternal cane. Planted in sugarcane, the North was an area of vibrant colour and great natural beauty. It occurred to her the procession might be heading to the cemetery via the South Pole.

Some five minutes later she arrived at the entrance to the hospital grounds. There was nothing to worry about, she kept telling herself. She had been assured of that by none other than Blaine Forrester, who had rung her with the news. She had known Blaine since her childhood. Her uncle thought the world of him. Fair to say Blaine was the son he never had. She *knew* she came first with her uncle, but his affection for Blaine, five years her senior, had always ruffled her feathers. She was *more* than Blaine, she had frequently reminded herself. He was the only son of good friends and neighbours. She was *blood.*

Blaine's assurances, his review of the whole situation, hadn't prevented her from feeling anxious. In the end Uncle Robert was all the family she had. Without him she would be alone.

Entirely alone.

The main gates were open, the entry made splendid by

a pair of poincianas in sumptuous scarlet bloom. The branches of the great shade trees had been dragged down into their perfect umbrella shape by the sheer weight of the annual blossoming. For as far back as she could remember, the whole town of Forrester had waited for the summer flowering, as another town might wait for an annual folk festival. The royal poinciana, a native of Madagascar, had to be the most glorious ornamental tree grown in all subtropical and tropical parts of the world.

"Pure magic!" she said aloud.

It was her spontaneous response to the breathtaking display. Nothing could beat nature for visual therapy. As she watched, the breeze gusted clouds of spent blossom to the ground, forming a deep crimson carpet.

She parked, as waves of uncomplicated delight rolled over her. She loved this place. North of Capricorn was another world, an artist's dream. There had always been an artist's colony here. Some of the country's finest artists had lived and painted here, turning out their glorious land- and seascapes, scenes of island life. Uncle Robert had a fine body of their work at the house, including a beautiful painting of the district's famous Poinciana Road that led directly to Moonglade Estate. From childhood, poincianas had great significance for her. Psychic balm to a child's wounded heart and spirit, she supposed.

Vivid memories clung to this part of the world. The Good. The Bad. The Ugly. Memories were like ghosts that appeared in the night and didn't disappear at sunrise as they should. She knew the distance between memory and what really happened could be vast. Lesser memories were susceptible to reconstruction over the years. It was the *worst* memories one remembered best. The worst became deeply embedded.

Her memories were perfectly clear. They set her on

edge the rare times she allowed them to flare up. Over the years she had developed many strategies to maintain her equilibrium. Self-control was her striking success. It was a marvellous disguise. One she wore well.

A light, inoffensive beep of a car horn this time brought her out of her reverie. She glanced in the rear-vision mirror, lifting an apologetic hand to the woman driver in the car behind her. She moved off to the parking bays on either side of the main entrance. Her eyes as a matter of course took in the variety of tropical shrubs, frangipani, spectacular Hawaiian hibiscus, and the heavenly perfumed oleanders that had been planted the entire length of the perimeter and in front of the bays. Like the poincianas, their hectic blooming was unaffected by the powerful heat. Indeed the heat only served to produce more ravishing displays. The mingled scents permeated the heated air like incense, catching at the nose and throat.

Tropical blooming had hung over her childhood; hung over her heart. High summer: hibiscus, heartbreak. She kept all that buried. A glance at the dash told her it was two o'clock. She had made good time. Her choice of clothing, her usual classic gear, would have been just right in the city. Not here. For the tropics she should have been wearing simple clothes, loose, light cotton. She was plainly overdressed. No matter. Her dress sense, her acknowledged stylishness, was a form of protection. To her mind it was like drawing a velvet glove over shattered glass.

Auxiliary buildings lay to either side of the main structure. There was a large designated area for ambulances only. She pulled into the doctors' parking lot. She shouldn't have parked there, but she excused herself on the grounds there were several other vacant spots. The car that had been behind her had parked in the visitors' zone. The occupant was already out of her vehicle, heading towards the front doors at a run.

"Better get my skates on," the woman called, with a friendly wave to Mallory as she passed. Obviously she was late, and by the look of it expected to be hauled over the coals.

There were good patients. And terrible patients. Mallory had seen both. Swiftly she checked her face in the rearview mirror. Gold filigrees of hair were stuck to her cheeks. Deftly she brushed them back. She had good, thick hair that was carefully controlled. No casual ponytail but an updated knot as primly elegant as an Edwardian chignon. She didn't bother to lock the doors, but made her way directly into the modern two-storied building.

The interior was brightly lit, with a smell like fresh laundry and none of the depressing clinical smells and the long, echoing hallways of the vast, impersonal city hospitals. The walls of the long corridor were off-white and hung with paintings she guessed were by local artists. A couple of patients in dressing gowns were wandering down the corridor to her left, chatting away brightly, as if they were off to attend an in-hospital concert. To her right a young male doctor, white coat flying, clipboard in hand, zipped into a room as though he didn't have a second to lose.

There was a pretty, part-aboriginal young nurse stationed at reception. At one end of the counter was a large Oriental vase filled with beautiful white, pink-speckled Asian lilies. Mallory dipped her head to catch their sweet, spicy scent.

"I'm here to see a patient, Robert James," she said, smiling as she looked up.

"Certainly, Dr. James." Bright, cheerful, accommodating.

She was known. How?

An older woman with a brisk, no-nonsense air of authority, hurried towards reception. She too appeared pleased to see Mallory. Palm extended, she pointed off along the corridor. "Dr. Moorehouse is with Mr. James. You should be able to see him shortly, Dr. James. Would you like a cup of tea?"

Swiftly Mallory took note of the name tag. "A cup of tea would go down very nicely, Sister Arnold."

"I'll arrange it," said Sister. Their patient had a photograph of this young woman beside his bed. He invited everyone to take a look. *My beautiful niece, Mallory. Dr. Mallory James!*

Several minutes later, before she'd even sat down, Mallory saw one splendid-looking man stride up to reception. Six feet and over. Thoroughbred build. Early thirties. Thick head of crow-black hair. Clearly not one of the bit players in life.

Blaine!

The mere sight of him put her on high alert. Though it made perfect sense for him to be there, she felt her emotions start to bob up and down like a cork in a water barrel. For all her strategies, she had never mastered the knack of keeping focused with Blaine around. He knew her too well. That was the problem. He knew the number of times she had made a complete fool of herself. He knew all about her disastrous engagement. Her abysmal choice of a life partner. He had always judged her and found her wanting. Okay, they were friends, having known one another forever, but there were many downsides to their difficult, often stormy relationship. She might as well admit it. It was mostly her fault. So many times over the years she had been as difficult as she could be. It was a form of retaliation caused by a deep-seated grudge.

Blaine knew all about the years she had been under the care of Dr. Sarah Matthews, child psychologist and a leader in her field. The highly emotional, unstable years. He knew all about her dangerous habit of sleepwalking. Blaine knew far too much. Anyone would resent it. He wasn't a doctor, yet he knew her entire case history. For all that, Blaine was a man of considerable charisma. What was charisma anyway? she had often asked herself. Was one born with it or was it acquired over time? Did charismatic people provoke a sensual experience in everyone they met? She thought if they were like Blaine the answer had to be yes. One of Blaine's most attractive qualities was his blazing energy. It inspired confidence. Here was a man who could and did get things done.

Blaine was a big supporter of the hospital. He had property in all the key places. The Forrester family had made a fortune over the generations. They were descendants of George Herbert Forrester, an Englishman, already on his way to being rich before he left the colony of New South Wales to venture into the vast unknown territory which was to become the State of Queensland in 1859. For decades on end, the Forresters pretty well owned and ran the town. Their saving grace was that as employers they were very good to their workers, to the extent that everyone, right up to the present day, considered themselves part of one big happy Forrester family and acted accordingly.

She heard him speak to the nurse at reception. He had a compelling voice. It had a special quality to it. It exactly matched the man. She saw his aura. Her secret: She was able to see auras. Not of everyone. That would have been beyond anyone's ability to cope with. But *certain* people. Good and bad. She saw Blaine's now. The energy field that surrounded him was the familiar cobalt blue. She knew these auras were invisible to most people. She had no idea why she should see them, *feel* them, as *heat* waves. The gift, if it was one, hadn't been developed over the years. It had just always been there.

Once, to her everlasting inner cringe, she had confided her secret to Blaine. She was around fourteen at the time. There he was, so handsome, already making his mark, home from university. She remembered exactly where they were, lazing in the sun, down by Moonglade's lake. The moment she had stopped talking, he had propped himself up on his elbow, looking down at her with his extraordinary silver eyes.

"You're having me on!"
"No, I swear."
He burst out laughing. "Listen, kid. I'm cool with all your tall tales and celestial travels, but we both know auras don't exist."
"They do. They do exist."

Her rage and disappointment in him had known no bounds. She had entrusted him with her precious secret and he, her childhood idol, had laughed her to scorn. No wonder she had gone off like a firecracker.

"Don't you dare call me a liar, Blaine Forrester. I see auras. I've seen your aura lots of times. Just because you can't see them doesn't mean they're not there. You're nothing but an insensitive, arrogant pig!"

He had made her *so* angry that even years later she still felt residual heat. She had wanted him to listen to her, to share. Instead he had ridiculed her. It might have been that very moment their easy, affectionate relationship underwent a dramatic sea change. Blaine, the friend she had so looked up to and trusted, had laughed at her. Called her a kid. She *did* see auras, some strong, some dim. It had something to do with her particular brain. One day, science would prove the phenomenon. In the meantime she continued to see auras that lasted maybe half a minute before they faded. Blaine-the-unbeliever's aura was as she had told him all those years ago, a cobalt blue. Uncle Robert's was pale green with a pinkish area over his heart. She couldn't see her own aura. She had seen her dying mother's black aura. Recognised what it meant. She had seen that black aura a number of times since.

A moment more and Blaine was making his way to the waiting room. Mercifully this one was empty, although Mallory could hear, farther along the corridor, a woman's voice reading a familiar children's story accompanied by children's sweet laughter. How beautiful was the laughter of children, as musical as wind chimes.

As Blaine reached the doorway she found herself standing up. Why she did was beyond her. The pity of it was she felt the familiar, involuntary flair of *excitement*. She was stuck with that, sadly. It would never go away. She extended her hand, hoping her face wasn't flushed. Hugs and air-kisses were long since out of the question between them. Yet, as usual, all her senses were on point. "Blaine."

"Mallory." He gave her a measured look, his fingers curling around hers. With a flush on her beautiful skin she looked radiant. Not that he was about to tell her. Mallory had no use whatever for compliments.

The mocking note in his voice wasn't lost on Mallory. She chose to ignore it. From long experience she was prepared for physical contact, yet as always she marvelled at the *charge*. It was pretty much like a mild electric shock. She had written it off as a case of static electricity. Physics. With his height, he made her willowy five feet eight seem petite. That gave him an extra advantage. His light grey eyes were in startling contrast to his hair and darkly tanned skin. Sculpted features and an air of sharp intelligence and natural authority made for an indelible impression. From long experience she knew Blaine sent women into orbit. It made her almost wish she was one of them. She believed the intensity of his gaze owed much to the luminosity of his eyes. Eyes like that would give anyone a jolt.

He gestured towards one of the long upholstered benches, as though telling her what to do. She *hated* that, as well. It was like he always knew the best course of action. She realized her reactions were childish, bred from long years of resenting him and his high-handed, taken-for-granted sense of superiority, but childish nevertheless. No one was perfect. He should have been kinder.

Blaine was fully aware of the war going on inside Mallory. He knew all about her anxieties, her complexities. He had first met her when she was seven, a pretty little girl with lovely manners. Mallory, the adult, was a woman to be reckoned with. Probably she would be formidable in old age. Right now, she was that odd combination of incredibly sexy and incredibly aloof. There was nothing even mildly flirtatious about her. Yet she possessed powers that he didn't understand. He wondered what would happen if she ever let those powers fly.

She was wearing a very stylish yellow jacket and skirt. City gear. Not a lot of women could get away with the colour. Her luxuriant dark gold hair was pulled back into some sort of knot. Her olive skin was flawless, her velvet-brown eyes set at a faint tilt. Mallory James was a beautiful woman, like her tragic mother before her. Brains and beauty had been bred into Mallory. Her academic brilliance had allowed her to take charge of her life. She had a PhD in child psychology. Close containment had become Mallory's way of avoiding transient sexual relationships and deep emotional involvement. Mallory made it very plain she was captain of her own ship.

The aftershock of their handshake was still running up Mallory's arm to her shoulder. She seized back control. She had spent years perfecting a cool façade. By now it was second nature. Only Blaine, to her disgust, had the power to disrupt her habitual poise. Yet there was something *real* between them; some deep empathy that inextricably tied them together. He to her, she to him. She was aware of the strange disconnect between their invariably charged conversations and a *different* communication she refused to investigate.

"I'm worried about Uncle Robert," she said briskly. She supposed he could have interpreted it as accusatory. "You told me it was a *mild* heart attack, Blaine. I thought he would be home by now. Yet he's still in hospital."

"He's in for observation, Mallory. No hurry." *Here we go again*, he thought.

"Anything else I should know?" She studied him coolly. The handsomeness, the glowing energy, the splendid physique.

"Ted will fill you in."

"So there's nothing you can tell me?" Her highly sensitive antennae were signalling there was more to come.

"Not really." His light eyes sparkled in the rays of sunlight that fell through the high windows.

"So why do I have this feeling you're keeping something from me?"

Blaine nearly groaned aloud. As usual she was spot-on, only he knew he had to work his way up to full disclosure. "Mallory, it's essential to Robb's recovery for you to be *here,* not in Brisbane. He's slowed down of recent times, but he never said there was anything to worry about. It now appears he has a heart condition. Angina."

"But he never told me." She showed her shock and dismay.

"Nor me. Obviously he didn't want it to be known."

Without thinking, she clutched his arm as if he might have some idea of walking away from her. He was wearing a short-sleeved cotton shirt, a blue-and-white check, with his jeans, so she met with suntanned, warm skin and hard muscle. She should have thought of that. Blaine had such physicality it made her stomach contract. He further rattled her by putting his hand on top of hers.

"You believe I have a moral obligation to look out for my uncle as he looked after me?"

"I'm not here to judge you, Mallory," he said smoothly.

"Never mind about that. I'm always under surveillance." Blaine had established the habit of meeting up with her whenever he was in Brisbane on business, which was often. His lawyers, accountants, stockbrokers, among others, were all stationed in the state capital. He made sure she could always be contacted. He was highly esteemed by her uncle, for whom he clearly stood in.

His hand dropped away first. It had made her uncomfortable feeling the strength of his arm and the warmth of his skin, but she wasn't about to waste time fretting about it.

"That's in *your* head, Mallory. It's not true. More like I've tried my hardest to be a good friend to you."

You difficult woman, you. He didn't need to say it; Mallory heard it loud and clear.

"Anyway, you're here now. You can give Robb your undivided attention for a few days."

"Whatever you say, Blaine. You're the boss." Heat was spreading through her. In the old days she had let it control her. Not now. As Doctor Mallory James, she was used to being treated with respect. "Uncle Robert and I are in constant touch, as you well know. Anyway, he has *you*," she tacked on sweetly. "Always ready to help. The figure of authority in the town."

"Do I detect a lick of jealousy?"

"Jealousy!" She gasped. "That's a charge and a half."

"Okay, make it sibling rivalry, even if we aren't siblings. You can't rule it out. I've known Robb all my life. My parents loved him. He was always welcome at our home. I remember the first time you turned up. A perfectly sweet little girl *in those days*, with long blond hair tied back with a wide blue ribbon. My father said later, 'Those two should be painted, Claudia and her beautiful little daughter.'"

"That never happened." A flush had warmed Mallory's skin. She wished she could dash it away.

"I noticed like everyone else how closely you resembled your mother," Blaine said more gently.

"Ah, the fatal resemblance! It was extraordinary and it impacted too many lives." She broke off at the sound of approaching footsteps. Sister Arnold was returning with tea.

Blaine moved to take the tray from her. "Thank you, Sister."

"Would you like a cup yourself, Mr. Forrester?"

How many times had Mallory heard just that worshipful tone? Nothing would ever be too much trouble for Blaine Forrester; tea, coffee, scones, maybe a freshly baked muffin?

"I'm fine, thank you, Sister." He gave her a smile so attractive it could sell a woman into slavery.

"You could bring another cup, Sister, if you don't mind," said Mallory. There was really something about Blaine that was very dangerous to women.

"No trouble at all." Sister Arnold gave Blaine a look that even a blind woman would interpret as nonprofessional.

"I don't drink tea," Blaine mentioned as she bustled away.

"At this point, who cares? Sister likes bringing it. Makes her day."

He ignored the jibe as too trivial to warrant comment. "You drove all this way?"

She nodded. "One stop. It would have been a whole lot quicker to fly, but I don't enjoy air travel, as you know." She was borderline claustrophobic but halfway to conquering it.

"That's your Mercedes out front?"

"It is." She had worked long and hard to pay it off. "I love my car. You did *assure* me Uncle Robert was in no danger."

"With care and the right medication, Robb has many good years left in him."

"I hope so." Mallory released a fervent breath.

"Ah, here's Sister back with my tea."

"Don't forget to give her your dazzling smile."

"How odd you noticed," he said, his sparkling eyes full on hers.

An interlude followed, filled with the usual ping-pong of chat, largely saturated with sarcasm, most of it hers. Dr. Edward Moorehouse, looking like an Einstein incarnation with his white bush of hair and a walrus moustache, hurried into the waiting room. A highly regarded cardiac specialist, he possessed a sweetness of heart and an avuncular charm.

"Ah, Mallory, Blaine!" He saluted them, looking from one to the other with evident pleasure. His head was tilted to one side, much like a bird's, his dark eyes bright with more than a hint of mischief. "How lovely to see you together. I hear such good things about you, Mallory."

Mallory kissed him gently on both cheeks, feeling a sense of warmth and homecoming. "Doctor Sarah set my feet on my chosen path."

"Bless her."

Dr. Sarah Matthews had guided Mallory through her severe childhood traumas: her terrible grief over the violent, sudden death of her adored mother, which she had witnessed, the later abandonment of her by her father, compounded by irrational feelings of guilt that she had lived when her beautiful mother had died.

"Wonderful woman, Sarah!" Moorehouse's voice was tinged with sadness. Sarah Matthews had died of lung cancer a couple of years previously, though she had never smoked a cigarette in her life. "We will always have a job for you if you ever come back to us, Mallory. No one has taken Sarah's place with the same degree of success. There are always cases needing attention, even here in this paradise."

She was aware of that. "Blaine tells me Uncle Robert

has had a heart condition for some time. I didn't know that."

"Robb wouldn't have wanted to worry you." Moorehouse darted a glance at Blaine, then back to Mallory. "He has his medication. Robb is the most considerate man I know," he said in his soothing manner.

Mallory wasn't sidetracked. "He *should* have told me. I needed to know."

"Don't agitate yourself, Mallory. With care and keeping on his meds, Robb has some good years left to him."

"Some?" She had to weigh that answer very carefully.

"All being well." Ted Moorehouse spoke with a doctor's inbuilt caution. "You must be longing to see him. I'll take you to his room."

"I'll stay here." Blaine glanced at Mallory. "You'll want to see Robert on your own."

"I appreciate that, Blaine," she said gracefully. "Give us ten minutes and then come through."

They found Robert James sitting up in bed, propped up by pillows. An ecstatic smile lit his still handsome face the moment Mallory walked in the door. As a consequence, Mallory's vision started to cloud. Outside his room she had steeled herself, concerned at how he might look after his heart attack. Now his appearance reassured her. She felt like a little girl again, a bereaved child. Uncle Robert was the one who had been there for her, taking her in. She couldn't bear the thought of his leaving her.

The ones you love best, die.

She knew that better than anyone.

Robert James, gazing at the figure of his adored niece, felt wave after wave of joy bubbling up like a fountain inside his chest. She had come back to him. Claudia's daughter. His niece. His brother's child. His family. He was deeply conscious of how much he had missed Mallory these past years, although they kept in close touch. He had accepted her decision to flee the town where he had raised her. She had strong reasons, and he accepted them. Besides, clever young woman that she was, she had to find her place in the larger world. He was so proud of Mallory and her accomplishments. Proud he had been her mentor. His whole being, hitherto on a downward spiral, sparked up miraculously.

"Mallory, darling girl!" He held out his arms to gather her in. What he really felt like doing was getting out of bed and doing a little dance.

"Uncle Robert." Mallory swallowed hard on the lump in her throat. She wasn't about to cry in front of him, though she felt alarm at the lack of colour in his aura. Love for him consumed her. He looked on the gaunt side, but resplendent in stylish silk pyjamas. Robert James was elegant wherever he was, in hospital, in private. Like her father, he was a bit of a dandy. There were violet shadows under his eyes, hollows beneath his high cheekbones and at the base of his throat. But there was colour in his cheeks, even if it was most probably from excitement. He had lost much-needed weight, along with strength and vitality; hence his diminished aura.

"It's so wonderful to see you, sweetheart, but you didn't have to come all this way. Ted says I'm fine."

"You *are* fine, Robb," Ted Moorehouse said quietly. He knew how much his friend loved his niece. Her presence would do him a power of good. "I'll leave you two together. You can take Robb home around this time tomorrow, Mallory." He half turned at the door. "I expect you're staying for a day or two?"

Mallory tightened her hold on her uncle's thin hand, meeting his eyes. "Actually I've taken extended leave."

"Why that's wonderful, Mallory." Moorehouse beamed his approval. "Just what the doctor ordered." He lifted a benedictory hand as he headed out the door.

"Extended leave! I feel on top of the world already." Robert's fine dark eyes were brimming with an invalid's tears.

Mallory bowed her head humbly at her uncle's intense look of gratitude. It was *she* who had every reason to be grateful. She pulled up a chair and sat down at the bedside. Her touch featherlight, she smoothed his forehead with gentle fingertips, let them slide down over his thin cheek. "I'm so sorry if I've hurt you with my long absence, Uncle Robert. I know Blaine finds it so. He's outside, by the way."

"He's always there when you need him." Robert's voice was full of the usual pride and affection. "To be honest, I don't know what I would have done without him. He's been splendid, a real chip off the old block. Not that D'Arcy ever got to grow old."

Mallory bowed her head. She wasn't the only one who had lost a beloved parent. Blaine too had suffered. D'Arcy Forrester had been killed leading a cleanup party after a severe cyclone. He had trodden on fallen power lines that had been camouflaged by a pile of palm fronds. His passing had been greatly mourned in the town. The reins had been passed into Blaine's capable hands.

Robert James's hollowed-out gaze rested on his niece. "Does Nigel know about me?"

Mallory's smile barely wavered. "I've left messages. I'm sure he'll respond."

"I won't count on it." Robert spoke wryly. "Stripped of the mask of learnedness, my brother is not a caring man.

What heart he had went with your mother. I would have liked to see him, all the same. We *are* blood."

Unease etched itself on Mallory's face. "Goodness, Uncle Robert, you're not dying." She tightened her grip as if to hold him forever. "You've got plenty more good years left to you. I'm here now. Father will be in contact, I'm sure." She was certain her father had received her messages. But her father hated confronting issues like illness and death.

Some minutes later, Blaine walked through the door, his eyes taking in the heartwarming sight of uncle and niece lovingly holding hands. "How goes it?"

"Wonderful, thank you, Blaine," Robert responded, eyes bright. "Ted says I can come home tomorrow."

"That's great news. I can pick you up in the Range Rover. To make it easy for Mallory, I can pick her up on the way."

So it was arranged, and they left the room.

She didn't so much walk as glide on those long, elegant legs, Blaine thought. Mallory moved like a dancer; every twist and turn, every smooth pivot. It was high time he dropped the bombshell and then stood well back for the fallout. He knew Robb hadn't told her. Robb simply wasn't up to it. It was part of Robb's avoidance program.

"Something I should tell you, Mallory." He hoped if she was going to shoot the messenger she aimed high.

"I *knew* there was something." Mallory came to an abrupt halt.

"Your psychic powers?" he suggested, that irritating quirk to his handsome mouth.

"Why don't you double up with laughter? What powers

I have—which you *don't believe* is true—do work. I've been picking up vibes that something wasn't right. I can see by your face you'd prefer not to be having the upcoming conversation." Normally she spoke quietly. She was quiet with her movements as well. She never sought to draw attention to herself, but with Blaine her usually controlled manner became by comparison nearly theatrical.

"How right you are. I don't think you could guess, so I'll get right to it. Jason Cartwright has a job at Moonglade. On the farm."

The shock was so great she felt like ducking for cover.

Blaine showed his concern. "Hey, are you okay?"

For a moment she was too dumbfounded to reply. "Okay? I'm the expert on okay. I'm actually delirious with joy. Jason at the farm! What luck!" Her blood pressure was definitely soaring well above her usual spot-on 119/76.

He didn't relish this job, but he had promised Robb he would bring Mallory up to date. Robb tended to pull in the favours. "I'm sorry to spring it on you. Robb has never told you for his own reasons, but it's something you obviously need to know now you're here."

Take your time.

Stare into space for a minute.

She felt more like shouting, only that would be so utterly, utterly unlike Dr. Mallory James. "I love Uncle Robert dearly, but we both know he evades difficult issues like the plague. I *knew* he was keeping something from me."

"Your psychic powers didn't fill you in?"

"Oh, bugger off, Blaine." Abruptly she stalked off to her car, unlocking the doors with a press on the remote. She felt like driving back the way she came.

Blaine caught up with her with ease. "We can handle this, Mallory."

"*We?*" she huffed, rounding on him. "*We* will, will we? I love that. Your offer of support only grates."

"It's well meant. I've another surprise for you."

Her dark eyes flashed. "Don't hang about. Get it out. It's a bigger surprise than Jason working at the farm?"

For a woman who hated to lose her cool, Mallory's dark eyes gave Mallory, the enigma, away. They were *passionate* eyes. "He *runs* it," Blaine bit off. "No point in stretching things out."

She tried to find words. None came. "Well, he's had such a rotten time, he deserves a break," she said finally.

"I share your dismay."

"Then why didn't you stop it?" She was trying without success to dampen the burn inside her. "You can do *anything* when you want to. I've seen plenty of evidence of that over the years. You're the fixer. You run the town."

"I've never said that."

"You don't have to. Does the Queen tell everyone she's the Queen? She doesn't have to."

"Are you hearing yourself?" He too was firing up. "Be fair. It was Robb's decision, Mallory. It was never going to be mine. I couldn't take matters out of his hands. Robb owns Moonglade and the business. I've never been a fan of Jason's, but he's not a criminal."

"He *is* a criminal!" Mallory declared fiercely. "He betrayed me. He betrayed his family, Uncle Robert, even the town. That's criminal in my book. Honestly, Blaine, this is too much."

He agreed, but he wasn't about to stoke the flames. "I can't expect you to be happy about it. He's good at the job. He works hard."

Mallory shook her head. "The golden boy! That makes

it okay for my married ex-fiancé to live and work on the doorstep? I suppose I can be grateful he wasn't invited to live in the house. Why couldn't Uncle Robert tell me himself? I don't give a damn how efficient Jason is. Uncle Robert—" She broke off in disgust. "It's the avoidance syndrome. It's rife among men." She propped herself against her car, in case she slid ignominiously to the ground. "Why does chaos follow me?"

"You're doing okay," he said briskly.

She waved off his comment. "What is *wrong* with Uncle Robb's thinking?"

"Obviously, it's different from yours."

"Ss-o?" she almost stuttered.

"If someone's decisions are different from our own, then we tend to assume it doesn't make a lot of sense."

"There's nothing wrong with my thinking, thank you." She became aware she was beating an angry tattoo on the concrete with the toe of her shoe. This wasn't like her. Not like her at all. Blaine found the terrible weak spot in her defences. "You didn't understand Uncle Robert's decision, did you?"

"The milk of human kindness? Blessed are the merciful, and all that?"

"I love the way you guys stick together."

"Oh, come off it, Mallory," he said, exasperated.

"We never know people, do we? Even the people closest to us. We always miss something. Uncle Robert needed to tell me. *You* of all people should know that."

"Damn it, Blaine, Jason's working at Moonglade is an outrage. It chills my heart. So don't stand there looking like business as usual."

He rubbed the back of his tanned neck. "It won't help to see it like that, Mallory. It's a done deal. You'd moved on. You didn't come back. It was well over six years ago."

"An astonishing amount of time. So you're saying *I'm* the one who is acting badly? Or am I an idiot for asking?"

"I don't think you're likely to hear the word 'idiot' in connection with you in a lifetime. Robb has a notoriously kind heart. He gave your ex-fiancé a job after it became apparent Harry Cartwright had disowned his only son. Robb is a very compassionate man."

"A sucker for a sob story, you mean. Okay, okay, *I* was a sob story. A seven-year-old kid who had lost her mother. A kid who was abandoned by her greatly admired, gutless father because I'm the spitting image of my mother. He couldn't look at me. I might have had two heads. I was his little daughter so much in need of a father's comfort, but my appearance totally alienated him. It was like I should have had plastic surgery, changed the colour of my hair, popped in baby-blue contact lenses. Ah, what the hell!" She broke off, ashamed of her rant.

"Mallory, I can't think of a single soul who didn't find your father's behaviour deplorable. You had a tough time, but you've come through with flying colours."

"An illusion I've managed to create."

"We all create illusions. I do get how you feel."

She raised her face to his, not bothering to hide her agitation. "How do you get it? Selma didn't run off from your wedding, so be grateful for that. Jason was an assassin. He stabbed me in the back, right on the eve of our wedding, remember? You should, you were there. You're *always* there, letting me know what a fool I am. Will you ever forget how the news of Kathy Burch's pregnancy spread like wildfire around the town? The disgrace. The humiliation. The shame. To make it worse, Uncle Robert had spent a fortune ensuring a fairy-tale wedding for me."

"I did warn you."

She felt the screws tighten. "Yeah, prescient old you!

You must get great satisfaction out of knowing everything you said about Jason came true."

"He wasn't the most desirable candidate for your hand. Certainly not the husband of choice."

"Not your choice for me."

"Not Robb's choice either, even if he avoided saying so, which is a great pity, but seriously not worth getting into now. It didn't make me *happy* to say what I said then."

"I don't believe that for one moment. You relished the breakup. I was under so much stress, but you, superior old you, had to punch my stupidity home."

An answering heat of anger was rising in him. A certain amount of conflict with Mallory was par for the course. "How unfair can you get? If I'd told you I thought Jason Cartwright was absolutely *perfect*, you might have broken off the engagement."

She stared at him, wondering in consternation if he had spoken a truth. "There's always friction between us, isn't there?" she said, angrily puffing at a stray lock of her hair. "Bottled up forces."

"That's what *you* want, Mallory. Not me." Blaine stared down at her. Radiance had a way of playing around Mallory. The hot sun was picking out the gold strands in her hair and at her temples. The delicate bones of her face he found not only endearing but intensely erotic.

"Jason was kicked out of his home and the thriving family real estate business for reasons unknown. Was it money?" Mallory pondered. "Money causes big problems. Were the twins robbing their father on the side? Surely Uncle Robert pressed Jason for some explanation?"

"None forthcoming to this day." Blaine fixed a glance on her narrow, tapping foot.

She stopped the tapping. "You've always been able to get to the bottom of things."

"Wasn't my place, Mallory, as I said."

"Well, I can't accept you don't have *some* idea as to what the breakup was all about. You have your little network. All the businessmen in town want to hook up with you. They all know Harry. What about the grapevine?"

"Oddly, the breakup hasn't become the talk of the town. It's a mystery, destined to remain so."

She gave another dismissive wave of her hand. "I don't like mysteries, especially when they impact on my life. His parents doted on Jason. Could the fallout have been because of *me*? That would make me very uncomfortable indeed."

"I think not."

"How can you be so sure?"

"I know that much, Mallory."

She felt another quick surge of anger. "Of course you do, and a whole lot more you're not telling. Jason married Kathy Burch. They have a little girl."

"Her name is Ivy, a cute little kid. Kathy, however, is a very subdued young woman these days. Marriage and motherhood have—"

"Taken their toll?"

"The short answer is yes. Kathy is very much under Jessica's thumb."

She took a deep breath. Counted to ten. "A bigger bombshell is coming? Jessica is still on the scene?"

"Try to pry her away from her brother," Blaine said, his tone bone dry.

"Can no one kill her off? Or at least start looking into it?"

"No way of doing it without landing in jail," Blaine said laconically. "Those two were always joined at the hip.

Jason and Kathy live in the old manager's bungalow, by the way. Robert remodeled it for them."

Mallory put her fingertips to her aching temples. "I didn't come prepared for these disclosures, Blaine. To think of all the phone calls, the e-mails, the visits, and never a word."

"Not so surprising, is it?"

She shook her head. "Not really. We both know Uncle Robert avoids unpleasantness. It's his problem area. As for *you*! You too left me completely in the dark."

"Mallory, I couldn't go over Robb's head."

"I had rights, didn't I?"

"You left, Mallory, telling us you were never coming back."

"Who would blame me? You're not the most compassionate man in the world, are you?"

"Compassion wasn't, still isn't, what you wanted," he said testily.

Mallory gave up. She would never win with Blaine. "I can't believe the Cartwrights would turn their backs on their only grandchild. Kathy might remain the outsider, but cutting off the little girl, the innocent victim, their own flesh and blood? The Marge Cartwright I remember was a nurturing woman."

"Maybe Jason is hitting back at his parents by not allowing them to see the child. She has a few problems apparently."

"Problems*?* What sort of problems?" Immediately Mallory started ticking off childhood disorders in her head.

"Health problems, and I believe she's a little wild. The whole town knows. Kathy is always at the hospital with her."

"How very worrying." Mallory's stance had softened considerably. "Is the child on medication? There are so many underlying reasons for behavioural problems. Sometimes it can be hard for a GP to differentiate. Kids are hyper for a wide range of reasons."

"I'm sure you're right, Doctor James."

Ah, the suavity of his tone! "Helping problematic children is my area, Blaine," she reminded him sharply. "I'd like to point out, while we're on the subject, I didn't allow bitterness over what happened to me and Jason to eat me away. What's past is past."

"Faulkner didn't see it that way."

"Okay, the past is never past. That way of yours of constantly having the last word drives me crazy."

"As I've suggested, it could be your bad case of 'sibling' rivalry. You were lucky you didn't marry Jason. He didn't break your heart."

"Did Selma break yours?"

He only shrugged. "Forget Selma. Look, I'm not in the mood for this, Mallory."

"Then you're welcome to go on your way. I'm not stopping you." She tilted her chin.

"Take a chill pill, why don't you."

She flared up. "Chill pill? I don't pop pills." She had been on antidepressants for some years. Occasionally she had panic attacks, but she worked to contain them without medication.

"Oh, for God's sake, Mallory! Why do you work so hard to misunderstand me? You're a psychologist. You know all about chill pills to control moods. I know this is difficult. If it helps, Cartwright is working hard. *Jessica* too."

For a split second she allowed her shoulders to droop. Then she straightened. No way was Blaine going to see her crumple. She'd do that when she was alone.

"Jessica Cartwright mightn't be a bucket of fun, but

she's extremely competent," he went on. "She's far better than Jason at getting the best out of the staff."

"That's her big rap, is it? Jessica Cartwright gets the best out of the staff. Does she do it with a whip? Jessica was the nastiest kid in the school. She tormented the life out of Kathy Burch, when Kathy had suffered enough with that appalling father. Dare I ask how she wrangled the job?"

"Good question."

"With no good answer. Uncle Robert never liked her. He once called her a little monster."

"Tell me who did like her? Being pleasant never caught up with Jessica. She needed a job. The prospect of her finding work in town was uncertain at best."

"Most people had had kids in school with Jessica," Mallory said tartly.

"She mightn't have a winning personality, but Jason's life doesn't seem to be complete without her."

"Repressed development. Jessica is the alpha twin. She's always been in charge. But Jason is a married man now. If Jessica is around she probably spends her time ensuring every day is a real *bad* day for her sister-in-law. It's cruel for Jason to subject his wife to Jessica's TLC. God forbid he does it on purpose." Mallory felt up to her neck in unwelcome disclosures. "She's not his identical twin. They don't share identical genetic material. Jason was as pleasant as Jessica was downright nasty. Having said that, twinship is a deeply symbiotic relationship. I hope it's not too rude to ask, but what now? Is there a way out?"

"Not at the moment. Jessica lives in an apartment in town."

"I expect you own the complex?"

"I expect I do," he said.

"Modesty doesn't come in your size, does it?"

"If you say so, *dear* Mallory," he drawled. "To try to balance the good with the bad, Jessica has stuck by her brother."

"She'd stick with him if he were a total nutter. I really liked the Cartwrights."

"And they *loved* you." He went heavy on the *loved.*

"It was what it was," she said soberly. "So you got me here knowing all this?"

"I got you here for *Robert.* You owe him."

Memory after memory was sidling up. All of them full of angst. "I do so love you when you're righteous!"

"Me, righteous?" He spread his shapely hands.

"That's one of your big problems, Blaine. You're most righteous when you're in the wrong. And this is wrong."

"Would you have come back had you known?" He pinned her with his luminous eyes.

"So you deliberately kept me in the dark?"

"What would you have done had I told you the truth?"

She averted her gaze. "You don't know the workings of my mind, Blaine."

"You don't know mine, either."

"What's that supposed to mean?"

"You're smart. You'll figure it out. One piece of advice. Take it slowly."

She searched his face. Blaine was a central part of her life, but hunkering down inside her bolt hole had become a habit. "You make that sound like I could be steering into dangerous waters."

"And so you could be."

"They know I'm coming?"

Blaine nodded. "I expect they're feeling their own brand of trepidation. But life has moved on. *You* have moved on, Mallory. You're Doctor James now, a highly regarded professional in your field. You could even be of help to the child."

The thought took the edge off her upset. "Only I'm certain Jason and his wife wouldn't want any help from me. Jessica was *never* my friend."

"I did tell you that as well."

"You did indeed." Between the heat and her sizzling emotions, she felt compelled to get away from him. "You know I've always thought you a complete—"

He cut her off, opening her car door. "No need to say it, Mallory. I can fill in the dots. And it wasn't *always*. Once we were good pals, until puberty got in the way."

"Puberty? Whose puberty?" she demanded, incensed.

"Why, yours, of course. I'm not a fool, Mallory. I know you hate it, but I know you too well."

"You'll need to do a lot of catch-up." With practised grace, she swivelled her long, elegant legs as she settled into the driver's seat. "You find this funny?" She caught the glint in his eyes.

"Not at all. I just hope you're relatively okay with it."

"Like I'm relatively okay with a Category Five cyclone. What time tomorrow?"

"Say eleven o'clock. Robert has a new housekeeper. Mrs. Rawlings. She lost her husband, Jeff, to cancer."

She nodded. "Uncle Robert did manage to tell me. I'm sorry. He told me plenty about your goings-on as well. We do so know he thinks of you as the son he never had. What did go wrong between you and Selma, anyway?" Her voice was edged with malice, when malice didn't come naturally to her. "I would have thought she was madly in love with you."

"You've managed to make that sound like one would have to wonder why."

"Just trying to spin your wheels. Besides, I didn't think you cared all that much what I thought."

"I'll let that one go as well. It was Selma who decided against an engagement," he offered with no loss of his iron-clad composure.

"It was the other way around, I fancy. She loved you, but you found you didn't love her, or not enough to get married. Had you a new conquest in mind?"

He made to close her door. "Let's swap stories at another time, shall we, Mallory?"

"Nothing in it for you, Blaine. I'm a closed book."

"Unknowable to everyone but *me*."

She could have cheerfully slapped him. Instead she found herself tightening her body against the odd tumbling inside her. "I assume that's your arrogance talking?"

"Not entirely. See you tomorrow."

He shut her door.

He walked away.

He didn't look back.